Shyly,
the ch

As she pursed her lips, he turned his head and she found herself mouth to mouth with him. To begin with he was very gentle, his lips brushing hers. Then he put both arms around her, and his mouth settled over hers and began to move in a way to which she instinctively responded by parting her lips and sliding her arms around his neck.

By the time he raised his head, she was breathless and trembling. "Oh... goodness!" she exclaimed. "I've never been kissed like that!"

"But you liked it?" he asked, smiling.

She buried her face in his shoulder. "Don't tease me...you know I did," she murmured.

Jago chuckled. "So did I. It's going to be a pleasure to teach you all the other things you haven't tried yet."

ANNE WEALE
is also the author of these

Harlequin Presents

and these

Harlequin Romances

Many of these books are available at your local bookseller.

For a free catalog listing all titles currently available,
send your name and address to:

HARLEQUIN READER SERVICE
1440 South Priest Drive, Tempe, AZ 85281
Canadian address: Stratford, Ontario N5A 6W2

ANNE WEALE

wedding of the year

Harlequin Books

TORONTO • NEW YORK • LOS ANGELES • LONDON
AMSTERDAM • PARIS • SYDNEY • HAMBURG
STOCKHOLM • ATHENS • TOKYO • MILAN

Harlequin Presents first edition January 1983
ISBN 0-373-10565-7

Original hardcover edition published in 1982
by Mills & Boon Limited

CHAPTER ONE

In the scurrying crowd of commuters who streamed off the eight-thirty train when it drew into one of London's mainline stations on a frosty morning in February, Savanna Bancroft caught the eye of passers-by because, even in flat-heeled shoes, she was as tall as most of the men around her; taller than some of them.

When she was wearing high heels, a man had to be exceptionally big to look down at her. Her father had stood six foot in his socks, and all his children had inherited his long bones and wheat-coloured hair. In the case of the four Bancroft boys, to be lanky was no disadvantage. For Savanna, in her early teens, to have legs like a colt and no bosom worthy of even the smallest bra had been a cause of deep depression.

Now, nineteen and no longer flat-chested, she was still on the thin side of slim, partly because, except when she was actually in bed, she was almost always on the go.

It wasn't that she was restless by nature. As the only girl in the family, with her mother disabled by arthritis, she had too much to do in the house to have time to relax.

All day she rushed about London from one appointment to the next. All evening she bustled about at home, doing the jobs which her mother couldn't manage.

Up to now, Savanna thought, she must be the least-dated girl in southern England. Until she was eighteen she had been totally absorbed in her studies. For the past year her evenings had been fully occupied in other ways.

Apart from the fact that most of the men she encountered in her working life were not interested in women, she had to have eight hours' sleep at night. Who wanted to wine and dine a girl who had to be in bed by eleven o'clock in order to rise with bright eyes at seven next morning?

Showing her season ticket to the dark-skinned ticket

collector at the barrier reminded her that, in a few days' time, she would be where his parents or grandparents had come from—the West Indies.

It would be her first assignment in a glamorous part of the world, and she couldn't help looking forward to it, even though her agent had warned her that she would be lucky to have any time for swimming in the warm sea, or sunbathing on the white beaches.

Apart from her height, there was nothing, at that hour of the morning, to make any of the male commuters give her a second glance. Dressed in trousers and a full-length raincoat, with her hair concealed by a knitted hat and her eyes by dark glasses, she looked very different from the girl on the cover of the new issue of *Vogue* which the man at the station bookstall was putting on display as she hurried past.

She had been in *Vogue* several times, although never before on the cover. But even if she had remembered that the magazine came out that morning, she would not have had time to stop and look at herself.

On the cover she was not wearing glasses, and her large, dark-lashed topazine eyes were made up to emphasise their jewel-like brilliance. Her lips, too, were outlined and shaded to make the most of their sensitive shape. With soft tendrils of silky blonde hair half hiding her forehead, and her chin snuggled into the collar of a fabulous fur, she looked ravishingly feminine and alluring.

And they say the camera can't lie! All done by mirrors and make-up—had been some of the teasing comments made by her brothers when they had seen the first *Vogue* photographs of her.

She had felt it was true. The camera, skilfully handled, could perpetrate fantastic lies; and almost anyone, taught to paint her face by an expert as Savanna had been, could create an illusion of beauty.

Really, she wasn't beautiful at all. It was merely a heaven-sent stroke of luck—for her family if not for herself—that Gerald O'Connor, a leading fashion photographer, had happened to be looking for a tall girl with a long neck, long legs, no hips, and an unblemished skin, and had spotted her before any of the thousands of other girls with the same basic qualifications.

If, at the time of her father's death, it had been suggested to her that she should surrender her burning desire to go to university for the trivial career of a fashion model, she would have dismissed it out of hand.

She had been only seventeen then. A year later her outlook had changed. The chance to make money had seemed like a gift from the gods; and her personal ambitions had become unimportant compared with the needs of her family.

The daughter of a couple who had adored each other, and planned every one of their five children, Savanna had grown up in the warmest kind of family circle. For her parents, or any of her brothers, no sacrifice was too great.

The disappointing thing was that, although Gerald was rapidly fulfilling his promise to make her England's top model, she was not earning nearly as much as she had hoped. Or rather she was making a lot of money but without being able to spend it on her family's needs. Too large a slice of her impressive income was whittled away by taxes.

So it was with several worries on her mind that she took her place in the queue for taxis, unaware that, as *Vogue*'s newest cover girl, she would excite much envy among her own sex; or that, later that day, on a Concorde flight to New York, a man would catch sight of her face and the course of her life would be changed for the third time.

Her flight from Heathrow Airport took off in the middle of the morning and lasted for eight hours.

She had been too excited to sleep much the night before. While most of her travelling companions were watching the movie, she slept. She slept not only through the film but while afternoon tea was being served, not stirring until Gerald nudged her. By the time she had stretched and was fully alert, the great aircraft was only a few thousand feet from the island which was their destination.

To anyone watching it from the ground, the time was early afternoon. But although they had put back their watches, according to the passengers' body clocks it was now six o'clock in the evening. For some days they would suffer from jet lag or, in medical terms, the disturbance of their Circadian Rhythms.

With Gerald O'Connor and all but one member of his party, the first sign of this came before dinner when they began to smother yawns, their drowsiness increased by the rum in their pre-dinner drinks.

Only Savanna, who had slept for much of the flight and who never drank spirits, ate her meal with her usual healthy appetite and showed no sign of drooping even when, far away in London, it was long past her usual bedtime.

'I can't keep my eyes open. I'm going to turn in,' announced Janey, one of the fashion assistants, after pecking unenthusiastically at her main course and refusing a pudding.

The others felt similarly weary. They were all planning to take a sleeping pill to prevent themselves waking up between three and four in the morning. But, although she had followed Gerald's instructions and asked the Bancrofts' family doctor to prescribe some mild tablets for her, Savanna was reluctant to use them except as a last resort.

While the others retired to their rooms, she went for a stroll through the lantern-lit gardens between the low buildings of the hotel and the sea in which they had swum within an hour of their arrival.

At this hour the beach was deserted. She had it all to herself; half a mile of powder-fine coral sand lapped by water clearer and warmer than any she had ever bathed in.

Remembering happy family holidays on the west coast of Scotland, in Guernsey and, one memorable summer, in

Brittany, she stood watching the sea, lost in thought until she was brought back to the present by a deep voice saying quietly, 'Good evening, Miss Bancroft.'

Startled, she turned to find the tall figure of a man standing near her.

'Good evening,' she answered uncertainly.

That he knew who she was suggested that he was on the staff of the hotel. But all the non-executive male staff wore a uniform consisting of white pants and boldly-patterned overshirts. It didn't seem likely that the manager or his assistant would be wearing jeans as this man was. Yet if he were a guest, how did he know her name?

He introduced himself. 'Jago Kindersley. How do you do?' He moved closer and held out his hand.

'How do you do?' Savanna echoed.

His unusual first name rang a bell. She felt sure she had heard it before. She put her hand into his, liking the strength of his fingers and the dryness of his palm.

The next thing he said was very odd. 'Good. I can't stand a feeble handshake in a man or a woman.'

It was a dislike which she shared, but it still seemed a strange thing to say, especially the 'Good.'

'Apart from ourselves, most of the people who arrived today seem to have gone to bed,' he remarked, as their hands drew apart. 'How is it that you aren't tired, Miss Bancroft?'

'I had a long nap on the plane.'

'You find air travel boring?'

In spite of the brilliance of the moonlight, it was difficult to see his face clearly because of the shifting shadows of the palm fronds rustling overhead.

She had an impression of dark skin stretched tautly over a bone structure very different in shape from that of the islanders. Their skulls and their features were rounded. His was an angular head, and a face chiselled rather than thumbed. High cheekbones. An aquiline nose. A chin aggressively square.

'On the contrary, I find it very exciting. So much so that I was tossing and turning most of last night,' she confessed. 'How is it that *you* aren't tired, Mr Kindersley?'

'Flying in from New York, I haven't suffered as much time displacement as you have. Also I have the knack of being able to sleep at will. In a mobile life, the ability to make up one's eight hours piecemeal is as useful as plastic money.'

'Goodness, yes, it must be invaluable. I wish I could train myself to do it.'

'It's a question of relaxation. Most people can learn to relax their bodies, but not always their mental tensions. Shall we take a turn along the beach?'

They were standing near one of the openings in the low wall which prevented the sand from encroaching on the well-kept lawns.

Apparently taking her assent for granted, he put his right foot on the wall and, bending, turned up his jeans. He was wearing French *espadrilles*, and when he took them off she could see that his feet were as brown as his ankles. He must spend a lot of time in the sun to be that dark colour all over—unless it wasn't a tan but his natural pigmentation. By moonlight it was difficult to tell.

'You can leave your sandals here. No one will take them,' he told her, with a glance at her slender feet. 'Did you buy them in Greece?'

'They were bought there, but not by me. They were a present from a friend who went to Rhodes for her holiday. I've hardly been anywhere yet.'

She withdrew a foot from one sandal which consisted of a leather sole held on by two straps, one across the tops of her toes, the second across her arched instep.

It had been her intention, before he had disturbed her reverie, to walk for a while by the sea's edge. But to stroll with a man she didn't know along a shore as sequestered as this one, particularly at its far ends, made her wonder if it would be wiser to return to her room and read herself to sleep.

He seemed to guess what she was thinking. His tone dry, he said, 'Have no qualms, Miss Bancroft. I have nothing in mind but conversation.'

Directed by Gerald, Savanna could look extremely sophisticated. She could also look angelically innocent as, in practice if not theory, she was. In her dealings with men she had a long way to go to catch up with her two closest school friends, Livvy and Clare. Neither of them would have flushed and floundered as she did.

'I didn't . . . that is . . . I . . .'

'To be wary is sensible,' he said. 'A beautiful model is as exciting a quarry to some men as a rich man to certain women.'

'How did you know I was a model? Have you something to do with the hotel?'

'Apart from staying in it—nothing. A woman on my flight to New York had a magazine with your face on the cover. When you came into the restaurant this evening I recognised you.'

'Really? You must have an exceptionally good memory for faces.'

'You have an exceptionally memorable face, Miss Bancroft.'

'Thank you, but I still think it was clever of you to place me. I was much more made up for that cover than I am at the moment. How did you find out my name?'

'It wasn't difficult. If you had noticed me in the restaurant, and had you been sufficiently interested, you could have found out mine. But you were intent on your meal. For a slim girl you have a surprisingly hearty appetite.'

'I didn't have much breakfast or lunch. Are you here on holiday, Mr Kindersley?'

By this time they were moving briskly along the expanse of tide-washed firm sand between the crystalline sea and the soft beach where pale, nervous crabs scuttled back to the mouths of their holes as the two tall humans approached.

Glancing at her companion, who was walking on the seaward side of her, Savanna estimated that he was at least a couple of inches taller than her father and much wider across the shoulders.

Peter Bancroft had been a very thin man to whose gan-gling frame his wife had never succeeded in adding an ounce of extra flesh. Jago Kindersley was lean rather than thin, and there was plenty of muscle cladding his broad back and deep chest. He looked as if, like Benjy, her third eldest brother, he could take a lot of pummelling in the region of his belt buckle without being hurt by it, and his close-fitting jeans showed long muscular thighs. He walked from the hips, moderating his loose-limbed stride to match her shorter step, although not as much as with a girl of average height.

By moonlight his hair and eyebrows looked Indian-black, but beneath the strongly marked brows his eyes were not the dark brown she had half expected. They were a much lighter colour, but whether blue or grey she could not tell.

In answer to her question, he said, 'No, I wouldn't call it a holiday, just a short break. I may not stay more than a day or two. It depends.'

'What do you do for a living?' she asked.

Having admitted to making enquiries about her, he could scarcely object to a little reciprocal curiosity.

'I'm an entrepreneur,' was his answer. 'If you know what that is,' he added.

'It means someone who brings together the components of an important commercial undertaking. In spite of my hair and my occupation, I'm not totally dumb, Mr Kindersley,' Savanna said coolly.

'I was hoping you wouldn't be.'

She stopped dead.

Two paces on, he checked and turned. 'What's the matter?'

'Why were you hoping I wouldn't be?'

He folded his arms across his chest, his left hand grasp-ing his right elbow, the other hand covering his biceps. Exposed by his rolled up shirt sleeves, his forearms were hard and sinewy, lightly covered with dark hair which thinned out between his wrists and his knuckles. In rela-tion to the rest of him, his hands were not large, although the long brown fingers looked as if they might fold into punishing fists if the need arose. There was a digital watch on his wrist, but he wore no rings, and no chains glinted inside the open collar of his dark-coloured shirt.

'However beautiful a woman is, she still needs a modicum of intelligence.'

The wind caught and tossed her hair. As she put up her hands to control it and her lifted arms tightened her thin shirt, she saw his glance shift to her breasts.

Forgetting that only instants before she had been appraising parts of him, Savanna felt a flash of annoyance.

She said, 'If, while I was concentrating on my dinner, you were picking me out as a possible diversion for your leisure moments, I think I should tell you that I shall be working non-stop. And even if I had time to spare, I shouldn't be interested in . . . in what you have in mind.'

She saw a flash of white teeth.

'You don't know what I have in mind,' was his bland response.

'Nothing intellectual, if you didn't even credit me with knowing what an entrepreneur is,' she said crisply, turning away to retrace her footsteps.

That patronising rider had touched her on a raw spot. It was one thing to give up her career plans in order to expedite the operation which might cure her mother's disablement and keep Joey, her youngest brother, at his expensive special school. That she could bear, and willingly. But to be taken for a pretty nincompoop . . . a feather-brained clothes horse . . . a sex object . . . *that* she could not bear. It made her hands clench with resentment.

Margaret, her agent, had warned her there would be men who would see her as a plaything or a status symbol, and it seemed that this man was one of them. His desirous appraisal of her body did not tally with his earlier assurance that he had nothing in mind but conversation.

On the strength of a few minutes' acquaintance, knowing nothing about her, he wanted her.

She half expected him to follow her, but he didn't.

When she reached the place where her sandals were beside his *espadrilles,* she saw that after she had left him he had gone to the extreme end of the beach and now was returning at a slow jog.

Perhaps he exercised the same way he slept, piecemeal, when and where he could. For a moment or two she watched him loping along the curving shoreline. At that distance he could have been mistaken for a man in his twenties but, close to him, she had judged him to be at least thirty, perhaps thirty-five. Certainly a lot older than herself, and probably married or divorced as most men were by that age.

Walking quickly and quietly to her bedroom, Savanna felt sorry for a wife whose husband, away from home, looked with desire at other women.

Livvy and Clare, with whom she still had discussions and arguments about life and love, thought that her ideas were old-fashioned. Their parents' marriages had broken up long ago, and neither of them expected to find a man with whom they could live happily ever after. According to them, that was fairy-tale stuff: not real life.

But Savanna was the product of a marriage between two people whose occasional disagreements had only ruffled the surface of their long and exclusive love affair.

She knew with absolute certainty that her father had never been unfaithful to her mother, or she to him. From their first meeting during their teens to the day of her father's sudden death, soon after his forty-fifth birthday, Peter and Mary Bancroft had supplied all each other's needs. They had been friends as well as lovers, setting a standard for their children which Savanna intended to cling to through thick and thin.

She woke up at seven, local time, and, having half an hour to spare before the call from the switchboard arranged by Gerald the night before, decided to swim before breakfast.

Apart from two youths raking the sand and re-grouping the reclining chairs, there was no one about on the beach.

The early sun was gentle on her bare skin as she took off her wrap. In preparation for this assignment, she had taken a course of artificial sunbathing at a Knightsbridge solarium, and her body was golden, not white. Even so she would have to be careful not to burn when the sun rose higher.

To be wearing a bikini in February, and to be deliciously warm in the kind of setting she had often looked at with longing on the covers of the travel brochures, filled her with a joie de vivre which she expressed by running along the beach and turning a couple of cartwheels before leaping into the invitingly clear jade-tinted shallows.

Unaware that her high spirits had been witnessed by someone other than the two West Indians, she duck-dived under the surface and swam as far as she could until her breath gave out and she had to surface, her long hair clinging to her shoulders like spun sugar.

She had been enjoying her solitary sea-frolic for some minutes before she realised she had an audience. Immediately, her unselfconscious pleasure in the Caribbean morning gave place to the discomfiture of being caught off guard by a man whose society she had hoped to avoid for the rest of his stay.

'Good morning. How did you sleep?' he called, dropping the towel which had been slung over his shoulder on to the sand beside hers.

'Good morning. Very well, thank you.'

Deliberately, she turned away and began to swim into deeper water. She knew it was a futile manoeuvre should he choose to follow her, but she hoped he would take the hint that she wasn't in a companionable mood—or not as far as he was concerned.

Yet even as she swam away from him, she knew the reason she had been annoyed with him last night was not only because she had recognised his desire for her, but because she had felt the same way.

His fine physique, and the virile assurance of his bearing, had excited a reaction she had never felt before—and did not want to feel again except for a man she knew and liked and respected.

To have been aroused by a stranger made her feel disgusted with herself. It offended the idealist in her, the romantic, the dreamer.

It wasn't that she was a prude. She had always liked poetry, and the erotic verses of the Golden Age of the English love lyric made her long to experience the raptures so graphically described by Cavalier poets such as Thomas Carew and Richard Lovelace. But it seemed a far cry from their descriptions of lovemaking to the short-lived sexual adventures which she saw going on all around her.

She swam well, having learned very young and thereafter competed with her brothers. But her crawl, although better than most girls', was no match for a powerful man's strokes. Jago Kindersley soon overhauled her, making it pointless to continue to exert herself.

She changed to a breast-stroke, and he to a leisurely back-stroke so that they were facing each other. Seen in sunlight, his eyes were an unusual true grey with no hint of blue in it. Cold eyes, in spite of the laughter lines at the corners of them. Hard eyes, matched by a mouth at once hard and sensual.

'Obviously you enjoy the sea. Do you snorkel?' he asked.

'No, and this will probably be my only chance to swim today. We start work immediately after breakfast.'

'Shall you object to my watching you do your thing?'

'Our photographer will,' she said crisply. 'Gerald doesn't encourage spectators.'

However, when Gerald O'Connor arrived at the beach a few minutes later and saw his protegée coming out of the sea, dwarfed by a tall, tanned man whose dark looks were the perfect foil for Savanna's blondeness, the photographer saw at once that the guy who had picked her up was as macho as she was feminine. If he could be persuaded to pose with her, the result could be some great pictures.

To Savanna, Gerald's arrival was a relief. She introduced them and went off to shampoo and shower, confident that he would know how to brush off Jago much more effectively than she could.

Although it was the first time she had been abroad with Gerald, she had worked on several outdoor locations with him. It was part of his style to involve passers-by in his pictures. Traffic wardens, street sweepers, postmen, office cleaners and many others had been seconded as background figures on previous assignments.

Last night he had spoken of using some of the hotel's waiters and maids, or possibly some of the countrywomen they had seen on the drive from the airport.

Contrast was what Gerald liked to achieve. The juxtaposition of a willowy model in expensive resort clothes with an outsize West Indian matron in a home-made dress and cotton headtie would be contrast at its most extreme.

When she joined the others for breakfast, and learned that Gerald had changed his mind and enlisted Jago as the principal member of her supporting cast, Savanna was horrified; the more so when she discovered that he was going to play the bridegroom to her bride in a honeymoon sequence.

'But he's not a professional. He'll be useless,' she protested.

'All he has to do is to look amorous, and he'll do that a hell of a lot more convincingly than most professionals,' said Gerald.

With this she was unable to argue, but it made her see that, if she couldn't deflect him from carrying out his new idea, she might be able to dissuade Jago from lending himself to it.

Making an excuse to return to her room, she went to the desk and asked for Mr Kindersley's number.

Her tap on his door was answered by a clear, 'Come in.'

She raised her voice. 'It's Savanna Bancroft. May I speak to you for a moment?'

The door opened. He must have come out of the shower only minutes before she had knocked. A towel was

wrapped round his hips, the whiteness of the fleecy
Turkish pile accentuating the bronze sheen of his torso.

Although, unlike Clare and Livvy, she was still a virgin,
the male body held no mysteries for her. Growing up in a
one-bathroom house with four brothers ranging in age
from twenty-four to sixteen, inevitably there had been
many occasions when she had seen all four without clothes
on. The boys had been brought up to respect her modesty,
and not to barge into her bedroom without warning; but
her parents had seen no reason to curb their sons' casual
attitude to their own nudity.

So why was it that, when the sight of a naked man would
not ordinarily have startled or embarrassed her, Jago
Kindersley in a bath towel made her draw back and feel
uneasy?

He, for a different reason, also stepped back a pace.
'Won't you come in?'

'No, thank you. I—I just wanted to say that perhaps
you haven't considered all the possible repercussions of
this idea of Gerald's.'

He folded his arms in the same way he had the night
before. It seemed to be a characteristic posture with him.

'What repercussions?' he enquired.

'I know it's only makebelieve, but your wife may not
like you pretending to be someone else's husband. She
may feel people will laugh at her.'

'I'm not married.'

'Oh . . . aren't you?' Did he mean he was not married
at present, or had never been married? 'Well . . . in that
case, perhaps you haven't realised that it will take more
than a day or two to photograph all the clothes we've
brought out. We're here for a week.'

'I'm my own master. I can spend a week here if I want
to.'

'But why should you want to? They won't pay you, you
know—or not much. You won't get the professional rate.'

'I'm receiving a strong impression that you aren't at all
keen on my taking part in this assignment,' he said dryly.
'I wonder why that is?'

She felt herself flushing at the mockery in his eyes.
Clearly he was aware of his effect on her.

'If you knew more about most male models, I don't
think you'd be keen either. They're nearly all homo-
sexuals.'

'So I believe; but I don't think anyone is likely to jump
to that conclusion about me. You asked why I had agreed
to O'Connor's suggestion. The answer is simple; I want to
get to know you better.'

She decided to be blunt. 'You mean you want to have
an affair with me?'

'No, I never have affairs with girls of your age. You're
a beautiful creature, Savanna, but don't overrate your
desirability. You'll be twice as attractive at thirty, and
certain women of forty, and possibly fifty, can give a man
just as much pleasure as a smooth-skinned young thing
like yourself.'

His mouth curled in a sardonic half-smile. 'The sexual
instinct is inborn, but making love is an art which I think
you have yet to learn.'

Her colour deepened. Baffled, she hurried away. If he
didn't want to go to bed with her, why did he want to
know her better? It didn't make sense, or none that she
could understand.

It was a difficult day. Jago, the amateur, did all that was
required of him with unruffled aplomb, but Savanna felt
as stiff and unsure of herself as she had on her very first
day in front of the camera.

She had gone to bed early, but was still sitting up with
the light on, when her bedside telephone rang.

She expected it to be Jago, but it was Gerald. He
wanted to come and talk to her for a few minutes.

The photographer's private life supported Jago's statement that some middle-aged women might have little to
fear from pretty girls. Gerald was thirty-six. His second
wife, Lolly, was at least forty, perhaps more, with a huge
bust and hips to match, and a wild shock of hennaed
hair. An inspired cook and genial hostess, she must also

have other talents. In spite of her unfashionable size, Gerald had never been known to make a pass at any of his models.

So it was with no qualms about his intentions that Savanna admitted him to her room, and climbed back into bed to hear what he wanted to say to her.

'You were off form today, Anny-lovey.' He rarely called her Savanna. 'What's up? More troubles at home?'

She shook her head. 'I suppose I'm still tired from the journey. I'll be better tomorrow,' she promised.

'I hope so. This fellow's a natural. The two of you look great together. He's some kind of tycoon, I've found out, so it's sporting of him to play ball. It must be that he fancies you.'

'I don't fancy him,' she said shortly.

'I don't know why not, for God's sake. The other girls do'—this being a reference to the magazine staff who were supervising the fashion side of the assignment. 'You could do a lot worse for yourself. You have too many worries, and not enough fun. It's time there was a man in your life. Why not this one who's loaded and can make things easier for you?'

'It's just not my style,' she said quietly.

Her hair was tied back with a ribbon, and her night-dress of flowered Liberty cotton had a shirred top and tiny puffed sleeves. Without make-up, with her slender arms clasped round her updrawn knees, she looked very young and unworldly.

'Maybe not,' Gerald agreed. 'But you'll have to take the plunge some time, and I don't want you falling for a local lad who'll resent your career and expect you to wash his shirts and cook his supper. Between him and your family, you'd be run ragged.'

'Don't worry. I have no intention of adding to my problems.'

'A rich boy-friend could relieve you of most of them. You have to be practical in this life. Take it from me, romance is highly overrated. As some wise man said, "The voyage of love is all the sweeter for an outside stateroom and a seat at the captain's table''.'

'You're a cynic, Gerald.'

'Yes: I see things as they are, not as they ought to be. When I was your age, life wasn't as free and easy as it is now. The first girl I fell in love with wouldn't live with me—it was marriage or nothing. So we married, and spent five years finding out it was a big mistake. A trial run would have saved us that bad experience. People are like clothes, you have to shop around and try on before you find out what suits you.'

Savanna shook her head in disagreement. 'Maybe your first wife was immature for her age. My parents married very young, and they *were* right for each other. Anyway, having a rich boy-friend wouldn't help me to find the right husband. Quite the reverse, I should imagine. The kind of man I want to marry wouldn't want his wife to have been around too much.'

'That's your mother talking,' said Gerald sagely. 'Ask your brothers what they think about it. My bet is they couldn't care less. They'll have been to bed with a few girls before they settle down, that's for sure.' He stood up. 'See you tomorrow.'

After he had gone, Savanna switched out the light and opened the curtains. The bedroom was air-conditiond, with a sheet of plate glass and a glass door between it and the balcony overlooking the gardens and the sea.

As she stood for a moment, watching the shimmering moon-glade between the shore and the reef, which was marked by a line of white breakers, the figure of a man appeared beyond the tall trunks of the palms segmenting the view.

It was Jago, loping along the shore as he had the night before.

Was it possible that, in spite of his denial this afternoon, he did want to have an affair with her? Gerald thought so, and he was much wiser than she in the ways of rich men of the world.

Although sometimes, working in a studio, he liked to

devise elaborate set-pieces using bizarre accessories, on location O'Connor's technique was much like that of a film director.

He would suggest a series of actions for his model to perform, then leave it to her to improvise variations on his theme while he darted about using yards of film to achieve a single brilliant action shot.

It was a method which made life more difficult for the fashion staff as it meant they could not pin and peg the clothes to look good from one angle only. But it was a way of working which suited Savanna.

Hitherto, even with onlookers, she had had no difficulty in carrying out his instructions to run, jump, dance, spin like a top, or do anything else he had asked of her. But waltzing by the Serpentine with a co-operative Cockney park attendant had been a hundred times easier than playing at honeymooners with Jago.

His attitude to it was that of someone taking part in charades at a party, and doing it to the top of their bent.

When Gerald asked for a lighthearted chase along a beach with no one else on it, Jago chased her, and caught her, and let her go; and did it again and again, making her feel like a mouse being played with by a cat.

Each time he caught her, he did something different; once snatching her up in his arms and striding into the sea as if he meant to drop her in the water; once making her fall on the sand with him, but on top of his broad brown chest so that there was never any danger of his hurting her; and finally pulling her close to him and looking as if he meant to kiss her.

Through it all, Savanna forced herself to radiate a bride-like enjoyment of these antics. But when he held her against him, and she saw the gleam in his eyes as his dark head bent towards hers, her bright smile faded. She trembled, forgetting it was only a pretence, that he wouldn't really force his mouth on hers, not with Gerald near, full of enthusiasm.

'Great! Marvellous . . . absolutely fabulous!' he was saying, while Jago loomed predatorily over her, using his superior height to sway her backwards, off balance, so that she instinctively clutched at his warm bare shoulders.

He was wearing only white linen shorts; she a sky-blue bikini with the matching Bermudas. The top of the bikini was no more than ordinarily skimpy, but it felt non-existent as his hand on her back pressed her closer to him, crushing her small, soft breasts against the hard wall of his body.

There was more than one swimsuit to model, and for each one her hairstyle was altered while Jago lounged in the sun and chatted to Gerald about his photographic equipment and his rise to the top of his profession.

Considering how different they were in every respect, the two men seemed to get on surprisingly well. Although that might have been because Jago was clever at drawing the other man out while revealing little about himself, thought Savanna, as she listened to their conversation.

When she was ready to model the black bikini which was the last of the swimwear, she went to join them.

'I'm ready when you are.'

Gerald had a cigarette between his lips and was fiddling with his lighter. Jago who, like Savanna, was a non-smoker, let his grey gaze slide slowly over the gentle contours of her body.

'According to my observations, the bikini has been superseded. It's smarter to wear a monokini and a string of beads,' was his casual comment.

She glowered at him. 'We're working for *Vogue*, not *Playboy*.'

'Yes, but he's right,' said Janey, who had overheard. 'The in thing to do is to knot the top round your leg, Savanna.'

'Although, of course, in real life a bride on this beach would be skinny-dipping,' Jago murmured, with a quizzical glint.

'Yes, but we must show part of the bikini,' said Janey, taking him seriously. 'Eileen, bring the gold rope necklace and the black Dior sun specs, will you? Savanna, take off the top and I'll fix it round your leg.'

Savanna glanced furiously at Jago. She had known that, sooner or later, she would be required to model a see-through shirt or a transparent nightgown. To that she had no objection as she felt that Gerald's attitude to her body was as impersonal as that of a doctor, and the photographs which he took of her would be for other women to identify with, not for a lascivious male readership to gloat over.

Once, looking for some Blu-Tack in the large attic bedroom shared by her three elder brothers when they were at home, she had come upon a magazine which she thought had probably been brought into the house by Benjy, the least intelligent of the Bancroft boys.

It had not been carefully concealed, merely put out of sight in a drawer. Rather guiltily, knowing that broadminded as her parents were they would not approve of that type of periodical, Savanna had looked through it.

What surprised her was that most of the models had looked what her mother called 'nice girls'. No matter how high the fees, how could girls with clear eyes and sweet faces have posed for those degrading photographs? She hadn't understood it then, and she didn't now. No matter how desperately urgent her family's need of money, there were some things she could never bring herself to do, and modelling for pornographic magazines was one of them.

Baring her breasts for the lubricious enjoyment of a stranger was another. But before she could say no, Jago said, 'In that case I'll go for a swim. Shout when it's okay to come ashore, will you?'

As he spoke, he unzipped his shorts to reveal his own brief black stretch-fabric trunks. The shorts discarded, he turned and sprinted into the sea.

'How very Edwardian of him,' said Janey, watching him take a header. 'Who would have thought he would be so gentlemanly? The way he was looking at you a moment ago, I thought he wanted to see you strip off.'

So had Savanna. As she watched Jago swimming away, her dark golden eyes were puzzled.

'Actually that French-cut bathing slip he's wearing is

almost the twin of hers, so maybe he should be in this shot,' said Janey to Gerald.

'No,' Savanna intervened firmly. 'If I have to be topless, I'd rather he wasn't around.'

The older girl stared at her in surprise. 'What difference does it make? We'll all be topless later on when the sun isn't so hot.'

She and the other girls, being white-skinned, were guarding against sunburn by working in loose cheesecloth trousers and flimsy but long-sleeved cover-ups.

'I shan't.'

'Why not? Everyone does now, unless they've got unsightly boobs.'

It was typical of Janey to use fashionable slang in preference to standard English. Her life was governed by what was in and what was out.

'Yes, but my mother's doctor says there are going to be some horribly prune-like bosoms around in ten years' time, so I'm not going to risk it,' said Savanna.

This was something she had invented. On hearing of her trip to the Caribbean, Doctor North had merely advised her to use a reliable sun cream and, every day, to drink a pint of water for every ten degrees of Fahrenheit temperature or, in terms of the metric system, a basic two litres a day plus a litre for every ten degrees of Centigrade temperature.

'Oh, did he? I didn't know that. I thought it was only faces which could become prematurely wrinkled,' said Janey. 'If that's the case, you'd better slap on some more oil for this shot,' she added, as Savanna unclipped the bikini top and handed it to her.

By this time Jago was in deep water, too far from the shore to see her in any detail as, presently, she paddled through the shallows, a half naked sylph with her eyes veiled by large smoky lenses as she lifted her face to the sun which was making the gilt tassels shine as they lay between her satiny breasts.

Why had he taken himself off with such unexpected and old-fashioned gallantry? she wondered. And why had she made that excuse not to join in the others' topless sunbathing as long as Jago was around?

What was it about him which made her feel unwontedly shy? More than shy. Nervous of him. Afraid. But perhaps not so much of him as of herself; of the feelings she had felt stirring within her when he had held her in his arms and seemed to be on the point of kissing her.

Before he returned to the beach, she had put on her bark-pleated sun top, and the others were packing up the props to return to the hotel for lunch.

They did not work that afternoon. Arrangements had been made in advance for them to spend the evening at an old plantation house where, its owners not being in residence, Gerald had permission to photograph evening clothes against a background of eighteenth-century elegance combined with twentieth-century luxury.

Fortunately, Jago's luggage included some evening kit which, although not designed for the tropics, was sufficiently light in weight to be wearable there.

Also, Janey had discovered, he had with him a dark brown silk dressing-gown which had caused Gerald to Telex to London for some trousseau underclothes and night things to be despatched to the island by air.

The house, with its high-ceilinged rooms opening on to a terrace on the ground floor and a pillared gallery above, appealed to Savanna's romantic streak. So did the selection of evening dresses made of cool cotton voile or silk chiffon in white and the sherbet pastels which set off a tan.

The evening session involved a good deal of standing about while Gerald and his assistant set up the supplementary lighting. The house had its own generator and was wired to the highest modern standards, but the soft old-world glow of candles and antique oil lamps was the effect which the photographer wanted to achieve.

There was a beautiful Spanish mahogany staircase with gilt-framed ancestral portraits grouped on the wall behind it. The first shots were taken there with Savanna wearing an apricot shoulder-tie dress and high-heeled gold sandals so that, standing two steps above Jago, for once she was looking down at him.

'I wonder if these people are genuine ancestors. I can't see much family resemblance, can you?' she said, to deflect his attention from her.

Being scrutinised by him, at such close quarters, was oddly unnerving.

'Perhaps they were bought for decorative purposes as some people buy books by the yard when they want an instant library,' he remarked, after glancing briefly at the portraits. 'Would you like to be painted?'

As he spoke, his keen eyes resumed their detailed appraisal, taking in her neck and shoulders, the hollow at the base of her throat, and the deeper hollow revealed by the low-cut décolletage.

'My parents had each of us drawn when we reached our eighth birthday,' she told him, striving not to mind the feeling of being under a microscope. 'My brothers were nice-looking children, but I looked more like a bush baby, all eyes and ears.'

'How many brothers have you?'

'Four. Three older than me, and one younger.'

'So it's probable that when you have children you'll also have more boys than girls.'

'I suppose so—if I have a large family. Most people stick at one or two. I doubt if my parents would have had five of us if they'd foreseen galloping inflation, or that my father would be killed before the boys were independent.'

'Has his death left your mother in straitened circumstances?'

'It has rather. Three of my brothers are very clever, especially the youngest one, Joey. His IQ is so unusual that any ordinary school would have been useless for him, so he goes to a school for exceptionally gifted children in Switzerland. He's only sixteen, but already he speaks fluent French and German,' she added, with affectionate pride.

'What's your own IQ?'

'Not worth testing,' she said, with a smile. 'Michael

and Richard are almost as brilliant as Joey, and Benjy and I are the dullards of the family.'

This was not strictly true, but Savanna had always had a specially soft spot for the brother nearest to her in age, and the only one of the young Bancrofts not to be blessed with a good brain. For this reason, although he had been hopeless in every field of academic endeavour and she only in certain subjects, she had always allied herself with him, bemoaning her failures at school and playing down her successes.

'However, as I'm lucky enough to be photogenic, it doesn't really matter that I was the despair of my maths mistress,' she said, neglecting to mention that in history and geography she had always been close to the top of her class.

'You are more than merely photogenic,' Jago told her dryly. 'I think you're too thin at the moment, but if you put on a few pounds your looks would match your brother's intelligence.'

'Put on weight! Are you mad?' she exclaimed, in mock horror. 'A plump model is an ex-model.'

'I wasn't suggesting you should become too plump. Just a little more curved here and there.' His hand closed on her waist and slid downwards from hip to thigh. 'You're not as undernourished as most of your kind, I agree. But the figure admired by other women isn't the one which turns men on.'

He had taken his hand from her thigh now, but the feel of it lingered, sharpening her awareness of their closeness.

'I'm not employed to turn men on but to show off clothes,' she said stiffly.

He gave her an amused look. 'I think it was Coleridge who said that men desire women and women desire to be desired.'

'By one man—yes. Not by all of them.'

He was smiling openly now. 'I don't think you know much about it yet.'

Before she could answer, Gerald announced that, the lighting being satisfactory, he was ready to shoot.

'Your left hand on Jago's shoulder, and your right on the handrail, please, Anny. With your body turned slightly this way. That's fine except for the facial expression. It's much too aloof for a bride, lovey. Let's see a little roguish smile . . . as if, having kept him waiting while you got dressed, you wouldn't mind too much if he took you back upstairs and undressed you.'

'I should be delighted,' said Jago, in an undertone.

He covered her hand where it lay on the smooth wooden rail, and his other hand returned to her waist.

'Roguish smiles went out with silent films, Gerald,' she said, hoping to hide her confusion with an air of nonchalence.

'Okay, a sexy smile, then,' Gerald amended.

'Is my expression satisfactory?' Jago enquired.

While one palm held her hand captive, the other was fondling her waist. His eyes were narrowed and intent.

'It's fine,' the photographer told him.

But the lighting was still not quite perfect, and they had to remain in the pose while his assistant carried out an adjustment.

By summoning all her professionalism, Savanna managed to maintain a provocative half-smile, but inwardly she was seething with mixed sensations, including being intensely conscious of the powerful shoulder beneath the black silk barathea on which her free hand was resting. The conservative cut of his dinner jacket, and the unadorned plainness of his shirt suggested that whatever form his tycoonery took—and she wished she had asked Gerald to elaborate on that disclosure—Jago did not suffer from any nouveau-riche leanings towards ostentation.

In a way she rather wished he did, for then she could have rationalised her wariness of him. But there was nothing about him—apart from his risqué aside a few moments earlier, and really Gerald was largely to blame for that—on which to peg her dubiety.

Physically, everything about him from his brushed back raven's wing hair to his well-scrubbed, neatly pared nails was pleasing to her. As close as they were, she could smell very faintly the clean aroma of his shaving soap, but none of the pervasive after-shave lotions used by less discriminating men.

Influenced by her father and brothers, she did not like men to be scented as strongly as women, or to give more time to their hair than was taken by a daily shampoo and a regular haircut. Any man sufficiently preoccupied with his looks to have his hair styled was too vain to be attractive to her.

'Okay, that one's in the bag. You can relax for five minutes while Anny gets changed for the next one.' Gerald was speaking to Jago.

For the next shot she wore a straight tunic of avocado crêpe-de-chine with plaited rouleaux straps and a matching girdle. Rhinestone waterfall ear-rings were her only jewellery.

This time, to her relief, they had to pretend to be playing backgammon, and there was no direct contact between them. But when she had put on the white dress, Gerald posed them on a sofa in the drawing-room, she with her feet up and Jago seated beside her, one long hard thigh pressed to hers as he leaned towards her, his forearm stretched along the backrest.

The unselfconscious ease with which he obeyed Gerald's instruction to kiss her hand would have made it clear—had it not already been obvious—that he must be a very smooth operator.

'Won't your business associates be amazed at your lending yourself to this sort of thing?' she asked while, once more, the lighting was being perfected.

'Amazed at my luck, I should imagine,' was his urbane reply. 'This dress is very becoming. You ought to buy it.'

'I should never wear it. I don't lead this kind of life. And even if I did, a dress like this would pay for a whole winter's fuel bills.'

'I suppose so.'

He sounded as if fuel bills meant as little to him as the cost of a ride on the Underground. Not that he was likely to use that crowded and uncomfortable form of transport. Probably he always took taxis, or was even grander and went about London reading the *Financial Times* in the back of a company-owned Rolls-Royce.

'Right: ready when you are,' said Gerald.

She pinned on her smile, and Jago again kissed her hand, his lips warm against her knuckles, making a quiver run through her.

They returned to the hotel in two cars, Savanna riding with Gerald and his assistant, and Jago driving the other girls. She had arranged for a light supper to be left on a tray in her room, and she did not see him again that night.

But she could not put him out of her mind, or dismiss the feeling that his co-operation was more than an un-motivated whim.

It was on their penultimate day on the island, when only one travelling outfit and the honeymoon lingerie remained to be photographed, that Gerald came to her room before dinner.

'Now that you've spent the better part of a week with him, what's your feeling about Jago, Anny?' he asked, after following her out to the balcony where she had been drinking iced water from the vacuum jug which the maids replenished several times a day.

'I'm not sure what you mean. I haven't any special feeling about him,' she answered untruthfully.

'He seems to have taken to you. Tomorrow he wants to take you on a picnic—just the two of you,' the photographer informed her.

'What? B-but he can't! We have work to do. And besides, I don't want to picnic with him.'

'Don't you? Are you sure about that?'

'Absolutely sure,' she said firmly. 'You told him I couldn't, didn't you?'

'Yes, but he isn't the type to take no for an answer if he's set his mind on something.'

'He argued about it? What cheek!'

'No, he didn't argue. I shouldn't think he ever does. He has more effective methods of getting his way,' remarked Gerald. 'To compensate me for the trouble of finding a reason for not being able to work tomorrow, he offered me this.'

He dipped two fingers into the pocket of his shirt and extracted a small folded paper.

Savanna looked at the cheque bearing Jago's bold signature, then raised incredulous eyes to his.

'He must be mad!'

'Or very much richer than I'm ever likely to be. If I want to cash it I have to give him the negatives of those topless shots we took on our second day here,' he added.

'*Oh!*' As the implication sank in, a hot angry flush suffused the gold of her sun-tan.

She would have torn the cheque to shreds, but he anticipated her reaction and whisked it away from her.

'Gerald . . . you couldn't . . . you wouldn't?' she expostulated, in shocked dismay.

'Don't fly off the handle, lovey. Think about it. If this is a tip to me for letting you off work tomorrow and handing over a few negatives, what's in it for you, ask yourself?'

Savanna drew herself up till her spine was a straight as a ramrod. Her soft mouth tightly compressed, she looked at him with icy contempt.

'I don't need to ask myself, Gerald; and I'm sorry you don't know me better than to think that I might, for one second, consider such a sickening suggestion. Keep your "tip". I don't care what you do. But I'm going to tell Mr Kindersley that he may be able to buy your co-operation, but he can't buy mine—not at any price!'

She sprang to her feet and brushed past him, fending off the arm with which he attempted to stay her.

A few moments later she was striding purposefully through the colourful shrubbery which separated her block from the one in which Jago was accommodated.

A white-haired West Indian gardener with whom,

normally, she passed the time of day whenever they saw each other, looked after her in surprise as she marched past a few yards away without even noticing him, her bearing stiff with indignation.

CHAPTER TWO

LAST time, she had tapped at his door. This time she pressed the buzzer, and continued to press until the door opened.

'Hello, Savanna,' Jago said calmly.

There were people passing along the path which ran the full length of the block.

She said, 'Aren't you going to ask me in?'

'By all means.'

He stood aside, and she stalked past him, into a room which she had expected to be the same as her own but which was considerably larger, with a screen wall between the sitting and sleeping areas. The bed was a double one, she noticed.

'Won't you sit down?' he suggested. 'What can I give you to drink?'

'Nothing, thank you,' she said furiously. 'I don't drink with men of your sort. I wouldn't be here, in the same room with you, if I didn't want you to know what I think of you and your kind!' She was shaking with rage, her eyes flashing.

'My kind?' Jago said mildly.

'Your kind,' she repeated, with a snap. 'The kind who thinks everyone has a price . . . that anyone will do anything if they're offered enough money for it . . . that all girls are whores, to be bought and bedded and forgotten. Oh! I can't tell you how you disgust me . . . you, and the hateful men like you. That you're not an old man makes it worse. You . . . you could have women for love.'

He said nothing, looking down at her with an expression she could not read. She had a feeling that her outburst had been a waste of breath; that there was no way she could pierce the thick, insensitive skin of a man who believed that everything in the world could be bought if one had enough money.

That her fury was all the fiercer for being shot through with disillusionment was a factor she was too worked up to recognise. At that moment all she was conscious of was an overwhelming need to get through to him, to dent the armour of his indifference.

Impelled by a blaze of temper completely foreign to her nature, she took one impetuous step forward and struck him with the flat of her hand.

Even before her palm had connected with his lean dark cheek, she was regretting an action totally at variance with her upbringing, and indeed with her everyday instincts.

Slender as she was, her right arm still had the muscle developed by several years of enthusiastic tennis, not only at school but on the grass court at Clare's house during the holidays. The slap didn't make Jago stagger as it would have done with a smaller man, but it had enough force to swing his head sideways.

The next instant she found herself with both arms pinioned and her spine arched like a bow as he held her helplessly captive, his face now as wrathful as hers had been moments earlier.

But his voice was controlled as he said, 'If you ever do that again, you'll regret it. My hand is much harder than yours, my girl, and don't think I won't hit a woman, because I will . . . here . . . and with interest.'

The single vigorous spank with which he demonstrated this threat made Savanna stifle a yelp. Her buttock smarting, she squirmed unavailingly to free herself. But the hand which was clipping her wrists was as inescapable as a handcuff, and his other arm was round her waist, pinning her to him.

'Let me go!' she demanded, through clenched teeth.

'When you've calmed down enough to listen to what I have to say to you.'

'I don't want to hear what you have to say. I've heard it already from Gerald.'

'What did he tell you?'

Realising she had no hope of escaping until he chose to release her, she forced herself to relax and submit to his hold on her. Striving for calm, she said bitterly, 'He showed me your cheque . . . your bribe to him. I don't know what men usually pay for pictures to gloat over in private, but I'm sure you could have bought several albums of dirty photographs for what you've just paid for a few shots of me in a monokini. Well, they're all you'll get for your money. Gerald may not object to our going on a so-called picnic tomorrow, but I do. I wouldn't "picnic" with you if you were the last man on earth!'

To her astonishment, Jago laughed and released his hold on her.

'Sit down, Savanna, and listen to me. *Sit down!*'—as she glanced towards the door.

The repetition wasn't shouted. If anything the second instruction was spoken more quietly than the first, but on a note of command which she didn't dare flout.

Reluctantly she chose the upright chair by the writing table, and sat down, giving him a mutinous glare as she did so.

'You're right,' said Jago. 'Not everyone has a price. But if you were me you would have learnt a long time ago that, when a man is very rich, a great many people will be nice to him—in every sense of that expression—in the expectation of being handsomely rewarded for their amiability. I didn't think you could be bought, but I wanted to be certain. I guessed the construction which Gerald would put on the cheque I gave him, and I didn't disabuse him of his ideas,' he continued sardonically. 'Evidently he conveyed them to you—or did you jump to those unpleasant and mistaken conclusions off your own bat?'

Ignoring his question, she asked, 'What do you mean—mistaken conclusions?'

'I offered Gerald money for the negatives in order to destroy them, not to gloat over the prints,' he sayd dryly.

'To destroy them?' echoed Savanna, mystified.

'I didn't wish them to be published.'

'Why not?'

'I want you to marry me, Savanna. And if you do, I don't want photographs of my wife's breasts appearing in a magazine, not even in *Vogue*.'

Her body sagged with the shock of a statement so incredible that at first she didn't believe she could possibly have heard him correctly.

'T-to marry y-you?' she murmured faintly.

'To marry me,' Jago repeated firmly. 'What you need is a drink,' he added and, turning, opened a cupboard which turned out to be a small refrigerator. She watched him dislodge some ice cubes and tip them into tall glasses. 'I know you don't care for spirits, but a small measure of rum won't hurt you. It will pull you together. This is called a rum float,' he told her, a few minutes later, when he brought one of the glasses to her.

With a hand not perfectly steady, she accepted the drink and sipped it, finding the taste unfamiliar but in no way unpleasant.

'You can't be serious about marrying me,' she murmured, watching his tall frame relax on the chintz-covered two-seater sofa.

'Perfectly serious, I assure you. Don't you remember my saying that I'd seen you on *Vogue* on board Concorde? When I reached New York I had checks made to find out if you were English or American. I came here specifically to meet you. To be recruited by Gerald to play the part of your bridegroom was better luck than I'd anticipated. I'm hoping the past week has been a dress rehearsal for our real honeymoon later this year.'

'But we don't *know* each other,' she protested. 'We only met a few days ago.'

'We have the rest of our lives to find out everything about each other. As soon as I saw your face, I knew it was the one I wanted to look at across the breakfast table for the next forty years,' Jago said quietly.

All at once, in a flash of perception, Savanna understood why Gerald's question *What's in it for you? ask yourself* had caused her to lose her temper and come blazing round here to tell Jago just what she thought of him.

She loved him.

All week she had been falling in love with him. Thus, the mistaken belief that he thought of her as a tart had been the cruellest of shocks.

'Come here.' He put out a hand and beckoned her to him.

Leaving her glass on the writing table, Savanna rose slowly to her feet and obeyed this much gentler command.

In her fury, she had stormed out of her own room without stopping to change the Turkish bathrobe and mules supplied to all guests by the hotel. Her hair was still damp from the shower, and she wore not a scrap of make-up, not even waterproof mascara and lip gloss.

When she came within reach, Jago took her by the hand and drew her down beside him.

'Have I been wrong in thinking that you liked me a little?' he asked quizzically.

'More than a little,' she admitted. 'But I think we ought to know each other for much longer than six days before thinking about marriage.'

'We shall have to be engaged for at least two months, because I have various commitments which will prevent me from taking time off for a honeymoon until early May. It was difficult to fit this trip into my schedule—I lead an erratic life, Savanna. Shall you mind a *mouvementé* existence? Presumably not, or you wouldn't have chosen to be a model.'

'I didn't choose. Gerald chose me.'

'But without any strings, I understand.'

'No—certainly not!' she said vehemently. 'Did you ask him that?—If there was anything between us apart from a professional relationship?'

'Yes. If I want to know something, I ask. Why not?'

'What did he say?'

'That, unlikely as it might seem in this day and age, he believed you to be still a virgin. Was he right?'

She nodded, blushing a little.

'Good. I prefer it that way.'

'Why? So that I shan't be able to compare you—perhaps unfavourably—with my previous lovers?' she asked, for the first time daring to tease him.

'No, I've never suffered from an inferiority complex—in any field,' was his dry response. 'However, as you will discover, one of the penalties of wealth is that it makes it very difficult to keep one's private life private. My marriage to a leading model is bound to attract a good deal of publicity and, inevitably, if there are any skeletons in our cupboards, the gossip writers will find them and rattle them. As you're a virgin, there's nothing they can write which will embarrass you. Nor is there in my case, as far as I'm concerned. But you may read things about me which will upset you.'

'What sort of things?' she asked uncertainly.

'I'm thirty-three. I haven't always lived as discreetly as I shall in future,' he told her. 'Any normal man of my age is bound to have a past, you know. Don't let it concern you.'

'No . . . no, I shan't,' she said gravely. 'As long as there's nothing shady about your business dealings. You don't make money from armaments, or anything of that sort, do you?'

He smiled, and shook his head. 'No, none of my activities is lethal, illegal or in any way dubious. Now, having demonstrated what a belligerent young woman you can be on occasion, how about a kiss to make it better?'—offering the cheek she had struck less than ten minutes earlier.

Shyly, Savanna put her lips to the taut brown skin between his cheekbone and jaw. As she pursed them in a light kiss, he turned his head and she found herself mouth to mouth with him.

To begin with he was very gentle with her; his lips brushing back and forth on hers which, at first, she kept closed. At this stage she was leaning against him, and he was still holding her hand as he had since drawing her down beside him.

Then, releasing her fingers, he put both his arms firmly round her, and his mouth settled over hers and began to move in a way to which instinctively she responded by parting her lips and sliding her arms round his neck.

The few kisses she had exchanged with friends of her brothers, after parties in her middle teens, were an inadequate preparation for being embraced by a man as experienced as Jago. By the time he raised his head, she was breathless and trembling, her heart pounding wildly against her ribs, her topaz eyes slumbrous beneath her dark silky lashes as she opened them to meet the slightly mocking grey gaze of the man who had induced her excitement.

'Oh . . . goodness!' she exclaimed, in a faint voice.

'Don't tell me you've never been kissed before. That I can't believe,' he remarked, relaxing his hold on her.

'Not very much . . . and *never* like that,' she admitted.

'But you liked it, I gather?'

She buried her face in his shoulder. 'Don't tease me . . . you know I did,' she murmured.

Jago chuckled. 'So did I. It's going to be a pleasure to teach you all the other things you haven't tried yet.'

She felt his hand slide down her back to rest on the place he had spanked with such painful vigour. This time his touch was a caress.

'You could have a long lesson now, if you like,' he said, close to her ear. His voice came from deep in his throat.

Quivering, she drew away. 'Will you be angry if I say No?' Before he could answer, she went on hurriedly, 'It isn't that I think it's wrong if two people really love each other. But I want to be absolutely sure before . . . before I go to bed with you. All this has happened so quickly. It . . . it could be an infatuation.'

Anxiously she studied his face for the first sign of his reaction.

'Not in my case it couldn't,' he answered. 'But in yours . . . yes, perhaps it might be.' He paused, his expression enigmatic. 'All right. As I've had the rare luck to find myself an old-fashioned virgin, I'll be an old-fashioned suitor and allow you to set whatever pace you please. If you want to be one of the few brides for whom a white dress is more than an obsolete convention, so be it. We'll go to bed on our wedding night. I can wait until then—if you can.'

He tacked on the afterthought with a glinting look which suggested that he doubted if she could.

'I—I must go back and dress,' said Savanna, as his gaze left her face and moved downwards to where, while she was in his arms, the front of the bathrobe had loosened, showing flesh which, although always visible at the beach, somehow seemed more provocative indoors.

As she pulled the robe closer about her, Jago said, 'Yes, it is rather a strain on my good intentions to have you here in my bedroom and, by the feel of it, wearing nothing under that bathrobe. But you may as well finish your drink.'

He stood up and fetched it for her. 'Unless you don't care for it,' he added, not rejoining her on the sofa but moving way to an armchair on the far side of the brass and glass coffee table.

'No, I like it. I've never had rum before. I hope it won't go to my head.'

'I didn't give you very much. What about this picnic tomorrow? Have you changed your mind? Will you come with me?'

'Yes, of course I will, now. But I think I ought to work tomorrow morning. There's the yellow trouser suit to photograph, and the underclothes and nightie.'

'I don't object to the trouser suit. But the other things—no,' Jago said decisively. 'From now on, the only person who is going to see you *en déshabille* is me. Will you mind giving up your career for me?'

'But Jago, I can't—not immediately,' she protested.

'Why not? Because of a contract?'

'No, nothing like that—I'm a freelance. But I need the money I'm earning. My family can't manage without it. I must go on modelling for a few years.'

'No, I don't want a part-time wife. I want you to travel with me. Looking after your mother and brothers will become my responsibility.'

'Oh, no—that's not fair,' she protested. 'I couldn't let you, and they wouldn't feel comfortable being dependent on you.'

'They'll have to adjust to it,' he said. 'Perhaps I should make it quite clear that, even though you are very young, I'm not, and therefore I want to have children as soon as possible. Does the thought that, a year from now, you could be a mother disturb you?'

'I—I don't really know,' she said hesitantly. 'Wouldn't it be nice to have a little time to ourselves before we start thinking about a family?'

'I've done my thinking already. I want several children, and I want to have them as soon as possible—which, however enthusiastically we make love, will not be this year,' he added. 'In your case, having children doesn't mean that you'll be tied down and hampered by them, as many women are. They'll have a nannie to look after them.'

It seemed to Savanna an oddly down-to-earth conversation to follow so swiftly on a proposal. But she said only, 'Yes, I suppose so,' and sipped the rum float, and tried to feel a sense of reality, instead of the feeling that the whole thing was a dream from which, shortly, she would wake up.

'As soon as we get back to England, I'll come and talk to your mother,' Jago went on. 'Whatever burdens you've been taking on your shoulders will be nothing to me, I assure you. You need have no compunction at transferring them to mine. Both physically and financially, they're much broader than yours are, my dear.'

'Yes, but even so . . .' she said uneasily. 'Anyway, I certainly don't mean to let Gerald get away with that ridiculously large cheque. To pay for those negatives is silly. He can easily make up some reason to explain why he wasn't able to develop and print them.'

'Let him keep it,' said Jago indifferently. 'It's little

enough compensation for losing his beautiful new discovery.'

'To me it seems a small fortune. Just how rich are you, Jago?' she asked him.

'Rich enough to buy you all those dresses you wore at the great house the other night,' he said lightly. 'Why do you frown? My income should make you happy. Most women enjoy spending money.'

'So do I—within reason,' she answered. 'But if you're really *extremely* rich, you must have a life style quite different from ours. I—I'm not sure that I can cope. For instance, what I know about giving large dinner parties is as little as you probably know about pot-luck and making ends meet.'

'If I want to give a dinner party, I have only to ring up one of the many hotels with a private dining-room. At present I live in hotels. You can spend our engagement house-hunting. I'm sure it won't be beyond you to find us a suitable place to live. I could see that you liked that plantation house. Something of a similar order is what I envisage for us.'

'You seem to have thought it all out, yet this time last week you'd never set eyes on me.'

'No, but I've been ready to take a wife for some time. As soon as I saw you on *Vogue*, I felt I had found the girl for me.'

'On the strength of a magazine cover?'

'Why not? Seeing you on a cover enabled me to study your face much more thoroughly than if our first meeting had been at some social occasion.'

'But a person's face is such a small part of the whole of them. There are so many other elements—their voice, their hands, their likes and dislikes, their sense of humour ... so many things. To come all this way to meet me, merely because my face had caught your eye, seems such a gamble,' she answered.

'What had I to lose?' he said carelessly. 'The extra air fare, and the couple of days which would have been wasted if the rest of you hadn't matched up to the promise of your lovely face. Not much to stake against the possibility of finding the woman I've been looking for.'

'Perhaps not.' She finished her drink and got up to go.

Jago rose to open the door for her. Before doing so, he put his hand under her chin and repeated the kiss which had played havoc with her senses; if not at such length as before, long enough to quicken her heartbeats and make her reluctant to leave him.

'Off you go. Be ready at seven. This evening we'll dine by ourselves,' he said, as he opened the door and propelled her gently over the threshold.

Savanna walked back to her room in a trance, once again oblivious to the gardener, who was still busy pruning a bush.

To her surprise and displeasure, Gerald was still on her balcony. She wanted to be on her own, to start getting used to the fact that, instead of returning to England with the uncharted future she had had on the day she left home, she would be going back as the prospective bride of a man who had swept into her life with the irresistible force of a West Indian hurricane.

'As you left your room key behind, I thought I'd better hang on for a bit,' said Gerald. 'What happened? How did he take it?'

'You misunderstood him,' she said coldly. 'You shouldn't impute your own base motives to other people. Nor should I have believed you could be right. May I have that cheque, please?'—holding out her hand for it.

'Why? What do you want it for?'

'To give it back to him. For you to cash it would put you on a par with a blackmailer, and I'm sure you don't want to be thought of in that light.'

'I didn't put any pressure on him. He gave me the cheque voluntarily.'

'As a romantic gesture of quite unneccessary extravagance, considering how small a favour he wanted from you. I'm sure if he rings up the Editor and explains the position, there'll be no question of them using the shots he objects to. And you'll make far more money if I let you have the exclusive rights to photograph my real life trousseau for *Hola* and *Paris Match*, and all the other magazines which thrive on features of that sort.'

'What are you talking about . . . your real life trousseau?' the photographer asked her perplexedly.

'Jago has asked me to marry him. That's why I was so upset when you gave me the impression that he had something else in mind. I've fallen in love with him, Gerald, and it seems he feels the same way.'

For some moments he looked as stunned as she had been earlier. Then he said, 'So I was right—he did have his eye on you.'

'Yes, but not in the way you implied. I told you you were too cynical. He's not that sort of person at all. Or not now. He may have been once, but not any more.'

Suddenly, in the same way that it had been a little while before she had felt the kick of the alcohol in the rum float, Savanna was beginning to feel an upsurge of happiness such as she had never experienced before.

Until his astonishing proposal of marriage, Jago's powerful physical attraction had been more worrying than enjoyable. She had seen it as a threat to her peace of mind; a force which might throw her off balance and make her act unwisely.

But now, in the context of an engagement, it no longer worried her. As the protagonists in a licit love affair, they were entitled to be violently attracted to each other. It was right and proper that they should be. From now on, whenever he looked desirously at her, she need not be nervous of his intentions. They could not be more honourable.

She felt so relieved and joyful that, when Gerald produced the cheque and handed it over to her, she forgot how angry she had been with him.

She said, 'Jago and I are going to have dinner *à deux* tonight, which is bound to make the others talk. But I'd rather you didn't tell them what I've just told you until I've asked him when he wants our engagement to be made public. Tomorrow I can pose in the yellow trouser suit, but not in the other things—he doesn't approve. And we can rely on you to get rid of the monokini negatives, can't we, Gerald?'

'Sure. As you say, I stand to make a lot more out of your whirlwind romance with England's answer to Onassis.'

'Is Jago on *that* level?'

'I don't know. Maybe not quite. But how old is he, for God's sake?'

'Thirty-three.'

'Give him time, lovey. He may end up richer than Onassis. According to the men I heard talking about him in the bar, soon after we arrived here, he's some kind of financial genius who's made most of his fortune simply by changing currencies at the right moment. Pretty risky, I should have thought, but then I don't know a stock from a share. But it might be as well if you're taking him for better *or* worse.'

'But of course. I love him, not his money,' Savanna said simply.

And she meant it.

Jago's wealth meant nothing to her personally, although she would be glad if it meant that her mother's operation could be expedited, and her brothers' futures made secure.

For herself, she would have been even happier to be marrying a man of ordinary means. The prospect of being mistress of a house which needed a large staff to run it was not alluring.

After Gerald had left her, she thought how much better it would have been, at least from her own point of view, if Jago had had the kind of income which would have allowed them to afford a country cottage and a tiny *pied-à-terre* in London, both of which she could have run single-handed.

To have too much money had always seemed to her to be as fraught with problems as having too little.

She wondered how Clare and Livvy would react to her news. They had both been inclined to mock her belief in a life-long relationship with one man as the best way to live.

When Jago came for her at seven, she was waiting for him in a dress she had bought in a Summer Sale, and carrying a shawl knitted for her by her mother in exactly the same shade of emerald, a colour which tended to look garish in the soft light in England, but which came into its own in the tropics.

He took her to dine at a hotel not much different from where they were staying, except that nobody knew them and they could sit and talk undisturbed.

'Do you realise I know nothing at all about your family . . . your parents, and your brothers and sisters?' she said, when they had chosen what to eat and he had finished studying the wine list.

'My parents are dead, so you'll have no problems with a mother-in-law. Not that you would have done anyway. My mother was a charming woman. I've only one younger sister, whose marriage has taken her to Cheshire. Her name is Susan, and her husband, Edward, is a surgeon—a nice chap, I like him. As they very rarely come to London, I sometimes fly up to Manchester and spend a weekend with them. Susan has strong family feelings. She had a close relationship with my mother, whom she still misses. She'll be delighted to have a sister-in-law.'

'What is she like? What are her interests?'

'Her husband, her children, and her house; although before she met Edward she was doing research for a well-known biographer. Now she has a pair of two-year-old twins to occupy most of her time, but she's a history graduate and she talks of a career later on, when the kids are at school. You needn't be daunted by her degree. No one ever takes her for an egghead—rather the reverse.'

Savanna was reminded of their first encounter, when he had put her back up by suggesting that she might not know the meaning of entrepreneur. Did he still think she wasn't too bright? Brainless enough to be nervous of people cleverer than herself?

'What about me, after I've produced your quiverful?

Will you mind if I take up my career then?'

'I doubt if you'll want to by that time. If you have eight babies at two-year intervals, you'll be in the second half of your thirties before the last one is born.'

'Eight babies!' she exclaimed, taken aback. 'But not even the Queen has *eight* children! I—oh, Jago, you're teasing again'—as she realised that although he wasn't smiling, there was a gleam of amusement lurking in his steady grey eyes.

He reached across the table for her hand. 'All right: if you think eight too many, I'll settle for four. I don't think we're likely to hatch any twins. That strain is from Edward's side of the family.'

'Supposing I couldn't have any children? Have you considered that possibility?

'An unlikely contingency,' he answered, adding, after a pause, 'You've never had any illnesses which might affect you in that way, have you?'

'No, I've always been extremely healthy.'

'I think it's a sensible precaution for people to have a check-up before they marry,' he went on. 'I have one every year, as a matter of routine, so I know I'm in good general health. I can't actually vouch for my ability to father children, but I have no reason to doubt it.'

For the second time that day it struck Savanna as somewhat prosaic for a couple so newly engaged to be talking about parenthood. But then Jago began to stroke the palm of her hand with his thumb, accompanying the caress with such an intent, ardent look that she became conscious of nothing but the excitement singing along her nerves.

Later a steel band played, and they danced on an open-air terrace lit by moonlight and coloured lanterns.

At first he held her very close to him. Unlike the night at the great house, when the feel of his shoulder inside his dinner jacket had been more disturbing than pleasurable, tonight she was able to enjoy the contact with his strong body.

However, after a short time, he loosened his hold, but

not before she had realised that dancing with her had rekindled the desire she had seen in his eyes at the beginning of dinner.

As he put a little space between them, she found herself wondering when was the last time he had made love, and with whom. Not very long ago, probably. But that was his past, and nothing to do with her. Their future together was what mattered. Could she hold him against all the women who, as Jago himself had remarked, saw him as an exciting quarry? And not only because he was rich, she thought, but because he was also a tall macho male with finely-articulated hands with which to caress them, and a mouth at once stern and sensual with which to kiss them.

It was not late when they drove back to their own hotel in the hired car. Where the road ran close to a beach, Jago slowed and drove off the macadam on to a stretch of firm turf which bordered the sand.

'It's so beautiful here,' murmured Savanna. 'I do think it's a shame that these islands haven't enough jobs to support all the people who were born in them. If I belonged here, I should hate being forced to go to England or America to find work. None of us wants to go back to London tomorrow. How must West Indians living there feel? Coming out here has made me realise how wretchedly homesick many of them must be.'

Jago said, 'The older ones—yes, I expect so. But don't forget that many people of West Indian origin are actually born and bred Cockneys or Liverpudlians. A beautiful environment is desirable, but it's not the most important thing in life.'

She had been gazing at the sea, but now she turned to look at him, the light being almost as bright as daylight, and the car an open one.

'What is the most important thing?'

His arm was along the backrest. He was playing with her moon-silvered hair which was loose on her shoulders, winding a strand round his forefinger. At her question, he shifted closer along the bench seat. His hand delved through the thick tresses to find the nape of her neck.

'At the moment, for us, this is,' he told her huskily, before he kissed her.

Very soon she knew he was right. Her whole body throbbed with excitement as he taught her many kinds of kisses; soft feather-light kisses on her eyelids, little nibbling kisses round her ears, and long, lingering, burning kisses—like brands on the skin of her throat—as he tilted her head back and traced a slow path down her neck to the top of her dress.

Her eyes closed, her mind in a whirl, her whole being engrossed by these new and lovely sensations, Savanna gave no thought to the outcome. She was incapable of thought. Only feelings governed her now; feelings which made her heart race, and her breathing rapid and uneven.

Even when she felt him beginning to unfasten her buttons, she seemed to be powerless to stop him. Her slim hands fluttered on his shoulders, but her body remained lax and yielding as his sure fingers opened her dress, and she waited to feel the heat of his lips on her breasts.

But Jago's ears, sharper than hers, had caught the drone of a motor. Not ungently, he released her and straightened. 'There's a car coming.'

Before its headlights swept the place where they were parked, he was once more behind the steering wheel, with a decorous space between them. As soon as the car had gone past, he switched on his engine and followed it.

Savanna, whose trembling fingers had been quite incapable of refastening her buttons quickly, and who had been holding her dress together, now began to do it up.

Stealing a sideways glance at Jago, she wondered what he was thinking, and why he had decided not to resume his interrupted caresses.

To be seen making love in a car—even if it was only a glimpse which the other driver would have had—was certainly rather offputting; but not to the extent of quenching her excitement. If she still felt all stirred up, presumably he did as well.

In the hotel car park, he pocketed the ignition key and came round to open her door for her. Neither of them had spoken during the second phase of the drive back, and his silence was beginning to make her feel ashamed of her abandonment while they were parked.

'Would you care for a nightcap?' he asked, as they walked towards the main block to pick up their room keys.

'I don't think so, thank you. Gerald says that night flights across the Atlantic are usually fairly uncomfortable. I think I'll try to make up some sleep.'

'Sleep can't be stored in advance. It can only be made good afterwards. Did you come over in the Economy Class?'

'Yes.'

'You'll be going back First Class with me. It's a good deal more comfortable.'

'Thank you, but I would rather go back the way I came—with the others. It wouldn't be nice to separate from them at this stage; especially as they don't know about us.'

'They will tomorrow, and I see no reason for you to consider their feelings in preference to mine. There's not enough leg room in the Economy Class for me. Everyone finds it cramped, and for someone of my height it's purgatory. You'll travel with me,' Jago said firmly, as they came to the porter's desk.

'Very well. If you insist.' She knew her tone was absurdly formal.

He took both their keys from the porter, and escorted her to the door of her room.

Having unlocked it for her, he handed her the key, saying, 'I won't come in to say goodnight. If I do, I'll be tempted to stay. I'm used to taking what I want when I want it, Savanna. It's a long time since I had anything to do with a young and inexperienced girl. I think it wouldn't be too difficult for me to sweep you off your feet. Earlier today I told you you could set the pace of our relationship. In future, don't rely on me to call a halt as I did tonight. Between now and May, there'll be many times when it will be up to you to control how far things go between us.'

He put his hands on her shoulders, and dropped a quick kiss on her forehead.

'Goodnight, my lovely. Sleep well.'

Then he was gone; his tall figure striding away through the shrubbery until, soon, he was out of sight, and she turned to enter her room.

A couple of hours later, remembering his injunction to her to sleep well, she wondered if he was asleep now. Imagining him sprawled in the wide bed, she moved restlessly in the twin bed which she was occupying.

Until tonight she had been only dimly aware of the overwhelming power of passion; and of the voluptuousness of her own nature. She could still feel his lips on her throat, and the aching longing to surrender herself to him utterly.

Although he, with his wider experience, seemed sure that it was not an infatuation on his side, how could she, with no experience at all, be equally certain of the nature of her feelings?

In that respect, an engagement of only two months seemed a short time in which to test the strength of their day-to-day compatibility. But when she remembered his kisses, it seemed a long time to wait before they could spend their nights together.

After the flight back to England, the First Class passengers left the aircraft before the rest; but all of them waited together for their baggage to appear on the carousel.

Savanna and the other girls, none of whom ran a car, had arrived at the airport by Underground, and it didn't occur to her that she wouldn't be concluding her journey home in the same way.

However, when Jago had retrieved all the girls' baggage for them, piled it on a trolley and pushed it through the Green side of the Customs hall, it turned out that he had a chauffeur-driven car waiting for him.

'If any of you live near Savanna, we can give you a lift,' he offered pleasantly.

But none of them lived in the same part of Kent as she did. The party broke up: Gerald and his assistant heading for the car park, and the fashion girls·taking over the trolley to push their cases to the Underground, while the driver carried Jago's case and hers to the waiting Rolls-Royce.

When they were ensconced in the back of it, being sped through the outskirts of London in a typical early March sleet shower, she said, 'Would you mind if I introduced you to my mother just as a . . . a friend, to begin with? I'd rather not spring our engagement on her without any warning.'

'By all means.· Whatever you wish. I'll just make a call to my secretary and see what's been happening in my absence. Excuse me.'

He lifted a section of the wide, padded armrest between them, and revealed a telephone receiver. Pressing a button, he waited for a moment before saying, 'Good morning, Elizabeth. I'm giving someone a lift home, but I'll be in the office after lunch. Has anything urgent come up since I spoke to you yesterday?'

Savanna looked out of the window at the sleet-lashed outer suburbs. They were cruising along a clearway flanked by semi-detached houses with all their windows closed. This could be because of the weather, because of the noise of passing traffic, or because there was no one at home, the wives in such houses being obliged to go out to work to help pay the mortgage and the bills.

Until recently, in spite of the glamour of her job, she had belonged to that world of mortgaged houses, small economical cars, and burdensome money worries.

Now, lapped in the spacious comfort of the Rolls-Royce with its thick Wilton carpet, pale grey leather upholstery and controlled temperature, she felt as if she were in transit between that world and Jago's very different one; just as, during the night, she had travelled from the balmy starlight of the Caribbean to this wet, dreary morning in England.

When he had finished talking to his secretary, she said, 'I haven't told you that my mother can't walk very well. In fact she can hardly walk at all.'

'Why is that?'

Briefly, Savanna explained her mother's condition.

'But you needn't worry that you're landing yourself with a crotchety invalid mother-in-law. She's incredibly brave and cheerful about it. I know she has a great deal of pain, but she never gives way to self-pity. She's a very positive person. When my father was killed, she was shattered . . . we all were. But now, instead of being miserable at having been widowed quite young, she thinks of herself as lucky to have had twenty-six years of happiness. If she weren't disabled, I expect she would marry again. I think some people have a talent for loving like others have a gift for music or painting. It seems a great waste of Mummy's gift for making a happy home for her to be left on her own when we all leave the nest.'

'She has domestic help presumably?'

'No, she does as much as she can, and I do the rest in the evening. Except for Benjy, the boys are only at home during the vacations, and not always then. But we've got them all very well trained. Why don't you come to supper tonight? By then I'll have broken the news to her, and you can meet Benjy and sample my cooking. It's not bad.'

'I should have liked to, but unfortunately I have an engagement which I can't break. I'm speaking at a dinner given by one of the livery companies,' he explained. 'As you probably know, most of them derive from the mediaeval guilds of the City of London which used to impose standards of quality and honesty on various crafts and trades. Nowadays the companies make generous grants to education, charity and research. I accepted the invitation a year ago, and I can't back out at the last moment.'

'Of course not. I wish I could hear your speech. What's your subject?'

'High finance—very dull,' was his answer. 'When we're married, I'm afraid you'll often have to sit through my speeches. You'll find it a great deal more boring than holding a pose while Gerald gets the lighting right,' he added dryly.

'Why?—Are you a particularly dull speaker?' she asked, slightly vexed by his assumption that his subject would be over her head.

'I hope not, but most wives are bored by their husbands' pet subjects. I've seen the glazed look in their eyes, and the concealed yawns.'

'Perhaps that's because they're bored not so much by the speeches as by their husbands *in toto*. I've noticed that, as a rule, people who go in for speechmaking do tend to be puffed up types, very pleased with themselves. Do you speak in public a great deal?'

While referring to bored wives, Jago had unfolded the morning paper which had been lying on his side when they entered the car, and begun to skim the front page.

Now he lowered the paper to look at her. 'Not often. Once or twice a year. Were you needling me, Savanna?' he added, with a narrowed glance.

'Yes, because you'd needled me, although unintentionally, no doubt.'

'Really? How did I do that?'

'By implying that, if I were present tonight, I wouldn't be able to understand you. Perhaps it will be too abstruse, but I find myself able to follow the speeches I hear on television . . . and sometimes to recognise them for the gobbledygook they are,' she added.

His lean cheeks creased with amusement. Keeping hold of the paper with one hand, he slid the other behind her and pulled her towards him.

'Come down from that high horse and kiss me,' he murmured, his eyes on her mouth.

The kiss would have gone on much longer, but Savanna, conscious that the driver must be able to see them in his mirror, pulled free.

Guessing the cause of her discomfiture, Jago said,

'Marsh is very well trained. With a girl in the back, he drives on his wing mirrors.'

It was meant as a joke—she knew that. But somehow it didn't amuse her.

She said shortly, 'And I suppose it doesn't matter what the hoi-polloi in the streets see. Who cares about them?'

His smiling mouth hardened. His gaze cooled.

'Cracks of that sort I like substantiated.'

She had already regretted the jibe which she knew to have been quite unjustified. He had never said or done anything to suggest that he looked down on people less affluent than himself.

'I'm sorry. It wasn't fair. It must be jet lag which is making me tetchy.'

'Could be. Have an early night.' Jago returned his attention to the paper.

Savanna recognised the snub, and knew it was not undeserved. Twice, in quick succession, she had been deliberately unpleasant, whereas neither of the remarks which had offended her had been intended to annoy.

Another girl, faced with Jago's withdrawal, might have reacted by pouting and removing herself to her corner, there to make matters worse by sulking.

But until two years before, she had lived with parents whose marriage had not been entirely a matter of luck. The Bancrofts, like all happy couples, had known how to stop minor tiffs from becoming major quarrels; and, by example rather than precept, had taught the technique to their children.

So it was because she had often seen her mother, and her father, eating humble pie with a good grace, that she laid both hands on his arm and, with a warmly repentant smile said, 'I *am* sorry—truly. It was horrid of me to say that to you when it's not half an hour since you demonstrated what nice instincts you have.'

His expression remained aloof, but he raised an eyebrow and said, 'Really?'

'By staying to hoist the others' luggage off the conveyor belt for them. Some men with a car waiting outside would have left them to manage by themselves. I thought it was very sweet of you.'

'I should call it the normal behaviour of any man in a baggage room where several of the women are known to him.'

'I shouldn't. Chivalrous manners are rare enough to be very much appreciated.'

'Not always. You'd be surprised at how often I've held a shop door open for one woman, only to have six march through it, none of them even bothering to smile at me.'

'That happens to everyone, and it's maddening.'

Not realising it could be pushed out of the way, Savanna moved round the armrest and perched on the edge of his side of the seat.

'If Marsh really never looks, can we kiss and make up?'

His charming smile appeared. 'With pleasure.'

He removed the rest, making more room for her to snuggle against him and offer her lips.

She was still in the circle of his arm, and they were both reading the book reviews, when she realised they had passed through the green belt and were nearing the town where she lived.

'Had I better give Marsh some directions?' she asked.

'No need. I gave your address to my secretary yesterday. She will have relayed it to him, and he will have found out the way there. It's part of his job.'

'But how did you know my address?'

'It was one of the facts I had checked when I wanted to know who you were.'

'What other facts do you know?'

'Your birth date. Your height. Your weight. Your vital statistics. Your telephone number.'

'Where did you get all that information?'

'I don't know the source—probably your agent. I merely rang up a friend who works for American *Vogue*, and left it to them to do the detective work.'

'I'm not sure I like the idea of those details being so easily available. You might have been some horrible old lecher plotting to seduce me.'

'I am plotting to seduce you—but in the most respectable way, in a bridal suite somewhere, with a marriage certificate in our luggage. Where would you like to go for your honeymoon?'

'Anywhere you choose to take me.'

He nuzzled her ear, his arm tightening round her waist. 'Just stay as beautiful and biddable as you are at this moment, and we'll be on a permanent honeymoon.'

'I hope so.' Savanna gave a sigh of contentment, the friction between them forgotten as she nestled against his strong shoulder.

'One thing is certain anyway,' she murmured, a few moments later. 'Although she's bound to be startled when I tell her about our engagement, my mother is sure to like you.'

But strangely, although she was usually the most welcoming of parents to any of her children's friends, Mary Bancroft's manner towards Jago was courteous but markedly reserved.

Probably he did not realise that she was not her normal friendly self, but Savanna sensed it immediately. Thinking that, in spite of her mother's assurance that all had gone well in her absence, some problem must have arisen, she cut his visit to a minimum.

'Thank you for bringing me home. I expect you want to get back to London if you're going into your office this afternoon,' she said, when the three of them had spent about a quarter of an hour making polite small talk.

'Yes, there's bound to be a good deal of work waiting after a fortnight out of the country, although I have a very able secretary who can take care of most things when I'm abroad,' he answered. He rose. 'Goodbye, Mrs Bancroft.' He bent to shake hands with her.

Watching them, Savanna saw the contrast between his tan and his fitness with her mother's pallor, and her drawn look, with an ache of compassion.

Leaving Mrs Bancroft in her chair by the sitting-room window, she went into the hall with him.

'You have our number, but I have no way of contacting

you. Do you really live in a hotel?'

'Yes, and this is the number.' He wrote it on the pad beside the telephone on the table by the foot of the staircase. 'But I'll call you later, after I've had a look at my desk diary and know how much free time I shall have in the next few days.'

Savanna's nod was somewhat abstracted. It was not that she wanted to say goodbye to him, but she was concerned to know what was behind her mother's manner.

Jago took both her hands in his and kissed them, one after the other.

'Goodbye for the moment.'

He released her hands, opened the door and went down the steps to the path which led past their plain front garden to the wooden gate.

At the back of the house there was a long narrow garden with a garage at its far end. The front garden was simply a space between the house and the roadway, and her father had grassed over the flower-beds inherited from his predecessor to save himself labour which he had felt was better applied to the garden at the rear.

The house itself was Edwardian, built of dark red brick with the many ornamental embellishments which had been fashionable at that period. It had a semi-basement kitchen with three floors above it, and it had been modernised to the extent of putting in central heating.

When she rejoined her mother, the Rolls-Royce was pulling away, and Mrs Bancroft was watching it with a troubled expression which cleared as she looked up at her long-legged daughter and said, 'So you enjoyed yourself, darling? The Caribbean really is as beautiful as it's made out to be?'

'More beautiful, if anything. The colour of the sea is indescribable, and it's as warm as bath water. Bliss!' Savanna was watching the departing car. As it moved out of sight, she said, 'But enough of my trip. What's been happening at home? Is everything *really* all right, Mother?'

'Yes, perfectly. Why do you ask?'

'I thought you seemed rather on edge while Jago was here . . . as if you'd be glad when he'd gone and we could talk privately.'

'I am glad he's gone,' her mother admitted. 'Does he want to see you again, Savanna?'

'Yes. He's going to ring up later on.'

'Oh, dear!' Her mother's worried look returned. 'I can see that it's tremendous fun to be whisked about in a Rolls, darling; and I haven't forgotten that you're nearly twenty and quite old enough and sensible enough to run your life without interference from me. So please don't be cross if, this once, I say, "Don't encourage him".'

Savanna's heart sank, but her tone remained light as she answered, 'When am I ever cross with you, dearest?'— stooping to give Mrs Bancroft a hug. 'But why don't you want me to see him again?'

'He's years too old for you, my dear. Presumably you know he isn't married, or you wouln't think of going out with him. But a man who's not married at his age is usually single because he prefers it that way—especially if he has money, and is tall and good-looking. You may be sure plenty of girls have tried to catch him, but he's eluded them. I should hate to see you involved with a philanderer.'

Before Savanna could say that, whatever Jago might have done in the past, he was not philandering with her, her mother continued, 'Even if he were several years younger, and more our kind of person, I should have reservations about him, darling. He has a charming manner, I admit, but underneath it I suspect he's a hard, ruthless man who rides roughshod to get what he wants. I didn't like him at all.'

CHAPTER THREE

LATER in the day Jago telephoned to say there were more matters requiring his attention than he had anticipated. It might not be possible for them to see each other again until the following Sunday, when he would like to give a luncheon party for her mother and her three elder brothers.

'Have you broken the news to your mother yet?' he asked.

'Not yet. I'll probably tell her this evening, about the time you'll be making your speech. I hope it goes well.'

'Thank you. Are you working tomorrow?'

'In the morning. The afternoon is free, so I shall be able to catch up with various household things which had to be neglected last week.'

'In a couple of months all that housework will be a thing of the past,' he told her. 'That's something we have to discuss—how to ensure your mother's comfort after you've left home permanently. I'll call you again as soon as I can. Goodnight, Savanna.'

She wished he had said, *Goodnight, darling*. The Bancrofts were a demonstrative family, free with hugs and kisses and loving words. But Jago had yet to call her by any endearment stronger than 'my lovely', which somehow had a different connotation.

As she replaced the receiver, she heard Benjy entering the house by the back door, and went through to the lobby where they hung up their raincoats to greet him. It was he, not her mother, who was the first to hear her news.

A couple of hours after supper, when Mrs Bancroft had turned on the television to watch a play, Savanna, whose real life problem made it difficult to concentrate on those

61

of the characters in a drama, went down to the kitchen to make her mother a pot of tea. She found Benjy there, the parts of a dismantled typewriter spread on the table, and a can of beer at his elbow. When not out with a girl, Benjy was always fixing something, either to save his mother money, or to make some for himself.

Outsiders regarded Benjamin Bancroft as a misfit, and a worry to his family. Although he had been to the same famous, fee-paying school as his scholastically brilliant elder brothers, he had done abysmally badly in all his exams and, since leaving, had been employed in a number of ways which the more conventional of Mrs Bancroft's friends thought unsuitable for a young man with his background.

At present he was working as a labourer on the site of a new public health centre. It was an unskilled job with no prospects, but it paid a high wage, part of which he contributed to household expenses, most of which he banked in his travel fund. As soon as he reached his target, he was setting out to see the world.

'Benjy, I need some advice,' Savanna said, sitting down on the opposite side of the table.

Her brother glanced questioningly at her. He had his father's blue eyes. His features were blunter than those of his brothers. Both Michael and Richard had a flair for making amusing ripostes which Benjy, less quick-witted, lacked. But he had his own sense of humour which, if slower, was also more gentle, more on her wavelength.

'What about?'

'I—I met a man while I was away, and he asked me to marry him.'

He whistled. 'That was quick work, wasn't it?'

'Yes, but that's how it happens sometimes. He's not an ordinary kind of man. He was flying to America, by Concorde, and he saw my face on the cover of *Vogue*, and made a special detour from New York to the Caribbean to meet me.'

'Some detour! Who is this guy? A millionaire?'

'He may be. He's very rich.'

'How old is he?'

'Thirty-three.'

'How many ex-wives has he?'

'None.'

'My advice is . . . grab him,' said Benjy.

Savanna couldn't help smiling. But then, swiftly serious again, she said, 'I want to . . . and it has nothing to do with his money. I've fallen in love with him. The trouble is Mother took an instant dislike to him when he brought me home from the airport this morning. She thinks he's too old, and a womaniser.'

'Aren't we all, given half a chance!' Benjy stopped work and drank some beer, reminding Savanna of her intention to put on the kettle.

As she rose to remedy her forgetfulness, he said, 'Obviously you haven't told her he wants to marry you, or she would have been talking of nothing else.'

'No, I haven't—not yet. I'd intended to tell her this afternoon, but after her criticisms of him I felt it might be better to wait. I didn't want to have an argument on my first day back.'

'If there's going to be trouble sooner or later, putting it off only makes matters worse,' said her brother. 'What's he like, apart from being loaded?'

'Very tall. Very dark. Very fit. His name is Jago Kindersley.'

'Jago? J . . . A . . . G . . . O?'

'Yes. It's an old Cornish name. His mother was born in Cornwall, and I shouldn't be surprised if her forebears included a Spanish castaway from the Armada. It would account for his black hair and the darkness of his tan. Perhaps for the name Jago, too. It may derive from the Spanish Iago.'

She glanced at the kitchen clock, wondering if Jago was on his feet now, giving his speech; or if, the dinner still being in progress, he was eating and making conversation with the women seated on either side of him.

As they were wives of the dignitaries of a livery company, it seemed unlikely that they would be notably attractive, although he would probably make them feel it—unless they responded to his charm with suspicion, as her mother had done.

'If he's fallen for you heavily enough to propose within a week of meeting you, how come he's not here this evening? Or is he tackling his mother, who's going to be equally hostile to you?' Benjy asked.

'His mother is dead.' Savanna went on to explain Jago's absence, and to mention the lunch party on Sunday.

'You can't ring up Richard and Mike until you've broken it to Mother.'

'No, I know I can't,' she agreed worriedly. 'Oh, Benjy, do you think she'll come round? The one thing I didn't bargain for was Mother taking against him.'

'She may come round right away when you tell her he wants to marry you. Probably she thinks he only wants to go to bed with you. She's still a bit uptight about Mike and Catriona, although she doesn't let them know it,' said Benjy.

This was a reference to his eldest brother's love affair with a fellow medical student who had announced, in front of Mrs Bancroft, that she had no intention of getting married because it would conflict with her career plans.

For anyone like Mary Bancroft who had never had a career, and whose entire adult life had centred round her husband and children, it was very hard to understand Catriona's determination to specialise in plastic surgery, or the young woman's clear-sighted acceptance that, to achieve her ambition, she would have to sacrifice much that was important to Mrs Bancroft.

'Perhaps you're right. I'll tell her tomorrow. I'll be at home in the afternoon.'

'Tell her now ... tonight,' Benjy urged. 'Otherwise you'll spend half the night worrying, and wake up with bags under your eyes. You know you always look like hell if you don't have a proper night's rest,' he added, with brotherly candour.

He cocked an ear towards the ceiling. 'She's turned off the TV. It must have been the kind of play she doesn't like—brass beds and four-letter words. Make the tea, and I'll come up and give you moral support.'

So it was that a few minutes later, when Benjy had carried the tea tray up to the sitting-room, and sat down to have a cup with them, Savanna mustered the courage to say, in rather a rush, 'I—I hope Mike and Richard are free this weekend. Jago wants them and us to have lunch with him. It's to be a celebration party.' Without pausing for breath, she went on, 'He's asked me to marry him, Mother. I would have told you right away, only you seemed not to like him. But I'm sure you will when you get to know him.'

It was to be expected that Mrs Bancroft's reaction would be much the same stupefaction which Savanna herself had experienced when Jago had first mentioned marriage.

Benjy's handling of the situation was not unlike that of his future brother-in-law. He said, 'What you need is a stiff sherry, Mother.'

He went to the corner cupboard where the drinks were kept, and came back with two glasses of Bristol Cream, one for her and one for his sister.

'I—I don't know what to say. I can hardly believe you mean this seriously,' said Mary Bancroft. 'To agree to marry a man whom you've only known for a few days . . . and who's so unsuitable for you . . . I can't take it in yet, Savanna. It's so extraordinarily unlike you. You've never been the giddy type of girl. I just can't think what's come over you.'

'Love has come over me, Mother.'

'In a week or less? Don't be absurd, dear. Love is something which grows with knowing. All you know about him at present is that you find him attractive. If in six months, or even three months, you both still feel the same way, one will begin to take it seriously. But as for a celebration party, or any kind of public announcement . . . that I cannot go along with, my dear.'

Ever since her mother's animadversions about him, immediately after his departure, Savanna had been worried that this would be her attitude to their news. Now, torn by divided loyalties, she sat silent and downcast, wondering how he would react to being told he was unacceptable.

'Can I put my oar in here?' asked Benjy. 'If this chap Jago is thirty-three, he at least ought to know *his* own mind; and there are other things he could have proposed which you would have liked a lot less, Mother.'

Mrs Bancroft's thin, pale face flushed. 'I'm aware of that, Benjy, and certainly it's something in his favour. But I've met Mr Kindersley. You haven't, and——'

'For a few minutes, Mother,' Savanna broke in. 'For a quarter of an hour at the most. Not for long enough to make a definite judgment.'

'Anyway, whatever we think of him, it's Savanna who's going to marry him,' said Benjy. 'I think a filthy-rich brother-in-law is exactly what this family needs. With Richard and Mike and Joey still being expensive passengers, and only Savanna and me supporting ourselves and contributing, we're barely keeping afloat.'

'To encourage your sister to marry in reckless haste merely because the man is wealthy shows a very immature outlook, Benjy. We're passing through a difficult period— yes. But it won't last for ever. Savanna's marriage will, I hope, last her whole life, as mine would have done if it hadn't been for Daddy's accident. It's at times like this I miss him so much. He would have taken the same view, and you would have listened to him, Savanna. You always took your problems to him, and acted on his advice.'

'But I was a schoolgirl then, Mother. I'm grown up now. I have to deal with my problems by myself—and I don't see why this has to be one. Benjy is right, darling. No one else can decide who is the right husband for me.'

'I'm not trying to decide for you, my dear. I'm merely asking you to wait. You're not twenty yet. How can you think of committing the rest of your life to a man who is virtually a stranger? Mostly, when marriages break down, it's because of a score of minor pinpricks which, cumulatively, make one or both partners' lives intolerable.

These are things which one doesn't discover in the first flush of love, Savanna. They only reveal themselves gradually. Please . . . *please* . . . be sensible about this. Wait a while, that's all I'm asking of you.'

'I don't think Jago will wait—or not very long. He's a man who, having made a decision, acts on it,' said Savanna.

'If he loves you, and you insist on a reasonable interval between your meeting and an engagement, he will have to abide by *your* decision. Marriage is essentially a give-and-take relationship. He can't expect to rule the roost completely.'

'Why not?—If I don't mind his doing so?'

'This pot of tea will be stone cold if someone doesn't pour it out,' said Benjy, reaching for it. 'I think we should all go to this lunch party, and enjoy a sample of the life-style he's offering Savanna, and then you should argue it out with him, Mother.'

'Don't be frivolous, Benjy. This is no laughing matter.'

'I'm not laughing, and nor is Savanna. She looks more like crying,' he said, with a sympathetic glance at her. 'I hope when I bring home a girl I'm serious about, you won't be like this about her. It's pretty deflating to anyone who's just fallen in love to have all the snags pointed out, Mum.'

'I do wish you wouldn't call——'

'Sorry. It slipped out, *Mother*,' he amended, with a trace of impatience.

He was too fond a son ever to irk her deliberately, although it amused him to outrage some of their neighbours, as on the occasion when, strolling in the town at lunch time, wearing cement-dusty overalls and carrying a carton from a fish and chip stall, he had encountered one particularly snobbish woman and invited her to try a hot chip.

One of Benjy's assets was his ability to adapt to any environment, and to be accepted by all kinds of people as one of themselves. He liked or disliked men and women for their fundamental human qualities, and was as happy in the company of some of his present workmates as with the friends of his schooldays.

For that reason Savanna was curious to see what he made of Jago. Although he might joke about the usefulness of Jago's wealth, of all her brothers Benjy would be the least influenced by it in forming his opinion of the man.

Seeing that there was little point in continuing the discussion tonight, yet relieved that, on his advice, she had at least aired the subject, she said, 'In spite of coming back First Class, I didn't get too much sleep last night. I think I'd better go to bed early.'

'Yes, I should if I were you, dear. We can talk things over again tomorrow,' said Mrs Bancroft.

Climbing the stairs being a difficult undertaking for her, she had made the former dining-room into a bedroom, with a prefabricated shower unit in one corner. Fortunately the house had already had a downstairs lavatory, but the basement kitchen was a great inconvenience. What was needed was a small lift, but the difficulty of installing one made the cost prohibitive.

Being worn out, Savanna slept well. However, when she took in her mother's early tea, she saw signs of a restless night in the circles under Mary Bancroft's eyes and the pinched look about her mouth. Pain frequently kept her awake, but last night, Savanna guessed, it had been worry which had done that. This was confirmed when she said, 'I've been thinking things over. Instead of the five of us being Mr Kindersley's guests on Sunday, I should prefer to receive him here. It will be less of a strain. You know what an effort it is for me to climb in and out of Michael's car these days; not to mention the double journey being a waste of his petrol.'

Savanna forbore to reply that she felt sure Jago would willingly send his more comfortable car for them. Nor did she point out that planning, shopping for and cooking a special lunch for six people at home involved a lot of extra work which she could have done without when her life was already very full. Seven people, if Mike brought Catriona.

But the last thing she wanted was to launch another argument, so she said only, 'Very well, darling, if you'd rather we had him here, I'll ring him up later this morning. I don't want to call him too early and risk waking him up.'

'What time does he normally get up? Or is that one of the many things you have yet to find out?'

'On the island he was a very early riser. But after attending a public dinner last night, and perhaps going to bed in the small hours, he could be forgiven for deciding to lie in this morning,' Savanna said mildly.

Later, on the train to London, she sat looking out at the bleak winter countryside, and wondering what she would do if her mother continued to find Jago an unacceptable son-in-law and he, in turn, was unwilling to meet Mrs Bancroft half way.

When Savanna herself had told him that she thought they ought to know each other for much longer before thinking about marriage, he had seemed to feel that a two-month engagement was an adequate delay. He had conceded, she remembered, that, in her case, it could be an infatuation; but not in his own.

How could he be so sure?

Because, in spite of numerous affairs, he had never before felt the way he did about her?

She would have liked to believe this explanation of his statement, but somehow she couldn't convince herself that, at not quite twenty, she was capable of enslaving an experienced man of the world so that never again would he look with desire at anyone else.

You're a beautiful creature, but don't overrate your desirability. You'll be twice as attractive at thirty, and certain women of forty and possibly fifty can give a man just as much pleasure as a smooth-skinned young thing like yourself.

She had a clear recollection of Jago's negligent answer when she had accused him of wanting to have an affair with her, and he had said she was too young.

On the same occasion he had told her that making love was an art which he thought she had yet to learn. Later he had found out he was right; she was the most virginal of virgins, inexperienced even in kissing.

Remembering those first thrilling kisses, she felt an upsurge of longing to be locked in his arms, 'the world forgetting, by the world forgot'.

As soon as she arrived in London, she dialled the number he had given her, and was answered by a girl on the switchboard of one of the most famous hotels.

'Who's calling?' the operator enquired, when Savanna had asked for Jago.

'Miss Bancroft.'

'Hold on, please.'

A few moments later, to Savanna's surprise, a man's voice said courteously, 'Good morning, Miss Bancroft. This is Matthews, Mr Kindersley's valet, speaking. He's out and about this morning, so I'm afraid I can't tell you where to reach him before lunch. May I take a message for you?'

'Oh, yes, thank you—if you would. He was going to give a lunch party for me and my family this weekend, but my mother would like him to spend the day with us. Do you happen to know if he has already made the arrangements he had in mind?'

'Mr Kindersley hasn't mentioned booking the room where he usually gives his private parties, but I can find out if he's done so, and ask the person in charge to await confirmation. Perhaps there is somewhere he can telephone you?'

The call gave her a further insight into the smooth-running luxury of Jago's life. Why hadn't he chosen a girl from that world to marry? There was no shortage of pretty faces among the daughters of the rich and influential.

As soon as I saw your face, I knew it was the one I wanted to look at across the breakfast table for the next forty years.

It wouldn't do for him to see me now, she thought ruefully, catching sight of her reflection in the window of one of the station kiosks, a wool cap pulled down to her eyebrows, her chin buried deep in a muffler because the cold seemed more piercing after a week in the sun.

I shall have to start looking glamorous all the time from now on, she reflected, as a taxi took her to her first appointment.

The ironic thing was that although she spent her working hours in furs, silks, cashmeres and luxurious evening dresses, the rest of the time she wore clothes chosen for cheapness and practicality.

Nowadays, her second brother Richard was the only well-dressed member of the family. He was at Oxford, hoping to achieve an honours degree in P.P.E., the university's name for the final examination in philosophy, politics and economics.

Clever, charming, and more than a little self-centred, Richard had a small income from funds left to him by one of his grandmothers, whose favourite he had been.

He spent it partly on others, and his unexpected gifts were always thoughtfully chosen, but mostly on presents to himself—old books, old prints, and good clothes, which he said lasted longer than cheap ones. He was probably right about this, but his sister, the only one of the Bancrofts who had any idea what his clothes cost, felt it wouldn't have hurt him to wait a few years for bespoke shirts and silk pyjamas.

Savanna returned home that afternoon to find that Jago had telephoned her mother to say he would be delighted to lunch with them; and the local florist, a member of Interflora, had delivered a box of three dozen long-stemmed red roses which did not have a card with them, but could only be from him.

Having divided them between two tall vases, one for the sitting-room and one for her own room upstairs, she rang up to thank him. As she waited for the number to answer, she found she could hardly wait to hear his deep voice. But when the switchboard connected her to his suite, once again it was Matthews who answered.

Jago was not there. He was spending the night in Paris, staying at the Plaza-Athénée.

'The number is 359 . . . 85 . . . 23, Miss Bancroft. Shall I repeat that?' asked Matthews.

'No, I have it, thank you. Goodbye.'

Savanna rang off, and sat down on the stairs, disappointed. She had wanted so much to talk to Jago. But to call him in Paris was out of the question. He might not be there. If he were, a few minutes' chat would cost pounds which they couldn't afford.

It seemed an eternity till Sunday. Knowing that an elaborate meal was not going to cut any ice with a man accustomed to the finest cuisine wherever he went, Savanna had settled for inexpensive and homely fare. For the first course, duckling, a cheaper alternative to smoked trout. For the main dish, a pot roast. For the pudding, apple tart and cream, always a favourite with her father and brothers and, it seemed likely, with all men.

Jago, not Marsh, was at the wheel of the Rolls when it drew up outside the Bancrofts' house at a quarter to one on Sunday.

'Impressive!' was Richard's comment, looking over his sister's shoulder as she stood by the window, awaiting Jago's arrival with mingled impatience and trepidation.

'I'll go and let him in.'

Conscious of an almost tangible feeling of expectancy as her family and Catriona waited to meet her rich suitor, she hurried from the room.

He was not at the gate, as she expected, when she opened the front door. On the point of running down the path to meet him, she checked, not wishing their greetings to be seen by anyone watching from the sitting-room.

Although Jago was hidden from view by the thickness of the beech hedge which retained its dead leaves through the winter, she could hear the expensive sound of the driver's door closing. A few moments later he appeared at the gate, one arm full of parcels.

He walked up the path, smiling at her, taking in the way she was dressed, which was the way he was dressed—casually, in trousers with a jersey and shirt. Hers were camel-coloured with a black shirt which emphasised the blondeness of her hair.

Jago's shirt and trousers were grey, like the car and his shrewd mid-grey eyes. His plain V-necked sweater was cashmere. A silk scarf was folded inside the open collar of his shirt. Reaccustomed now to looking at pale faces, Savanna saw his brown face and hands as strikingly bronzed.

'Hello. Have you missed me?' he asked, as he mounted the steps.

She nodded. She had meant, very swiftly, to break it to him that, as far as her mother was concerned, their engagement was not a *fait accompli*. But when he stepped over the threshold and bent his tall head towards her, the kiss he pressed on her lips put everything out of her mind but her gladness at seeing him again.

Prevented as he was by the parcels from embracing her with both arms, his one-armed hug and quick kiss were affectionate rather than passionate.

'I gather you've telephoned several times. I'm sorry I haven't been there, but I've been exceptionally busy. I'm not always as inaccessible as I've been for the past few days.'

'It doesn't matter,' Savanna assured him. 'Thank you for the gorgeous roses. I read the report of your speech.'

'Did you indeed? Very dutiful of you to scour the papers for it.' He moved towards the sitting-room door. 'Are your brothers here today? I'm looking forward to meeting them.'

Had the situation been reversed, and it had been she who was about to enter a room full of his relatives, she would have been twitching with nervousness. But obviously Jago was completely at ease.

She opened the door and re-entered the room, a step ahead of him.

'My mother you've already met. Let me introduce the rest of the family. Mike first, as he's the eldest . . . and this is his friend, Catriona, who is also reading medicine.'

After bowing and smiling at Mrs Bancroft, who was seated beside the log fire which they lit on special occasions, Jago had deposited his parcels on the upright chair by the door. Now he shook hands with Michael Bancroft and the dark-haired, sturdily built Scots girl.

Next, Savanna introduced Richard and, finally, Benjy who, having wrung Jago's hand with a grip which made most people flinch, but not his prospective brother-in-law, asked, 'What can I get you to drink, sir?' as if he were addressing someone many years his senior.

The Bancroft men were drinking lager, the women sherry, as Jago noted before he answered, 'I'll also have beer, if I may.'

'What very exciting-looking parcels,' remarked Catriona, in the pause which followed.

'They're one or two things I picked up in Paris, Savanna,' said Jago.

'For me?'

'For you.'

'How kind of you. Thank you.'

'Aren't you going to open them?' said Catriona, when the other girl made no move towards them.

'Oh . . . yes . . . yes, of course,' Savanna said hastily.

But when she would have returned to the chair where the parcels were lying, he stopped her, saying, 'No, they can wait, but this can't.'

Before she realised what he was about, he had taken a small leather box from his pocket, opened it, removed something sparkling, put the box away and possessed himself of her left hand. A moment later he had slipped the ring to the base of her third finger, and was lifting her hand to his lips.

The whole thing was done very swiftly and un-obtrusively so that, had they not been the centre of attention already, it might have passed unnoticed, except for the kiss on her knuckles. Over that, he lingered a little.

For Savanna, as he let go her hand and she had a clear view of the jewel now adorning it, it was a moment at once wonderful and terrible.

Clearly it had never crossed Jago's mind that her family wouldn't welcome the engagement. How would her mother react to this turn of events?

Her pleasure shot through with the fear of an embarrassing scene, she gazed at the diamonds which symbolised the bond between them. Not an unbreakable bond, but not one to be set aside lightly.

'It's beautiful, Jago,' she murmured, raising her eyes to his face. Then, mustering her courage, she turned to show it to her mother. 'Isn't it, Mother? Isn't it lovely?'

Don't be angry. Don't spoil it, her tawny eyes pleaded.

Mrs Bancroft took her daughter's outstretched hand to study the ring more closely.

'Yes, very beautiful,' she agreed.

For an instant, Savanna thought it was going to be all right: that her mother was going to accept this development without fuss, at least for the moment.

'However, I should have appreciated the courtesy of being consulted beforehand,' Mrs Bancroft went on, turning an unsmiling gaze on Jago.

'You mean you haven't told your family about us?' he asked, flashing an interrogative glance at her daughter, one black eyebrow arched in surprise.

'Yes . . . yes, but . . . you see . . .' she faltered.

'But *you* have not conferred with us, Mr Kindersley,' her mother put in. 'As you are a stranger to us, I think it would have shown a greater degree of consideration had you made yourself known to us properly before taking this precipitate step.'

'You mean you would have liked me to ask permission to marry Savanna?'

'It would have been more gracious.'

'You've used the word precipitate, Mrs Bancroft. It suggests that, had I been gracious, I might have been graciously sent packing,' was his dry response.

'I should certainly have counselled caution. Savanna is very young, and——'

'But of age, and no longer in need of parental consent to her marriage. As for myself, had I felt there was anything about me which Savanna's family might object to, probably I should have consulted you. But as I have neither a previous marriage, uncertain prospects or anything else to make me ineligible, I assumed that, if

Savanna was happy, you would be too.'

'Many people would consider your age to be a disadvantage,' said Mary Bancroft. 'Thirteen years is a considerable gap,' she added, ignoring her daughter's imploring, 'Oh, Mother, *please*——'

'But one offset by the fact that, unlike a much younger man, I'm in a position to provide her with every comfort, including the clothes and jewels which her beauty deserves.' Half turning away from his hostess, Jago said, 'You're her eldest brother, what is your view of our engagement, Michael?'

Earlier, Michael had been inclined to agree with his mother that for Savanna to return from a week in the Caribbean committed to marry a man whom none of them knew, was an act of impetuosity which she would almost certainly regret.

Now, however, after flashing a troubled glance at his mother, he said uncomfortably, 'Surely the purpose of an engagement is for people to test whether they're right for each other. As long as you aren't intending to rush into marriage too quickly, I—I have no objection.'

Mrs Bancroft looked angrily at him, but before she could speak her second son intervened.

'My opinion,' said Richard smoothly, 'is that we should defer this conversation until later. Wherever her future may lie, at this moment Savanna's place is in the kitchen attending to our lunch.'

'Oh, heavens—the roast potatoes!' she exclaimed.

With a look of apology at Jago for deserting him, she fled to the basement to check that the potatoes she had left in the oven were not becoming too well browned.

She was followed, some minutes later, by Catriona.

'Anything I can do to help?'

'No, it's all under control, thanks. What's happening upstairs now?'

'Richard is chatting to Jago, and Mike and Benjy are smoothing your mother's ruffled feathers. I must say I can't understand why she should be put out. Except that it's happened very suddenly, your Jago seems to personify everything most mothers hope for in a son-in-law. Can I feast my eyes on that gorgeous ring for a minute?'

Rather than hold out her hand, Savanna slipped the ring off and offered it for the other girl to take from her.

'It must be worth . . . goodness knows what? If it were mine, I should be terrified of losing it, or having it pinched. Anyway, I haven't the hands, or the nails, to set it off,' said Catriona, comparing her stubby fingers and short, unvarnished nails with Savanna's elegant hands.

Lunch was served in the conservatory at the side of the house. Warmed by a radiator and with sea-grass matting on the floor, it made a pleasant place to eat now that the indoor dining-room was no longer available.

It was a successful meal. The food was well cooked and complemented by three bottles of claret provided by Richard, who considered himself to be something of a connoisseur. The conversation flowed smoothly and, by the time they were eating biscuits and cheese, Savanna could see that her mother was mellowing towards Jago.

Having crossed swords with her earlier, he had been at pains to be charming; and his charm, when he chose to exert it, was a force which a woman of any age would find it hard to resist.

Afterwards everyone except her mother, and Richard who usually managed to slide out of any domestic duties, helped to clear the table.

'In a family of this size, I'm surprised you haven't a dish-washer,' said Jago, seeing Benjy, in a plastic apron, beginning to wash up by hand.

'We have two—me and Savanna,' quipped her brother. 'You're excused today,' he said to her. 'Mike and Cat will dry for me. Why don't you two go for a walk?' He looked at Jago. 'It will give us a chance to discuss you, and you to discuss us,' he said, with a grin.

The older man laughed. 'A sound idea, Ben. Better get your raincoat, Savanna. Mine's in the car.'

'Did Benjy tell you he doesn't really like being called that except by the family, and to say Ben when I introduced him?' she asked, as they set out down the road.

'No, It was a guess on my part. He's a nice chap, your brother Ben. I like the way he takes some of the weight off your shoulders without being asked. Would your mother be affronted if I arranged for a dish-washer to be installed?' Jago added. 'There's plenty of room for it, and it's something which every large family needs. In the States, you wouldn't find a prosperous family without one.'

'We aren't a very prosperous family. Even when my father was alive, we had problems making ends meet. The thing is that when we were born, his income seemed equal to sending his sons to his old school. You might have foreseen what was coming, had you been his age. But Dad didn't. Inflation hit us like a hurricane, and then he was killed and . . . well, you can imagine. But that's no reason to batten on you.'

'Allowing me to give you a dish-washer hardly comes into the category of battening. Why is your mother opposed to our marriage?' he asked.

'For the reasons she gave you—the age gap, and the suddenness of it. I'm sorry she was so quelling when you first arrived. I should have warned you about her attitude, but already I think she's coming round. And if the boys like you, as they obviously do, that will bring her round more. She's not really a martinet. She has a lot of pain and worry, and it makes her appear more severe than she ever used to be. Don't write her off because of that scene before lunch.'

'I'm hardly likely to write off my future mother-in-law,' he said dryly. 'It's natural for her to be concerned for your happiness. Do you like that ring? If it's not what you'd set your heart on, it can be exchanged.'

'I hadn't set my heart on anything because I hadn't thought about it. I adore this ring,' she said, spreading her hand to admire it. 'It's gorgeous. I only pray I never lose it.'

'If you do, it doesn't matter. It's insured.'

Savanna stopped short, her topaz eyes shocked. '*Jago!* How can you say that? This isn't just *any* ring. If you'd bought it at Woolworth's it would still be irreplaceable to me.'

He tilted an eyebrow. 'Would it?'

'Of course.'

'But you wouldn't be equally afraid of losing a Woolworth's ring, my dear,' he said cynically.

'No, because if I left this somewhere, the chances are it would be stolen. A Woolworth's ring I might get back. Anyway I'm going to take very good care not to lose it.'

She glanced up and down the street, saw no one about, and stood on tiptoe to brush a kiss on his cheek. At once his strong arms closed round her, and her kiss was returned—on her mouth.

He had not kissed her properly, like this, since their last day in the West Indies. And her long lashes fluttered to rest, she felt a tremor of pleasure at being held so firmly and possessively. Jago made her feel small and fragile, and enjoyably helpless.

'Mm . . . like Baked Alaska,' she murmured, when he raised his head.

'Baked Alaska?' He was still holding her close.

'That pudding with ice cream inside hot meringue. Don't you see the connection? Cold cheeks but warm mouths . . . nice.'

He looked at her soft, smiling mouth, and something fierce flared in his eyes.

'Delicious!' he agreed huskily, and kissed her again, at greater length.

The sound of a child's bicycle bell brought Savanna back to earth. As she and Jago broke apart, she turned dazed eyes towards the small, woolly-hatted figure who was pedalling energetically along the pavement in advance of a man with a push-chair and a woman leading a toddler.

She was still not fully recovered when they and the couple passed each other.

The man nodded. 'Afternoon.'

Both he and his wife looked over-fed and sedate, as if it were a long time since they had kissed in the street and longed to be in bed with each other, thought Savanna.

For that was how Jago's persuasive kisses had made her feel. If the onus for keeping their relationship on a footing acceptable to her mother rested on her, as he had said it would, it was not going to be safe to kiss him anywhere *but* in public.

By the time they returned to the house it was just beginning to drizzle, and the lamps were alight in the sitting-room, making it look very cosy as Jago opened the gate for her.

In the hall, he helped her to take off her raincoat before removing his own light-coloured windcheater. She had pulled a comb through her hair and was putting on lipstick at the mirror above the telephone table, when she saw his reflection behind hers.

Watching her over the top of her head, he slid his arms round her, his brown hands stroking her breasts, finding the shape of them through her loose-fitting sweater.

Savanna stopped using the lipstick, her own hand suddenly shaking as his strong gentle fingers rekindled the feelings damped down by their brisk two-hour tramp.

Although conscious that at any moment someone might come out of the sitting-room, she found herself leaning against him, mesmerised by the gleam in his eyes and the slow caress of his hands.

'Jago . . . don't!' she gasped, twisting to face him and burying her face in his shoulder.

His fingers searched for her chin, and he tilted her face up.

'You don't like my touching you like that?'

'I like it too much,' she admitted. 'Oh, darling, what is it you do to me?' Her arms crept round his neck. She clung to him. 'I love you. I can't wait to be your wife.'

'In two months from now you will be. I want you, too,' he said softly. 'Now I think we'd better join the others.'

That night, preparing for bed in the pale blue silk-lined cashmere robe which had been one of Jago's presents, with another—an enchanting artificial lemon tree, nine inches tall including the miniature Versailles pot—

standing on her dressing-table, Savanna felt a good deal easier in her mind than she had before his visit.

He had stayed to have tea by the fire. After he had gone, none of her brothers had had any faults to find with him, and even her mother had admitted that a second encounter had made her amend if not revise her original opinion.

Even so, as she turned out the light and lay down on her side to gaze at her engagement ring in its open box on the night table, the diamonds shining in the glow from the street lamp outside their garden, she still felt a certain unease. A feeling that it was all too good to be true. There had to be a flaw somewhere. There *was* one: she could feel it in her bones. Yet somehow she couldn't pin it down.

CHAPTER FOUR

THE announcement of their engagement in the *Forthcoming Marriages* column of a reputable national newspaper was quickly picked up by the sensational press. One morning, on the train, Savanna saw a number of people immersed in the *Full Story on Page 3* behind the front page headline *Model to Wed Millionaire Playboy*.

When the train reached London, she bought a copy of the paper and read it in the taxi taking her to her first appointment. Since no one had been in touch with her, or with Jago as far as she knew, the so-called report had been concocted from information from other sources and from the reporter's imagination. Savanna felt as if she were reading about a stranger. She hoped the description of Jago as a rakish member of the jet set had equally little verisimilitude. If Mrs Bancroft read it, which it was to be hoped she would not, it would confirm her worst fears.

With him, the reporter had had more to work on. Clearly he had featured in the paper's columns on previous occasions when his name had been linked with other women. There were photographs of three who had failed to hold him permanently, with potted accounts of their relationships. With one of them, an actress, he was said to have been inseparable for nearly two years.

Although, on the island, Jago had warned her that this dredging up of his past was inevitable, she could not help being wounded by the public exposure of his amorous past for the gloating delight of readers who would probably absorb it as gospel.

During the day she was in contact with Margaret, who said she was under pressure to reveal Savanna's address.

'And if they don't get it from me, they'll find it out somehow—they always do. There's just no escape from the Press. My advice is to give them what they want and get it over,' said her agent.

'But why should I have to be interviewed against my will?' Savanna protested. 'I don't want all the details of my home life laid out for public inspection. My family will hate it, especially my eldest brother. Pictures of me in the scandal rags will embarrass him horribly.'

'I don't know why. If he doesn't read them, presumably his friends don't either. Don't let it get you down, my dear. The worst that can happen is that they will hang about outside your house until you've given them the answers they want. They won't actually force their way in and badger your mother. With any luck, it will be a nine days' wonder; not even that if something more sensational—hold on a moment, will you?'

There was a pause, after which she came back on the line to say, 'My secretary has just put her head round the door to tell me someone else wants to know where to find you. Don't worry—not a Press hound: your boy-friend. I'll ring off and give him your number. Call me back, would you?'

Savanna replaced the receiver, wondering what was so urgent that Jago needed to speak to her during working hours. He had taken her and her mother to the theatre the night before, booking a box so that Mrs Bancroft, who found it difficult to sit still for long periods, would be able to change her position during the performance.

Tomorrow night they were dining together. Tonight he was entertaining some business associates from Germany.

The telephone rang. When she answered it, Jago said, 'The Press has latched on to our engagement. I think you may be subjected to a certain amount of harassment in the next few days. As I can't be with you all the time, and I don't want you to be put through too much third degree stuff, I've arranged for someone else to look after you.'

'Is that necessary? Will it be as bad as that?'

'Maybe not, but I'm taking no chances. Politicians and

show business types can cope with the limelight. They love it.'

Was he thinking of his 'close friend', the actress?

'But although the cameras won't upset you, the questions may not be so easy to handle,' he continued. 'It takes a tough cookie to survive a barrage of personal questions, and you're not the type to stay cool under that kind of pressure.'

Was that a criticism? she wondered.

Aloud, she said, 'Who is going to look after me?'

'Miles Masters. He's the younger brother of a man I shared a study with at school. Recently Miles has spent some time guarding the children of an Italian manufacturer who was worried about them being kidnapped. But I gather there's a girl in England whom he wants to see more of, so he's come back to this country, and at present he's free to protect you from being hounded by the Press. What time are you finishing work today?'

It was arranged that Miles should collect Savanna from the salon where she was having her hair cut.

When Jago had rung off, she re-dialled Margaret's number and told her it no longer mattered if her address was released because now she had someone to protect her if any Pressmen became too pressing.

Her first sight of Miles was from her seat under a dryer hood—her hair was too long and thick to be blown dry— when he walked into the reception area and spoke to the girl behind the desk.

She indicated that he should take a seat, which he did, but not until he had paused by the short flight of steps leading down to the hairdressing area and scanned the faces of the clients.

To Savanna's surprise he recognised her, and smiled. She smiled back. Until then she had thought he was calling for someone else. He wasn't the burly, rugger-playing type she had expected, but a lightly-built man in his late twenties, of medium height, with medium brown hair, and medium looks—neither noticeably attractive yet not unattractive. She judged that when she was wearing flat heels as she was at the moment, he might top her by an inch. In high heels, she would be the taller.

He chose a chair from which they could still see each
other, but he didn't look at her again. She watched him
glancing through a copy of *Harpers & Queen* and evidently
finding an article which interested him, because after a
bit he stopped flicking over the pages and began to read.
She wondered how he had landed the job in Italy. He
was not at all her idea of a bodyguard.

The Italian who always did her hair knew that, when
she came for a cut, she didn't want elaborate styling. He
took out the clips which had held it in large loose curls
under the dryer, then gave it a vigorous brushing with
two bristle brushes.

He had already remarked on her engagement, asked
when the wedding was to be, and hoped she would want
him to dress her hair for it. Now, passing the brushes to
his assistant, he used his fingers to pull a soft airy fringe
across her forehead, and loosen the rest into an artfully
tumbled mane of pale gold silk.

'Thank you, Luigi.' She slipped some coins into his
pocket, and followed the assistant to the coats rail to ex-
change her pink cotton wrapper for a black quilted
jacket.

Her guardian was on his feet when, having dealt with
the bill with her bank card, she turned to join him.

'Miles Masters, at your service, Miss Bancroft,' he said,
holding out his hand. Although lacking Jago's height
and breadth of shoulders, he had latent strength in his
handshake. His eyes were hazel. There was a scar across
his right cheekbone.

'Hello. How did you recognise me, sitting down under a
dryer?' she asked.

A model had to be exceptionally famous for her face to
be known to the opposite sex.

'Jago described you.'

'What did he say?' she asked, as he opened the door for
her.

'That I should look for the most beautiful girl, and she
would be you.'

Her face lit up. 'Really? What a nice thing for him to say—but not very helpful. We all look terrible with our heads in a dryer, and you might not like my kind of face. Thank you'—this as he pushed open the outer door.

'The car is round the corner,' he told her. 'I was lucky to get a free meter. I should think there are very few men who wouldn't like your face, Miss Bancroft,' he added pleasantly, but as a statement of fact rather than a compliment.

Savanna gave a smiling shrug. 'My brothers aren't greatly impressed by it, and I haven't got used to the fact that Jago seems to be. For how long has he asked you to look after me, Mr Masters?'

'For as long as is necessary. As I'm supposed to be a friend of the family, rather than a hired watchdog, I think we should use each other's first names. Mine, as you may know, is Miles.'

She nodded. 'Your elder brother and Jago were at school together, I believe?'

'Yes, their last year was my first year.'

So he must be either twenty-seven or twenty-eight, she calculated.

'My brother was head boy of his house, and Jago was head of the school, which made him, in my eyes, as awe-inspiring as the Headmaster,' Miles continued. 'On Speech Day, at the end of my first year, his short speech of thanks to the long-winded and boring Distinguished Guest was received with terrific applause. I remember my parents discussing it afterwards, and prophesying a brilliant future for him. That was fifteen years ago. My brother thinks now that, given another ten years, Jago will be one of the most influential men in the country.'

It was a statement which made Savanna conscious of how little she knew about the man she was in love with. If his gifts were so highly thought of by those who did know him, would she be able to live up to him? Being much younger than he was, and having had her education cut short by Gerald's discovery of her at a time when money seemed of paramount importance, would she ever be able to keep pace with a brilliant husband and the clever men and women who were his friends?

The car was a small saloon belonging, she noticed, to a car hire firm. Miles put her into the passenger seat before going round to unlock the driver's door. Before he reached it, she had leaned across to unlock it and push it open for him.

'Thank you.' He slid behind the wheel. 'Would you put your seat-belt on, please.'

She obeyed, but needed his assistance to extract it fully from the reel and then to adjust it to fit her.

'Don't you usually wear a belt?' he asked.

'I don't often travel by car. There's a good train service from where we live, and on working trips outside London, I'm usually in the back of the car.'

'What about going out in the evening?—Before you met Jago?'

'I didn't,' she answered succinctly. 'You may find it odd, but I led a very sheltered life until I met him,' she added, with a smile. 'The only man I know who roars around in a fairly fast car is my brother Michael, and as he and his girl-friend are medical students, they always use belts, having seen the results when people don't.'

'Yes, so have I—pretty horrific. And, with a face like yours, worse than madness to chance windscreen cuts.'

He didn't refer to his own scar, so presumably he had come by that in some other way.

'You've been working in Italy, I believe? How did that come about? I mean how does one become a bodyguard?' Savanna asked, as they followed a taxi which was cutting through the side streets of Belgravia to avoid the heavy traffic in the main thoroughfares.

'I was in the Services for a while,' was all he said. Obviously he didn't want to talk about it.

She tried another tack. 'What did you think of Italy? It's a country I long to visit. All the nicest things in London seem to be made there. I should think the shops must be marvellous.'

'Yes, the Italians are very strong on good design. I liked

Italy, but my job there—keeping an eye on a couple of children—wasn't really up my street. It paid well. I saved some money, and learnt to speak passable Italian, so it wasn't entirely a waste of time.'

'What are you thinking of doing next?—When you've finished looking after me?'

'Ah, that's the problem. I came back to England to look up a girl who I hoped might have missed me more than she expected to when we said goodbye. She hadn't; and, seeing her again, I realised she'd been right to send me packing. We weren't right for each other. So now I'm in the market for whatever adventure offers itself.'

His openness about the girl surprised her in view of his evasive reply to her earlier question. Could it be that he'd left the Services under a cloud? Been cashiered?

No: because if that were the case Jago would know about it, and would not have entrusted her to him.

By road, at that hour of the day, the journey home took considerably longer than by rail, but it didn't seem tedious to her. She found Miles a pleasant companion.

Outside the Bancrofts' gate was a car from which, as they pulled in beside it, two men emerged.

'Brace yourself. Those are newshounds,' said Miles.

Savanna stayed where she was while he went round to open her door. She heard him say, 'Good evening, gentlemen,' and ask which paper they represented.

It was the one which had already printed a largely cock-and-bull story, and which never mentioned a woman without giving her age, the colour of her hair and, unless she was old, her measurements.

One of the men was a photographer. Accustomed to facing bright lights, and prepared for the flare of his flashbulb, she neither blinked nor flinched when he snapped her stepping out of the car.

But without Miles' reassuring presence, she might have been flustered by the questions which the other man fired at her. Some she answered; some Miles expertly parried. When asked who he was, he said, 'A friend of the family.'

They wanted to come into the house and photograph

her there, with her mother, but Miles wouldn't have it.

'I'm sorry, but Miss Bancroft has had a busy day and needs to relax now. I have Mr Kindersley's authority to say that if you want to take pictures of them together, you can do so at seven tomorrow evening, at his hotel, before they go out to dinner.'

'That's fine, but we also want some pictures of Savanna at home,' the photographer persisted.

'Sorry, Miss Bancroft is tired. Goodnight, gentlemen,' was Miles' firm reply, as he shepherded her through the gate and latched it behind them.

Walking up the path, she heard one of them say, his voice carrying in the quietness of the tree-lined road, 'That bloke is no friend of the family. He's a strong-arm man hired by the boy-friend.'

'That's what I think,' agreed the other. 'Can't say I blame him. She's not the type I expected. Seems a nice girl, not one of the go-getters.'

'Thank you,' Savanna murmured sotto voce, and saw Miles grin.

But moments earlier there had been something in his manner which made her understand why the two men hadn't gone on arguing with him. Jago had used the expression 'a tough cookie' during his telephone talk with her, and she had a feeling it was an apt description of the man who had brought her home tonight. Easy-going and mild-looking normally, but, when occasion demanded, a very tough cookie indeed.

Miles' arrival came as no surprise to Mrs Bancroft. She, too, had had a call from Jago. When it emerged that Miles had instructions to stay at the house all evening and spend the night at the nearest hotel, she surprised her daughter by insisting that he should make use of Joey's room.

Next morning he drove her to London, and for the rest of the day he was always somewhere near at hand until, at six, he saw her to the door of Jago's suite.

Meeting Matthews for the first time, she found him to be a middle-aged man with grey hair and a kindly warmth in his eyes which reminded her of her father.

Jago had not yet returned from his day's activities, and the valet showed her where she could change her clothes. Having no glamorous evening things, and feeling that tonight it would be wiser to veer towards dignity rather than glamour, she had rushed out during the day—accompanied by an unembarrassed Miles—and bought a long, narrow skirt of black wool crêpe, and a shirt of black silk. Linked by a soft black kid belt, the combination of these classically plain and undating separates had a simple elegance which she hoped would please her future husband and act as a visual counterbalance to any exaggerated text which might accompany the photographs he had agreed to have taken.

'Mr Kindersley returned while you were dressing, Miss Bancroft. He won't be long changing. Would you care for a glass of sherry while you're waiting for him?' Matthews enquired, when he found her wandering round the sitting-room.

Savanna shook her head. 'You don't happen to have any unsweetened orange juice, do you? It would steady my nerves much better than sherry.'

She was sipping the refreshingly cold fruit juice when Jago appeared and made her heart leap with pleasure at the sight of his tall, lithe figure striding into the room, making the atmosphere zing with the vital force of his energy. Not for him the late-day fatigue of the tired businessman. Fresh from the shower—she could see that his hair was still damp—he looked as if the day was just beginning.

'May I kiss you, or will it ruin your make-up?' he asked, removing the glass from her hand and putting it aside.

Coming towards her, he had already scanned her appearance, taking in what she was wearing, and the way her pale hair was brushed back and clasped at the nape of her neck to make her look older and more poised. Her only jewellery was his ring, and the pearl beads which went with the gold pins she had worn since having her ears pierced.

Savanna shook her head. She was wearing make-up, but most of it was round her eyes.

'Does that mean I can't kiss you, or that it won't hurt your make-up?'

He was teasing her. He was going to kiss her whatever she said. He was looking at her mouth with an anticipatory gleam which made her quiver inside. She drew in her breath, her lips parting, her lashes flickering with the shyness revived by the interval since their last time alone together.

Jago bent, his mouth alighting on hers feather-gently, their lips barely touching, but the warmth of his breath intermingling with her own quickened, uneven breathing.

His hands came to rest on her hips, but so lightly she scarcely felt them until they moved up to her waist, then behind her to spread on her back, warm and firm through the thin black silk. But he didn't draw her against him. There were still several inches between them.

When he touched her lips with his tongue, her body recoiled like a gun from the sudden sharp shock of excitement which raced down her spine and made her slender thighs tremble.

Minutes later, when he straightened and moved back a pace, she was uncrushed and undishevelled, only her inner self disturbed.

'There you are: every hair in place.'

His grey eyes gleamed with amusement. She could see that he knew what he had done to her; that, without even pressing her to him, he had made the blood burn in her veins, and all her nerves tingle with longing for more of that soft, sensuous kissing which no one had shown her before him.

'I saw this today. It's on approval, so don't be afraid to say if it isn't your style,' he said, taking out of his pocket a rope of unusual beads and handing them to her.

'Oh, but it is!' she exclaimed. 'What sort of beads are they, Jago?'

'Cloisonné and pink jade, carved. I was buying a net-

suke for myself, and they caught my eye. They're old, but
the tassel is new, of course.'

Savanna examined the beads more closely. The ones he
had called cloisonné were decorated with enamel in many
colours, with fine lines of metal in their design. Alternating
with them were the semi-translucent rose-coloured jade
beads, spaced by knots of thick silk, the rope finished with
a handsome tassel.

'Put it on. Let me see how it looks,' Jago commanded.
She obeyed him.

'Yes, I like it on you. It looks well with black. You
must keep it.'

'Thank you, I'd love to . . . but . . . but I haven't given
you *any*thing,' she said regretfully.

'On the contrary, you give me pleasure every time I look
at you—and even more when I touch you. Come here.'

He had moved a few paces away to appraise the beads
from a distance. Now, almost reluctantly, she went towards him, half dreading, half longing to feel him savour-
ing her lips again.

Before she reached him, his manservant entered. 'The
representatives of the Press have arrived, sir.'

'Then you'd better show them in, Matthews.'

In the brief interval between the valet's withdrawal and
their visitors' entrance, Jago looked at her with an expression in which she read irritation at being interrupted,
a resigned acceptance that the coming interview was a
tedious necessity, and the promise that when it was over
he would again demonstrate his power over her senses.

The interview went smoothly, because he dominated
the Pressmen as easily as he dominated her. As they had
on the island, they posed together for photographs. When
urged to kiss her, he did so—on the back of her hand.
They sat side by side on a sofa, their fingers interlaced,
her face lifted attentively to his as he answered their questions, or ignored them, as he chose, never as they chose.

Afterwards he took her out to dinner, feeding her on
delicious things she had never tasted before; gulls' eggs
with rock salt and very thin brown bread and butter;

breasts of chicken cooked in sherry and cream and sprinkled with finely chopped truffles; praline ices with kissel, a hot fruity blackcurrant sauce.

'How are you getting on with Miles?' he enquired, during dinner. 'I haven't seen him for some time.'

'I like him. So do Mother and Benjy. He's a very ... comfortable person.'

'Not always,' Jago said dryly. 'They're a tough lot, the S.A.S.'

'He was in the Special Air Service?' she asked, with quickened interest.

She remembered watching, on live television, the famous rescue by the men of the Special Air Service of twenty people held hostage by terrorists in the Iranian Embassy in Prince's Gate, a terrace of tall, dignified houses overlooking Hyde Park.

Occasionally Savanna went there to buy her mother embroidery wools from the house occupied by the Royal School of Needlework, not far from the burnt-out ruin of the former Embassy.

Everyone who had seen the programme had felt proud of the brilliantly executed rescue of fifteen men and five women whom the terrorists had threatened to murder at half-hourly intervals. The operation ranked with the Israeli rescue raid on Entebbe, and had focussed the attention of the nation on a crack force of daring men who would have preferred to avoid the ensuing publicity for their Regiment.

To discover that Miles had belonged to this military élite showed him in a new light, and explained his evasive reference to it, and also the instinctive recognition by the reporter and photographer who had been waiting for her outside her house that he was not someone to tangle with.

'I wonder why he left it?' she pondered.

'To please the girl he wants, I believe. Foolish of him!' was Jago's rider.

'Why do you say that?'

'Because girls should take men as they find them—and vice versa. Nothing is more unwise than to try to change people. If a man has a bent for that kind of soldiering, he can't be converted into a desk-bound commuter, or whatever it is she wants him to be.'

'She doesn't want him—nor he her now.'

'He told you that?'

'Yes, last night, driving me home.'

'Unusually forthcoming of him. According to Guy—his brother—Miles keeps his cards close to his chest, and rarely confides in his family or anyone else. I wonder why he's made an exception of you,' he said thoughtfully.

'I asked him what he was going to do next.'

'Which didn't oblige him to discuss his love life with you. I hope he's not going to be even more foolish and fall in love with you now.'

'Of course not! I'm engaged to you.'

'That doesn't stop other men wanting you. Even our marriage won't do that.'

'It stops me wanting them,' she said gently.

'Nevertheless I shouldn't have engaged him to look after you had I known the affair was over.'

Prompted by a sudden longing to hear Jago say something as gallant as his description of her to Miles, she gave him an impish smile. 'Am I really so irresistible?'

Instead of the ardent assurance she had hoped for, he said merely, 'A man on the rebound is peculiarly susceptible.'

'I don't think he is on the rebound. It sounded as if the fire had burned out on both sides.' She decided to change the subject. 'You told me you saw these beads while buying something for yourself. A netski .. was that the word?'

'That's how it's pronounced. It's spelt n-e-t-s-u-k-e.'

'What exactly is it?'

He put his hand in his pocket and produced a small object which he placed on the white damask cloth near her wine glass. It was a piece of ivory, carved to represent two mice on a cob of maize. Savanna picked it up and turned it between her fingers, examining the exquisite detail of the animals' beady eyes and hair-fine whiskers.

'It's enchanting. But why these holes?'

'Because netsuke were used to fasten pouches to belts, or to fix the ends of a sash. I began to buy them as an investment, and now do it for pleasure as well. I have rather a fine collection, although not to compare with the one in the Victoria and Albert Museum. The next time I go to look at it, I'll take you with me. Perhaps, somewhere else in the museum, you'll see something which you'd like to collect. I should like my wife to be able to enjoy my resources with more discrimination than the woman whose only interest is in clothes.'

'Sometimes clothes can be an investment,' she said. 'Fortuny dresses, for instance. Christie's auctioned a Delphos, which is a long gown of pleated silk, and it fetched three and a half thousand dollars. And it was his most popular design, in production for over forty years, so examples aren't particularly rare.'

'Yes, I've heard of Fortuny,' he answered. 'Perhaps, if his things appeal to you, we might find you a well-preserved white dress in which to be married. But possibly you would rather have your wedding dress specially designed?'

'I haven't thought as far ahead as that.'

'Only ten weeks ahead. We're going to be married on the ninth of May. But you needn't worry about the arrangements. They'll all be taken care of. You and your mother have only to make certain choices. All the practical side will be handled by members of my staff.'

'Is it going to be a very large wedding?' she asked.

In occasional daydreams about her future, before she had met Jago, Savanna had vaguely visualised having a quiet, informal, close-family-only kind of marriage; the honeymoon being more important than an elaborate and costly ceremony.

'As far as I'm concerned, a register office with you and the necessary witnesses would satisfy me. But I should think that your mother, as you're her only daughter, would prefer to see you married in the traditional way,' said Jago, turning to cast his eye over the selection of cigars in a humidor which had been wheeled to his elbow.

'I didn't know you smoked cigars,' she commented, when he had decided he didn't wish for one.

'Sometimes I smoke Davidoff cigarillos or, if I want to switch off for an hour or two, I'll have one of their No. 1 Havanas. But there are other ways of relaxing, and I'll give up the few I do smoke if you find it objectionable.'

'I don't mind the smell of cigar smoke. It's like the smell of good cooking. Cigarette smoke is what I can't bear.'

'You may not like cigar-scented kisses,' said Jago quizzically.

They were seated opposite each other, and he moved his leg under the table, rubbing his knee against hers and his calf against her calf.

She tried to look serenely unruffled both by the pressure of his leg and his expression, but it wasn't easy when he fixed her with that glint of devilment, and talked of kisses with a blithe disregard for anyone listening.

'To . . . to get back to the wedding. I do think a register office is rather soulless. A quiet church wedding is what I should prefer.'

'Unfortunately that presents difficulties. I don't want to invite half my friends and offend the other half. It's better to have all or none, and not only is your parish church too small to accommodate my guests, there's no local hotel which can put on a suitable reception. With a lot of people flying in from Europe, it'll be easier to have it in London; the service at St Margaret's, Westminster, and the reception at my hotel.'

Savanne quailed. St Margaret's was the setting for many of the largest and most fashionable London weddings. She had never seen herself being married there, and did not relish the prospect. But if that was what Jago wanted, she could only acquiesce.

'Don't worry,' he said, 'you'll enjoy it. I shall keep a watching brief on the preparations and make sure you don't become frazzled. Have you any idea where you'd like to go for our honeymoon?'

'No, none. I—I'll leave it to you.'

'Very well, it shall be a surprise. A few weeks of peaceful seclusion in which to adjust to your new rôle as the beautiful Mrs Jago Kindersley.'

There was no mistaking the possessive satisfaction with which he was looking at her. Remembering Miles' remarks about windscreen injuries, Savanna found herself wondering how Jago would react if she were to be badly cut about, her looks spoiled by ugly lacerations.

Naturally her face, which had attracted him to her in the first place, must be an important element in his feelings towards her; just as his own dynamic features were part of the reason she loved him.

If he were to be terribly scarred, she knew it would not alter her love. But would his for her diminish if he could not show her off proudly?

He said, 'If you're free this Saturday and Sunday, we'll fly up to see my sister. She's impatient to meet you, but she can't come south at the moment.'

The weather being milder that evening and, as they had come from his hotel to the restaurant in a taxi, not in the Rolls, Savanna suggested walking back.

Jago agreed. 'I often take a walk at this hour,' he told her. 'But are your shoes suitable for walking?'

She nodded, lifting her skirt to show him a black-stockinged ankle and a lowish-heeled black patent lace-up with a ribbon in place of a shoelace.

'Hm, reasonably sensible—but I think you could do with a fur in place of that light cloak,' he said, referring to the velvet opera cloak of pre-World War One vintage which was her only evening wrap.

'Perhaps Father Christmas will bring me one,' she said lightly, thinking that when next Christmas came she would like to be able to give him a very unusual netsuke.

'You could do with one before that, my dear. The spring isn't here yet, and may not start till late April. Have you any free time tomorrow? I'll take you to Maxwell Croft and——'

'No, no—please, Jago, no!' she protested. 'I loved your presents from Paris, and these beautiful beads which you've given me. But I don't want any more presents— not until we're married. If my father had been alive, he would have insisted on contributing as much as he could towards the wedding. As things are, it will all fall on you. The fact that you can afford it is neither here nor there. I was brought up to give as well as take. Too much taking makes me uncomfortable.'

'You're over-sensitive,' he told her. 'Your family's financial difficulties make you see these things out of perspective. For me to give you a fur is no more than for you to give your mother a bunch of daffodils.'

Their end of the street was deserted. Jago put his arm round her shoulders and drew her against him.

'You will give—have no doubts on that score. And I shall take you, my lovely. Often, and with a pleasure which, as you know nothing about it, you can't yet weigh against other pleasures.'

In the light of the street lamps his features looked harsh and remorseless, but his deep voice was quiet and caressing as he murmured, 'Even sable isn't as strokable as a woman's skin. Food and wine are very enjoyable, but not to be compared with making love.' He gave a soft, mocking laugh. 'And you're so refreshingly innocent that you don't even know that I'm making love to you now.' He put his lips close to her ear. 'Trying to make you as impatient for May the ninth as I am.'

'But I am impatient,' she whispered, trembling. 'I love you. I want to be yours in every possible way.'

She hoped that he might stop walking and put both his arms round her. There was no one about to see him embrace her, and she longed to be held close and kissed.

But he walked on, making her wonder if admissions such as she had just made were better left unspoken. Perhaps, in spite of his claim, too much eagerness didn't please him as much as a measure of reserve. But it wasn't in her nature to hold back, to dissimulate.

When they entered the foyer of his hotel, she was

surprised to see Miles there, reading. She had not expected to see him again before tomorrow.

Jago explained, 'I'm flying to Munich in the morning, and I want to be up at five-thirty, so I asked Miles to run you home tonight.' He beckoned the younger man to them. 'Hello, Miles. How are you? Come upstairs and have a nightcap with us.'

'Thank you, but I won't if you don't mind. I've already had a couple of beers this evening, and I'm quite happy to wait. This is a very good book'—displaying the cover of a recent best-seller.

'I applaud your good sense with regard to drinking and driving,' said Jago, 'but your tact is unnecessary. I want to talk to you. Savanna and I have also had our quota of alcohol. We'll drink coffee,' and he swept them both into the lift.

Evidently Matthews was off duty as he used a key to open the door of his suite.

As he took her cloak, Savanna said, 'I feel a bit wind-blown. Is there somewhere I could tidy my hair?'

'Use my bedroom. I'll show you.'

He crossed the room to the door he had emerged from earlier. It opened into a lobby with built-in cupboards on either side, and an inner door leading into a spacious bedroom.

'The bathroom's through there,' he said, indicating another door. 'I prefer your hair loose as you usually wear it.' He withdrew.

Savanna looked around her. The most striking feature of his bedroom was its view. One whole wall was a floor-to-ceiling window, the curtains left open to reveal a wide view of London by night.

Facing this scintillating prospect was a large double bed, its cover removed, the top sheet neatly turned down on one side, but no pyjamas in evidence.

The colour scheme was restfully neutral, ranging from the milky coffee of the twisted wool pile of the carpet to the natural linen covers of the armchairs. An indoor tree, its container concealed in a huge wicker basket, stood in one corner. A nude statue, its head and arms missing, stood on a plinth in another, dramatically lit from below.

It looked Greek: the art of a time when harmonious proportions mattered more than size. Savanna concluded that, like the several fine oil paintings, it was Jago's personal property. If it represented his ideal of the female body, her only resemblance to the statue was in her height.

Undoing the clasp which had held her hair back, but for one silky tendril blown loose by a gust of night wind, she shook it free, then quickly combed it.

When she rejoined the men, Jago was already pouring out coffee from a glass jug of the kind which attached to a gadget which made proper coffee very quickly. The tray, with its jug of cream, and a dish of *petits fours* and handmade chocolates, must have been left ready by his valet.

They both rose to their feet as she came back, and she saw them looking at her hair.

'I wore it the other way to look less "dumb blonde" for the Pressmen,' she said explanatorily.

'I shouldn't have thought that was necessary. You haven't a dumb blonde's face,' said Miles with a smile.

She smiled back. 'I hope I haven't.'

'If you had, we shouldn't be getting married,' Jago said crisply. 'A pretty face is no compensation for an empty head.'

Something in his tone made her say, 'Did you have my school records checked as well?'

'No. As Miles says, you look intelligent.'

'Appearances can be deceptive.'

'A few hours in your company was enough to prove otherwise. Try one of these'—offering her the dish of sweetmeats.

Savanna took a black chocolate which, guessing it had a liqueur filling, she did not risk biting into.

'I didn't think models ate these,' commented Miles, as he chose one for himself.

'I eat everything that's offered to me.'

'You missed lunch,' he reminded her.

'Yes, but think of the huge breakfast we had.'

'We?' Jago queried, raising an eyebrow.

'Mrs Bancroft invited me to make use of her youngest son's room while I'm keeping an eye on Savanna,' the young man explained.

'I see.' Jago turned to her. 'Why did you miss lunch?'

'I had some shopping to do.'

'Very foolish of you to skip meals. Don't allow her to do it again while she's in your charge, Miles. You were also dragged round the stores and made to miss your lunch, presumably?'

'I've been on more exacting exercises. We only went to two shops. Judging by what I know of my mother's and sister's shopping habits, I should say Savanna was an exceptionally fast, decisive shopper. More like a man in that respect.'

'And what higher praise could there be than that?' she retorted impishly.

Miles gave his rare, lopsided grin, as Benjy might have grinned at her after some brotherly badinage. Yet she sensed that Jago was not pleased by their banter. She remembered what he had said about Miles during dinner. Was he going to turn out to be jealous?—Irrationally jealous of men who, in her eyes, could not be compared with him?

Yet there was nothing of the jealous lover in his manner when, about twenty minutes later, he rose to fetch her cloak for her, thereby indicating that it was time they went on their way.

'I thought there was something you wanted to talk to me about,' said Miles.

'Nothing specific—merely to renew our acquaintance. Savanna and I are spending the weekend with my sister, after which it may not be necessary to continue your surveillance. But I'll let you know about that.'

He walked with them to the lift which connected the suites on the top floor with the underground garage where Miles had been able to park the hired car. In the other man's presence, Jago's goodnight embrace was confined to a hand on her shoulder, and a light kiss on her cheek.

'Marsh will collect you at eight on Saturday morning. Pack what you're wearing tonight, and some flat shoes for walking on Sunday. Goodnight.'

'Thank you for a lovely evening. Goodnight.'

Savanna went down in the lift with Miles, wishing it was Jago who was taking her home. But if he had to be up at five-thirty, it was understandable that he wanted to be in bed by midnight.

Thinking of his bed, and its wonderful vista of lights, she found herself half regretting that theirs was not the usual relationship between people with marriage in view. If it had been, she could have stayed with him.

Not that she would have liked deceiving her mother by pretending to be spending the night with Clare and Livvy in the flat they were sharing in Hampstead; nor would she have liked Matthews knowing that she and Jago were sleeping together.

How many women had shared that great bed with him? she wondered. The thought did not trouble her greatly. It was only the future which caused her a peculiar unease. Was it all too good to be true? Must something happen to spoil it?

They were crossing the Thames before she realised she had not said a word to Miles since leaving the hotel.

Seeking a subject for conversation, she said, 'Jago tells me you used to be in the S.A.S.'

'For a time, yes,' was his offhand answer.

'Is it something you're not allowed to talk about?'

'No, but for security reasons the Regiment is inclined to keep itself to itself. Most of the people who are or have been in it tend to prefer action to talk.' He glanced at her. 'But I'll tell you anything you want to know if you'll gratify my curiosity about something you said to him this evening.'

She hesitated. 'What was it?'

'You asked if he had had your school records checked as well. As well as what?'

She gave a soft laugh. 'As well as my address and telephone number, and various other checkable facts.'

Curious to know his reaction; she explained how she and Jago had met.

'Does it sound crazy?' she asked.

'For two ordinary mortals—yes, insane,' was his candid comment. 'But perhaps not for people like you two.'

'We are ordinary mortals . . . or I am.'

'You behave like one, I agree. For a girl with your looks, you're the least spoilt stunner I've ever met,' he told her, with another sideways glance. 'All the same, one wouldn't expect you to fall for an average sort of man, and Jago isn't.'

'No, he isn't,' she agreed, in a thoughtful tone.

Nor was Miles himself, and yet somehow, for all his reserve, she found him less daunting than Jago. She fell silent, fingering the beads he had given her, and remembering the way he had kissed her, deliberately exciting her senses while appearing to remain in full control of his own emotions. Would she ever be able to stir him as wildly as he had stirred her? Somehow she couldn't visualise him losing control of himself.

To her surprise, Jago flew the plane himself on their journey to the north of England.

'I learnt in a Beagle Pup when I was nineteen, and I had an American Cessna for ten years before I bought this French plane. There's no need to be nervous,' he assured her, as they reached his aircraft.

It was an Avion Robin HR 100, painted blue and white, with the wings below the cabin rather than above it as they were on the nearby Cessna which he pointed out to her.

They had to climb over the wing to enter the cabin. But as Savanna was wearing trousers and low-heeled shoes this presented no problem. Having checked that she was properly strapped in her seat, Jago then gave all his attention to the business of take-off. Watching his long brown fingers moving confidently over the switches of the Robin's instrument panel, she had no doubt that he was a skilled and careful pilot.

When they were airborne, he said, 'The disadvantage of this plane is that it needs almost twice as much runway as the Cessna. One of the reasons for the Cessna's popularity is its short field performance. You can get it off the ground almost anywhere, but the Robin needs half a mile to clear fifty feet.'

'So you don't like it as much as your last plane?'

'I think it has a number of drawbacks. As you may have noticed, the way the whole side of the cabin slides forward when one wants to get in and out is not good design for wet weather. But, having said that, it's a marvellous aeroplane to fly—a pilot's plane rather than a businessman's. When we land, you'll see what an excellent view of the airfield we'll have, and the low wing configuration makes for a much softer landing. Also, of course, the Robin has a higher ceiling and a faster cruising speed than the Cessna. On balance, I'm very happy with it.'

'How much does it cost to run a private plane?' she asked, more to satisfy Benjy's curiosity than her own.

'About a tenth of one per cent of the cost of the aeroplane per hour,' said Jago. 'Which means that a Cessna bought for twenty-five thousand would cost about twenty-five pounds an hour. This plane costs roughly fifty pounds an hour, not including hangarage. It's an expensive way to travel, but I enjoy it and can afford it, so why not? After we're married you can learn, if you like.'

He paused to take a large vacuum flask out of the canvas carrier he had brought on board and put on the floor by his seat. Handing it to her, he said, 'Time for coffee. There are mugs and biscuits in the carrier.'

As Savanna poured out the coffee, she said, 'I feel I should learn to drive before I think about flying—although it's nice to know you think I'm capable of it.'

'Women are capable of a good deal more than they're given credit for. The last time I was in America, I read a report of a woman who was out for an afternoon flip in a light aircraft with her husband when he collapsed at the controls. She didn't know how to fly, but somehow she managed to keep the plane airborne. She must have been almost demented with shock and fear, but she kept a grip on herself.'

'What happened?'

'A flying instructor at an airfield heard her calling frantically for help, and he took off and found her, and flew alongside giving directions. She got the plane down in one piece. That's a test of nerve which a lot of men would fail.'

'What an appalling experience!'

'Yes, and perhaps I shouldn't have mentioned it until we're on the ground again. But I had a check-up quite recently, and it's very unlikely that I'm going to collapse on you,' he said, with a smile.

'I've had a check-up, too. You'll be pleased to hear there's no reason why I shouldn't produce little Kindersleys as efficiently as a battery hen lays eggs,' Savanna replied, with an edge in her voice.

If he heard it, he chose to ignore it. 'Splendid. Who did you see? Your family G.P.?'

'Yes. He was surprised. Most girls go to see him for the opposite reason—they don't want to have children immediately.'

'Or, if they do, they can't afford to,' he answered dryly. 'Women have gained a lot of new options recently, but that one's been lost—the right to be a full-time wife and mother.'

His sister Susan, who met them at Manchester, turned out to be a warm, direct, easy-going personality, bearing little physical resemblance to her brother except in her height and colouring. Her features were softer than his, and she had brown eyes which held no critical reserve as she greeted her future sister-in-law.

'I feel I know you already,' she told Savanna. 'When I saw your face on the cover of *Vogue*, I thought you had that special something which takes a model to the top— little guessing that my brother was going to snap you up first,' was her greeting, as she held Savanna's hand in hers. 'It's about time he settled down. I was beginning to wnder if he'd ever find the right girl.'

'I don't know why. I'm five years younger than Edward was when he married you,' remarked Jago.

'He hadn't tried and rejected dozens before me,' said his sister. Then she hastily changed the subject, obviously feeling that she had made a gaffe.

At her suggestion, Savanna sat in the front of the small car during the half an hour's drive which it took to reach Susan's house on the outskirts of a pretty village in Cheshire.

This gave Jago the whole of the back seat to accommodate his broad shoulders and long legs, and allowed Susan to talk to his bride-to-be while keeping most of her attention on the other traffic.

By the time they turned into the drive of a large detached family house with a double garage, the well-kept but labour-saving grounds screened from the adjoining properties by tall evergreen hedges, Savanna knew she was not going to have any difficulty in establishing a comfortable relationship with her sister-in-law.

The twin babies, William and Emily, were at home in the care of Susan's part-time housekeeper. With their round cheeks and button noses, Savanna found them enchanting. But although Jago petted them briefly, it was clear that he wasn't much interested in them. There was, however, no doubting his affection and respect for his brother-in-law when that evening Edward came home after a long day in the operating theatre.

The age gap between him and his wife was even wider than between Jago and Savanna, which she would have found reassuring had it not been for the realisation that although Susan did not advertise her intellectual powers, she was a graduate and therefore in much better mental shape than Savanna felt herself to be.

Explaining that he was playing golf early the next day, Edward went to bed at ten.

'No need for you to come up yet, my dear,' he remarked to his wife, when she would have accompanied him.

'I'm an owl married to a lark,' she explained to their

guest, when her husband had left the room. 'Jago burns the candles at both ends. How about you, Savanna?'

'As a rule I'm a lark.'

'Off you go, then. We'll see you in the morning,' said Jago.

She was about to protest that, tomorrow not being a working day, it wasn't necessary for her to go to bed as early as this, when it struck her that he might wish to talk to his sister privately.

'Well . . . if you won't think it rude of me?' she said to Susan.

'Not a bit. I want you to feel completely at home. As you may have noticed, there's a kettle in your room if you want to make early tea or coffee.'

Savanna stood up. 'So I saw. What a good idea. Goodnight, Susan. Goodnight'—this to Jago, who was in the act of rising.

He went with her to the door which he opened. The hall was in darkness, Edward having turned off the lights.

'Wait a moment.' Jago left the room ahead of her.

As he touched the switches which illuminated the upper and half landings, she followed him into the dimness of the hall, out of sight of the chair occupied by his sister.

She expected and hoped that he would take the opportunity to kiss her goodnight with greater ardour than he could have done in front of Susan. He did kiss her, but not with his arms round her, and not with any suggestion that he would have liked to be going to bed with her.

His mouth brushed hers, lightly and briefly. 'Goodnight. Sleep well.' His tone was matter-of-fact.

He did not linger by the newel post as reluctantly, disappointedly, Savanna mounted the staircase. Before she had reached the turn, he had returned to the sitting-room and closed the door.

CHAPTER SIX

WHEN Savanna woke up the next morning under a fern-patterned duvet on one of the twin beds in Susan's green and white guest room, she was startled to see from the small quartz clock on the night table that it was long past her usual waking up time.

Then she remembered that it had been well after midnight before she had put out her light. After that she had remained awake for a long time. The book she had been reading had not succeeded in taking her mind off her disappointment at the tepidity of Jago's goodnight kiss.

It had been about half past eleven when she had heard some faint sounds which indicated that he and his sister were retiring for the night. She knew, because Susan had mentioned it, that he had been given the visitors' room with the double bed because it was better suited to his size than a single bed.

Now, at ten past nine in the morning, he would be up and about, as would the rest of the household. What a nuisance Susan must think her, still to be upstairs at this hour.

Jumping out of bed, she padded across the thick ivory carpet to the vanitory unit to brush her teeth. Her usual sleepwear was a gaily striped knee-length nightshirt, but for this visit she had brought with her a pair of peach-coloured silky pyjamas which had been a present from Richard. They were edged with pale blue piping, with a mandarin collar and fastenings in the Chinese style. The silk being synthetic, not real like that of her brother's pyjamas, they had survived her restless night without crumpling.

She had just finished using a mint-flavoured mouthwash when there was a tap on the door. Thinking it must be her hostess, Savanna called 'Come in' and turned.

But the apology she was about to make died unuttered at the sight of Jago opening the door with one hand, a tray balanced on the other.

'Good morning.' He closed the door behind him. 'I thought you might still be asleep. For a professed early riser, you were giving a good imitation of a dormouse when I looked in half an hour ago.'

'I know ... it's disgraceful. I'm sorry. I hardly ever oversleep. It must be because I was reading late.'

'It doesn't matter. It does people good to ignore the clock from time to time. I always do when I stay here. Edward is on the golf course,' he went on, 'and Susan and the twins are out. We have no one to please but ourselves, so hop back into bed and have breakfast there for a change. I had kidneys and bacon myself, but Susan seemed to think you would prefer something lighter. We're having roast lamb for lunch.'

Savanna climbed back into bed and pulled the quilt over her legs. She had yet to brush her long hair, which now she raked back with her fingers in an attempt to make it look less tousled.

The tray was the kind with short legs, but instead of placing it across her lap, Jago put it on the chest next to the night table, and sat down on the edge of the bed.

'First, a good morning kiss,' he said, smiling. 'I have shaved, if you notice.' He reached out for one of her hands and held it against his hard cheek for a moment before turning his lips into her palm.

Her fingers fluttered against the taut brown skin of his jaw. She swayed towards him, her free hand going to his shoulder, feeling the hard bone and muscle under the chestnut brown velour of his bath-robe. He was wearing pyjama trousers but not, apparently, a jacket. Where the robe gaped, his chest was bare, the bronzed skin inviting her touch. But as yet she had not the confidence to slip her hand inside the cloth and search for his heartbeat.

His arm slid round her waist, drawing her closer to him. He kissed her lips. This time there was nothing perfunctory about the pressure of his mouth. It was warm and lingering—the kiss she had wanted last night but which he had withheld, leaving her restless with longing.

When he let her go she was trembling. Opening dazed eyes, she watched him lean across the space between the beds to get hold of the second pillow which she had removed from her bed before lying down the night before. Before she could protest that it was wasteful, he had taken the two pillows from the other twin bed and piled all three behind her in addition to the one she had slept on. Pressing her back against this luxurious mound of feathers and down, he began to kiss her again, his fingertips softly caressing the long smooth lines of her throat and the delicate skin behind her ears.

As one kiss merged with another, Savanna lost all track of time. The persuasive movements of Jago's mouth worked like a drug, dulling her normal reactions while arousing strange new responses.

He made her feel like a candle melting in the sun . . . like a tree with all its leaves quivering in a gust of wind . . . like a swimmer floating in a warm sea.

When at last he took his mouth away, she gave a soft murmur of protest, not wanting the long kiss to end, and those lovely sensations to stop.

For some moments she lay with closed lids, her breathing shallow and rapid, unwilling to open her eyes and break the spell he had put on her.

When she felt the brush of his fingers and realised that he was releasing the blue silk toggles from their loops, her breathing ceased altogether. For long seconds she lay like a statue while he undid the top of her pyjamas and laid bare her small untouched brests.

When he kissed the warm hollow between them, she gasped and a shudder ran through her.

'No, Jago, you mustn't . . . oh, please . . .'

'Why not?'

His deep voice vibrated through her as he kept his lips where they were.

She looked down and saw his dark hair, and felt a

primeval instinct to delve her hands into its thickness, and press his head to her body.

Instead, she said faintly, 'You promised . . .'

He raised his head.

'What did I promise?'

His eyes were amused as he ran the tip of his forefinger around the still visible outline of the left half of her bikini top.

'You . . . you promised not to do this until . . . we were married.' Her voice came out a hoarse whisper.

'I promised not to seduce you. I didn't say I wouldn't touch you at all.'

As his finger moved in slowly diminishing circles Savanna shrank back against the pillows, not because she objected to his touch or found it distasteful, but because she was afraid of her own reaction when he reached the centre of the circle.

'Yes, but . . . but one thing leads to another,' she murmured, through dry lips.

His smile mocked her rosy-cheeked confusion.

'Very true. But not in this case.'

'W-why not in this case?'

'Because you may lose your head, but I shan't lose mine,' he said dryly. 'Nor is there time to do more than play with you a little. My sister will be back in half an hour, and it will take longer than that to give you your first lesson in love.'

Her colour deepened. 'How do you know you won't lose your head? How can anyone say that for certain?'

'At your age they can't. At mine one has learnt self-control.'

It irked her to feel herself acutely responsive while Jago remained calm and unmoved. She wanted to see his hard grey eyes become bright with desire, and his fingers shake as they touched her.

'Are you sure?' Recklessly she reared up from the pillows, locking her arms round his neck, pressing herself to his chest, offering her parted lips.

This time he kissed her more fiercely, his hands sliding

round behind her to caress her bare back under the jacket.
When he ran his short, well-kept nails up and down both
sides of her spine, it sent shivers of delight along her
nerves.

As far as she was concerned, the embrace could have
gone on for ever; but after a while he removed her arms
from round his neck and pressed her down on to the
pillows.

She saw that, although he was breathing slightly faster
than usual, he was far from being carried away. His fingers
were steady as he covered her and dealt with the fastenings
of her jacket, while she lay there with heaving breasts and
limbs which felt limp and trembly, as if she had run too
fast and too far.

'Your coffee will be getting cold,' he said, as he slipped
the knot on the collar through its loop.

'It d-doesn't matter. I don't like it too hot,' she
murmured, half relieved and half sorry to be modestly
covered once more.

Not that her breasts were now invisible. The thin stuff
clung to their contours, and she saw Jago looking at the
signs of how deeply his kisses had stirred her.

Smiling slightly, he put his hands on her shoulders, pinning her to the pillows. He bent his head, not to her mouth
but lower, to the bud-like shapes outlined by the silky
fabric.

She gasped, instinctively resisting a caress which
suddenly she felt to be more a test of her reactions than a
passionate urge on his part. Yet when his mouth touched
her, her momentary struggle changed into a spasm of
pleasure which made her gasp with the shock of it.

A few moments later Jago rose from the bedside and
placed the tray across her legs. Then he walked away to
the window which overlooked the grounds behind the
house.

Watching him as he stood looking out at the garden,
his hands thrust into the pockets of his robe, Savanna
wondered if his control was not as complete as he had
vaunted.

She herself was trembling so violently that she dared not pour out any coffee for fear of spilling it on the pretty pale green linen place mat which had a pocket at one end containing a matching napkin.

With an unsteady hand she took up a spoon and forced herself to start eating a mélange of chilled grapefruit segments with orange and melon arranged in a shallow glass bowl.

She had calmed down a little by the time Jago turned from the window, his expression impassive and all sign of any interior disturbance which he might have felt erased from his dark compelling features.

'W-where has your sister gone this morning?' she asked.

'To see an old lady who has no one else to keep an eye on her. Susan doesn't go to church, but she takes the Ten Commandments a good deal more seriously than many who do. She has a much nicer nature than I have,' he added sardonically.

A few minutes later he left her to finish her breakfast and get dressed.

The bedroom had an adjoining shower where Savanna had a hot shower followed by a cold one. Having dried herself, she returned to the bedroom to lie down again for five minutes to allow her deodorant to dry completely before she put on her clothes.

Before she stretched out, she locked the door. She could imagine what would happen if Jago decided to come back for the tray and found her lying totally naked.

Thinking about what had happened earlier, she felt her insides contract with rekindling excitement. Her breathing quickened, and she found herself longing for the moment when he would make love to her properly instead of, to use his own phrase, merely playing with her a little.

She wasn't sure that she liked that expression. It made her sound like a toy; a diversion merely, not the person of supreme importance to him, as a truly beloved wife should be.

For the first time, it struck her sharply that Jago had never actually *said* he loved her.

Suddenly she had an overwhelming need to hear him say those three simple words—I love you.

When she went downstairs, Jago was in the kitchen, reading one of the Sunday newspapers.

'Have you already washed up your breakfast dishes?' she asked, seeing no sign of them on the drainer.

'No, they're in the dishwasher. Susan waits till there's a full load before she turns it on,' he answered, without raising his glance from whatever he was reading.

Savanna added her breakfast things to those already in the machine. Jago continued to read, a slight frown contracting his well-marked dark eyebrows. She could see now that it was an article on the leader page which was engaging his attention. She moved to his side to read the headline.

She hoped he would look up and smile at her, or perhaps put his arm round her hips. But evidently he was too absorbed in the views of the paper's political columnist to feel any affectionate impulses.

She read the first couple of paragraphs before her attention wandered to the crispness of Jago's dark hair, the strong brown column of his neck, and the high hard slant of his cheekbone as he leaned over the outspread paper.

When she laid a hand on his shoulder, he seemed unaware of her touch. He was still in his dark chestnut robe, and the velvety feel of the fabric seemed somehow to accentuate the masculinity and power of the body beneath it.

Sooner than she expected, he finished reading and switched his attention to her. Turning away from the table, he spread his legs and drew her down to perch on one of his thighs.

'Sorry . . . was I neglecting you, my lovely?'

For the second time that morning something in the way he expressed himself struck a jarring note.

'Not at all. I don't expect you to concentrate on me every minute of the day,' she said coolly.

'No, that I shall not do,' he stated. 'In general, during the day you will have to make your own amusements. I shall only be able to concentrate on you at night.'

The gleam in his eyes made her blush. She would have sprung up, but he held her firmly where she was.

'Kiss me, Savanna.'

Softly-spoken, it was still a command, and one he would make her obey if she tried to refuse him. Not that she had any wish to refuse him. It was only . . . she pushed the unease out of her mind, and pressed her lips lightly against his half-smiling, sensual mouth.

He had made her initiate the kiss, but it wasn't long before he took it over, holding her head between his hands so that she could not escape the warm, hungry pressure of his lips.

When he let her go she was trembling again; bemused by the surging emotions he could so easily arouse in her.

'Oh, Jago, I love you . . . I love you so much,' she whispered passionately.

It was a spontaneous expression of her deepest feelings. She had said it without any thought of hearing him echo her admission. But when, without saying a word, he would have kissed her again, she was conscious of something lacking.

Jerking her head back, she murmured, 'You . . . you haven't said that you love me.'

'Do you need to be told?' he asked huskily. 'Can't you tell the effect you have on me?'

Bright colour flared in her cheeks as, deliberately, he made her aware of his readiness to make love to her.

'Th-that isn't what I meant,' she stammered. 'Yes, I *do* need to be told, Jago. All women do.'

A curiously shuttered look came over his face, blanking out the amorous mockery which had been in his eyes seconds earlier, hardening the curve of his mouth into a stern, disciplined line.

She knew then, before he spoke, that her sense of unease had been justified. There *was* something wrong with their relationship.

He pushed her gently off his lap, and stood up and moved away, ostensibly to pour some more coffee from the jug keeping warm on the hotplate of his sister's automatic coffee maker.

Savanna watched him with a sinking sense of panic; knowing that in a few moments he was going to tell her something which would dissolve the bright haze of her happiness like a strong wind.

'Do you believe in astrology, Savanna?' he asked her abruptly.

The question baffled her. What had astrology to do with their feelings for each other?

'No . . . no, I don't, actually.'

'Nor do I. Nor am I superstitious. If I spill salt, I don't throw a pinch of it over my shoulder. If I break a mirror, I don't expect seven years' bad luck. I'm an educated twentieth century man, and I don't believe in any of that nonsense—including the idea that being "in love", as it's called, is the proper basis for a marriage. All the evidence is that it's not.'

There was a silence while she digested this statement.

'Wh-what do you consider the proper basis for marriage, then?' she asked at last.

Before he could answer, there was the sound of a car entering the garage which was connected to the kitchen by a small utility room.

'Susan's back,' he said. 'We shall have to continue this conversation later.'

'But I——' Savanna's protest that she couldn't wait until later died on her lips as she realised the impossibility of discussing this thunderbolt he had lobbed at her until they had the certainty of privacy.

Meanwhile she had to have a few minutes alone to pull herself together. If Susan were to see her now, she would know at once that something was wrong. Any woman, coming into the kitchen at this moment, would sense the tension in the atmosphere.

'I—I'm going up to make my bed,' she muttered.

She had made it before coming downstairs, but neither Jago nor Susan were to know that.

On reaching her room she walked across to the window,

standing almost on the spot where, less than an hour ago, Jago had stood while she lay in bed, still quivering from the ecstasy of his kisses.

Now all that tremulous excitement had been doused by his arbitrary announcement that love, as she understood it, had no meaning for him. It was merely superstitious nonsense.

She remembered how, the day he had asked her to marry him, he had said, *As soon as I saw your face, I knew it was the one I wanted to look at across the breakfast table for the next forty years.*

And she, foolishly, had chosen to take it as a way of saying he had fallen headlong in love with her. Yet down in the depths of her being, at the level between subconscious and conscious thought, she had suspected that he was too experienced, too worldly, too cynical to share her own outlook on life.

Young men fell in love. Sometimes much older men developed intense infatuations which made them behave impetuously, and often foolishly. But not men in their early thirties; especially not rich, attractive men who could have all the women they wanted.

She should have known that. She *had* known it, and chosen to ignore it.

The sound of the door opening made her hurriedly compose her face into an untroubled mask before turning to face her hostess. But Susan would have knocked before entering, she realised a second or two later, watching Jago shut the door behind him.

'I came up here to be private. What do you want?' she asked stiffly.

'I don't want to have you working yourself into a state for no good reason,' was his brisk reply. 'I'd hoped this issue wouldn't arise, but since it has, it had better be tackled immediately. You won't enjoy your lunch if you're upset.'

'Are you surprised that I'm upset? What girl would not be, after being told by her fiancé that he doesn't love her?' she enquired, in a voice which shook.

'Ask yourself which you would prefer: a bridegroom so besottedly in love that he thinks you're the perfect woman, and consequently is certain to be disappointed; or one who's chosen you while still "of sound mind", as they say?'

Before she could answer, he went on, 'A lasting marriage has to be built on solid foundations, not romantic illusions, Savanna. I'm prepared to cut my losses in my business life from time to time, but not in my private life. We'll marry, and we'll stay married. Divorce is not my style.'

'Your style? What about my style? Have you only seen it from your side? Hasn't it occurred to you that I might not want a husband who didn't love me?'

He came closer and laid both his hands heavily on her slim shoulders. 'I like you. In the long run—and marriage is a long run—that's the most important thing. Girls of your age are brainwashed into thinking that being in love is the be-all and end-all of existence. Liberated they may be, but not from that particular delusion. Not yet.'

Suddenly, to her consternation, she began to cry, her soft mouth working uncontrollably, hot tears brimming over her eyelids and trickling down her cheeks. It was ages since last she had wept; not since having to give up her ambition to go to university.

Jago gave vent to a sound which she couldn't interpret. Perhaps it signified exasperation. At the same time he pulled her into his arms and held her against him.

'There's no need for this, silly child.'

He held her close to him with one arm, while his other hand fondled her head, smoothing her thick silky hair and caressing the nape of her neck with light, gentle fingertips.

Savanna strove to control herself. Even in her shock and misery, she was still aware of the latent power in the tall, strong body close to hers.

Presently the hand at the back of her head slid round to tip up her chin. When she tried to resist the upward pressure, not wanting him to see her with moist eyes and blurred mascara, he used such force as was necessary to tilt her head back so that he could kiss her wet cheeks.

Her breathing, already irregular from the bout of tears, became even more uneven as she felt him tasting her tears with his lips and tongue. Before long she had forgotten everything but the longing to feel his mouth on hers.

Her hands which, a few moments earlier, had attempted to push him away, now crept up his chest to his shoulders, circling the collar of his robe until they met behind his neck. Her body no longer needed the iron grip of his left arm to keep her pressed tightly against him.

Her outraged feelings had evaporated; swept away by the powerful narcotic of his overwhelming physical power over her. It was impossible to think clear-headedly—to think at all!—while his mouth roved over her face, exploring her eyebrows and eyelids, the short straight bridge of her nose, the delicate texture of her cheeks and the smooth young sweep of her jaw. Time and again he came close to her parted lips, only to move his mouth away again until she was crazy with longing.

'Kiss me . . . please kiss me,' she whispered, when she couldn't stand it any longer.

'With pleasure.'

Softly he covered her mouth with his, tasting her lips in the same way he had tasted her tears.

His gentleness ended abruptly when, impelled by blind instinct, she tried the same caress on him. The diffident touch with her tongue-tip seemed to electrify him. She felt all his muscles harden, and the speeded-up beat of his heart. His kiss became wild and devouring. It was as if she had touched a secret spring, releasing a fierce primal force. His hands, which had been at her waist, moved possessively over her hips and then to her neat trousered bottom, where his fingers spread, pressing her to him.

Neither of them heard the tap on the door. It was only when it opened and his sister walked in that Jago jerked up his head and glared at her.

'Oh . . . I'm frightfully sorry,' she apologised. 'You said

Savanna was making her bed, and I thought you'd come up to dress.'

Already he had recovered himself. 'I did; and I'd better get on with it.'

He released his hold on Savanna, and walked past his sister, out of the room.

'I'm sorry I burst in like that. I assumed you were alone,' said Susan.

'It doesn't matter. I . . . we . . .' Savanna broke off in confusion. She felt acutely embarrassed at being caught in such an abandoned embrace.

'I thought you might be interested to see our bedroom,' Susan explained. 'It's just been re-done with paper and curtains which I bought in America. Edward's parents spend every winter in Florida because the climate is so much better, and they can play golf more often than they could here. This year we spent Christmas there with them, and I fell in love with the way Floridian houses are decorated. Come and see what I mean.'

Hardly able to make sense of what she was saying, but obedient to her beckoning gesture, Savanna followed her out on to the landing. As the other woman led her to the master bedroom, she seized the chance to snatch a tissue from her pocket and quickly blot her mouth and eyes. An anxious glance in a mirror as she passed it reassured her that her eye make-up had survived the emotional storm fairly well.

When Susan opened the door of the room she shared with her husband, Savanna saw at once why she was so proud and pleased about her new décor. Although it was an overcast morning, the room seemed to be full of sunshine; an illusion of summer created by the design of lime green leaves and vivid lemon-coloured flowers on the puffy white quilt, and on the wall of the alcove behind the bed.

'In America this is called a comforter,' said Susan. 'This one is an outline comforter because it's quilted round the outline of the pattern.' She lifted a corner of it to show the thick but featherweight filling between the cotton and the backing.

She crossed to one side of a large window and pulled

the cord which controlled floor-length curtains which matched the design of the comforter but were made of a type of stiffened voile which combined semi-transparency with a crisply pleated heading.

'These give privacy without shutting out the light during the day, and at night I draw these white lining curtains behind them,' Susan explained.

'They're lovely.' Savanna forced herself to look and sound enthusiastic as indeed, at any other time, she would have been.

'When you're decorating your house, you should make Jago take you to America before you make any decisions,' the other woman continued. 'I used to think the French and the English produced the best furnishing fabrics, and the Italians were the tops for clothes and shoes. But now I think American soft furnishings are probably the best, and as for their towels and bedlinens—you've never seen such gorgeous colours. I could have filled several suitcases!'

She chattered on at some length, giving Savanna more time to compose herself.

Suddenly Susan stopped talking about bathroom accessories, and said, in quite a different tone, 'Perhaps I should mind my own business, but it seemed to me that you and Jago might have been making up a lovers' quarrel when I barged in on you just now.'

Savanna shifted uneasily. 'I . . . it wasn't exactly a quarrel. Just an argument.'

'But he'd made you cry—I could see that. Don't let him bully you, Savanna,' Susan said earnestly. 'I'm very fond of my brother, but that doesn't blind me to his faults. He's an exceptional man, with all the defects of his qualities. He's a leader—and sometimes a tyrant, if people don't stand up for themselves. You're much gentler and less sophisticated than we'd expected you to be. You mustn't let Jago bully you.'

'He doesn't,' Savanna protested. 'He's been wonderfully kind and generous to me. My only concern is that I'm not up to his weight. As you say, he's an exceptional man. Apart from being photogenic, I'm just an ordinary girl. Can I make him happy? I ask myself.'

'You underrate yourself, my dear. It was obvious from your conversation at dinner last night that you're very intelligent as well as very beautiful. I think you'll make him extremely happy—provided you stand up to him when necessary. Now I'd better go down and attend to the lunch. You could lay the table for me, if you would. Edward should be back before long.'

Before Jago reappeared, his brother-in-law had returned from the golf course. For the next two hours it was as if nothing had happened to disturb the calm surface of the engaged couple's visit to the north.

Savanna's appetite for the excellent lunch which Susan had prepared was less hearty than usual. But no one noticed this because she and Jago had not eaten many meals together, and her host and hostess probably thought that, being a model, she never ate very much.

While he was helping himself to the Stilton which followed the home-made apple pie, Edward announced that, having exercised all morning, he was going to spend the afternoon by the fire with the Sunday papers.

'We're going for a tramp,' said Jago. 'What about you, Sue? Will you join us?'

His sister shook her head. 'I've taken up jogging—did I tell you? I've been doing it for nearly a month now. Every weekday, but not on Sunday. While you two are flying back to London tomorrow morning, I'll be out in my track suit, jogging around the park and back. Do you exercise regularly?'—this to Savanna.

'No, but I don't sit down much normally.'

'She needs plumping up, not fining down,' remarked Jago, appraising as much as he could see of her above the level of the dining-table.

Was that remark an indication that he was disappointed with what he had seen of her figure in the bedroom that morning? she wondered unhappily.

But from the very beginning, in the Caribbean, when he had seen her in various bikinis, he had known she was on the slender side, as she had to be for her work. Some of her fellow models were almost completely flat-chested, and had to wear fibre-filled bras to give them any curves at all. At least she could fill a 34C.

But if Jago didn't see her with the redeeming eyes of love, was by temperament a perfectionist, and his preference was for more voluptuous feminine flesh, what hope had she of holding him?

In order to walk in the real country, rather than in a nearby public park where his sister did her daily aerobics, Jago borrowed her car to drive them a few miles from the house to an area of fields and woods.

They did not talk much on the way; and after he had parked the car and they had begun their walk, his remarks concerned the weather and the countryside rather than the subject which weighed so heavily on Savanna.

At last, unable to ignore it any longer, she said, 'This morning you called me "silly child". Is that how you think of me?—As a child?'

He slanted a faintly amused glance at her. 'Did it rankle?'

'I wouldn't say that exactly. But although I was very fond of my father, and I've missed him a lot since he died, I'm not looking for a father-figure husband,' she answered evenly.

Jago received this statement with a reflective silence. At length, he said, 'The difference in our ages makes it inevitable that, in certain respects, you seem very young to me—younger than most girls of your age. By the time you're twenty-five, the gap will have closed. I consider a ten-year gap to be an advantage.'

'Why?'

'Because when two very young people marry, neither of their characters has stabilised. By the time they've both matured, they may find themselves seriously incompatible. People change as much between the ages of twenty and twenty-five as they do between fifteen and twenty. Did you know that, technically, physical adolescence is defined as from fourteen to twenty-five in males, and from twelve to twenty-one in females? I'd say mental immaturity lasts several years longer. My character is set for life. Yours is still malleable. In other words, I can bend you to my will,' he finished, on a note of raillery.

Savanna was not amused. 'What if I resisted the bending process?'

'I don't think you would.'

'*I* don't think you know very much about me. I may be young, but——'

'I know things about you which you don't know yourself,' Jago interjected dryly.

'What do you mean?'

'This, for instance.'

Before she realised what he was about, he pulled her into his arms and brought his mouth hard down on hers, resuming the kiss which Susan had interrupted.

She tried to resist, to pull free, to wrench her face aside. Her efforts were futile. His powerful arms held her fast, and his lips were equally inescapable. Nor did her resistance last long.

Within a few seconds she no longer wanted to break away. It was as much as she could do to remain passive. Even that became impossible as the kiss continued, reanimating the warm, pliant, eager response he had made her feel earlier.

Once she opened her eyes for a second, fearing that he might be watching her, might be kissing her merely as an exercise. But his lids were closed, his dark lashes fanned on his cheeks.

Against her will, her body surrendered to him. When it ended, her arms were round his neck. If he had removed them and released her, she would have staggered and fallen. Dazedly, totally disorientated, she stayed in the circle of his arms, her face hidden against his shoulder.

Jago said, 'Before we met, you didn't know you could feel like that, did you? I did. Your eyes, your mouth, your reactions to me were all clear indications that there was a fire waiting to be lit inside that virginal exterior.' He spoke into her hair, his voice deep and slightly husky. 'You're a lovely girl now, but not as beautiful as you'll be when we've spent a night making love, and that fire is really well alight.'

He felt her chin, and tilted her face up to his. 'It's only smouldering at the moment. You may think otherwise. But how you feel now is nothing to how you will feel when . . .' a pause to nibble the lobe of her ear, sending frissons of pleasure down her neck, '. . . you're in bed with me.'

She had no doubt that he was right but, closing her mind against the vision of their naked bodies entwined, she managed to push herself free, although only because Jago allowed her to.

'I . . . I'm not sure now that I'm ever going to be in bed with you,' she said, in an unsteady voice. 'If you're not in love with me . . . I'm not sure I want to be your wife.'

'It's too late to back out now, my dear,' he answered lazily. 'You've passed the point of no return.'

'It's never too late to back out if one has any serious doubts—not even halfway up the aisle,' was her angry retort. Seeing the scepticism in his eyes, she went on, 'I—I suppose you're thinking that, if our engagement was broken, no one would believe that *I* had broken it? They would think it must be you who had changed your mind. I wouldn't care about that. Marriage is too important to allow oneself to be influenced by other people's opinions.'

'That was not what I meant.'

They were standing a yard apart now, and his fists were tucked into the vertical slit pockets of the shower-proof windcheater he was wearing, unzippered, over his sweater.

'You love me—or so you've said. Are you sure you can kill that feeling? If you can't, how will you feel in a year's time; knowing that you could have been my wife, enjoying all the best things in life? Because I shan't be waiting for you to change your mind, Savanna. I intend to marry this year. It may take a little time to find someone else who suits me as well as you do, but it won't be impossible.'

She drew in an uneven breath, her nails digging into her palms.

'Don't you think it would have been fairer to tell me this was your attitude *before* our engagement?'

'If I had, we shouldn't be here. I wanted you. I knew I could make you happy. I acted for the best—our best.'

His arrogant conviction that he was right made her furious.

'And how long do you intend being faithful to me? Until I'm pregnant with your son and heir, I suppose,' she exclaimed, on a bitter note.

'As long as you never refuse me—or not without a very good reason—I shall never be anything but faithful,' he told her steadily. 'Naturally there have been women in my life before you—it couldn't be otherwise at my age. But there's never been more than one at a time, and most of them were, within limits, lasting relationships. I'm not an inveterate womaniser. A willing wife is all I shall need from now on, and I think you'll be more than willing.'

The mocking gleam with which he tagged on this last remark made Savanna's cheeks glow with sudden colour.

'It—it seems to me you only want a wife as a . . . a sex object,' she said stiffly.

'If you mean that I want my wife to give me what many men receive only from their mistresses—pleasure and amusement—yes, you're right. What kind of wife would you rather be? A housekeeper-wife? A career-wife, struggling to crowd two lives into one?'

He moved closer and, taking her by the hand, began to stride on along the secluded woodland path, not so fast that she had to hurry to keep up with him, but with a leisurely swing.

'A hundred years ago you would have had little or no say in the matter of marriage,' he went on. 'Your suitors would have applied to your parents, and the one they considered most eligible would have been selected on your behalf. Not all those marriages were unhappy.' He glanced down at her. 'Think of yourself as a Victorian girl. Would you be in despair if your parents had chosen me to be your husband? Would you hell! You'd be thanking your lucky stars for a man who wasn't old enough to be your father; who would give you unlimited pin money and a life of considerable luxury; and who didn't make you dread the mysterious "duty" which your mother hadn't fully explained.'

'Yes, that's probably true,' she conceded. 'But I'm not a Victorian girl, Jago. I've been brought up completely differently. It isn't possible for me to think in those terms.'

She gave him a searching upwards glance. 'If you knew how I felt, why couldn't you at least have pretended to . . . to be in love with me? Why spring the truth on me now?'

'I wouldn't have done so if you hadn't forced the issue. I never lie in answer to a direct question.'

'I think you've behaved abominably,' she said, in a low, angry voice. 'You must have known how deeply unhappy this would make me, but you obviously didn't give a damn as long as you got what you wanted. My mother was right to oppose our engagement. I should have listened to her.'

'You're making a fuss about nothing, but only time will prove it to you,' was his even reply. 'Twenty-five years from now, when the first of our children are grown-up, and you're still a beautiful woman because you've been well taken care of, you'll wonder why you were upset. I can give you everything you want—houses all over the world, clothes by your favourite designers, jewels, flowers, books, fine wines, a chef, a nannie, good seats at first nights, any car which takes your fancy. If you consider all that, plus what promises to be a highly satisfactory pleasure bond, to be unequal to the blind hopes and reckless promises on which most marriages are based, you're not using your intelligence.'

'What do you mean . . . a pleasure bond?'

'It's a term coined by Masters and Johnson, who are well-known American researchers, to refer to a good sexual relationship. Our pleasure bond isn't forged yet, but the auguries are good, wouldn't you say?'

As he spoke he swung her hand upwards, pressing his lips to the soft, veined inside of her wrist.

'Don't try to deny that I know how to excite you, Savanna.'

She jerked her wrist free. 'That's only one aspect of marriage.'

'It's the keystone of marriage,' Jago answered incisively.

CHAPTER SIX

BECAUSE there was nowhere at the Bancrofts' house to hang it—the skirt was far too voluminous to fit inside a normal wardrobe—Savanna's bridal dress was kept at·the designer's workroom until the morning of her wedding.

She had chosen who she wished to design it but, before she and the couturier had discussed the dress in any detail, Jago had made several stipulations concerning her appearance on the day. He wanted the dress to have a full skirt and a train, and he wanted the headdress to incorporate an antique diamond fillet which had been in his possession for some time, having been bought as an investment and kept in his bank ever since.

His insistence on a spectacular train and the costly diadem had raised no objections from the designer, but Savanna had been thinking in terms of a simple dress and a coronet of country flowers.

She gave way with a good grace because she knew she had no alternative. If Jago had made up his mind about something—anything!—that was how it was going to be, and as he was paying the piper he had every right to call the tune.

That, if he had been in love with her, he would not have cared what she wore as she walked up the aisle, was a thought to be pushed to the back of her mind.

In the end, however, she had to concede that although it was far more elaborate than the one she had had in mind, the dress was extremely beautiful. She had seen it many times before it arrived at the house. It had required half a dozen fittings, including an extra one because since being measured for it she had lost several pounds in weight, making her already slender waist even narrower.

At ten on the morning of the wedding, her hairdresser,

Luigi, came to the house to do her hair in the style devised by Savanna and her couturier.

Probably Jago would expect his fillet to be worn in the manner of an Alice band, with a cloud of tulle floating from it. But after studying Savanna's face with its broad, high, intelligent forehead—usually concealed by a soft fringe—and the long graceful lines of her neck, the designer had decided that the fillet ought to be worn as such, round her forehead, an inch above her eyebrows.

It had been her suggestion that the band of diamonds should be entwined with a length of the smallest and freshest of real ivy leaves, and he who had agreed and added that the leaves should also be incorporated into the thick plait which would show off her neck and her small shapely ears.

Tests had been made to ensure that ivy could be used in this way without wilting before the ceremonies were over, and had proved successful. But what Jago would think of his diamonds being combined with ivy, and of a long trailing bouquet of lilies, ivy, honeysuckle and cow parsley, remained to be seen.

'You don't seem to be at all nervous,' Luigi remarked, as he applied a pair of bristle brushes to the heavy swathes of her shining clean hair.

'I'm not at the moment. Probably I shall be later.'

'Perhaps not. You're used to being stared at while you're working. It's my Maria who is nervous. She's never been to a grand wedding before,' he told her, with a grin. 'It was kind of you to ask us both. It's helped her to get over the depression after losing the baby.'

Not all Luigi's clients were privy to the circumstances leading up to his own marriage, or the reason for his wife's recent melancholy. He was more inclined to listen to customers prattling than to disclose the facts of his private life.

But Savanna was not one of the self-absorbed women who made up the majority of his clientele, and she knew a good deal about him. Not long after the beginning of her career as a model, Luigi, the son of Italian parents but himself a born and bred Londoner, had gone to Italy for a holiday. While there, he had looked up some cousins of his mother's, and had fallen in love with their daughter, a shy country girl as different from the girls with whom he worked as it was possible to be.

Savanna's quick intuition had made her sense his exuberance after that holiday, and his impatience during the time before he could return and marry Maria. She had been equally quick to detect that all was not well when one of her appointments with him had been on the day after Maria's miscarriage.

Learning that his wife was going to be in hospital for several days, and knowing that she was too shy to have made many friends since coming to England, Savanna had made a point of going to visit her.

It had not been an easy visit because Maria's English was still limited, and she had been heartbroken over the loss of her child, and fearful that it might happen again and deprive Luigi of the sons she wanted desperately to bear for him.

To learn from Savanna how lovingly he had sung her praises since returning from his Italian holiday had seemed to comfort her a little.

When the time had come to make a list of Bancroft wedding guests, it had been natural to include the Lascaris, as well as all the other people who had played a part in her short-lived career.

Even so the bride's guest list was far shorter than that of the bridegroom, who had friends from all over the world coming to see him married, and who, last night, had given a lavish dinner party for all his overseas guests.

Savanna had not been present. They would not meet her until today, at the reception. But that was some hours ahead, and meanwhile she was feeling strangely calm and detached.

After Luigi had finished doing her hair, he went home to put on his hired morning dress, leaving Savanna to apply her make-up. This could have been done for her by a professional cosmetician, but she preferred to put on her face by herself. When anyone else made her up, no matter how skilfully, she felt they tended to overdo it. There were occasions when she liked to do dramatic things with her eyes, but not on her wedding day. Today she wanted to look as natural as possible.

Having made up, she took off the robe which she had been wearing since she got up, and began to put on the underpinnings for the dress which was due to arrive within the next quarter of an hour.

First a white lace bra. Then a suspender belt to hold up sheer white silk stockings. Then, after putting on gloves to avoid any possibility of snagging them, the stockings themselves. Then a pair of white satin French knickers trimmed with handmade white lace. Then a full-length white organdie underskirt, specially made to support the wedding dress.

At Jago's insistence, her shoes had been made by Clive Shilton, the designer of the beautiful silk slippers, with hand-painted soles, worn by Lady Diana Spencer for her wedding to the Prince of Wales.

Because the Royal bride had been almost as tall as her bridegroom, her slippers had had half-inch Louis heels. Savanna was equally tall, but not by comparison with Jago, so the heels of her wedding shoes were higher.

They were made of glove-soft white kid, with rosettes of embroidered tulle on the toes, and a design painted in silver on the instep part of the white leather soles. Like the Princess of Wales' bridal slippers, which had had the gold initials C and D on either side of a tiny heart, Savanna's shoes had her initials and Jago's, and the date of their wedding, painted close to the heel.

As she slipped her narrow feet into them, she wondered if they would ever be worn again, by her daughter or, years hence, her granddaughter. They were the first pair of handmade shoes she had ever possessed and, as she took a few turns about the room, she might have been barefoot on grass, so comfortable were they.

For her 'something old' and 'something borrowed' she had a small silver-beaded purse just large enough to contain a lawn handkerchief and a lipstick. It had been lent to her by Clare, who had a collection of 1920s evening purses. It would be left in the car during the wedding service.

Her 'something blue' was a pale blue silk garter made by her grandmother for Mrs Bancroft's wedding. Her mother, who had had plump legs as a young woman, had worn it above her knee. On Savanna's long slender legs it could be worn at mid-thigh.

As she lifted the underskirt and rested her foot on the dressing stool to slide the garter carefully over her silk stocking, she heard a vehicle draw up outside the house, and going to her window, she saw the couturier's delivery van.

Fortunately, it was a perfect May morning, and the fitter who had come to dress her—and who also would be at the wedding—was able, assisted by the van driver, to carry the tissue-swathed dress from the van to the house without risk to the delicate fabric from rain or gusts of wind. No doubt, had the weather looked doubtful, the dress would have been protected by plastic as well as by clouds of tissue, thought Savanna.

She heard them admitted to the house by Catriona, who had spent the night there in order to help Mrs Bancroft to dress.

Michael was giving Savanna away. Richard and Benjy would soon be on duty as ushers, while Joey, the youngest of her brothers, was assigned to look after his mother in her new wheelchair.

Savanna's friends, Livvy and Clare, were her brides-maids. But she would not see how they looked in their apricot dresses and chaplets of honeysuckle until she arrived at the church.

'Here we are, Miss Bancroft. Were you worried we might be late?' asked the fitter as, with her robe thrown over her shoulders, Savanna met them at the door of her room.

'Good morning, Mrs Harris. No, I felt sure you'd arrive on the dot—as you have. Good morning'—this second greeting being for the driver.

"Morning, miss. Lovely morning for your big day,' He
was carrying the train of the dress while Mrs Harris held
a hanger aloft in one hand and supported the skirt with
her other arm.

When the whole thing had been carefully laid down on
Savanna's bed, the driver withdrew. Mrs Harris took off
her hat and the jacket which matched her pale blue dress
before beginning the task of removing all the plastic clips
which held the long sheets of tissue in place.

As she worked, she chatted about other brides and their
dresses. She did not say so, but Savanna guessed that it
was not usual for the couturier's clients to live in com-
paratively modest houses in the outer suburbs.

Before Mrs Harris had finished unwrapping the dress,
Jago's Rolls-Royce arrived to deliver the diadem and the
bouquet, and then to take Richard and Benjy to the
church before returning for the bride. Her mother,
Catriona and Joey were being transported by hired car.

Every detail of the arrangements had been worked out
by Jago's secretary in consultation with him; and if there
were any hitches it would not be for want of careful
organisation beforehand.

Jago's chauffeur had been instructed to deliver the
diadem to Michael. Her brother brought it upstairs himself, accompanied by the florist who had designed and
made the bouquet, and who was going to add the ivy to
the diadem and to Savanna's thick ash-blonde plait.

As well as the case containing the diadem, Michael had
been given a smaller box. This, when she opened it,
proved to contain an exquisite pair of diamond drop ear-
rings, probably of the same period as the fillet, judging by
their colour and style.

'Oh, Miss Bancroft, what gorgeous ear-rings! Aren't you
the lucky one!' was the fitter's exclamation when she saw
them.

'Aren't I?' Savanna agreed.

She wondered if Mrs Harris and the florist thought
Jago's wealth was part of his attraction for her. If only

they knew how much happier today would have been for her had he been a poor man who loved her..

Half an hour later she was ready; the dress of embroidered cream tulle moulded tightly over breasts and waist before falling in tiers to her feet. The bodice was lined with cream silk, but the long fitted sleeves were transparent, showing off the delicate embroidery. The neckline was low but decorous. Her veil was a circle of double tulle, only embroidered at the edges, flung over her head and secured by a single pin so that it could be swiftly removed during the signing of the register, leaving her completely unveiled for the return down the aisle on her husband's arm.

She went down the stairs very slowly and carefully, for the silk tulle was as fragile as gossamer.

When she joined her brother, who was waiting for her in the hall, he exclaimed, 'You look fabulous, Savanna! Jago's a damned lucky fellow. There's just time for a glass of champagne, and then we must be on our way.'

They did not talk much on the drive into central London.

Once Michael reached for her hand, and squeezed it, and said, 'It's a shame Father isn't here today. He'd have been enormously proud of you—as Mother will be when she sees you. Are you as calm as you look?'

'At the moment, yes. I feel it may all be a dream. When I realise it's not, I may start quaking like a jelly,' Savanna confessed.

'I expect Jago's the one who is nervous. It must be quite an ordeal, hanging about in front of several hundred guests, waiting for one's bride to arrive.'

'It won't worry him,' she said with certainty. 'Anyway, he won't be there yet. Probably he's still in his suite, chatting to Christoper, or even attending to last-minute business matters.'

Jago's best man, whom she and Michael had met at the wedding rehearsal, was Miles Masters' elder brother. Miles himself would not be present. He was on a walking tour in France.

Although the wedding had received a great deal of advance publicity, she was not prepared for the size of the crowd awaiting her arrival at the church.

As Michael stepped down from the car, she saw Clare and Livvy hurry forward to deal with her train. Policemen were preventing photographers and craning onlookers from stepping on to the wide piece of red carpet which led from the kerb to the porch. Inside the porch she could see her couturier hovering, waiting to make the final adjustments to her veil and train.

'Isn't she a picture, bless her!' a female voice exclaimed loudly, as Savanna emerged from the Rolls-Royce.

The momentary blaze of the photographers' flashbulbs was accompanied by a concerted murmur of oohs and aahs, and one or two cries of 'Good luck, dear!'

As she paused while her friends spread her train, she saw, peering through the gap between two policemen, the face of a small, elderly woman, her eyes full of sentimental tears at the sight of a bride.

Would her mother be in tears? she wondered. Why *did* women weep at weddings? For 'remembrance of things past'? For pity, because the bride's bright dreams might soon give place to disillusionment? That couldn't happen in her case. She was already disillusioned. When Jago promised to love her, it would be a form of words merely.

As they entered the porch she could see, through the arched inner doorway, the crowded interior of the church and a profusion of hats in all the fashionable spring colours. Of her bridegroom there was no sign: He must be just out of sight at the far end of the aisle.

Her brother tucked her arm through his. 'Ready?' he murmured.

Savanna nodded, and as she did so, her calm disintegrated. Suddenly she felt utterly panic-stricken.

As the organ boomed out the chords which were their cue to advance, she saw women close to the aisle half-turning to catch the first possible glimpse of her dress.

With her head high, she pinned on a smile and walked slowly, gracefully forward. No one, least of all her own family, must guess that she longed to turn tail and run.

At the measured pace—approximately one step a second—they had practised at the rehearsal, they moved up the aisle. Conscious of the many eyes upon her, she fixed her own gaze on on the glittering gold threads of the altar frontal, specially made at the Royal School of Needlework for use at weddings.

Then, as they approached the chancel steps, a tall figure stepped into view, and Savanna's breath caught in her throat at the sight of Jago preparing to take his place beside her.

He looked superb in evening kit; even more so in morning clothes. She knew that these were not hired because she had heard him mention to Michael that his life involved enough functions to justify owning his own morning coat.

She had thought it would be black, with a light-coloured waistcoat. But in fact his coat was light grey, and the quality of the cloth and its impeccable tailoring, combined with his splendid physique, made him look extraordinarily distinguished. A pearl grey silk tie, and a white carnation in his buttonhole, served to emphasise the darkness of his colouring except for his steady grey eyes which, exactly as she had anticipated, showed no sign that he felt anything but his habitual calm self-confidence.

Savanna surrendered her bouquet to Livvy before the four of them—herself and Jago, flanked by Michael and Christopher Masters—moved into position for the service.

'Dearly beloved, we are gathered here in the sight of God, and in the face of this congregation, to join together this Man and this Woman in holy Matrimony; which is an honourable estate, instituted of God in the time of man's innocency, signifying unto us the mystical union that is betwixt Christ and his Church . . .'

As the Bishop who was taking the service began the preamble, she had to take several deep breaths to stop herself starting to shake.

Something of the terror inside her must have communicated itself to Michael on whose right arm her hand was still resting. He put his left hand over hers, and kept it there while the Bishop said:

'I require and charge you both, as ye will answer at the dreadful day of judgment when the secrets of all hearts shall be disclosed, that if either of you know any impediment why ye may not be lawfully joined together in Matrimony, ye do now confess it.'

Thinking about the secret in her own heart, she was only dimly aware of the Bishop turning to her bridegroom.

'Wilt thou have this Woman to thy wedded wife, to live together after God's ordinance in the holy estate of Matrimony? Wilt thou love her, comfort her, honour, and keep her in sickness and in health; and, forsaking all others, keep thee only unto her, so long as ye both shall live?'

'I will.' Jago's answer came swiftly and firmly.

As the Bishop turned to Savanna and repeated the promise, her mouth was so dry she was afraid that when she tried to speak no sound would come.

Probably the pause before she answered was only a fraction of a second, but to her it seemed an eternity before her lips framed an almost inaudible, 'I will.'

'Who giveth this Woman to be married to this Man?'

Michael took her hand from his arm and stepped slightly to one side, leaving her nearer to Jago.

At a sign from the Bishop, he took her right hand in his. She could feel him watching her as he said, 'I Jago take thee Savanna to my wedded wife, to have and to hold from this day forward, for better for worse, for richer for poorer, in sickness and in health, to love and to cherish, till death us do part, according to God's holy ordinance; and thereto I plight thee my troth.'

Strangely, the firm clasp of his hand steadied her more than her brother's gesture of encouragement.

She was able to make her vows to him in a steadier voice, if still a low one.

As he slipped the ring on her finger, she stole a swift

upwards glance through the filmy meshes of her veil, and felt her heart lurch with love for the strong-featured face at that instant intent on the ring.

They did not kneel for the prayer, but stood with bent heads while the Bishop appealed for God's blessing before, re-joining their hands, he said solemnly:

'Those whom God hath joined together, let no man put asunder. For as much as Jago and Savanna have consented together in holy wedlock, and have witnessed the same before God and this company, and thereto have given and pledged their troth either to other, and have declared the same by giving and receiving of a Ring, and by joining of hands; I pronounce that they be Man and Wife together. In the name of the Father, and of the Son, and of the Holy Ghost. Amen.'

For Savanna, the rest of the service had little meaning. She only half-heard the hymns and the Bishop's very brief address. All she could think of was that she and the tall man beside her were now inseparably bound for the rest of their lives.

Presently, in the vestry, for the last time she used the signature *Savanna Bancroft*. From now on she was Savanna Kindersley . . . Mrs Jago Kindersley.

'What about your veil?' murmured Livvy.

'Oh, yes . . . I almost forgot.' She felt for the pin which secured it.

Jago was speaking to Michael while her mother, wheeled there by Joey, was signing the register.

Livvy took charge of the veil and handed back the bouquet. Then it was time to return for the walk down the aisle.

Smiling, Jago offered her his arm. As they left the vestry, he said, 'You make a ravishing bride.'

He pressed her arm to his side, his eyes taking in the details—her brushed back blonde hair and bared forehead encircled by his band of diamonds and the tendril of tiny green leaves.

She could see the pride in his eyes; but pride of possession was not the same thing as love.

Going down the aisle, trying to look as joyous as the music he had chosen for their wedding march, the first person she recognised was her new sister-in-law. Susan was looking very attractive in a primrose suit and a hat made of massed silk primroses.

Savanna smiled at her, and at Edward, before turning to look at the other side of the nave where the most noticeable of her own guests was Gerald O'Connor's wife Lolly, her ample curves swathed in royal blue chiffon. Gerald was not beside her. He had been given a place on the aisle so that, during the signing of the register, he could leave his seat and go to the porch from which he intended to take the first photographs of the bridal pair.

Among others whom Savanna noticed were Margaret, until recently her agent, and Janey, one of the fashion assistants who had been on the fateful trip to the Caribbean a few months earlier.

But there wasn't time to recognise more than a few faces, and most of those at whom she smiled were Jago's guests and strangers to her.

It was the time of day when office and shop workers, after taking advantage of the fine weather to have lunch out of doors in the many oases of greenery which that part of London offered, were on their way back to work. It looked as if some of them would be late. The crowd outside the church seemed to have doubled, and now there was a mounted policeman in attendance as well as those keeping the red carpet clear.

A cheer went up from the onlookers as she and Jago stepped from the subdued lighting of the church into the early afternoon sunlight made more dazzling by the flashes from many cameras. There was even a shoulder-held television camera trained on them. At the same moment, the bells of the church began to chime the news of the happy occasion to everyone within earshot.

Instead of leading her straight to the waiting car, Jago stopped, and again she saw the gleam of possessive satisfaction in his eyes as he gave the photographers time to take their pictures.

'Give the bride a kiss!' one of them shouted.

Her husband lifted her hand from his forearm and kissed the back of her fingers. Ignoring the suggestion that he should kiss her more demonstratively, he urged her towards the car, climbing in first to give her the nearside seat and make it easier for her bridesmaids to gather up the yards of her train and arrange it round her feet.

This done, the door of the car was closed, the Rolls glided forward and, apart from Marsh on the other side of the glass partition and the onlookers on the pavement, they were alone.

'Feeling better now that it's over?' Jago asked quietly.

She nodded. 'I'm afraid I made some mistakes. I should have let go of Michael's arm as soon as we reached you.'

'I doubt if anyone noticed. A bride is expected to be nervous.'

'Weren't you . . . just a little bit . . . inwardly?'

'I wasn't the star of the occasion—you were. Everyone in the church, including me, was dazzled as you came up the aisle.' He reached for her hand, holding it lightly in his, feasting his eyes on her as he had coming out of the vestry.

She remembered the ear-rings she was wearing. Letting go of her bouquet, she put up her free hand to touch one.

'Thank you for these. They're beautiful.'

Her wedding present to him had been a Japanese box-wood netsuke in the form of a hare, bought from a specialist dealer who had assured her it was of excellent quality.

She had·hoped that Jago would be pleased with it, but had not expected that he would have it with him in an inside pocket of his morning coat.

Taking it out, he said, 'I was surprised that you'd remembered my interest in these little things. This is a very good example. Nothing could have pleased me more.' For the second time he lifted her hand and kissed it.

For a moment she could almost believe they were like all the normal newly-married couples who loved each other and expected to live happily ever after.

In some ways the reception was more of a strain than the service. With such a large number of guests, it would have been impractical for the bride's widowed mother to welcome everyone, or for the bride and groom to receive the congratulations of all those present.

Instead, it had been arranged that they should mingle informally, with Mrs Bancroft's three eldest sons acting as subsidiary hosts.

For about three-quarters of an hour, Jago and Savanna circulated, speaking briefly to his closest friends and the guests from abroad, merely smiling at others.

Then it was time for the best man to propose a toast to their health in a very brief speech, to which Jago replied equally briefly before helping her to cut the first slice of the many-tiered wedding cake.

At this point in the proceedings Savanna was able to swallow a little champagne and to eat one smoked salmon sandwich and a small, delicious *bouchée à la reine* of fragile, buttery puff pastry filled with a curled anchovy.

She needed the brief refreshment to sustain her through another half an hour of maintaining an appropriately brilliant smile and trying not to sound mechanical as she thanked people for their good wishes, and answered their enquiries about the honeymoon by explaining that its location was a secret to which even she was not privy.

At last the customary hour and a half of mingling was over, and it was time to slip away and, with the help of her attendants, to extricate herself from her finery.

As both Livvy and Clare had pierced ears, Jago's presents to them had been classic diamond stud ear-rings which would never go out of fashion. He had suggested these himself, and Savanna had agreed that they would be most acceptable mementoes.

'What about your diamonds, Savanna?' asked Clare, as they helped her to undress. 'Are you taking them away with you?'

'No, Marsh is going to take charge of them, either to take them to Jago's bank, or perhaps they're going to be put in the safe at the hotel. Although I don't know where we're going, I'm sure it will be somewhere quiet, not a place where I'll need any jewels.'

When she had asked Jago what sort of clothes she would need, he had said a bikini, a few casual cotton separates, and something to dance in would be ample.

Her going-away clothes were a suit of pale topaz silk with a pleated skirt and short sleeves, and a saucer of fine cinnamon straw tilted forward over her forehead and secured by a matching ribbon slipped under her plait, from which Clare had very carefully removed all the ivy leaves. A lizardskin clutch bag matched her sandals.

Her bouquet was going to be placed on her father's grave; her dress and veil packed in a large box. Considering how prolonged and complex the preparations for this day had been, Savanna found it hard to realise the wedding was now almost over.

Jago had changed into a suit when she rejoined him. It only remained to say brief farewells to their close relations before stepping into another car. The Rolls in which they had arrived was taking her mother and brothers home.

As they drove away from the reception, Savanna wondered how long it would take them to reach their secret destination. She felt exhausted; every fibre of her being drained of vitality by the weeks of emotional strain culminating in the gala performance which had just ended—at least as far as the two principals were concerned.

Now what she longed for more than anything was a pot of tea, and the freedom to crawl into bed and sleep for twelve hours, if not longer. Instead of which she had to muster the energy for the journey to wherever they were going, and then be suitably appreciative of the special dinner which Jago would have arranged.

When that was over he would expect her to be a co-operative partner in her first experience of lovemaking. At the moment, bone-tired as she was, the thought of so much still to come made her feel like bursting into tears.

To her relief, Jago seemed equally disinclined to talk as the car slid through the moderate afternoon traffic.

'Your mother looked very nice today. I approved of her hat. There were one or two shockers—did you notice?' was his first remark, after they had been driving for three or four minutes.

'The purple feather thing, do you mean? Who was that woman?'

'The wife of one of my executives.'

They relapsed into silence. Savanna wondered if Jago were tired, too. He didn't look it. She was limp. He was merely relaxed.

She looked at her hand, her left hand, now bearing the unusual ring he had chosen for her. It was designed as a plait of three precious metals, platinum and two shades of gold. Unlike a single metal wedding ring, it would look well with all kinds of other rings.

Her eyes were still on the ring when she felt the car swoop down an incline and thought they were entering an underpass. When she glanced up, she saw that it was an underground garage.

'Where is this?' she asked, in surprise, having assumed they were on their way to an airport, or to one of the main railway terminals.

'You'll see.'

As the car drew to a halt, Jago sprang out and turned to help her alight. Leaving the driver to close the door, he said, 'Thanks very much,' and slipped something into the man's hand.

'Thank you, sir.'

The driver touched the peak of his cap and smiled at Savanna before Jago took her by the elbow and steered her towards a door with an illuminated sign above it— LIFT.

It wasn't until they stepped into the lift that she recognised the carpet and realised that she had been in the lift before. They were underneath Jago's hotel.

'Why have we come here?' she asked him.

He pressed the button which would take them straight up to his suite.

'We're spending the night here. The place I've chosen

for our honeymoon is several hours' journey from London. I think you've had enough for one day. You need some rest now.' He paused. 'Disappointed?'

'Oh, no . . . relieved,' she admitted. 'I do feel rather done in—but I'm sure I'll perk up in a little while,' she added hastily.

'Coffee and a sandwich will make you feel better. You've had almost nothing to eat. Nor have I, and I'm hungry,' he remarked.

'A pot of tea is what I really fancy. I don't very often drink it, but somehow I feel like it now. Is that very prosaic of me?' she asked, trying to inject some lightness into her voice.

'Not at all. Have whatever you feel like.'

The lift door slid open. They stepped out into the lobby, and walked to the door of the suite.

Jago opened it with a key. 'We shall be alone here,' he told her. 'Matthews is taking a holiday. He has a sister in Ireland. He was at the service, but not at the reception. He should be in Dublin by now.'

As they entered the suite, he went on, 'I asked him to leave some snacks for us. Later on, we'll have dinner sent up from the restaurant. While I'm making the tea, why don't you have a hot tub? It's the best relaxer I know of.'

'That would be lovely,' she agreed.

'I'll show you the bathroom. This way.'

He went ahead of her, leading her into the bedroom where once she had tidied her hair and seen the nightscape of London, and the statue of a naked woman. Now the view was of misty green tree-tops, their newly opened leaves still unblemished by the fumes from the traffic below.

She thought by referring to a hot tub Jago had meant an ordinary hot bath. But when she walked into the bathroom, she saw that instead of the conventional rectangular bath there was a large circular pool sunk into a carpeted dais. The pool was already full of water and, when Jago touched a switch, the still surface began to swirl and bubble, activated by several jets in the sides.

'Ten minutes in there and you'll feel a new woman,' he told her. 'I'll go and attend to the tea.'

He pressed another button, and quiet, soothing background music mingled with the sound of the moving water.

When he had left her on her own, she began to undress, hanging her going-away dress on one of the hangers in an alcove between two of the seven or eight panels of floor-to-ceiling mirror in which she could see herself reflected from many different angles.

There was also a large recessed shower cabinet in which to cool off after a hot tub, and an abundance of towels, from all-enveloping bath-sheets to matching face-cloths.

The tub, the shelves and the towel rails were all made of a material like dark tortoiseshell, and the carpet and towels were the dark apricot colour called tiger lily. The faint drone of an air extractor accounted for the fact that, although the bathroom had no windows, the steam from the eddying water was not condensing on the mirrors.

It took her only a few moments to remove her few scanty undergarments and drape them on a cushioned bench. Having stepped out of her shoes, and peeled down her gossamer stockings, her last task was to take off her jewellery.

Then she stepped on to the dais and dipped one foot in the water which, as far as she could judge, was heated to about ninety degrees. Moments later she was sitting on the ledge which formed a seat round the pool, the water almost up to her collarbones, and her legs stretched out towards the centre.

She had read about the craze for jacuzzis, hydrotherapy pools and spas which had swept America and now had caught on in Europe. But this was her first experience of being lapped by warm, gentle crosscurrents. She noticed a waterproof bath pillow lying on the dais and stood up to reach for it. With the pillow tucked behind her head, she was even more comfortable—totally comfortable. It was bliss to be alone and at rest. She felt grateful to Jago for his consideration in bringing her here for the first difficult night of their marriage. For it was a difficult situation; being the inexperienced bride of a man who had slept with many women before her, and who she knew did not love her.

She sighed, closing her eyes for a moment, the better to enjoy the swirling movements of the water and the lulling sound of the music.

'Your tea, madam.'

She opened her eyes to find Jago setting down a tray.

'Have two or three of these sandwiches,' he advised, pouring tea from a silver pot into a porcelain cup. 'They're smoked salmon, turkey, and cream cheese with cucumber. Want a towel to dry your hands? I'll get you one.'

Having supplied her with tea, something to eat, and one of the fluffy-piled towels, he left her alone again.

Savanna drank the hot tea, ate two brown bread and salmon sandwiches, and began to feel less like a rag, although still unbridally drowsy. She remembered reading that Bernard Levin, the well-known London newspaper columnist, made a habit of cat-napping in his bath before going out for the evening. Perhaps if she dozed for a few minutes . . .

The next thing she knew was that Jago was saying her name, and this time he wasn't bending over the dais, fully dressed. He was in the pool with her, facing her, his elbows propped on the rim as he watched her wake up and blink at him.

'I don't think you should stay in too much longer. I keep this tub cooler than many of them, but even so it can be enervating to stay in too long,' he remarked.

The water was no longer swirling. He must have turned off the jets.

'How long was I dozing?' she asked him.

'Not long. Only two or three minutes.'

His foot touched hers under the water, and it wasn't an accidental contact. The soft pads of his toes moved gently over her instep, and he watched her reaction, smiling slightly.

'Does it make you shy to get out of the water in front of me?'

'I suppose it does a little.'

'It's something you'll have to get used to.'

'I know.' But she didn't move.

She had a feeling that the moment she stood up he would grab her and take her in his arms, and she wasn't ready for that yet. She had thought it wouldn't happen until later . . . tonight, after dinner . . . with the lights out.

'Doesn't it ruin the carpet to drip water on it?' she asked.

'It's a synthetic carpet, so a certain amount of water does no harm. But, if you notice, I put out a bath mat. There's also a towel ready for you.' He indicated the mat he had spread on the dais, and the several towels folded beside it.

'Oh, so I see . . . thank you.' But still she hesitated.

Now that the water was quiescent, Jago must be able to see a good deal of her already. As she could of him—if she looked. But she was being careful not to look.

'Perhaps I should get out first. I'm not shy,' he said, on a teasing note.

He stood up and sprang out of the tub. She had a brief glimpse of his long thighs and muscular buttocks before he wrapped a towel round his hips, using another to dry himself.

His body was still almost as brown as it had been in the Caribbean. Only his backside was paler, although not as white as her white parts because of his much darker skin tone.

Growing up outnumbered by brothers, Savanna had seen male backsides before. But none of the Bancrofts' three sons was as tall or as well-built as Jago. Seeing his sinewy thighs for the first time since the West Indies, and the masculine lines of his backside, so different from her soft behind, sent a shiver of apprehension through her. He was so big and strong. Would he hurt her? Without love to make him tender, would the first time be miserably painful?

'Out you come, Savanna.'

He was holding up a large bath-sheet, ready to envelop her in it. Instinctively taking a deep breath to steady her nerves, she stood up and stepped on to the ledge, the water streaming from her body. She saw his grey eyes sweep over her in a single comprehensive glance, and then she was wrapped in the towel.

As if he knew what she'd been thinking, he said quietly, his voice slightly husky, 'Don't be nervous—I'm not going to hurt you.' Then, still holding the towel in place for her, he kissed her softly on the mouth.

If anything could have reassured her that, even without being in love with her, he was prepared to make allowances for her inexperience, it was that first restrained kiss—their first kiss in private as man and wife.

'Poor little tired, nervous bride,' he murmured, his lips to her cheek. 'But there's nothing to be afraid of, I promise you.'

'I'm not . . . not really,' she murmured. 'Well . . . perhaps a little . . . *oh*!'

The last exclamation was caused by being suddenly swung up in his arms.

He carried her out of the bathroom, through the dressing room, into the bedroom.

'This hairstyle is very attractive, but I like you better with it loose. Why don't you undo it?' he suggested, as he carried her to the wide bed which had had its cover removed, and the clean sheets turned down on one side.

He put her down in a sitting position on the side of the bed.

'It's too bright in here. I'll draw the curtains.' He walked away.

Quickly Savanna rearranged the towel into a sarong, and raised her arms to feel for the pins which secured the perfect French pleat her stylist had put up that morning.

The curtains were controlled by switches. At the touch of a button they swished across the wall of glass, to be stopped by Jago a foot before they met in the middle.

The room became restfully shadowy, just one narrow bar of sunlight falling across the expanse of thick carpet.

Savanna put the handful of pins on the night table, and shook her head from side to side, trying very hard to remain calm as Jago came back to join her.

Naked but for the small towel which covered him from hip to mid-thigh, his tanned skin as smooth as brown silk, he looked very different from the man who had stood beside her at the reception, clad in immaculate morning clothes, making urbane replies to the people congratulating him.

He sat down beside her, close to her. As her trembling hands fell to her lap, he stroked the loose swathes of her hair, looking at it, feeling its texture, still smiling faintly.

With his left hand, he picked up her left hand and looked at the gleaming new ring. The sapphire was still with her ear-rings and pearls in the bathroom.

'Do you like this?' he asked.

'It's beautiful, Jago. You have excellent taste.'

'I think so, too—whenever I look at you. Did you hear the murmur of admiration which went through the church when people saw you coming down the aisle?'

She gave a mute shake of the head. Her throat and her lips were dry, and she didn't seem able to breathe properly.

He began to kiss her knuckles and fingers, while his other hand slid through her hair to find the nape of her neck and gently caress it. Presently he stopped playfully toying with her fingers, and drew her closer to start kissing games with her mouth. His lips were not dry as hers were, from the tension coiling inside her. His were warm and supple and persuasive, so that after a little she found herself starting to respond instead of being passively submissive.

'Put your arms round my neck,' he told her softly.

Her eyes closed, Savanna obeyed him, linking her hands behind his head and feeling him press her softness against the hard wall of his chest.

He kissed her for a long time, sometimes freeing her

mouth to explore the delicate skin of her eyelids, or to nibble the lobes of her ears.

It was all very slow and unhurried, with none of the fierce impatience she had imagined and dreaded. She became more and more relaxed, all the tension melting away, and excitement beginning; the excitement which, in the past, she had always fought to control, but now need not fight any more.

She felt Jago loosen the towel until it slid down to her waist, exposing her small ivory breasts. But he did not immediately touch them. His hands returned to her back, and his fingertips slid down her spine, making her give an involuntary purr of pleasure.

'You like that . . mm?' he asked lazily.

When she murmured assent, he did it again.

Her cheek resting on his shoulder, and her lips very close to his throat, she inhaled the faint scent of his aftershave and the warm, clean smell of his skin.

When, taking her wrists, he loosened her hold on his neck and made her lean back on his arm, she did not resist, although a fresh wave of shyness swept her as she felt him unwrap the towel from her hips and thighs.

Lightly, his hand brushed her knee and slid slowly up her slim thigh. Her eyes almost closed, her hair cascading over his supporting arm, she saw him appraising every line and curve of her body, first with his eyes and then with his palms and fingertips.

Her skin, still warm from the hot tub, was acutely sensitive to his touch as his hand reached her hip and paused there. When he half-clenched his fingers and drew his nails lightly across the soft golden plain of her belly, just below her navel, she had to smother a gasp at the strong, almost painful response which the action induced.

When he did it again, in the opposite direction, she gave a convulsive shudder and her hands gripped the discarded towel, half wanting to clutch it around her but knowing he would not allow it.

Jago's palm passed over her waist and moved slowly upwards to fondle her quivering breasts. Her breathing quickened and she began to shiver uncontrollably. Beads of moisture broke out on her forehead and upper lip. When she felt the warmth of his lips directly over the spot where her heart was thudding like a trip hammer, her shivering intensified.

Moments later a gasp did escape her when his lips reached the tip of her breast and sent shooting-stars of pleasure along every sensitised nerve.

When, a little while later, he lifted her further on to the bed, and pulled all the pillows together to make a soft mound behind her and have both his hands free, Savanna opened her eyes and whispered, 'What's the matter with me? I . . . I can't stop this shivering.'

'It doesn't matter. Forget it.' His voice had a slightly ragged edge, but his hands remained steady and gentle as he resumed his caresses, kissing her throat, breaking down her inhibitions with the irresistible delight induced by the things he was doing to her.

Very soon it wasn't enough for her to lie still. She found herself impelled to touch him, to plunge her fingers into the thickness of his dark hair, to feel his strong neck and shoulders.

His skin was as smooth as her own, yet subtly different; like fine polished leather stretched over a hard under-surface of strong bone and springy muscle. Her own flesh was softer, more plastic. Did it please him as much as the feel of his taut skin pleased her?

She was filled with a strange, feverish impulse to make her spine bend like a bow, arching and stretching her body as if it might ease the increased violence of her tremors.

Jago's mouth came down hard over hers in a long, hungry, sensual kiss to which she responded eagerly, all shyness forgotten.

Later, she woke up to find him wearing a dressing-gown and opening a bottle of champagne. He had unpacked her night things for her. She wore the virginal white nightgown to eat a delicious light supper for which, refreshed by her sleep, she was unexpectedly hungry.

Eating caviare, and listening to a recording of Debussy's *Nocturnes*, she wondered if, before they went to sleep for the night, Jago would make love to her again. She found herself hoping he would.

Whatever else was lacking in their marriage, she had nothing to complain of in the tender expertise with which he had introduced her to physical love.

By the following evening they were installed in a white-walled, white-shuttered villa on a hill between Vale de Lobo and Albufeira on the south coast of Portugal, in the region known as the Algarve, the name deriving from the Arabic words for the south—Al Gharb.

A short drive from Faro airport, the villa had been lent to them by friends of Jago who used it themselves for only a few weeks each year. Luxuriously furnished, and serviced by a Portuguese maid who came in for four hours each day, the house offered a choice of beaches not far from its own large garden and swimming pool.

From the spacious, airy master bedroom occupying the whole of the upper floor, they looked across pinewoods to the ocean. The bedroom had its own walled terrace where they could sunbathe in privacy without any clothes on.

At first Savanna was shy of lying on a towel-covered air-bed without her bikini, but when she jibbed at removing it, Jago laughed and kissed her, successfully distracting her attention while he untied the strings of both parts. Then he insisted on applying her sun cream for her, which led to his making love to her. After which she was shy no longer, and abandoned herself to the golden warmth beaming down from the cornflower sky as freely as he had just made her abandon herself to him.

At night he would watch her swim, naked, in the illuminated pool while he sat on the deck with a long drink. That, too, was a lovely sensation. When she came out he would wrap an enormous towel round her, and they would stroll back to the house through the lantern-lit garden to dine by the light of two candles and the innumerable stars in the now black and velvety sky.

The heat, the beauty of the place, the wine which they drank at all hours, the delicious seafood and salads prepared for them by Maria, all conspired to lull Savanna's doubts about the future.

She lived entirely in the present, and a great deal of the present was spent in her husband's arms, an experience which swiftly became the most intensely pleasurable of all the sensual delights the Portuguese villa had to offer.

Sometimes they walked through the pinewoods to bathe in the sea. The water was clear, and still cold enough to be invigorating.

Once, on a breezy day when the surface was a little choppy and Jago swam a long way out—to him the confines of the pool were like a small exercise yard to a big dog—Savanna lost sight of him. There were wind-surfers and water-skiers skimming back and forth. For a few minutes she was terrified that one or other might have hit him.

She was on the brink of panic when she saw his distinctive arm strokes. She felt a wash of relief. The incident gave her a glimpse of what she would feel if she lost him.

But how much would he care if she were killed?

An echo of the conversation they had had while staying with his sister came back to her.

I intend to marry this year. It may take a little time to find someone else who suits me as well as you do, but it won't be impossible.

About a month after their return to London, Jago had to go to America. It was to be a gruelling coast-to-coast trip, leaving no time for relaxing or sightseeing.

'I won't take you with me this time. Why not spend a few days with your mother?' he suggested.

Mrs Bancroft and her two youngest sons were now in the competent hands of a living-out housekeeper who ran the house with great efficiency and also did most of the cooking.

Savanna went to the airport to see Jago off. As he had made love to her before breakfast, perhaps it was unreasonable to feel disappointed because his farewell embrace was somewhat perfunctory.

That night, when she went to her room, it seemed very small and cluttered compared with the luxurious spaciousness to which she had already become accustomed.

The bed in which, at one time, she had seldom remained awake for more than two or three minutes because she had always been tired by the end of those long days of working at her job and at home, now seemed crampingly narrow.

Although it was summer, the weather was cool enough for her to have switched on the electric underblanket. It made the bed warm, but it was a poor substitute for the living warmth of Jago's chest against her back, his long legs behind her legs and his hand enclosing one of her breasts, which was the way they usually slept.

In New York it would be early evening. Jago would be having dinner, talking business; not thinking of her, not missing her.

The days of his absence seemed endless. It was on her last day at home, after she had been out shopping and was unpacking a pot plant which the florist had put in a carton and supported with crumpled newspaper, that Savanna caught sight of her husband's face.

She spread and smoothed the sheet of paper. It was a page from one of the popular dailies aimed at readers more interested in scandal and sensation than in a responsible presentation of serious news and events of genuine importance. It was not a paper she ever saw except on the news stands. The page which carried Jago's picture was the paper's gossip column, composed of short, spicy paragraphs about film and pop stars, television personalities and the more colourful politicians.

The text accompanying the photograph hinted that, although recently married, he had already resumed a relationship with the actress who had been his close friend several years earlier. It was all done by innuendo; carefully avoiding anything libellous.

Twice in the space of ten days he had been seen leaving the expensive West End apartments where the actress had a flat. Perhaps he had other friends living there, the columnist conceded.

But if he and his former love should meet in the lobby or the lifts, it must cause her some pangs, if not him. According to the writer, her name had not been linked with anyone else's since the end of her association with Jago. Friends said she had been madly in love with him, and had never got over the break between them.

Savanna read and re-read it, feeling shocked and sick. This was what she had feared, but much sooner than she had expected.

Her first reaction was to tear the page into small shreds, drop them in the waste bin, and try to forget she had seen the malicious paragraph. For what motive other than malice could a man have for writing such cruel exposures of the frailties of the rich and famous? How he must envy and resent them to make his living by spying on them, or paying equally unpleasant people to supply him with snippets of gossip, half of it probably having little or no foundation.

However, try as she would to dismiss what he had written about Jago as spiteful rubbish, she found it impossible not to credit the story with some truth.

CHAPTER SEVEN

JAGO was expected home for dinner. By four o'clock Savanna was back in central London, having her hair done. She had made the appointment with the intention of looking her best to welcome him home, but now she was dreading the reunion.

Should she tell him what she had read, and see how he reacted? No: what was to be gained by bringing her fears into the open? Better by far to behave as if nothing had happened—if she could.

At six o'clock she was ready and waiting for his arrival in an outfit by Giorgio Armani. He and Gianni Versace had long been her favourite designers, and now she could afford to buy their clothes. The Armani outfit consisted of a cream silk blouse with a pair of knickerbockers gathered into a band at the knee, and patterned with dark blue and cream leaves on a coffee-coloured ground. With the pants Savanna was wearing opaque blue stockings and low-heeled pumps. There was also a band-collared, seven-buttoned light wool jacket to wear over the blouse out of doors.

It had cost a great deal of money and the pants would go out of fashion. But the blouse and the jacket were classics which would be wearable for years. Long before they grew shabby, their cost per wear would be less than that of cheaper but less enduring garments.

Cost per wear was an attitude to clothes expounded to Savanna by an American model, and one she would have liked to adopt earlier, but the drains of her income had made it impossible.

Now, as Mrs Jago Kindersley, she could have succumbed to the attractions of all the most transitory vogues without overspending her dress allowance. But her time as a model had made her resistant to most of the extremes of fashion. However, the knickerbockers were fun and very feminine, and at the time of buying the outfit she had thought they would amuse her husband.

In that supposition, she had been right. When Jago walked into the sitting-room and saw her standing by the window, her hands in the vertical pockets of the new Italian pants, his grey eyes lit up with smiling appreciation of the casual chic of her appearance.

'Hello. Did you have a good trip?' she enquired, with a cool little smile.

He came swiftly to where she was standing.

'Excellent, but five days is too long without this'— taking her in his arms, and pressing his mouth over hers.

Savanna tried to pull back, but his embrace was too firm for her resistance to be noticeable, and once his lips were on hers it was futile to deny that for her, too, five days had seemed a long time to forgo the strong clasp of his arms, and the sweet surrender to his kiss.

Her eyes closed. For those first few moments in his arms, nothing mattered but being pressed against him, his hands roving over her back, his mouth moving hungrily on hers, as if it were weeks rather than days since the last time they had held each other.

At last he raised his head. 'Let's go to bed,' he said huskily.

Savanna shook her head, partly in rejection of the suggestion, partly to clear it of the drug-like effect of the long, passionate kiss.

'Matthews will be unpacking your cases.'

'I told him to leave it till later.'

'You didn't!' she exclaimed in dismay. 'Oh, really . . . - what must he think?'

'That I want to be alone with my wife—a very natural desire in the circumstances.'

He had slackened his hold sufficiently for her to free herself. 'I've only just dressed . . . and I had my hair done this afternoon,' she said awkwardly. 'We're going out tonight. Had you forgotten?'

'No, but I see no reason not to go to bed on that account. We have two hours in hand—ample time. Your hair will survive.'

He took her by the hand and began to lead her towards their bedroom.

With an open show of reluctance, Savanna allowed herself to be taken there. As they crossed the threshold, she said, 'But I've only just done my face, Jago . . . and I . . . I'm not in the mood now.'

He closed the door and turned the locking device on the knob. Ignoring her remark, he said, 'I've brought you some presents. One of them is in my suitcase. I expect Matthews has put it in the dressing-room.'

While he went to fetch what he had brought her, Savanna remained in the bedroom, trying to make up her mind what to do when he returned.

She was remembering the day he had told her that as long as she never refused to make love—or not without a very good reason—he would never be anything but faithful to her.

Clearly he didn't consider the fact that she was ready for their evening engagement an adequate reason to deny him the welcome he wanted. If there was no truth in the columnist's allegations—and Savanna clung to the hope that there might not be, or at least not yet—to refuse him would be asking for trouble.

Jago returned with a flat box. As he handed it to her, he said, 'I bought you a teddy. I've no idea why it's called that, and the salesgirl couldn't enlighten me. Perhaps they're obtainable here, but I've never seen you wearing one and it struck me as rather a fetching garment.'

Savanna opened the box and unfolded the leaves of tissue paper to reveal an expanse of oyster satin trimmed with palest dove grey lace. She could see at once that it was silk satin and handmade lace. Jago must have bought it from a shop specialising in the most expensive kind of lingerie.

'Try it on,' he said. 'I'm going to have a quick shower. I shan't be five minutes.'

Alone again, she shook out the teddy. It was styled like a loose one-piece bathing suit with tiny hooks and eyes to fasten the join between the legs. The cups and a panel down the front were of unlined lace with more lace at the hips. The rest was made of the sleek, lustrous satin.

At any other time she would have been delighted to receive such a charming and luxurious piece of underwear, but the seeds of suspicion sown in her mind by the gossip column now were tainting all her reactions.

Unwillingly, she undressed and slipped the teddy over her head. It fitted perfectly, emphasising the fuller contours of her body since she had gained a few pounds. The cobwebby lace clung to her breasts, and the bias-cut satin gave a voluptuous roundness to her hips and buttocks. Ladylike and restrained in its colouring, in cut and design it was deliberately seductive.

Jago returned, wearing a bathrobe and vigorously rubbing his wet hair. He walked round her—prowled was the word which came into her head—his hard eyes glinting appreciatively.

'I'm beginning to see a connection between this kind of teddy and the other. It makes you look very cuddlesome.' He flung the hand towel on the carpet, and reached out a long arm to pull her to him. 'I have something else for you, but that can wait until later.'

Savanna had been house-hunting for two months, and was beginning to wonder if she would ever find a place which complied with Jago's requirements and which also appealed to her, when she decided to try another estate agency, one less well known than those which advertised in the glossy magazines.

It was an impulsive decision inspired by a small advertisement in one of the Sunday newspapers. On Monday she called at the office and talked to the owner of the agency, who turned out to be an American married to an Englishman. Her name was Nancy Southworth, and her business had sprung from her successful efforts to track down attractive apartments for friends from her country who needed to live in Europe for periods from several months to two or three years.

She had been a professional agent for a little more than a year but, after half an hour's talk with her, Savanna felt she might turn out to be more helpful than some of the established agencies which, in spite of her clear-cut requirements, were inclined to send her to see places which were completely unsuitable.

Not that such time-wasting mattered, when she had so much time on her hands; but it was a rather pointless exercise to look at houses which, had she been given the details in advance, she could have ruled out unseen. Most of the agents seemed to think her incapable of reading a floor plan or digesting a written description. Obviously they knew she was the wife of a very rich man, and were more concerned to sell her one of their most expensive properties than to pay attention to her reasons for not liking many of the houses they had on their books.

If Nancy recognised her new client, and was mentally rubbing her hands in anticipation of a large commission, she concealed it better than some of the others.

'At the moment I've only two places which come close to fitting your bill,' she said, after making a list of the factors which Jago considered essential. 'The snags are that one is three or four miles farther out of London than the distance you've stipulated, and the other is a super house but it needs a lot of modernisation and redecoration. You couldn't move in in less than six months, I would say. But it really is a gorgeous old place, with terrific potential. As a matter of fact I'd love to have it myself, but my husband won't hear of it. He insists on living in London, and I guess he's right. Neither of us has time in our lives for several hours' travel every day. But if we were younger, and planning a family, I'd want them to grow up at Merryhill.'

'I don't think a distance of under five miles is too important. Where are these houses?' asked Savanna.

'They're both in Buckinghamshire, and within a dozen miles of each other. If you like to suggest a convenient time, I'd be happy to run you out there—they might be a little difficult to find if you don't know that area well. If your husband will be looking at them with you, I'd advise going along without me. Frankly, from my own past experience as a buyer, I think having an agent along can be inhibiting. But for a woman to view a large empty house on her own can be a little scary.'

'My husband is too busy to look at houses until I've approved them. I'd be glad of your company, Mrs Southworth.'

'Good, then let's fix a date, shall we? Would Friday morning be any good to you? We might not get back until early afternoon, depending how interested you were. If neither place appealed to you at all, we'd be back in London by lunchtime.'

'Friday would be fine.'

As Savanna went on her way, she found herself looking forward to spending some time in Nancy Southworth's company. Marriage was proving a somewhat lonely existence.

This would be remedied as soon as they found another home. But meanwhile, with Matthews taking care of all the domestic arrangements, her mother housebound and none of her former colleagues having any time to spare during the day, she found time hanging rather heavily. Perhaps it was partly by comparison with the rush of her life before marriage that the days seemed three times as long now.

She knew there must be many women who would envy her ample leisure, and the generous allowance which Jago had put at her disposal. She not only had hours free for window-shopping, but the means to buy almost anything which took her fancy. But the life of a rich, idle woman didn't really appeal to her. She longed for more fulfilling activities than beauty treatments and clothes shopping. At present, when she wasn't house-hunting, her most useful occupations were learning to drive and attending an exercise class. She also read a great deal, but somehow had not regained the academic impetus disrupted by her father's death and the consequence of it.

Part of the reason was that it hardly seemed worthwhile to embark on a programme of classes or even a course of self-tuition when she might soon be involved with doing up a house, and very likely pregnant as well.

The frequency with which he made love to her made her feel it could not be long before Jago's wish to start a family was on the way to being fulfilled. She was in his arms much more often than she had expected to be, given the nature of their marriage. There were times when she wondered if it were normal for a husband to continue, after the honeymoon, to be as ardent as he was.

Very often he would kiss her awake and make love to her before breakfast. Sometimes he would come home for lunch, and from time to time while they were eating she would look up from her plate to find him watching her with a fixed intensity which she knew meant that, when lunch was over, he would take her to bed for half an hour.

During these rapturous interludes she surrendered herself to the pleasures of the moment, and each time seemed better than the last. Jago was never selfish in his love-making, although he would leave her soon afterwards, returning to give her a final kiss before, having put on his clothes, he was ready either for breakfast, or to continue his crowded schedule.

It was then, when he had left the bedroom, leaving her to make a more leisurely recovery from the languor which followed the frenzy, that certain disturbing thoughts would creep into her mind. Would his desire for her wane from the day she told him she was expecting a child? How could she hope to hold him when her body became bulky and ungainly? How could she endure the agony of suspecting that he was unfaithful to her?

She knew that each time they made love she became more deeply addicted to the exquisite feelings he gave her, and which she felt sure she would never experience in the arms of anyone else. But she had no confidence at all that making love to her was better for him, if as good, as the times he had spent with the women who had preceded her, and those who might—would!—succeed her.

On the evening of the day of her visit to Nancy Southworth's agency, Jago seemed preoccupied by an impending political crisis which, if not averted, would have serious effects on commerce.

He spent part of the evening watching an hour-long programme in which politicians and union leaders were interviewed and expressed their attitudes to the crisis. Savanna saw his mouth harden with impatience when they made statements of the kind which she knew he found exasperating.

The news bulletin which followed the programme made his jaw muscles clench. Afterwards he disappeared into his study to make a Transatlantic call, and she decided to go to bed early and continue reading a book which, perhaps foolishly, she was keeping in a locked drawer in her dressing-table, out of Matthews' sight as well as Jago's.

For a reason which might have disappointed him, but had been a relief to her, it was some days since Jago had held her tightly in his arms and pressed his mouth hungrily on hers. As she sat up in bed, reading the book, Savanna found herself longing for him to join her. But she thought it would probably be midnight or later before he came to bed.

He needed much less sleep than she did, and if he did retire early he would often read far into the night, using a narrow beam of light which had been specially installed so that his nocturnal habits would not disturb her rest.

Frequently he rose very early to work from perhaps five o'clock until, at six-thirty or seven, he would shower, shave and come to wake her up, his face smooth, the minty tang of his toothpaste flavouring his kisses.

Now, stirred by the book she was reading, she longed to be able to get up, go to his study and entice him to come back to bed with her. But she lacked the confidence to make that kind of approach to him. Theirs was not the sort of relationship in which she could take the initiative, and probably it never would be, she thought, with a sigh.

About ten minutes later the door opened and Jago strolled in. Savanna controlled an impulse to thrust her book under the bedclothes, like a child caught reading after lights out time. Supported by his pillows as well as her own—he used only one to sleep on, but the bed was made up with two on each side—she was sitting with updrawn knees, her thighs forming a book-rest.

She expected him to go to the dressing-room, and then spend some time in the bathroom, giving her a chance to put the book away and be reading a magazine when he reappeared.

Instead, he walked to the bedside. Usually he changed before dinner and spent the evening in casual clothes, but tonight he was still wearing a suit. As he untied his tie and unbuttoned the collar of his shirt, she was pierced by a thrust of excitement at the thought of the strong, virile body concealed by the well-tailored cloth.

He sat down on the side of the bed, just beyond the hump made by her knees. As he pulled the tie free of his collar, his glance flicked from her hair to her shoulders, and then to her gauzy nightgown made of two layers of chiffon, white over peach, with a narrow peach binding and fragile shoulder straps.

'I thought you might be asleep. Good book?' he enquired.

She nodded. 'Are you coming to bed now?'

'That depends. If you want to go on reading, perhaps I'll do some more work.'

She closed the book and put it aside on the night table. 'I can finish it tomorrow. I was only reading because you seemed to be busy.' She smiled at him. 'Can't the work wait?' she suggested, longing for him to kiss her.

'By all means, if you're feeling neglected.'

'Not neglected exactly, but it would be nice to . . . talk.'

His eyes mocked her. 'Talking wasn't what I had in mind.'

Savanna veiled her eyes with her lashes. 'Well then . . . whatever you like.'

Long fingers took hold of her chin and tilted her face. 'Very dutiful, but what would you like, Savanna? And don't tell me that you'd like whatever I'd like, because I don't buy that kind of bromide.'

An urge to tease him for a change made her say demurely, 'But, Jago, it was you who told me to think of myself as a Victorian girl, and be thankful that you weren't an old man who would make me dread . . . that side of marriage.'

'To which you replied, I remember, that since you were a modern girl it wasn't possible for you to think in those terms,' was his dry reply. 'If you want to make love, say so. If not, I'll leave you to read.'

Considering how long they had been married, it was absurd to be shy with him. But words played no part in their physical relationship. They made love in a silence broken only by the small gasps and stifled murmurs which she could not always repress, and later by his laboured breathing. To admit that she wanted him to stay was not easy for her.

Her cheeks hot, she said, in a low voice, 'I—I would like to make love.'

'So would I, but I need a shower. I'll be back in four or five minutes.'

As he rose and took off his coat, his eye fell on the book she had put aside. To her dismay, he picked it up and glanced at the title, his left eyebrow arching as he read it.

'Why are you reading this?' he asked.

'I . . . it caught my eye at the library. I thought . . .' Her voice died away as he sat down and riffled through the pages, pausing at some which were illustrated.

'Thought what? That you might be missing something?'

'No . . . no, of course not,' she protested. 'I—I wanted to be sure that you weren't.'

'If I were, I should tell you.' He tossed the manual aside and went off to shower.

But would he? Savanna wondered uneasily. Or would

he turn to someone else?—An experienced woman of the world, well versed in the arts of love at which she, all too clearly, was still an inhibited beginner.

Late on Thursday night, Nancy Southworth rang up to tell Savanna that she wouldn't be able to take her to see the house in Buckinghamshire the following day.

'My husband's father has been taken ill, and I have to be with my mother-in-law as long as his condition is critical. She has no daughters of her own, and we have a very close relationship. However, I've arranged for someone else to take you to see the houses, and I hope you'll forgive me for letting you down, Mrs Kindersley.'

'There's nothing to forgive. Please don't worry about it. I know how traumatic it can be when illness strikes unexpectedly. We've had the same thing in our family. Don't give our appointment another thought. I'm sure your assistant will be an excellent deputy,' Savanna said sympathetically.

'He's new to the job. But I've briefed him, and he'll do his best. It's good of you to be so understanding.'

'Not at all. How could I not be? Is your father-in-law still at home, or has he been taken to hospital?'

They discussed his illness for a few minutes. Then, with repeated apologies, Mrs Southworth rang off, leaving Savanna to recall the dreadful days when her own father's life had hung in the balance, and she had done all she could to support her mother through the hours of agonised waiting.

It had been arranged that the estate agent's assistant, whose name she had forgotten to mention, would call for Savanna at nine-thirty. She waited for his arrival with a hopeful feeling that today, at last, she might find the house she was looking for.

In the light of Nancy's remark that they might be out for some hours, she had asked Matthews to make up a lunch basket containing a light meal for two. The weather forecast had promised a hot day, and it was in her mind that they might be able to picnic in the grounds of one of the houses—unless the assistant turned out to be un-congenial, which didn't seem likely in an occupation which called for an outgoing, sociable personality.

Being ready ten minutes beforehand, she told Matthews she would answer the doorbell when it rang.

A minute or two before the hour, her guide signalled his punctual arrival. But when she opened the door, it was not a stranger who confronted her.

'Good morning,' Miles Masters said pleasantly.

'Miles! What are you doing here?'

She had almost forgotten his existence.

'I'm standing in for Nancy Southworth. How are you, Savanna?' He offered his hand.

'I'm fine. How are you?' she responded, as they shook hands.

'Pretty fit, thanks.'

'Come in. I—I didn't know you were in real estate now. It doesn't seem your sort of thing.'

'It isn't, and I'm not—or only temporarily. My sister-in-law is a neighbour and friend of Mrs Southworth's. When she heard that old Mr Southworth had had a stroke, and Nancy was worried about losing an important client, she suggested me as a stopgap. Which I would have been happy to be even if the client had not been someone I knew.'

'I see. What a nice surprise. Shall we set out at once, or would you care for some coffee first?'

'It's not long since I had breakfast. Have you eaten yet?'

'Oh, yes—an hour ago. I'll just fetch a sweater—in case the weather-forecasters are wrong—and then I'll be ready to go.'

'What's this?' Miles enquired, when she returned with a jersey and the lunch hamper.

'A picnic, in case we're still out at lunchtime,' she explained. 'But perhaps you want to get back to London as soon as possible?'

'No, I'm at your disposal all day. A picnic in a country garden sounds much nicer than my usual pub lunch.'

He took charge of the basket, and they left the apartment and took the lift down to the underground garage.

'I thought you would probably have left England by now,' Savanna said, as they stood side by side in the lift. 'I remember you said you were in the market for whatever adventure offered itself. Has nothing come up yet?'

Miles shook his head. 'Not so far. The field is narrower than it used to be. Two or three of the various leads I've followed have turned out to be illegal; and a number of suggestions which have interested me, such as skippering one of the motorised rafts which take parties of sightseers down the rapids in the Grand Canyon, are ruled out by red tape. Most of the countries I'm interested in seeing discourage foreigners from working there. It's an understandable policy, but it makes it hard for a man or a girl to work their way from place to place without running foul of the law.'

'Yes, I suppose you need work permits everywhere except in the Common Market countries?'

'Exactly: and I've already seen as much of Europe as I want to. It's the New World which attracts me now, especially the wilderness areas. But there are a lot of other people who want to get away from it all. Every time the American National Parks advertise for a warden, they receive about a thousand applications, including quite a number from women. If nothing offers pretty soon, I may spend six months back-packing through some of the wild country over there.'

'All by yourself?' queried Savanna.

'I expect so. Most men of my age are shackled to their career prospects, and I've yet to meet a girl I liked who wanted to live off the land for any length of time.'

'I wouldn't mind doing that—if it was what Jago wanted,' Savanna said thoughtfully. 'I should worry a bit about how I could cope, miles from anywhere, if he broke his leg or had any kind of serious accident. What does happen to people in those circumstances? Are there any facilities for rescuing them if they do get into trouble?'

'I don't know. I shouldn't think so. They take their

chances as the original pioneers did. It's good for people
to have no one to depend on but themselves. Too much
pampering isn't good for individuals, or for nations
either,' Miles said briskly.

'That's what Jago says. He doesn't think people should
be mollycoddled, but neither does he believe the sur-
vivalists who preach that Western civilisation is on the
brink of total breakdown.'

'And what do you think?' Miles enquired. 'Or, now
that you've lost your independence, do you just go along
with his views?'

They had reached the car, and he had opened the passenger door for her. In the act of stepping in, she paused.
'That's a very cutting thing to say, Miles. No, I don't
"just go along" with my husband's views. I admire his
mind, and I listen to what he has to say. But I still form
my own opinions, some of which coincide with his.'

'I'm sorry. I didn't mean it the way it may have
sounded.'

Savanna tilted a delicate eyebrow. 'Didn't you?'

He looked a little shamefaced. 'Well . . . maybe I did,
but I apologise.'

'Why? Why did you mean it?'

He studied her for a long moment. 'Perhaps because,
although it's none of my business, I feel you were very
young to give up an interesting career and commit yourself to Jago's life-style. As I see it, the twenties should be
flexible years, not in any way predetermined.'

'But I never wanted to be a model. That was forced on
me by my father's premature death and the need to earn
money,' she answered. 'If Father had lived, I expect I
should be a history student now, and Jago and I would
never have met.'

She climbed into the car, and turned to put her sweater
and bag on the back seat. This time Miles didn't have to
tell her to fasten the seat-belt as he had the first time they
met. Nowadays she did it automatically.

'Anyway,' she went on, as he drove the car up the ramp
to street level, 'I don't believe anyone's life is ever com-

pletely flexible, however much they try to avoid being pegged down. There are always determining factors, even if they're negative ones such as not being able to get a work permit. As Jago's wife, I'm actually much freer than I was before. I used to have hardly a minute to call my own. Now I have several hours a day. Given a choice between stewing in a hot, stuffy studio and going into the country to look at houses, I know which I'd rather be doing.'

'What kind of house are you looking for?'

'A large family place in a secluded position, but close to a village or a small market town. I've looked at dozens, but none of them has been quite right. Do you know the area we're going to? Mrs Southworth felt they might be difficult to find unless one had been there before.'

'I know the area intimately. It's only a few miles from my parents' place. In fact my mother knew Miss Atkinson, the last owner of Merryhill. I rang her up last night to ask. Apparently the old girl was nearly ninety when she died, but still fairly active in her garden. She was the kind of woman who's pretty well extinct now: unmarried because she spent half her life dancing attendance on elderly parents. She was middle-aged before they died, and from then on her passion was gardening. According to Mother, she didn't give a damn about the condition of the house, but spent every penny on plants and paying a man to do the heavy work.'

'That tied in with what Mrs Southworth said about the house needing a lot of renovation to make it habitable.'

'Which do you want to see first—Merryhill, or the other place?' asked Miles.

'The other one, please.'

They were silent for a while. It was strange but, although she hadn't seen him for a long time, or thought about him, Savanna felt as if she were in the presence of an old friend. Miles must feel the same towards her, or he would not have been so outspoken in his attitude to her marriage.

Presently he asked if she would mind if he switched on

the radio for a programme in a series he had been following.

It turned out to be about great composers, the talk interspersed with passages from the subject's works. Savanna also gave her attention to it, silently surprised by the discovery that Miles had a serious interest in classical music.

Within an hour of setting out they had passed through suburbia to the countryside which today was looking at its best with a clear blue sky overhead, and green vistas of meadow and wood on every side.

The first house they went to look at had been built in the early 1900s to a design by Sir Edwin Lutyens. His houses were enjoying a new vogue as examples of the last period of English architecture when, labour being cheap and incomes not heavily taxed, mansions could still be erected with solid wood doors and other refinements now beyond the means of private patrons, unless they had Jago's means.

However, one look at the exterior and Savanna knew this was not the house she had in mind. She walked through its empty rooms out of curiosity, but the lavish use of dark oak panelling, and the massive staircase rising from the sitting-room-cum-hall, were not attractions in her eyes.

A long verandah on the south side made the other reception rooms dark even on a hot summer morning. In winter they would be gloomy.

En route from there to Merryhill, they stopped in a village where the cake shop had an old-fashioned tea room adjoining it. They had coffee and buttered fruit scones, and Savanna bought some free-range eggs and a jar of honey with part of the comb in it.

The late Miss Atkinson's house was close to a similar village a few miles farther on. The drive was barred by a gate secured with a padlock and chain, but Miles had the key to the padlock. Thick shrubberies hid the house from the road, and the first fifty yards of the drive were overhung with branches, making Savanna fear this was going to be another dark house.

Then the drive emerged from deep shade into sunlight, and the thickets of holly and laurel gave place to overgrown lawns surrounding a Regency house with paint peeling from its walls and an air of years of neglect. But the graceful pillars of the portico with, above it, a canopied balcony and a cast-iron railing with a typically Regency lyre motif, made Savanna's heart leap with excitement.

'This is it! I'm sure of it,' she exclaimed.

'Steady on. It may be riddled with dry rot, death watch beetle and God knows what else,' warned Miles, looking amused by her excitement.

She didn't wait for him to walk round and open the door for her, but sprang out and hurried across the weed-tufted remains of a gravelled sweep towards the sun-blistered front door.

Although the house was empty, the ground floor windows were screened by dingy lace curtains which had probably been chosen by Miss Atkinson's mother, and hung there, unwashed, for many years. They were Victorian in taste, and ruined the appearance of the tall Georgian windows.

'Oh, do hurry, Miles,' she urged, as he followed her at a more leisurely pace.

There were several large keys on the ring labelled 'Merryhill', and it took him a minute or two to find the right one for the lock on the front door.

When at last he pushed it open and stood aside for her to enter, Savanna took a deep breath and braced herself for the disappointment of discovering that, in spite of its attractive façade, the interior of the building did not tally with Jago's requirements.

She knew he would not be influenced by the romantic appearance of the place. A man who selected his wife for practical reasons would never buy a house for impractical ones.

The long hall was flooded with sunlight slanting through the dusty panes of a window at the top of the staircase and a glass door with a graceful fanlight at the back of the hall. To the right, the door standing open, was a large room, also full of sunshine. She went in. It was the drawing-room; spoiled by a dark red flocked wallpaper.

In her mind's eye, Savanna saw the walls painted with a soft apricot emulsion, the bare floorboards carpeted, and several Regency mirrors reflecting books, flowers and watercolours.

'It would need completely re-wiring,' was Miles' comment, indicating the room's only socket outlet of an outdated type unsuited to take modern plugs.

'And re-plumbing, I expect,' she agreed.

A quick reconnaissance of the whole house to form an overall impression took about half an hour and confirmed her intuitive certainty that, as far as she was concerned, this was the place they were seeking.

Next they explored the large garden. After a year of neglect—the house had not come on the market immediately because Miss Atkinson had left it to a nephew in Canada, who, when eventually he had been traced, had instructed that it be sold—the garden was not as she had left it.

Unweeded, unpruned and showing signs of youthful trespassers who had done a good deal of damage and left some unsightly litter, it needed an imaginative eye to recognise how it had looked, and could look again.

'I'm hungry. Shall we have lunch now, or is it too early for you?' she asked, after touring the grounds.

'I'm peckish too,' Miles agreed. 'Wait here, I'll fetch the hamper.'

They ate on an old stone bench, dappled with patches of lichen, at the end of a lavender walk, the bushes busy with bees.

Pâté, wholemeal bread and green salad were accompanied by a flask of Matthews' home-made lemonade, refreshingly cold to their palates. Fresh peaches, and a second flask of coffee, rounded off their open-air meal.

'How about strolling down to the pub for a drink?' Miles suggested afterwards.

'Why don't you go?' she answered. 'I want to look round the house again, and make notes and also take photographs.'

'You won't mind being on your own?'

'Not a bit. In fact I'd prefer it. Then I can take my time without feeling it's a bore for you.'

'Being with you could never be a bore, Savanna.'

Somewhat abruptly he turned away and walked off.

She watched him go, a little disconcerted by the unexpected compliment. But she didn't think about it for long. The house drove out all other thoughts. Would Jago like it as much as she did? When would he have time to come and look at it? Would someone else snap it up before he had made a decision?

About an hour later, glancing out of one of the upper windows, she saw that Miles had returned and was lying on his back in the long grass at the front of the house. His eyes were closed, and although she watched him for several minutes, he did not stir. The heat of the summer afternoon, and whatever he had drunk at the pub, had conspired to send him to sleep.

Relieved that he wasn't in a hurry to be off, she used a whole roll of film to snap all the features which gave the place its character and charm.

He was still asleep when she locked up and put her camera and notes in the car. But when she nudged his foot with the toe of her sandal, he woke very quickly, sitting up without using his arms as levers, which she knew was a sign of strong stomach muscles, and looking much more alert than most people did when roused from a nap. Perhaps that instant alertness was a result of his S.A.S. training.

'What did you think of the pub?' she asked.

'It's a free house which hasn't been spoiled by most brewers' mania for red plastic and mind-bending carpet patterns. It still has the original oak settles and Windsor chairs, and the landlord's wife makes the sausage rolls and Scotch eggs. Not that I tried them, having eaten beforehand, but they looked good. The beer is good too.'

'I'm not sure that Jago ever drinks it, but he may on
occasion. Perhaps we ought to be getting back . . .
although it seems a pity to waste this lovely afternoon,'
Savanna added regretfully.

'Let's not waste it, then. Let's walk for a while. You
don't want to go overboard for the house and then find
you're down-wind from a broiler house or a pig farm.'

'All right, let's explore for an hour. But I mustn't be
later than five.'

'What happens at five?' asked Miles.

'Nothing, but I like to bath and change before Jago
comes in about six.'

'It will be much later than six if you move out here,' he
pointed out.

'Not really, because he'll come home by helicopter, not
by road. That's why a sizeable paddock was one of the
vital prerequisites.'

To her delight, her enthusiasm for Merryhill made Jago
rearrange his schedule to see the place the next day. He
liked it as much as she did and, subject to certain precautions such as having it surveyed, was prepared to buy it.

The day before the house became theirs, Savanna
passed her driving test and thereafter was able to drive
herself backwards and forwards. Jago wanted the house
to be habitable by Christmas.

'By then you may be pregnant and not up to running
yourself ragged, as women invariably do when they're
choosing furnishings,' he said. 'Even with a decorator to
help you, putting the place in order will take up a lot of
your time.'

By this time Savanna had reason to believe that she
was pregnant. A few days later, unwilling to go to a doctor
yet but impatient to know what was happening inside her
body, she bought a test kit which was said to be ninety-
eight per cent accurate. Two hours after she had carried
out the simple instructions, the result was positive.

Although it would be a long time before there was any
visible sign of it, the tiny embryo of their first child was in

existence; a mysterious little being of unknown sex already dependent on her to supply it with vital nutrients and to avoid everything which might harm it.

As she had never smoked or drunk spirits, and had always eaten plenty of raw vegetables, wholegrains and natural yogurt, the confirmation that she was responsible for someone else's health as well as her own did not call for any marked change in her previous régime.

It seemed unlikely that Jago, with much else on his mind, would have noticed the one clue to her condition. She could keep the baby a secret for some time. Not that it made much difference if he was already being unfaithful to her. But perhaps he wasn't. She kept hoping against hope that he wasn't, and would not be, until the un-gainliness of her figure gave him a better excuse than he had at the moment.

Recently she had read an article in a magazine which had taken the view that women were asking the impossible to expect any man to be an exciting lover and a faithful husband. A virtuoso lover would never be content with only one woman. A man who never looked at anyone but his wife would probably be an unimaginative lover.

Whether or not the article had any force in it, or was merely a provocative piece churned out, tongue in cheek, by a journalist, Savanna felt sure that no man with Jago's sexual appetite would be able to abstain from making love for several weeks, as must be the case towards the end of her pregnancy and for a time afterwards.

If he loved her—yes. With love, all things were possible.

In the weeks which followed she saw a good deal of Miles. The friend whose flat he had been borrowing had returned from abroad, and now Miles was living at home until he took off on the next phase of his life. This meant he was close enough to Merryhill to come over and work in the garden.

Jago had told Savanna to call in one of the leading landscape gardeners. But she was reluctant to do this, pre-ferring—with Miles' help—to reclaim the garden herself.

Once the overgrown lawns had been scythed to a mowable length by an elderly man from the village, and she and Miles had cleared the worst of the undergrowth, it might be that the garden would do very well as it was without any professional redesigning.

Preoccupied with the house, and with thoughts of the baby, she saw no reason to discourage Miles from spending more and more of his time at Merryhill. As far as she was concerned, his assistance was invaluable and his friendship comfortable. Much of the time they spent in different parts of the grounds, only meeting for a shared picnic lunch.

She did not mention him to Jago because she suspected that her husband would be incapable of a straightforward friendship with a woman unless she was many years older than himself, and would not understand the sisterly affection of her feeling for Miles, or his brotherly attitude to her.

Once it crossed her mind that it was a little strange that his parents—met briefly at the wedding—had not suggested that he should bring her to lunch with them, and to wonder if they were unaware of the time he spent at Merryhill.

She would have expected his mother at least to ring up and express some pleasure in having them as fairly near neighbours. But it might be that Mrs Masters, who had looked rather frail at the reception, was not equal to much entertaining. As Miles rarely mentioned his parents, she didn't know a great deal about them.

When a long hot spell was followed by several days of rain, she busied herself in London, looking for antique furniture and going round all the kitchen and bathroom showrooms.

Although it was wonderful to be free to choose anything she wanted, the habit of being careful with money was too deeply ingrained for her to be carried away by the *carte blanche* which Jago had given her.

One afternoon, she returned from a shopping expedition to be met by his manservant. It seemed that Miles had arrived about half an hour earlier and insisted on waiting for her to return.

'Hello, Miles. What brings you here?' she asked, as she entered the sitting-room.

'I've come to say goodbye, Savanna.'

'Goodbye? When and where are you going?'

'To the States, on the first available stand-by flight. I've delayed too long already. It's time I moved on.'

She wondered what had precipitated his decision.

'I shall miss you,' she told him sincerely.

'I shall miss you, too.' He paused before adding, 'More than I should miss another man's wife. At first, when Jago came to see me, I was furious with him for suggesting there might be more than friendship between us. But afterwards I realised he was right. On my side there *is* more than friendship. Given the smallest encouragement, I would be in love with you, Savanna. But you've never given me that encouragement. I have no idea how you feel about me. I only know that you're not really happy with him.'

She blinked at him, stunned by this revelation of feelings she had not suspected; but most of all by the fact that Jago had been to see him.

'W-when did he come to see you?'

'This morning. He's been having us followed. Obviously he's wildly jealous of every man who looks at you, and I can't say I blame him—although I think he's a fool not to realise that you aren't the kind of person who would ever do anything underhand.'

'We've been followed? I can't believe it. Followed by whom?' she expostulated.

'By a private detective, I suppose. But never mind that at the moment.' He came closer, and laid both his hands lightly on her shoulders. 'Tell me the truth. You're not happy with him, are you? You try to hide it, but sometimes your face gives you away. One day at the house when you didn't know I was watching, your eyes were full of tears. You wanted to cry . . . and I wanted to take you in my arms and comfort you,' he added, in a low tone—a more emotional tone than she had ever heard him use before.

Savanna drew back, deeply disturbed by his revelation of feelings she had not suspected of fermenting beneath his calm, casual friendliness; and even more shocked by what he had said about Jago having them followed. Shocked, and angrier than she had ever been in her life.

'Miles, you've misunderstood,' she began distractedly. 'I—I had no idea you had any . . . warm feelings towards me. At least, not warmer than friendship. I thought you were just killing time. If I'd thought . . . if I'd guessed——'

'You haven't answered my question. You aren't happy, are you?' he persisted.

She hesitated. 'Not entirely, but——'

'I knew it wasn't working out. Frankly, I never thought it would. You were dazzled by him . . . not seeing straight. But you don't have to stay with him if he's making you miserable.'

'He isn't. You don't understand, Miles. I love Jago. I always shall. The only thing wrong with our marriage is that he . . . he doesn't feel quite the same way about me. If he's jealous, it's only possessiveness. It wouldn't wreck him if I left him. He would be very angry, I expect, but he certainly wouldn't be heartbroken.'

'Then why must you stay with him? You deserve more than pride of possession. God knows, you're incredibly ornamental, but it's not your looks which made me love you. It's your gentleness, and——'

She cut him short. 'Please, Miles . . . don't go on. I'm desperately sorry you feel like this, but you must put me out of your mind. You're wrong if you think I regret my marriage. I don't. If I've been a bit . . . moody recently, perhaps it's because I'm expecting a baby.'

She saw him flinch, and knew there would be no further argument.

'I see,' he said heavily.

'And I'm sure, when you get to America, you'll soon feel differently yourself. You've been at a loose end, and lonely . . . oh, Miles dear, forgive me if I've unwittingly hurt you. I didn't mean to—truly I didn't.'

'I know that. It isn't your fault. The fact is that any man who spent much time with you would be bound to love you,' he answered. 'I must go—I shouldn't have come. Goodbye, my dear. Take care of yourself.' Pressing her hands between his palms, he squeezed them for a moment. Then, with a muttered, 'I can find my own way out,' he was gone.

With Miles gone, Savanna could hardly contain her impatience for Jago to come home. She found it almost unbelievable that he had been having her spied upon while at the same time being unfaithful to her.

They had an engagement to dine with some friends of his that evening, and ordinarily she would have had her bath and probably put on her make-up before he returned. But tonight she had no intention of going anywhere with him. He would have to think of some excuse for her absence, if not for his own. There was no possibility of her putting on a happy bride act when inwardly she was seething with rage and resentment.

As she waited for him, she paced restlessly up and down the length of the sitting-room, her hands clenched into fists and thrust into the pockets of her trousers, every line of her body taut with contained anger.

By the time he arrived her rage was already at boiling point, but, although usually he was quick to notice anything untoward, tonight he seemed unaware of anything strange in her manner.

'What did you do with yourself today?' he asked, after saying hello to her.

'Nothing special,' was her clipped reply. 'A very dull day for your watchdog. As a matter of interest, what does it cost to have me shadowed?'

CHAPTER EIGHT

In the act of crossing the room, Jago checked and glanced sharply at her. 'What are you talking about?'

'About the man who keeps me under surveillance and reports all my movements to you. Where I go . . . who my friends are . . . my lovers!' Her voice was sharp with angry sarcasm as she flung the last word at him.

There was a brief pause before, with no sign of discomfiture, he said, 'You've been talking to Miles.'

'Yes. He came to say goodbye. He didn't stay long. Your watchdog will tell you exactly how long . . . and whether it was long enough for me to commit a final act of adultery with him,' she tacked on bitterly

It took Jago three strides to reach her, and grip her by the upper arms.

'Stop this nonsense, Savanna! You know perfectly well I don't suspect you of anything of the sort.'

'Then why have me followed?'

'For the same reason that I've had someone watching me for the past couple of weeks.'

'Watching you?' she echoed blankly.

'I didn't mention it because I didn't want to alarm you unnecessarily. Just over a fortnight ago, someone—probably a harmless crank—threatened to injure me. Abusive letters and telephone calls are not uncommon in the lives of anyone permanently or even temporarily in the public eye. I've received various threats from time to time, particularly after expressing opinions which upset fanatics and extremists. However, the police considered this particular threat might be a serious one, and they advised certain precautions. It seemed possible that if the author of the threat was unable to strike at me, he or she might try to harm you. That's why I had you shadowed, and that's how it came to my notice that Miles was spending more time with you than I considered good for him.'

The discovery that he had been in danger drove everything else from her mind.

'Why didn't you tell me? I'm your wife, I have a right to know such things!'

'You would have been upset and worried. As your husband I have a right to protect you from needless anxiety, particularly now when, although you've chosen not to mention it, I think you may be expecting our first child. Am I right? Are you pregnant, Savanna?'

'I—I'm not sure yet. I may be.'

'And if so, you're not happy about it?—Or that's my impression,' was his comment.

'It's not being pregnant that I mind,' she said, in a low tone.

'It's not?' Jago sounded surprised. 'What is it, then? I can tell that something is weighing on you. I concluded it must be the baby; that you would have preferred to postpone it. Perhaps I was wrong to impose my wishes on yours. But you won't lose your figure for some time yet, and I've been reliably assured that it need leave no permanent effects. You'll be just as beautiful afterwards.'

'I'm not concerned about my figure . . . or about being pregnant. I should be very happy about it, if——'

'If what? Come on, out with it. What's on your mind?'

Savanna knew then that she had to tell him, not merely because she had already admitted to being under pressure, but because she could no longer endure the cruel uncertainty of recent weeks.

'Even though I haven't lost my figure yet, I seem to have lost your . . . undivided attention, Jago. It appears to be common knowledge that you've resumed a relationship with someone you knew before me. In those circumstances, is it surprising that I'm not overjoyed at the prospect of having a baby?'

His dark brows contracted and his fingers tightened on her arms.

'What crazy nonsense is this? First you jump to the conclusion that I suspect you of infidelity; now you're accusing me of it, which is even more foolish.'

Savanna drew in a long shaky breath, bracing herself to put the question which would either relieve her anguish, or intensify it beyond bearing. Jago might prevaricate, but she did not think he would lie if she had the courage to ask point-blank.

'Are you saying there are no other women . . . n-not even one?'

His hands slipped down her arms to close round her slender wrists. But the denial she longed for did not come. He said only, 'I suppose by "common knowledge" you mean the scurrilous innuendo published in one of the gossip columns? Who drew your attention to it? I might have known someone would.'

'No one. By an unfortunate chance, I happened to see that particular issue of the paper.'

'But it didn't occur to you to ask me if there was any truth in it?' he said irritably.

'What was to be gained by confronting you with it? It was only what I'd always known would happen eventually. I shouldn't have brought it up now if I hadn't been so furious at the idea of you suspecting *me* of being unfaithful.'

'Will you believe me if I tell you that you're the only woman I've made love to, or wanted to make love to, since we met in the Caribbean?'

She raised her eyes to his face, and saw that he was looking down at her with an expression of great gravity. Yet how could that statement be true?

'I should like to believe it, but it's very difficult. Do you deny that you did go to see the actress who used to be your . . . friend?'

'No, I don't deny it—or that I've been to see her regularly since then. But if you'd asked me about it, I should have explained the reason for my visits to her.'

'What was the reason?'

Jago said heavily, 'She's seriously ill . . . dying, in fact.

She knows it, but she doesn't want the world to know it. It seems the least I can do is to give her a little of my time in the short time she has left to her.'

Immediately Savanna was seized with pity for the actress, and regret for her unfounded suspicions.

'How terrible! If only you'd told me. Why did you keep it a secret?'

'The relationships I had before I knew you are something I prefer to forget. If I'd told you that Charmian was merely a friend, it would have been a lie and—knowing how warm-hearted you are—I felt you might want to come with me when I went to see her. To have told you the truth, which is that for a year or two she and I amused ourselves together——'

'The paper said she·was in love with you,' she interrupted. '*Did* she love you?'

His mouth tightened. 'Unfortunately—yes, I believe so. When the time came for us to separate, she would have liked to continue the affair. This was all a long time ago ... when you were in your early teens. But I've always regretted hurting her, and now she needs friendship very badly. She has no family, and not many close friends. I owe her a few hours a week. It won't be for very much longer.'

It was she who went to him then, putting her hands on his chest and looking up into his face with no guard on her own expression.

'I'm sorry,' she said contritely. 'How rotten of me to believe that despicable columnist! Only, you see, I can't help being miserably jealous. If you loved me, it would·be different. But when it's all on my side ...'

Jago put his arms round her and pulled her against him. Speaking over the top of her head, he said, in a low voice, 'But it isn't all on your side, Savanna. I've been in love with you for some time; perhaps since before we were married, although I didn't recognise my feelings until one morning quite recently. I woke up and watched you sleeping, and knew just how much you meant to me.'

She stood very still in his arms, hardly daring to believe

she had heard him say, in plain words, that he was in love with her.

'Why didn't you tell me?' she murmured, at last.

'I thought it might be too late. It's a long time since you gave any indication that you still felt warmly towards me. It seemed entirely possible that you'd begun to cool off—except in bed. But now I want your heart as well as your body. Are you sure I still have it, Savanna?'

'Oh, yes—yes! How can you doubt it?' Her face still hidden against his broad shoulder, she slipped her arms round him and hugged him. 'I could never love anyone but you.'

'I thought I could never love anyone—until you proved me wrong,' he said quietly. 'I wanted to take Miles apart when I found out how often he'd been seeing you. Oh, I knew it was innocent enough—neither of you is the type to do anything underhand. But love, as I'd just discovered, can catch people unawares. With his S.A.S. background, he cuts a much more heroic figure than I do.'

At that she lifted her face. 'Not to me. Never to me. You are my *beau idéal*, and always have been.'

'God knows why, after the way I trod anything but softly on your dreams, my poor little love.'

'But my dreams only began when I met you. Before that I never gave much thought to love. I was more ambitious than romantic. Oh, Jago, say it again—that you love me,' she pleaded softly.

'I love you, and want you, and need you . . . for the rest of my life.'

He bent to kiss her; the first kiss she had ever received with the certainty that he cared for her.

One kiss led to another, and soon they were locked in their bedroom, rapidly shedding their clothes, as impatient to lie down together as lovers united at last after prolonged separation.

Today Jago did not draw the curtains, but today Savanna had nothing to hide when he came to the bed where she was waiting for him with smiling lips and eyes bright with relief and happiness.

'This has always been wonderful, but I was afraid to admit it in case you became bored with me,' she explained, as she melted into his strong arms. 'Darling . . . do you realise I never dared to call you that before?'

'You never looked at me like this before either. It was always as if I were taking you against your will . . . forcing you to respond to me.'

'If only you'd known how I really felt!' She drew his head down and gave him a warm, wanton kiss, the first of its kind she had ever ventured.

Much later, they remembered the dinner party.

'I'll ring up and say you're not well,' Jago decided, reaching for the telephone.

'No, no, Jago, you can't. It's not fair to spoil Eleanor's table plan. Tell them we shall be fifteen minutes late. I can dress as quickly as you can, and put my face on in the car.'

'To hell with Eleanor's table plan. She'll have to manage without us. If you think I can sit through a dinner when I want to be in bed with you——'

His powerful hands held her captive, and she tried in vain to break free from his caressing imprisonment.

'She won't believe you,' she objected. 'If I hadn't been well I'd have rung her up hours ago.'

'Not necessarily. When my sister was pregnant with the twins she had to chuck several engagements at the last minute. Eleanor has a sharp ear for a nuance, and she likes nothing better than to be first with a piece of news.'

While he dialled their hostess's number, Savanna relaxed against him. She felt a little guilty but, like him, she wanted to stay where she was. These first hours of total rapport were too precious to be sacrificed for a social obligation. Even now she could scarcely believe that this dynamic man, with his brilliant brain and foreful character, had actually admitted to loving and needing her.

The call took only a few moments. Then he replaced the receiver and returned his attention to her, smoothing back her tumbled blonde hair, delicately stroking her face with the backs of his knuckles.

Suddenly, to her astonished delight, he said softly, *'Western Wind, when wilt thou blow, the small rain down can rain? Christ, if my love were in my arms and I in my bed again!'*

There were lines written long ago in the sixteenth century by an unknown poet; lines Savanna had always found touching and poignant. That he knew them too, and should choose this moment to quote them, set the seal on her new-found happiness. She knew she had been right to give her heart to him.

Harlequin Plus

A POET'S RAPTURE

Savanna, Anne Weale's heroine, longed "to experience the raptures so graphically described by Cavalier poets such as Thomas Carew and Richard Lovelace." To help you understand the sort of rapture Savanna wanted to feel, here is a poem by Thomas Carew, a seventeenth-century English poet, famous for his elegant and polished amorous verse.

Secrecy Protested

Fear not (dear love) that I'll reveal
Those hours of pleasure we two steal;
No eye shall see, nor yet the sun
Descry, what thou and I have done;
No ear shall hear our love, but we
Silent as the night will be.
The God of love himself (whose dart
Did first wound mine, and then thy heart)
Shall never know, that we can tell
What sweets in stol'n embraces dwell.
This only means may find it out,
If when I die, physicians doubt
What caus'd my death, and there to view
Of all their judgments which was true,
Rip up my heart, Oh then I fear
The world will see thy picture there.

Now's your chance to discover the earlier
books in this exciting series.

Choose from this list of great
SUPERROMANCES!

SUPERROMANCE

Complete and mail this coupon today!

Worldwide Reader Service

In the U.S.A.
1440 South Priest Drive
Tempe, AZ 85281

In Canada
649 Ontario Street
Stratford, Ontario N5A 6W2

Please send me the following SUPERROMANCES. I am enclosing my check or money order for $2.50 for each copy ordered, plus 75¢ to cover postage and handling.

☐ # 8	☐ # 14	☐ # 20
☐ # 9	☐ # 15	☐ # 21
☐ # 10	☐ # 16	☐ # 22
☐ # 11	☐ # 17	☐ # 23
☐ # 12	☐ # 18	☐ # 24
☐ # 13	☐ # 19	☐ # 25

Number of copies checked @ $2.50 each = $_____
N.Y. and Ariz. residents add appropriate sales tax $_____
Postage and handling $_____.75
                     TOTAL $_____

I enclose_____.
(Please send check or money order. We cannot be responsible for cash sent through the mail.)
Prices subject to change without notice.

NAME_____
(Please Print)
ADDRESS:_____ APT. NO._____
CITY_____
STATE/PROV._____
ZIP/POSTAL CODE_____
Offer expires May 31, 1983   30156000000

His hand slipped do [...]
pulse in her neck, po [...]
pressure of his massa [...] only have to
ask," he said softly.

Her eyes had fluttered shut. They snapped open.
"Now you're being purposely obnoxious. Besides,
this won't help you. It will interfere with what I'm
trying to teach you."

"Teach me." He touched her waist, making her
insides feel as quivery and airy as soap bubbles.
"Teach me, Annie," he repeated more strongly, an
air of desperation in his words.

"Cliff, you can have everything you had before,
believe me. The accident hasn't made you any less
attractive."

"Then come here."

His hand closing on the bare skin of her arm was like
the first blast of shower spray in the morning. She
had to brace herself for it.

He felt her stiffness. "I can have women, I just can't
have you, is that it?"

Dear Reader:

It's October and there's no stopping our men! October's *Man of the Month* comes from the pen of Leslie Davis Guccione, whose books about the Branigan brothers have pleased countless readers. Mr. October is Jody Branigan, and you can read all about him in *Branigan's Touch*.

Coming in November is *Shiloh's Promise* by BJ James. You might remember Shiloh from his appearance in *Twice in a Lifetime*. We received so much positive feedback about this mesmerizing man that we knew he had to have his very own story—and that he'd make a perfect *Man of the Month*!

Needless to say, I think each and every Silhouette Desire is wonderful. October and November's books are guaranteed to give you hours of reading pleasure.

Enjoy!

Lucia Macro
Senior Editor

TERRY LAWRENCE

BEFORE DAWN

SILHOUETTE *Desire*

Published by Silhouette Books New York

America's Publisher of Contemporary Romance

Books by Terry Lawrence

Silhouette Desire

Cabin Fever #465
Before Dawn #526

TERRY LAWRENCE

told her fifth-grade teacher she wanted to be a writer. He sent her home with a note to her mother saying, "I believe Terry possesses a gift and should be encouraged." In the twenty years that followed, that encouragement has come from family, friends and other teachers, all of whom made it easier for her to achieve her dream.

She lives in northern Michigan, where she divides her time and attention between a word processor, a cat and four breathtaking seasons.

One

Annie Rosetti had few rules she lived by. Accept your-self for what you are. Be honest. Don't get too hung up on what others think. And *never* get involved with a heartstoppingly handsome man. Watching Cliff Sulli-van stride down the beach, she had a sinking feeling he'd be the exception to the rule.

It was that period in mid-August when even the breeze off the big lake couldn't cool things down. Maybe that justified his wearing nothing but threadbare cutoffs and weathered Topsiders. Annie could almost feel the ra-diating heat of the sun on his bare chest. She squeezed her eyes shut, shook her head and patted the black dog beside her.

Okay, so Cliff Sullivan was Blond, Bearded, Brawny and Beautiful. Annie tried to think of another word that began with a *B* and spelled trouble. Bothersome was as close as she got.

Oh, yes—and Blind.

Cliff stopped fifty feet away, planted strong hands on narrow hips and shouted for his dog. "Kane! Damn you, get back here!"

He reminded her of the blinded Samson, tearing down the temple in a rage. But she seriously doubted that Samson wore black wraparound shades, and every fiber in her body insisted that Samson had never been that good-looking.

"Kane!"

The black Lab whose leash Annie held barked and lunged, almost yanking her arm out of its socket.

"Over here!" she called out.

She watched Cliff half turn in their direction. Anyone else would think the man wore dark glasses because they made him look so damn good. She would have. And she would have steered clear. Even now a tiny voice inside her was shouting a warning. This was not a man to get mixed up with. But—

He needs me and he doesn't even know it.

Damn.

Cliff strode in the direction of his barking dog. Watching the anger and strength he put into something as basic as walking, it was obvious to Annie that he was a man who did nothing halfway. He'd been avoiding her art therapy classes at the hospital just as bullheadedly. But she and Cliff Sullivan were about to collide.

As she watched him walk toward her, she scanned the sand for anything that might get in his way. He wasn't using a cane. From what she'd heard, he wouldn't. For someone who'd been blinded only three weeks before in a blasting accident, he didn't hesitate.

He's either very confident or completely denying his limitations, Annie thought. Meanwhile the dog at her side was barking his fool head off.

"Kane!"

"I've got him."

"Quiet!"

Not easily affronted, Annie couldn't prevent a startled "What?" from escaping her.

"I was talking to the dog," he spat.

Annie took a deep breath and decided she might as well be direct. "You've been avoiding me."

He stopped within ten feet of her. His hair was sun-bleached with darker strands underneath; his beard was long stubble. Neither the heavy stubble nor the sunglasses could hide the emotions flickering across his face: confusion, frustration, anger.

"Say that again," he demanded.

He was reaching, getting her to talk so he would know which direction to turn, Annie figured. "If you want to know where I am, you're right on target."

He stiffened.

Annie counted to ten while waiting for him to speak, the sound of the waves and sea gulls punctuating the silence.

Finally Cliff stuck his hand out, seemingly deciding to ignore the whole blindness issue. "May I have the leash?"

"You're not going to hit him, are you?"

He appeared surprised for a moment, until the anger reemerged. This time it was directed at himself. "How can I hit him if I can't even find him? Please?" He ground the word out between his teeth.

Annie placed the leash in his hand, Kane's cue to leap on his chest. "Down, damn it!"

Despite the show of anger, Annie glimpsed the way his hand lingered momentarily on the back of the dog's neck, giving it an unobtrusive squeeze. When he shoved the dog down, the robust Lab interpreted it as play and immediately assumed the position—paws down, rear end in the air, his whole body swaying with each energetic wag of his tail.

Annie had to laugh. There was something about the way a dog rebounded from rejection and temporary setbacks. Unlike some people. She studied Cliff a moment. "How old is he, your dog?"

"Eight months of trouble."

"A little young to be a seeing-eye dog, isn't he?"

"You mean a little untrained?"

"Uh-huh."

Cliff paused. He was beginning to pick up on so many subtle clues about this unseen woman. He could hear her smiling, and that surprised him. He'd figured that by this time he'd be contending with pity. "He's not really a seeing-eye dog."

"And you're not really blind?"

Cliff straightened at that one, pulling his shoulders back, the muscles on his chest taut. No, he wasn't blind. At least, he wouldn't be after the operation. "It's temporary. Is it that obvious?"

"Kane was dragging this harness through my tomato plants, the kind guide dogs use." He flinched as she unexpectedly put the harness in his hand, then flushed at his own response. His fist tightened around the square leather bar.

Knowing apologizing would only make it worse, Annie took a moment to chalk up a few more impressions. He hated talking about it. And, God, how he hated being helped.

She took a chance and laughingly asked, "So where'd you get those crazy shades?" One of them had to relax; if he didn't, he'd crack.

"I like 'em dark," was all he said.

Her voice came out huskier than the crashing of the waves. "And I like 'em blond," she said, almost to herself.

Cliff smiled automatically, thrown off balance by the sound of flirtation in her voice. Maybe he was imagining it. After all, how could he tell if he couldn't see? "That's a problem?"

On him even half a smile was gorgeous. Annie's heart skittered like a sandpiper chased up the sand. "It is when they don't like me."

He mulled that over a moment. "They must be blind."

Annie's smile widened, and she chuckled so he could hear it. That might have been the first joke he'd made about his sight since the accident. She was careful not to pat herself on the back for making progress so soon; they still had a long way to go. If only she could get him into her class...

"I work with the blind, you know. My name's Annie Rosetti."

Her progress ended quickly as he muttered an ugly curse. "The hospital sent you."

She crossed her arms. "Sorry I didn't get around to that sooner. You *have* been avoiding me, Mr. Sullivan."

If he could see, he'd be looking down at her. "I don't need to make baskets," he sneered.

"Pottery. And I believe we have a date for two o'clock tomorrow. You've already broken four of them."

"I won't be seeing you." A miserable play on words. Cliff clenched his jaw when he realized it. A wave of fury washed over him. She'd known who she was talking to all along. He hadn't. It was an underhanded trick, and she had the gall to laugh. His gut tightened at the sound and his mouth compressed in a thin line.

"Maybe you won't be seeing me, Cliff, but I promise I'll be seeing you."

She looked him up and down once more. Virile, vital and ready to lash out at something, anything. Trouble is, fate was hard to hit. "You've got a lot of anger built up in you—"

"So you're a psychologist-potter, is that it? Have clay, will diagnose?"

Cliff damned himself for making her laugh again. Encased in a world of milky white light, her laughter was the last thing he wanted. There was an earthiness there that struck a chord in him. He didn't like coy women, and this one sounded uninhibited, sexy and much too pleased with everything he said.

"Caught me analyzing without a license. Honestly, Cliff—"

Did she always pause after his name, or did he imagine that, too?

"—stop by my class. You might learn something—like how to deal with your handicap. I mean, training a pet to be a seeing-eye dog is one way—"

"I'm blind, damn it. Not handicapped, not disabled. I hate those bloody euphemisms. And for your information, I don't need to learn to live with anything, because this condition's temporary."

"Probably." If he expected an argument, she wasn't going to give it to him. From what she'd gathered at the hospital, the kind of corneal scarring he had could often be cured with a transplant. They did them every day downstate. But the waiting list could take months, and the procedure wasn't guaranteed. "So what are you going to do temporarily until this little setback clears up?"

"I'll get by."

They were butting heads, getting nowhere. Difficult as it was, Annie let the silence stretch, let him turn and walk away, Kane leading like a sturdy black tugboat.

Ten feet farther down the beach, Cliff stopped. Why, he couldn't have said. It wasn't polite to just turn his back on her. Then again, he hadn't been feeling very polite for the past three weeks. Caged, was more like it.

He faced her, he hoped, and nodded toward the straining dog. "He's been in a kennel for a month. They exercise them, but he really needs to run."

So do you, Annie thought. Body honed as only a runner's could be, he'd probably worked out every day before the accident. No wonder he was a seething mass of energy.

But more importantly, he was talking. Innate politeness, loneliness—she'd never know. Either way it was an opening. Annie did everything but jump at it. She sauntered up beside them instead.

"I'm not up for a run, but how about a good long walk?" Not waiting for an invitation, her footfalls hissed softly ahead of them in the sand. Man and dog had no choice but to follow.

He'd been rude, Cliff knew. He'd been biting off everybody's head lately. Just because he had a better than average excuse...

He'd also been a real jerk about those therapy classes they'd tried to get him into at the hospital. Hell, as long as he had his brother staying with him at the beach house, what did he need with therapy? Playing with clay wasn't going to teach him a damn thing about how to get through this nightmare, sane.

Eventually his thoughts strayed to the woman walking beside him. She'd tricked him, tracking him down on the beach without introducing herself. He tried to get worked up about that again, but he couldn't. Somehow it was a relief just having someone there. He tried to picture her. There was something about her voice. It was smooth, one or two notes lower than typical. A woman's voice, not a girl's. She could be anywhere up to forty and matronly as a TV nurse.

They walked in silence. Cliff waited for the inevitable question about the explosion that had blinded him. She didn't ask.

"Ow!"

"Halt." He jerked the dog to a stop when the word itself didn't work. "What is it?"

Annie put her hand on his arm to steady herself as she pulled off one of her rubber thongs. "Little stones in the sand. One got into my sandal."

Her hand was small, cool on his skin. "Flip-flop," he corrected automatically.

They both stood amazed for a moment.

"Very good," she murmured.

Even Cliff was impressed. Every day he was able to put more together by using his other senses. Not that it helped anywhere near enough. For example, it didn't tell him anything about what she looked like. That his curiosity couldn't be satisfied only added to his frustration. At this point in his life, he had no business being curious about any woman.

"Your hearing is very acute," Annie commented.

"Sounds like another diagnosis," he replied curtly.

"Oh-oh. Better report me to the AMA."

Although her barefoot steps were softer without the slap of thongs, Cliff could just as easily follow the gentle sounds. He imagined her feet, and from there, since he couldn't picture her face, he contented himself with trying to picture her legs.

"Blond or brunette?" The question popped out. He was startled he'd even spoken.

Annie smiled, careful to keep it out of her voice. "Who, me?"

She noticed he was seething again. Oh, he hated asking for anything, didn't he? But she couldn't help feeling good. He was reaching out, seeking some form of contact.

"Yeah, you," he growled. "I know what Kane looks like."

Her smile widened. She'd reward him for that. "Medium brown hair, brushing my shoulders. Remarkable only for its total frizziness. I hold it back with combs most of the time."

"About five foot five, right?"

She whistled, one clean musical note that showed she knew how.

Cliff smiled. Nailed it, as his brother Dave would say. He was getting good at this.

"How did you figure that one out?" she asked.

"The length of your stride, how much shorter it is than mine. Sometimes it helps to have an engineering background."

"This is soft sand," she argued. "It's clumsy to walk on and you're on the hardpack by the water."

"Therefore?"

"Therefore, my steps are shorter because the terrain is more difficult, and *that* was an educated guess."

He grinned. "Darn right."

"Do you guess weights, too?"

"You wouldn't like it if I was right."

"Give it a shot."

"One-twenty?"

"You're right. I don't like it," she admitted, laughing. At least he was taking some pride in the sharpening of his other senses. That would help them both.

He couldn't resist one more. "You're not wearing a bathing suit, even though you're on the beach."

Now she *was* impressed. The fact was that she had nothing on under her sundress except some silk panties. "Superman, right? You wear those shades to hide your X-ray vision."

"I can hear the fabric flapping. It has to be a dress. Simple."

"Ah." It was an Indian cotton, a complicated blue vine printed on a gray background, imported by an artist friend of hers. Tentlike and comfortable, flimsy and cool, she liked to toss it on for beach walks. With the breeze picking up, the dress flapped around and between her legs with every step. "Of course, I could be wearing a bathing suit under it."

"Could be."

"Anything else, Amazing Kreskin?"

"You're carrying those flip-flops in your left hand. I can feel the sand sprinkle my leg when you swing them."

"Oh, sorry." Yes, she was. Especially after she glanced down at those legs. Golden and hairy and built like the towers Samson toppled. Muscles rippled with every step. No wonder he wanted to run. She felt like running herself. In the opposite direction.

"Anything else you want described?" he asked.

"I'm not wearing anything else—" Blood rushed to her cheeks. She knew if she stopped to stare at that grin on his face, they'd be here for hours. Fortunately the dog intervened by lurching to the right and panting excitedly. "Looks like Kane wants to head up there," she said, pointing in the direction the dog was lunging.

Cliff's mood abruptly changed. He had to pay more attention to his surroundings. No more walking on the beach, drifting, thinking, working out problems. Just getting to and from home was a problem now.

"He's probably heading for the cottage," he said.

"Cottage! Looks more like House Beautiful. Peaked roof, lots of glass, bleached siding and matching snow fence?"

He silently thanked her for the clues. It was his place. "Keeps sand from drifting against the house."

Kane barked his barrel-chested bark until they reached the gate. There was an uncomfortable pause while Cliff wound the leash around his fist. He'd have to thank her for getting him here. He used to be polite; lately he was beginning to hate every thank-you. Each one seemed like another bar on his cage.

"Excuse me if I'm bad at this. I haven't always depended on the kindness of strangers."

Annie smiled, knowing that if he didn't see it, he'd hear it in her voice. She touched his arm to reinforce it. "We'll be seeing more of each other, Cliff." She used his name softly but definitely. "When I'm not working at the hospital, my studio is just down the beach."

He nodded, but made no promises.

Then a young man came out of the house and jogged down the path toward them.

"Who's this?" she asked.

Cliff muttered under his breath, knowing his brother Dave would be eyeing the woman with him, asking himself the same question.

Dave obliged by stating it out loud. "And who is this lovely lady?" He was using his smooth-talk voice, or a twenty-year-old's idea of one. "Still picking them up on the beach, bro?"

Cliff cringed.

Dave looked blandly back and forth, but it was obvious he was wondering how much Annie knew about Cliff's disability.

She stuck her hand out for a firm shake. "I'm Annie Rosetti, art therapist at the hospital. We've been chasing after your brother to stop on by for the past week."

"Oh, yeah? Why don't you, big brother?"

Cliff scowled blackly. "This is all I need, nagging at home."

"Could be fun." Dave shrugged. He looked Annie up and down and blushed when he got caught. Just because he was living in his much older brother's bachelor pad on Lake Michigan didn't mean he was nearly as smooth as Cliff when it came to the ladies.

"Are you staying here, Dave?" Annie asked.

"Yeah. Until break is over. Then back to the books."

They chatted. Cliff listened. Annie said goodbye. As she walked off down the beach, Kane dug under the fence post until it was completely revealed.

"She's waving," Dave said to his older brother. He filled in Kane's hole with the toe of his tennis shoe.

"Great."

"Another day, another sunny mood."

"Don't quote Mom."

"Maybe you need one. A mom, I mean."

The good-natured bickering subsided. Cliff let the wind buffet him, listening to the waves crash. Why was he still facing the direction she'd headed as she walked away?

Or maybe he wasn't. How would he know?

He turned toward the house, Dave at his side. "At least you don't run off. The damn dog got away from me and tore up her garden."

"Maybe you should try a cane instead. With a *C*."

"Very funny."

Cliff kicked off his Topsiders on the deck and slid the glass door open. The inside of the house was cool and, as he knew from years of coming here on every available weekend, shadowy and dark compared to the glaring white sand. It had been one of the bigger shocks of the past three weeks to realize that he didn't know this place like the back of his hand; he was still bumping into things.

While Dave gave Kane a fresh bowl of water, Cliff found the couch and mulled over how obvious his first question should be. "So what did she look like?"

Dave snickered. "Wondered how long that would take."

"Think you know me too well, kid."

"Been following you from afar for a long time. Exploit after exploit," he said suggestively.

Cliff lapsed into an imitation brogue he used only in the family. "Mother of mercy, you'd think I wrote home about it."

"I can guess."

"You, kid, have a wild imagination. My sex life is nothing like what you imagine. In fact, it's *all* imagination right now."

"So what about her?"

"That's what I'm asking you. Would she be worth looking up when I can see again?"

"Could be. Is she married?"

"Didn't ask."

"Divorced with four kids and too proud for child support?"

"Didn't ask. She knows I'm blind."

Cliff could almost hear Dave grinning. "So I noticed. You finally told somebody."

"No, I didn't. She knew who I was all along. She tracked me down so I'd take her art class."

"Oh." The disappointment was palpable. "Does she get paid by the student?"

"Thanks for the compliment."

Dave frowned, then gave up on his brother's sarcasm.

Cliff elaborated. "You think that's the only reason a woman would look at me?"

"You didn't see the way she was looking at you."

"Oh, yeah?" The smile was all male.

Dave handed him a can of beer. Cliff knew because he'd heard the hiss of the pop-top all the way across the open living room. The bubbly liquid was cold and strong. He stretched his feet on the coffee table, and Kane flopped, panting, on the floor beside him. He reached down and petted him. Heck, it wasn't the dog's fault that eight months into his puppyhood his master had been rendered useless.

Dave plunked down on the sofa, his heavy feet jarring the table. "Ask her yourself. What she looks like, I mean. See if she's interested."

"And how am I going to do that? Hobble down the beach with a white cane, tapping on doors until I find her cottage?"

"Take her class."

Cliff frowned and muttered something about nagging.

"Might get on her good side," Dave added. "You could score some brownie points for when you can see again."

Cliff downed the second half of his beer and grinned. "Dave?"

"Yeah?"

"Did studying me for twenty years really teach you to be that devious?"

Two

―――――

Whaddya think, two or three hours?" Dave opened the car door and escorted his brother to the hospital wing containing Annie's classroom.

"Two should do it. Just drop me here." Cliff shouldered his way through the doors alone.

It was the smell that assaulted him first—disinfectant. Must buy it in fifty-gallon drums, he thought wryly. He felt waxed linoleum beneath his feet, heard nurses in rubber shoes, hushed voices. The memories they evoked weren't pleasant. The oldest ones never ceased to be painful. He had yet to come to terms with the most recent ones.

Three weeks ago he'd woken in a hospital and been told about the explosion in the mine. Something about a faulty charge and a flash, sand particles embedded in his eyes. Bandages had been applied and removed, tests run;

fingers had stretched his eyelids open, shining a penlight at him that looked like the sun behind a heavy cloud.

After two weeks of that sort of treatment combined with unrelenting questioning from the Bureau of Mines people and a half-dozen safety inspectors, all the proper reports had been filed. Meanwhile, the doctors had admitted there was nothing more they could do. They put him on a waiting list for cornea transplants at the University of Michigan and sent him home.

But instead of going to his apartment, he'd chosen the cottage, 150 miles to the south in what was still considered northern Michigan. The local hospital, this hospital, would keep him updated on his waiting-list status.

The first time he stopped by, the staff suggested he learn survival skills by taking therapy classes. But he hated working out on treadmills; they only reminded him of how much better it was running outdoors—fresh air, sunrises. He had no interest in home health care, either. Dave would help him out there. Then they made the mistake of presenting him with a white cane. He broke it across his knee.

Their last suggestion was the art class. Pottery—as if that was a survival skill!

But here he was, listening to the art room fill up: listening to people chatting, electric wheelchairs humming by, a metal walker clicking and scraping across the floor. He'd been escorted to a stool by a nurse. There he sat, restless, vaguely angry, waiting for the class to start. *Let's get on with it.* He didn't give two bits for art he couldn't see. Art for a mining engineer meant graph paper, drafting pencils, computer graphics. What did they call this charade? *Tactile arts?*

But maybe the doctors were right. Maybe it would take his mind off the milky white room he was trapped in. It was like watching people moving behind a linen curtain. Like bandages that never came off.

After a few minutes it was obvious that everyone was waiting for Annie Rosetti. Judging by how quickly he picked out her footsteps as she came through the door, so was he. Hers was the steady go-ahead stride he'd learned on the beach. Today she was wearing sandals, he guessed, flats. Listening to a few more steps, he knew he was right.

Annie wasn't surprised to see Cliff in her class. She'd been warned he was coming. The shock was seeing him smile. Maybe he'd heard her enter. Maybe it was some private thought. It was impossible to tell behind the dark glasses. She tried to feel a twinge of sympathy for his handicap, but she felt absurd feeling sorry for anyone who looked that virile, that mysterious, that just plain dangerous.

Annie smiled. Dangerous? Only to her common sense. He'd probably swallowed some pride to be here. *Because he needs my help,* she reminded herself. That, she would willingly give.

"Class, I'd like to introduce you to our newest member, Cliff Sullivan." He stiffened, she noted, and the smile froze before disappearing completely.

"Cliff, since you can't see, I'll tell you who's here. Emily is on your left. She's in a wheelchair from multiple sclerosis. Bob is to her left, with cerebral palsy. Grant was paralyzed from the chest down in a diving accident."

"Hi," a young man said.

Cliff barely nodded.

"And Susie is on your right. She has arthritis."

"Hi, Cliff." Her voice was very young. Nodding again, Cliff wondered with a pang how young.

"I tell you this," Annie continued, "not because anyone here is identified by his or her disability, but they will be identifiable to you by their sounds. The electric wheelchairs are Emily's and Bob's, Grant uses the hands-on type to keep his muscles looking great—" laughter all around "—and Susie uses the walker. And for your information," she announced, to the other class members, "Cliff is blind."

"Temporarily." It was the first and only word out of his mouth, and already he regretted it. No one else was here temporarily. Just because he didn't belong was no reason to insult people.

Attitude. Annie knew the difference it could make. Grant had adjusted so quickly, modifying his very first wheelchair for racing so that he could remain involved in athletics. Cliff wasn't adapting; he was denying. She had to reach him.

She started with the indirect approach, including him in the group. "Since we have a new member, I get to stand up and give my speech."

Groans and laughter met her announcement. Cliff grimaced but found himself leaning forward for more of her voice. It was the only familiar thing here.

She began, punctuating her words with emphasis. He could almost see her hands darting as her voice rose and fell, fists clenching or fingers pointing. As she moved, he caught a sense of the room's dimensions, never losing track of how far away she was at any given moment.

"I don't care what you can't do," she said. "I want to know what you *can*. And you want to know. That's why you're here. There is something worthwhile in every one of us. Something beautiful. Maybe you don't think so. Maybe others look at the outer shell and see something broken. Don't let anyone judge you by the outside. Show me the inside, what you can *create*."

She moved slowly around the room, laying a hand on a shoulder, touching an arm, her passion and her belief in her work obvious. She approached Cliff last. The closer she got the more suspicion radiated from him. She had one two-hour class in which to gain his trust, to get inside those defenses.

"Some people may dismiss this as mere basket weaving, but I believe in this class. Anything that comes from inside you is beautiful, is worthwhile. Let's get started."

Music began, a salty calypso playing as softly as a Caribbean breeze. Cliff heard the whir of the chairs and people moving past, heard the tinkle of paintbrushes in jars, running water, another page being turned on a drawing pad. Somewhere in the jostle, he lost the sound of her walking.

"Cliff?"

He started and cursed himself. She was right beside him.

"Sorry to startle you." Her voice was warm, her hand resting lightly on his shoulder. "I want to show you this wheel."

She reached around to throw a switch. He heard the potter's wheel start to spin and felt the fabric of her dress sweep and catch against his shirt as she came around behind him.

"This is the clay we'll be using." She plopped a cabbage-sized lump into his hand.

Cliff said the first thing that came into his mind. "Feels like plastique."

"Plasteek?"

"Plastic explosives. Got enough here to blow a good-sized building sky-high."

She laughed lightly. "Well, I've never heard that one before. Tell me more."

He almost did, but it would mean talking about his work, setting charges to loosen tons of rock and ore in the open pit mines of Michigan's Upper Peninsula. It would also mean talking about the explosion. "Just show me what to do with this, Doc."

She settled herself on a stool. "If you could see the getup I'm wearing, you wouldn't think I looked much like a doctor."

"I can hear it. You have bells on?"

"Little Indian bells on the belt, hammered silver. It was made by an artist friend."

Close friend? he wondered. "And bracelets?"

"Always, though they'll come off once we get into the clay. Here, you'll need to wear this." She flapped a cloth in front of him and tried to direct his arms into the smock.

"Oh, no, I'm not." He wasn't about to put on another of those ridiculous hospital gowns.

"You'll get spattered with wet clay."

"I'm not a baby. I don't wear a bib."

"It's an artist's smock."

"No!" The mouth was firm, the jut of his jaw outlined even through the beard. The furrow between his brows was deep and unyielding.

Annie sighed. "Guess it'll have to come out in the wash. By the way, does Dave do that or do you?"

Cliff frowned. Just because he hadn't memorized the washer cycles yet didn't mean it was any of her business. He squeezed the clay so hard it was indented with the shape of his fingers.

Annie wrapped her hands around his and said in a tone of gentle teasing, "You're getting ahead of me, Cliff.

Kneading the clay is next." Her fingers threaded with his, pressing softly.

He almost choked. An image of their legs entwined in the same way rocked him to the core. At the same time the smell of her perfume came to him, soft, seductive. He wanted to turn his head and follow that scent to its point of origin, the side of her neck perhaps, or beneath her ear. To put it bluntly, he wanted her. Physically. Immediately.

She continued to touch, to knead, mouthing soft, encouraging words that had his blood racing even while his mind told him what an idiot he was. He was blind. To her he was nothing but a student. If he kept that thought firmly in place, maybe he could get through this thing without making a complete ass of himself.

"All right, teach, what do I do with this useless lump of clay now?"

"Well," Annie replied, trying not to sound surprised at his sudden cooperation, "we center it on the wheel and start it spinning."

Two hours of hell, that's what Cliff had been through when the music stopped. His shoulders were stiff from hunching over the wheel and his back ached. The concentration needed when one couldn't see was tremendous; a pounding headache was proof of his efforts. But those were only aches and pains.

For two hours he'd had Annie's perfume, Annie's voice, Annie's arms reaching around him, intermingling her fingers with his in that yielding clay, guiding his hands up and down the wet and spinning shape. He'd made two pots, both round and full at the bottom, tapering at the neck. Like a woman. And when she'd shown him how to dip his fingers inside to hollow out the pot, he'd thought he'd break in two.

If this was supposed to relax him, it sure as hell wasn't working. He felt clumsy, tense, helpless and aroused all at once. He felt like a wounded bull in a pottery shop, and Art with a capital *A* wasn't about to assuage him.

Bidding the other students goodbye, Annie watched Cliff get up to leave and sensed every piece of hard-won progress about to slip down the drain. How was he going to get out of here with all those easels and stools in the way? "Cliff? I don't see Dave outside. Why don't you wait a minute while I clean up?"

"No thanks." He had to get out. He kept hearing her swishing around in that dress, that body, that darkness. Every time she walked by he caught the sway of fabric and the sound of bells. What would he do alone with her in this room? Correction, what did he want to do that he was a fool to even dream of?

He was leaving. Now. And he'd be damned if she'd see him shuffle. He took one solid stride and kicked the water bucket next to the potter's wheel. He'd been using it all through class to rinse his hands and moisten clay. He remembered it the moment lukewarm water sloshed over his pant leg and down into his shoe.

He felt like an idiot, and he knew he looked like one. At least the string of curses he let loose was creative. He kicked the bucket halfway across the room.

Annie tossed her smock on the floor. "Damn it, Cliff, I don't tolerate tantrums in class."

"I'm not in your class anymore!" Refusing to mince or hesitate, he stormed forward. Until he hit the wheelchair.

"Hold on a second, man," Grant said, rolling backward, "Let me get out of your way."

"Uh, sorry." He'd thought everyone else was gone.

"Yes, you are sorry," Annie replied tartly, coming up behind him. "You should be. You're also free to leave." Putting the flat of her hand firmly on his back, she steered him on a path through the easels. When there was a straight line to the door, she let go with a slight push for emphasis. "Eight paces, turn left in the hall."

Cliff stopped and turned toward her. To argue, apologize or curse, he couldn't have said. He wanted to break something, hit something, run until his heart pounded like a bass drum in his ears. But no words came, so he walked, hand extended, until he hit the door and slapped it wide open. He executed a neat turn and marched out, quietly calling himself every name in the book. One thing was certain: he was never coming here again.

Dave entered the other end of the hall just in time. "Hey, look out! Stretcher at twelve o'clock."

They looked a lot more like brothers when they frowned, Annie thought, watching from the art room door. Fortunately Dave caught on quickly to her hands-off method. She wasn't helping Cliff because it wasn't the kind of help he'd accept. He'd make it down that hall alone.

He'd do it all alone.

Annie muttered a curse of her own. The man was impossible. Inflexible. His conduct inexcusable.

The hard part was, she could still feel his back under her palm, the slip of fabric against skin as she pushed him out the door, still see his determined walk. It took a lot of courage to walk like that, pretending nothing was wrong, refusing to be slowed down by the simple fact that he couldn't see. Either way he still needed her help. Maybe more than ever.

They would meet again.

Maybe she should add *inevitable* to her list.

* * *

Two days later at 7:00 a.m., watching Cliff jog down the beach with Kane, Annie's plan was made.

She'd been thinking since Tuesday, when the sound of Dave's car had faded outside the hospital and she'd realized she'd been listening to it go. She was determined, too. Cliff had to adjust, to accept himself as he was. But he was proud. She couldn't emphasize his limitations. She'd show him all the things he was still capable of. The months of waiting for his operation would go more easily. And if the operation failed, he'd be that much farther along.

Besides, she knew if she let him simply walk away, he'd haunt her forever.

At the moment it was Kane who was doing the tormenting. Drawn to the water like any Lab, he wanted to play in the waves. No matter how straight a path Cliff maintained, Kane veered to the right with every sixth step. Nikes splashing in the water, Cliff cursed and tugged the dog back as they zigzagged their way down the beach. Annie waited until they were directly across from her house.

"Care if I join you?"

Cliff stopped as if he'd heard a rattler. Actually it was her voice and the sound of bracelets. He steeled himself. "We're heading for the showers. Or the dog pound," he growled.

"Looks like Kane's already had a shower. Hi, beast." She let the overgrown pup slurp her hand. It gave her a moment to take in Cliff's soaked shoes. "Did you two stop for a swim?"

He didn't take kindly to teasing.

She'd been watching them all along, he thought, in which case she already knew damn well they'd been in the water more than out. "I'm not coming back to the hospital."

"I'm not asking you."

He paused, jaw tight. "Then why are you talking to me?"

"I have a proposition."

Not the kind he wanted to hear, he thought.

"I promise you'll never have to come to class again, if..."

"If?"

"If you come to my studio instead. Cliff, Dave's not going to look after you forever."

"I don't need forever."

"You need more than a few weeks. The waiting list could take months, and Dave has to go back to college."

"I'll get by."

"On what? Is he teaching you anything? Or do you blow up every time you hit a snag, until he backs down and does everything himself?"

She'd hit a nerve. Dave wanted friendliness and good times. He'd cater to his brother rather than fight.

"I've had experience, Cliff. I can deal with the anger."

"Is that why you kicked me out of class?"

"You bothered another student. That's not allowed."

"I didn't see him."

They both let that excuse lie.

"I thought they'd all left, that we were alone," Cliff said finally. Thought it, wished it, dreaded it.

"Then the tantrum was for my benefit?"

Yes. It was because of her, because she was a woman he wanted so unreasonably and couldn't have. "It won't work, whatever your proposition is. Kane, home!"

The dog took off in the direction *he* wanted to go, after a flock of sea gulls settling downwind.

"Wrong way," Annie called.

Halting, they came slowly back to the sound of her voice. Sprinkling his request with expletives the dog would never understand, Cliff said, "Just point us in the right direction and drop it, okay?"

"Not okay."

He thought he could hear her folding her arms across her chest, bracelets jangled then muffled, voice tight.

"I can teach you everything you'll need to know when Dave's gone. How to use the can opener, the stove, how to set up the medicine cabinet. Whatever you need for daily living, you'll learn. How to run a washing machine, for instance."

"I know how. I'm not going back to the hospital."

"Accept my proposition and you won't have to. I'm talking about my house. It's better than any classroom. We'll have a real kitchen, real stairs and carpeting."

Kane wanted to stalk the gulls. Cliff let him, following at the other end of the leash. Annie anxiously kept pace, fully aware Cliff hadn't said no.

"And what if I knock over a bucket of dirty water in your living room?"

"My studio is impervious to dirt."

"Your studio is in your house?"

"Semiattached. It's actually a heated garage with concrete floor, a drain and a kiln."

"I could break a lot of pottery, you know."

"I'm not Cliff-proofing my house for your sake. You'll simply have to learn to live with what's there." Annie smiled, a disguised philosophy if she ever heard one.

"So now I'm living there," he said.

"Every day, ten to two. We'll fix lunch, do dishes, run a load of wash, all the things you need to learn. We might even make some pottery. Only catch is, you have to put up with me."

Kane, who had come to a complete halt pointing at the squawking birds, lunged. The gulls scattered and screeched. Cliff reined him in while mulling over Annie's offer.

They'd be spending time together, a lot of it. Alone in a way they'd never be in a classroom. Did this woman have any idea how she was tempting him? On the other hand, maybe she'd never even considered that aspect.

Still breathing hard from the workout with Kane, Cliff was aware of how little he was wearing. The warm southern wind chilled the sweat off his skin, and his nylon running shorts clung to him. He felt on display and there was no way to gauge her reaction. Did she even notice?

He decided it was high time he found out whether she saw him as a student or a man. "If I spend that much time at a woman's place, I usually know a little more about her."

Annie's heartbeat sped up. At least he was thinking about it. She tried to sound cool. "What do you want to know?"

"Starting from absolute scratch, what do you look like?" He looked down at her, those flat black glasses suddenly reflecting her upturned face. With the blunt prickly beard, he could have passed for a dissolute movie star.

Her mouth was suddenly dry. Even though she knew he couldn't see her, his prolonged scrutiny produced the strangest sensation. "Didn't Dave describe me to you?"

Not enough. Cliff didn't reveal how coy his brother had been, suckering him into going to her class. Not that it was Dave's fault anymore—against his better judgment, Cliff wanted to know. He wanted to get out of this self-enclosed prison. He wanted a reaction. "I'd like to see for myself."

Annie had to find her voice first. "All right." She reached out and put her hand on his shoulder so he'd know where she was. Then she touched his chin, tilting it so that he was looking right at her. "I'm directly in front of you."

The minute she took her hand away she wanted to touch his beard again, to feel his shoulder muscles bunch and relax beneath her other hand. She mentally corrected that. What she most wanted was to touch and not get burned. Which was crazy and, with Cliff Sullivan, she sensed, impossible. She clenched her hands at her sides and hoped the tension didn't show in her voice.

"I'm five-five, as you guessed before. You figured out my weight. I have frizzy brown hair that looks like I overperm it."

"Do you?"

"Been that way since I was born. Maybe my mother was frightened by a Brillo pad."

He smiled. "You have some weird ideas."

"Just trying to be honest. I used to do everything but iron my hair to make it behave. Go ahead."

He paused, uncertain, so she lifted his hand.

"You can't see, so touch. Brillo, right?"

He smiled grimly, shaking his head slightly. He patted her hair awkwardly, then pleased himself by catching a strand that was being toyed with by the wind and combed it back in place. This was so intimate, touching a woman's hair. The kind of thing he usually did when pulling a woman toward him to kiss her. He dropped his hand to his side. "All right."

Annie had to swallow, clear her throat, something. Her voice felt as hoarse as his sounded. "Not exactly the classic pageboy," she croaked.

"No."

"I used to dress very understated and preppy."

"Was your family well-off?"

"My husband's was."

"Husband?"

It wasn't something she liked talking about, but she knew he was going by verbal clues alone, so she filled in the details. "Ex-husband. I was the perfect wife while it lasted, or so I thought. Guess I didn't measure up."

"In whose opinion?"

"Ken's."

"And who appointed him God?"

She smiled, then squeezed his shoulder to show she meant it, saying, "Thanks for that one." He was surprisingly easy to talk to, even without visual feedback. He had a very mobile face, little tics, smiles, frowns. "I wish I'd had you around back then. You would've saved me a lot of trouble."

"How so?"

"I've always been what my Mom calls 'artistic.' In her vocabulary that means funky Bohemian clothes made by friends who are into fabric, a lot of jewelry and plenty of color. Needless to say, I wasn't preppy material. Ken wanted to change me, and I wanted to change to keep him. I was so eager to fit in." She sighed, briefly remembering the past. "He left me anyway."

Cliff's face was unreadable. "Must have been tough."

Her shrug took in the sky, the sand, the whole crazy world. She wished he could see it; it was harder to put into words. "We're all stronger than we realize. Trite but true. I know now I'd never have been happy that way. I'm just me now, unapologetic."

She was about to add something, instead she slipped her hand into the crook of his arm and they started walking.

Sometimes she wished she could change back, be as accommodating as she used to be, quick to align her opinion with others'. No more. She was honest and blunt, and her true friends cherished her for that. But some people, she glanced warily up at Cliff, had trouble accepting it. Some men, she reminded herself, wanted a woman more in their own image.

Although they'd lapsed into silence, Annie didn't seem to feel the need to fill it with chitchat. Cliff liked that. He also liked the way she matched him stride for stride. He made sure they kept on the packed sand by the water's edge. That meant she stayed close by his side. She felt good there. Right. Maybe too good. Every now and then the back of her hand stroked his bare waist. That's when he realized his hand had covered hers where it rested in the crook of his arm.

Her perfume was still there, enticingly reaching him whenever the breeze died down. "Your artist friends make clothes and bells and bracelets. Do they make perfume, too?"

His hand was already reaching, catching Annie's nod.

"This one makes potpourri, too," she said, suddenly breathless as he lifted her hair, bending carefully forward to inhale the delicate scent of her neck.

That was accidental, she told herself when his lips skimmed her skin. She tried to breathe shallowly, aware of how dangerously close her breasts were to touching his chest, suddenly aching for just that.

His quick breaths fell on her neck; her eyes fluttered closed. His hand was on her shoulder, steadying her, as if she had any intention of moving. She must be completely crazy. "Cliff."

He turned his head as she turned hers. Chins collided. Embarrassed, he backed away. His hand fell, the backs of his fingers accidentally brushing her breast, discovering the upraised nipple.

For five stultifying seconds nothing was said.

"Uh, sorry," he muttered, color flooding his face.

"You don't have to be embarrassed," she said quietly, as much to herself as him.

"By what?" He pulled his shoulders back.

"Why not be honest?"

"I am," he insisted with a tug on Kane's leash.

"You touched my breast and you're embarrassed, that's what. You're also mad at yourself for doing something dumb."

Mad? He felt mortified, embarrassed and furious. Also as clumsy as a fifteen-year-old at a drive-in. Where was his old suave way with women? Just because he hadn't used it lately shouldn't mean he'd lost it completely. If everything were normal, what would he do in this situation? Try humor.

"You don't have to make up excuses for me, Annie. Where I come from, copping a feel is considered a coup."

"You did that on purpose?"

She didn't sound convinced. All right. As Dave would say, punt. "You didn't describe those to me. It's nice to know who I'm talking to." Lord, that came out crudely. Maybe she'd slap him instead of the pity or revulsion he imagined in her eyes.

Annie was sure Cliff was covering up his embarrassment. She just wasn't *completely* sure. She'd enjoyed his touch. That she shouldn't have, didn't change anything. The memory of the sensation still tingled on her skin, repeating as her breasts rose and fell against the fabric of her dress. The tiny hairs on her neck still prickled.

He was so handsome, so masculine. No matter how she wanted to overlook that for the sake of their relationship, her body wasn't buying.

"Guess private lessons won't work," he said, listening to her silence. His face was immobile, unreadable. Convinced she was embarrassed by this whole scene, Cliff knew exactly where he stood with her. Nowhere.

"May I ask why not?"

"That's obvious," Cliff replied. "I'm too clumsy. And too tempted." He carelessly brushed the back of his fingers over her breast again, surprised at how quickly the nipple hardened. She responded to him. And he could feel his own body responding. Maybe it wasn't a lost cause.

Annie stepped back awkwardly in the soft sand. "We can, we *should* keep this strictly teacher and pupil."

Not on his part, Cliff promised himself silently. He was just beginning to realize how much he needed someone to react to him as a man, to convince him he was just as desirable, just as strong, just as normal as ever. He didn't want her sympathy; he wanted her response. And he was getting it.

He felt his confidence rise. He knew as sure as the sun beating down on his back that she wouldn't buy an outright courtship. She wanted to teach. Okay, he'd go along to get along. Let her teach him Pottery and Dishwashing 101. Meanwhile he'd teach her he was every bit the man he'd always been. And then some.

"Tomorrow at ten, then?"

Annie nodded, rooted to the spot. He touched her arm, his thumb grazing the inside of her elbow, doing strange things to the pulse inside it. "Uh, Cliff, maybe we need some ground rules here."

"Don't pull away," he said softly. "We have no eye contact. This is the only way I can see you."

The request was stated so simply that she couldn't refuse.

"Ten?" he asked again.

His fingers found her cheek and her nod. His touch was gentle, his face impenetrable once more. He turned and followed Kane toward the cottage.

Did he have any idea how she reacted to him? Annie mentally shook herself. She had to keep this professional for his sake. Emotions would get them both mixed up. She was going to help him, and for that, she'd have to gain his trust.

But who was getting close to whom? And who most needed to heed those words of warning?

Three

———

Annie pursed her lips in contemplation, trying to make this piece of clay better, a thinner wall, a more fluid shape. Unfortunately, every time she thought she was onto something, her concentration shifted to Cliff Sullivan.

Willing her hands to be steady as the pot spun, watching thin finger-width notches circling and building, she was aware of how tightly her arms were clamped to her sides, the pressure on the side of her breasts, the sensation, slight, of the nipple he'd touched, hard-tipped and pushing against fabric. A gentle, aching throb. She had a sudden desire to run her fingers across it, but they were clay-smeared.

The pot, its walls too thin, began to cave in.

"Bah!" She shut the wheel off with an angry flick of the switch. Straightening her aching back, she stared purposefully at the shelves of unglazed pots. She had work to do if she was going to be ready for the art fair this weekend. Which one was she scheduled for? It didn't matter; she wouldn't have anything to sell if she didn't get some production going.

"So what about Cliff Sullivan?" she asked the empty room. If their lesson tomorrow went as badly as their art class had, they were doomed to failure.

Used to working with three-dimensional objects, Annie examined the man from another perspective. Obviously he'd been abashed about that touch, at first. Maybe sexual attraction was getting in her way, not his.

At least they'd made some positive steps. She remembered with a flash the first time he'd smiled; she'd been joking about good-looking blond men. But they don't like me, she'd said.

"Words to the wise," she muttered, cramming some clay into a ball and starting over.

The second time he'd relaxed was their walk on the beach, his guessing her height, practically showing off the skills he'd picked up.

Then he'd touched her. In a sense that was good; he was reaching out. He'd found her cheek to check on her nod.

Annie sat up straighter and took a deep breath. There was that sensation in her breasts again, full and tingling. She could blame it on the week of the month, but she knew exactly whose fault it was.

"So he can flirt." She sighed and returned to the analysis. "He knows how. It makes him feel comfortable around me." No doubt that would be the best way to reach him, provided she could take it as lightly as he did.

That was the trick.

Applying patterned indentations to a vase with a small tool, she considered it. By the time she finished, her mouth was as taut as the wire she drew under the clay to separate it from the wheel.

Could she honestly say she wasn't interested?

Yes.

Would she believe it?

No.

She was challenged by the stubbornness in him, drawn to the hurt, attracted to his strength. She'd learned to accept herself exactly as she was. It was taking Cliff Sullivan as much strength, if not more, to deny what he'd become. Contradictory as it might seem, she admired anyone with that kind of courage, the sheer willpower to face reality and say, "No, I won't accept it."

One of the combs loosened in her hair as she bent over to set the vase on the workbench. If she didn't push it back, it might fall and nick her carefully applied pattern. If she did, she'd get clay in her hair. What the heck. She pushed it back anyway. She'd gotten clay in her hair more than once. She wasn't exactly the glamour type.

"And that, Annie Rosetti, is undoubtedly what Mr. Gorgeous is used to."

She'd made a major, painful mistake with her ex-husband, one she didn't want to repeat. Physical attraction was one thing, but you didn't build a relationship on it. Unfortunately some attractive people never learned that. Her ex-husband for one. Cliff Sullivan for another?

Or was she judging him on *his* looks? Seeing through to the inner person was something she firmly believed in. It hurt when you were judged on the surface as she had been judged. And found lacking.

"Cliff wouldn't do that." Cliff was blind; he couldn't. Did that make him safe?

Annie shook her head slowly back and forth. She was applying an awful lot of thought to a man she barely knew. Rinsing her hands off, she pried clay from under her fingernails with an old file.

So what was a woman to do? The answer was surprisingly easy. Help the man. Teach him what she could. After all, he was a student, not a lover.

And she was determined to keep it that way.

The next morning Annie knocked on the glass doors of Cliff's cottage. If she was to regain control of this situation, she had to take the first step.

"Morning, Dave," she called, peering inside.

"Hi. Bring a mop?" he whispered conspiratorially.

"Why? Did he kick over—" Annie stopped with a flinch when she realized it was a joke. At least Cliff had told Dave about the debacle in class. Talking it out might have helped. "Actually, we're going to walk over to my house."

"Come on in. He's upstairs. Classes are at your place now?"

She gave him the address and phone number in case he needed to get in touch during the day, and explained that she was fitting Cliff in prior to her weekday afternoon sessions at the hospital. During the summer months and into the fall, Saturdays and Sundays were reserved for traveling to art fairs.

"You can do that for a living? Don't answer that. Here he is now," Dave announced.

Cliff stopped halfway down the open staircase. Annie swallowed hard. He was wearing cutoff jeans and little else. Droplets of water clung to him from his morning shower. A cotton shirt was slung carelessly over his shoulder. He reminded her of a hunter carting home a lion's pelt. That's when the caffeine from her morning coffee hit all at once, and her pulse set up an erratic hammering.

The frown she recognized from yesterday's class was firmly in place, anchored by glasses as dark as Cliff's mood.

He hated being on display. Who was staring at him now? If Dave didn't speak up, he'd find his kid brother and gladly strangle him.

Then she spoke. "Hi, Cliff."

His stomach contracted at the sound of her voice. She was speaking from the bottom of the stairs; he could almost picture her looking up at him. He pulled the shirt off his shoulder. Slowly. He wasn't going to fiddle with finding which end was which right now. If she liked the view, let her look.

Better yet, let her remember yesterday. Not the art class, but the touch on the beach. He'd had plenty of doubts assault him since the accident, more than a few related to how he'd be perceived as a man. In class, feeling clumsy and buffoonish, with that easy sensuality of hers surrounding him, taunting him, he'd been insecure and frustrated. But it had occurred to him after he'd left the beach yesterday that he'd regained something by touching her, something he wasn't about to lose. She saw him as a man now.

The black mood began to lift. This blindness was a temporary thing. As Dave said, he could lay the groundwork now for winning Annie later. In the meantime he'd be limited to flirting but not following up. That might be its own brand of frustration, but it sure as hell beat loneliness.

Shallow? Maybe. But all the while he'd be subtly winning her. The idea made his whole day.

A slow smile curved his features. "Hello, Annie." His teeth were perfect and white, in two evenly spaced rows. He knew it. Now Annie knew it.

She swallowed, afraid it sounded like more of a gulp in the suddenly silent house. "Hi." She'd already said that.

"So, teach, ready to do it? Your place or mine?" He took the stairs one slow step at a time, grinning as he came.

Annie had that sinking sensation in her stomach again, like falling over a cliff.

Cliff? She blinked. These mood swings of his were throwing her off balance. What was he up to now? Strutting. Sexy. That walk oozed male confidence. Out of the blue, a thought whispered in Annie's ear. Maybe he'd gotten a call from an old girlfriend.

Her heart sank with her smile. Of course. Talking on the phone was something he could do. He wouldn't be blind on the phone; he'd be himself. That would make anyone feel better, put the world back to rights.

Next question, would this old flame pay him a visit?

Or was Annie making it all up? He'd never mentioned— She'd never asked—

She took a deep breath, chased those thoughts out of her head and spoke in her "now, class" voice. She was sure no one noticed the quaver located somewhere near her abdomen. "First thing we're going to do is walk down to my place, counting paces so you can learn the way. When we get there, I'll show you around the kitchen. Then we'll make lunch."

"Lunch? You don't have to do that for me." Cliff ducked his head and scratched his beard with the back of his knuckles, stealing the gesture from a James Dean movie.

Dave's grin was almost loud enough to break the stretching silence. He'd never seen his brother turn it on like this. But the lady was holding her own.

Barely.

Annie recognized twenty-four-karat charm. She might not be impervious to it but that didn't mean she was amused. "You'll be the one doing the cooking, Cliff. You have to learn to do these things by yourself."

He came to a stop at the bottom of the steps and leaned one hip against the railing. "Some things are more fun with two."

Dave choked down a laugh. Whistling a sprightly tune, he suddenly became fascinated with finding Kane's leash as the dog pranced beside the door.

Annie wasn't about to be cowed. "Dave," she emphasized for everyone's benefit, "won't always be here. As for Kane, if he'll behave himself in the house, he can come down the beach with us."

"Oh, *he'll* behave." Cliff smiled, finding the sliding door with little trouble and opening it for her. He stopped on the deck to shrug into the body-fitting knit shirt, grinning wider when his head popped out of the opening, sunglasses still in place. It was as if he'd known she'd be watching. "After you," he said softly.

Every step of the way they silently counted paces. A sound method, it prevented conversation. One look at Cliff's cocky grin and Annie knew there were words that needed to be said; boundaries had to be drawn.

Cliff switched the leash to his other hand so that Kane was on the outside, and casually took her arm. He was whistling the tune he'd picked up from his brother. It didn't help when Annie recognized it as "Na Na Na, Hey Hey, Goodbye." She wasn't about to give up. Or give in.

The tension built with each step. The feel of his fingertips made her keenly aware of the softness of her own skin. Since when was her inner elbow so sensitive? By the time they reached the cottage, her stomach felt as hollow as the wooden deck off her living room sounded.

"Let's just concentrate on the task at hand," she said. That seemed a foolproof path. "You need to operate a can opener first."

"No house tour?"

"Oh, of course." He was right. She'd been so eager to get down to an actual lesson, she hadn't thought of that. And that grin! If he thought he was getting to her, let him believe it. If his touch actually had her picturing showing him the bedroom instead of the living room—

"Can openers! You've got to—"

"Learn this stuff. I know, but, babe—" he laughed softly "—I don't even know where the hell I am yet."

She flushed. Men never called her babe. And if they did, she was sure it wouldn't have that strangely comforting, seductive result. In the meantime her jitters were making a shambles of their first lesson. One thing at a time, Annie. Stick to details. "We're on the living room floor."

"Sounds kinky. But I'm game if you are."

She resoundingly ignored him. "There's a fireplace on the right-hand wall, with a grouping of furniture in front of it. I haven't reorganized anything for your sake, it's all as it was, and it's going to stay that way."

"Is it, now?"

She also ignored the teasing lilt in his question. "As we turn left here, we'll go directly into the kitchen. You can distinguish that by the tile floor." Annie glanced down. He was still barefoot, still had hairy bronze legs like oaks, and those loose-fitting cutoffs were more snug across the front— Her gaze shot back to his face so fast that she could have sued for whiplash.

Tile. Cliff could have recognized it just by Kane's nails clicking as he padded across it. "Okay if I let the dog go?"

"Sure."

Leash unhooked, Kane sauntered to the front door, sniffed the braided rug, circled three times and collapsed with an audible huff, seemingly content to watch the birds and waves for the rest of the morning.

"Don't tell me—he's lying down," Cliff said.

"Right."

"So why is it the world's laziest dog wants to turn every walk into the Boston Marathon?"

Annie shrugged and smiled, unaware for a moment that he couldn't see it. Breathing a prayer of thanks for Kane's interruption, she proceeded with the lesson. "The kitchen is basically two rows of cupboards and appliances on opposite walls, with an eating island in the middle."

"Any hanging copper pots?"

She glanced above the island. "Good point. Yes, a few, and a rack of glasses."

He lifted a hand cautiously above his head and touched crystal. She watched his long, blunt fingers circle a rim. It was dry, no note sounded, except the one deep inside Annie. "Very nice," he said.

Why had she never noticed his voice was so low? "Thank you," she replied.

"Would you like to make lunch?"

That came out sounding entirely too much like something else on her mind.

"Lunch!" She fairly pounced. "Yes, lunch, well, if you'll come down here to the pantry at the end of the counter, we'll get the ingredients."

She described the organization of the shelves, which she *had* rearranged for him: dry goods, napkins and paper towels on top, crackers and cereal on the next shelf, then canned goods, et cetera.

As lessons go, it wasn't too bad. He got the bread out of the breadbox, mayonnaise out of the fridge—confused at first by a pickle jar until he heard the slush of pickle juice—found lettuce in the crisper and set it all out on the island. The can opener for the tuna wasn't too hard, either, except that it required her hands closing over his.

Cliff wasn't about to let that one go. It was as close as she'd let him get since they'd entered the house. "Hands-on teaching, my favorite method." He smiled.

They sat down to eat, Annie choosing a stool on the opposite side of the island. When the meal was almost finished, Cliff saluted her with his beer bottle. "Now that you've wined and dined me, what's next?"

"We clean up."

"Not my ideal way of ending a date." He pursed his lips in a mock pout.

Which only made Annie's eye linger on his lips that much longer. They were moist from the beer. Maybe they tasted of tuna and the saltiness of potato chips. He quirked one side of his mouth, as if aware of her stare. She felt suddenly guilty. "This isn't a date," she said softly but firmly. "I want to teach you."

"That's all?"

"That ought to mean everything to you in the months ahead."

He joined her at the sink to rinse dishes. "Having some company along the way would be nice."

Annie was surprised at how he'd read her thoughts. Company was nice. To her it meant a small circle of friends, easygoing, relaxed, not the tension and zing of awareness she felt every time Cliff was around. That he used every opportunity to bump her, touch her or skim her hands with his while rinsing dishes under running water, didn't help.

But blindness as an excuse only went so far. One look at him told her he wasn't a clumsy man. On the other hand, requesting he keep his distance would be tantamount to admitting he was getting through. She retreated to the island and began to clean off the scraps of food left on her plate.

"I'd appreciate it if you didn't feed him from the table," Cliff said.

Annie looked up in surprise. Of course, he'd probably heard Kane's tags jangle as the dog padded over to where the food was, but there wasn't any way he could have heard her tear off that little piece of crust.

"It's those big brown eyes," he said, smiling grimly. "They'll get you every time." He'd had brown eyes. Before. They appeared milky white now, or so the doctors told him. Not the kind of eyes a woman would want to gaze into.

"Sorry, fella." Annie patted the dog on the head, comparing those imploring eyes to Cliff's sheltered ones. She'd wanted to discourage his flirting, not start him brooding again.

Annie remembered her resolve from yesterday. He was a pupil, so she came up with another task. "Why don't you bring over some laundry tomorrow? You'll need to learn that."

"I know how to do that." His reply was surprisingly brusque, the smile gone as he turned back to the sink.

"Maybe I'm overchallenging you," she said, and immediately bit her tongue. No man would admit to that, especially this one. "I don't want you getting frustrated by learning too many things at once."

"I'm not."

"So what's the problem with laundry?" She hadn't missed his frown.

"I already know how. I've known for years."

"You have to relearn things. I mean, who's going to do your underwear?"

"Who says I wear any?"

"No?" Her mind went blank except for the knowledge that underneath those comfy stretched-in-all-the-right-places cutoffs was more of the bare skin she'd seen this morning. In a way it was a good thing he couldn't see, or she would have been caught staring.

Cliff leaned back against the counter, crossing his arms and those legs, and kept talking. At that moment Annie was grateful for her stunned silence. He didn't offer personal information easily.

"It was a bad habit I got into as a teenager. Not that I do it anymore. When they pulled me out of the mine, I'm sure I was wearing fresh underwear, just like Mom would have wanted."

Annie chuckled. Learning about his past was helpful, but asking about the explosion itself might be too direct. "I bet your mother was upset, after the accident."

"She died, years ago. When Dave was five."

"I'm sorry. How old were you?"

"Nineteen. She was in and out of the hospital for a number of years before that. My assignment was always laundry. I figured out pretty quick to wear as little as

possible, for as many days in a row as I could manage."
Cliff chuckled this time. "When the going gets tough, the
tough minimize."

"I haven't heard that one before."

"Personal philosophy of mine." He took a step toward the island, found his beer with a motion like
sweeping crumbs off the Formica, and swallowed the last
of it. "It was a bad time, especially her first few operations. Dad was working extra shifts and didn't know
what to do with two boys at home. We all handled it as
best we could. I cut a lot of classes, quit a couple of
sports, baby-sat Dave and took it day by day. You travel
light when you have to travel fast."

Annie didn't wonder that he kept so much to himself.
As a teenager he'd gone from a normal home to complete disruption of his family life. Almost four weeks ago
he'd gone from seeing to not seeing in seconds. So he was
traveling light, letting no one near. What was his philosophy, 'When the going gets tough, the tough minimize'?
Yes, she thought, and they hold it all inside.

She came around the island to touch his arm. "I'm
sorry I asked, but thank you for telling me."

He grinned slightly and cocked his head. "Anytime."
Standing so close, it wasn't hard for him to reach up and
find her cheek. Sliding the backs of his fingers over her
skin, he thought he felt that fine peach fuzz women have.
He never remembered his fingers being that sensitive. His
thumb stroked her lips, the lower one full, the tiny row
of teeth behind.

His fingertips were wet, slippery from the soap. Dia-
mondlike bubbles caught the light and dissolved in his
palm. As he traced her cheekbone, Annie felt the cool
trail of water where his breath met streaks of wetness.

For a searing instant she envied him the ability to narrow everything down to touch. If only she could touch his beard the way he was touching her cheek, or his lips the way he was running his fingers over hers. She had the sudden urge to dart her tongue out and lick the moisture off the tip of his thumb. "Please," she breathed.

"All you had to do was ask," he replied seductively.

"That's not what I meant."

"No?" A wry smile was his only reply to her haltingly spoken words. As far as he was concerned, he knew exactly what she meant.

Annie shook her head, momentarily dislodging his hand. It was soon back, palm to cheek, so gentle she wanted to stay right there and nuzzle against it. This time the word, "Don't," came out, slightly shaky.

"I never force, Annie." His hand slipped down her cheek and found the pulse in her neck, pounding slowly against the slight pressure of his massaging thumb. Her head tilted, her shoulder rose. She liked that. She also liked his fingertips tracing her collarbone through the filmy cotton dress. And when he got to her breast, a warm handful with a nubbing peak... "You only have to ask," he repeated softly.

She wanted to ask, ask for things she had no right even imagining. Things that had nothing to do with her helping him, more like him pleasuring her. Her eyes had fluttered shut. They snapped open. "No!" She stepped back, startled by the sensations that rocked her as his thumb did something delicious to her left breast.

"I was under the impression I could touch anything I could identify. Isn't that part of our lesson?"

This time she slapped his hand down. Anger was easier. "Now you're being purposely obnoxious."

"And aren't you being a bit of a tease?"

"This won't help you."

"Wanna bet?"

"It will interfere with what I'm trying to teach you."

"Teach me." He touched her waist, making her insides feel as quivering and airy as soap bubbles. "Teach me, Annie," he repeated more strongly, an air of desperation in his words.

There was so much he wanted to be. How could she deny him the chance to be a man again? "Cliff, you can have everything you had before. Believe me. The accident hasn't made you any less attractive."

"Then come here."

His hands closing on the bare skin of her arms was like the first blast of shower spray in the morning. She had to brace herself for it.

He felt her stiffen. "I can have women. I just can't have you. Is that it? And how am I supposed to meet these women?"

"So you want me because I'm available." It was the perfect opportunity to take offense. Annie used it.

"I want you period, damn it. And don't run away! I need to touch you when I talk to you, otherwise how do I know where you are?" He ran his hand over her cheek again. "I can't tell if you're stifling a yawn or rolling your eyes."

"You can't touch everyone you talk to."

"No, but I need to touch you."

Annie felt a pang. Here she was so busy protecting herself that she was forgetting her duty to him. It took guts to admit need like that, especially for someone as determined to go it alone as Cliff. It was a step she had to acknowledge. "I'm here," she said, touching his face in return.

Now they were getting somewhere. Cliff flinched at how self-centered his words sounded. Annie was being helpful, sensible. And he was acting like some randy teenager, trying to gain control over this crazy situation by being macho, wanting her to dance to his tune, to prove he was still good for something. "I'm sorry," he mumbled.

He found his way to the kitchen island and whistled for Kane. With one hand under the dog's collar, the other searched for the leash coiled on a chair.

"You don't have to go," she said, her voice husky and soft.

"I'm doing this all wrong. You should have kicked me out ten minutes ago."

"We can keep this professional, you know."

"Not if you keep doing that."

He motioned downward with his chin, and Annie realized her hand was on his chest, fingertip inches away from the hair that coiled at the open V-neck. "Sorry."

"You want me to be a student instead of a man," he said, not yet resigned to playing by her rules.

"You haven't stopped being a man, Cliff. Believe me."

She didn't have to touch him; her voice did it for her, soft, concerned, keeping him rooted when he knew he'd be better off leaving. It was the way she paused when she used his name, making him picture her mouth, her teeth touching her lower lip, coming to rest there. Were those lips moist, or dry and slightly parted?

He could drag her to him and kiss her until there was no doubts. His tongue forging into her mouth, her lips forming themselves around it, her body moulded to his.

The only thing stopping him was the fact that he didn't know exactly where she was.

Or what she looked like.

Or how she might be looking at him at this very moment.

Who was he kidding?

"All right," he said stiffly, "I won't bother you anymore. You're the teacher. I'm the pupil."

He'd stay with it, if only to hear her say his name a few dozen more times. He'd risk her stray touches, her determined concern. Whether the lessons worked or not didn't matter to Cliff anymore. He got the distinct feeling that around Annie Rosetti the most important lesson he'd learn was just how far his self-control stretched.

"Thank you," Annie said, but the words lacked enthusiasm. He was saying what she wanted to hear, but his abrupt mood change made her feel like an emotional elevator ride had come to a sudden, bumping halt.

Four

The dark Cliff was back, Annie noticed as they crossed through the kitchen for the next day's lesson. *The Dark Cliff* sounded like some kind of Gothic novel, she thought, trying to work up a smile. The tension that entered the house with him didn't allow for more than a mirthless smirk.

"This door leads outside," she began, taking him through the kitchen. "There's a flagstone path, as you can tell."

"I can feel it."

Because he was so heedless of obstacles, barging ahead, she kept a lookout for anything he might bump into. "Good. Six paces and you'll be at the garage door."

"Got a lawn mower needs fixing?"

She laughed, or tried to. That didn't come out right, either. Although they were supposed to be on formal terms, his withdrawal bothered her more than ever. Was it because she'd drawn lines when he'd tried to reach out yesterday? No going back now. "This is my studio. I like it separate from the house because of the kiln."

Kane trotted in as they entered, nose to the concrete, tail wagging as he circled the room.

Cliff just stood in the doorway. "He won't knock anything over, will he?"

"No, he's fine. Will he stay if we open the garage doors? I'll be firing the kiln and it gets stuffy in here."

"He'd better," Cliff growled. "Kane! Sit."

Annie had to guide Cliff's hand to the garage door latch. "We'll lift together, but be careful. It sticks in the middle."

With one heft the door swung upward so fast that it clanged against the rail stop and bounced back. Pulled off balance, they brushed against each other, only inches apart, as they listened to the clang fade in the big room. She could smell his cologne. No, it was something subtler—a spicy soap.

"That was easy," she said, trying to sound encouraging instead of nervous.

A breeze blew in and a jangle of sound surrounded them.

"What's that?"

"Chimes," she replied, fixing a comb in her hair.

"You collect them?"

"I practically live off them. They're my best sellers. It's a basic pot shape turned upside down, with hanging elements made from cookie cutouts or long painted strips of clay."

"Let me see."

She took his hand, leading him past sawhorses with plywood tops that stood in for tables where numerous pots were drying.

Following the remaining tinkling sound, Cliff reached up. Touching dangling strips, he felt the rasp of rough clay on one side, smooth glaze and slightly raised paint on the other.

And he felt her hand. It fitted his perfectly, firm, good-sized, not callused, but not flimsy, either. He ran his thumb absently across her fingertips.

It was a moment before Annie noticed. She was watching his face relax at the bell-like sounds. His head tilted back, and she took in his strong neck, the mixture of blond and brown hairs in his beard.

"These sound the way you smell," he said softly.

He could tell by the sound of her indrawn breath that her lips had parted. She wanted to say something, he knew, but she had to think it through first. This was going to be harder than he thought. He'd told her he wouldn't bother her anymore, but she wasn't about to give him the same distance, let him crawl off to some cave and lick his wounds. Not Annie. She wanted to help. She wanted in. So did he.

He abruptly let go of her hand and listened to her retreat to what sounded like a wooden chair scraping on the concrete.

"Ninety-degree turn to your left, three paces, and you'll find a chair to sit down on," she said in her businesslike manner.

Cliff found the chair and sat, legs out, crossed at the ankles. He wore khaki shorts and a navy blue polo shirt.

Downright formal for him, Annie thought wistfully, preparing her glazes. That was how it would have to be if she had any hope of teaching him things he didn't already know. But how did you teach someone to live again? How did you grade it?

If there was a grade for being aware of him as a man, she'd be valedictorian by now. She noted where his shirt sleeve ended and his biceps began, how the nubs of his nipples pressed against his shirt. Did it mean what it meant on a woman? Was it the same as the way her body reacted when she thought of his touch?

"So you don't just teach," he said, scratching aimlessly at his chin. "You sell these things?"

She took a deep breath and dispelled the images that looking at his body created. At least someone had the sense to make common conversation. "Pottery is my main source of income, although teaching is more regular. I work the art fair circuit in the summer, teach an adult education class at the community college in the winter, therapy classes year-round. Mornings I work in here, catching up on my inventory."

"Sounds very professional."

"Gotta earn enough to keep me in clay and paint." She tried to sound bright and nonchalant. It fell flat.

He wasn't smiling, he wasn't teasing, he wasn't flirting. He was remote. He was waiting for something, some sign from her. One she couldn't give.

Cliff listened to her puttering around a while longer. He wanted the wind to blow, more chimes to sound. There was something magical, something of her in them, saying things she was too cautious to say. Or so he'd like to think. "What are you doing?"

"I'm firing up the kiln."

"Anything I can do?"

She had to be honest. "Actually, not much right now."

You can say that again, he thought.

Annie was still talking. "This part is mostly visual. I'm doing a little handpainting and glazing while the others are fired."

She tried to work and watch him at the same time, the hair on his arms, the sturdy legs, the tapping foot betraying his restlessness.

The chimes rang, and he turned and listened. Kane lifted his nose to sniff the air but didn't move from his chosen spot on the cool concrete. They got through another few minutes.

"What are you doing now?" he asked.

"Putting this one in the kiln."

He heard the rumble and hiss of the heat. He'd never noticed heat had a sound before and the smell of it, dry and powdery, made his nostrils twitch and distend.

She closed the heavy door with a thud and set a timer to ticking.

"My eyes are fine," Cliff said, apropos of nothing. Maybe that was what she was wondering. Maybe it was holding her back. Fear of his appearance without the glasses might be a shallow reason, but it was understandably human, easily forgivable.

"They're milky-looking, so I've been told. They'll be normal again after the operation. Brown."

"Oh."

His jaw was tight, his fist clenched on his thigh. He scratched his beard until she thought it would rub off. She wanted to get these pieces finished before lunch, but he was feeling useless and she was spending half her time watching him. "Would you like to do something?"

"Such as?" His voice was soft, his face relaxing briefly, a flash of bittersweet smile.

Annie's stomach dipped. No, she hadn't meant that. She thought they'd come to some sort of agreement. So far he'd respected it, although it was costing him every minute he sat there. "I meant something useful. You look bored."

Bored? *Honey, I'm set, wired and ready to explode,* he thought wryly.

"How about lunch? You breezed through it so easily yesterday, I thought you could try it on your own today."

Cliff thought of a couple other things he'd been doing on his own lately. "Right. Lunch." He was up and out of his chair and through the door.

Annie sighed and combed her thick hair with her fingers. She never ceased to marvel at how he walked, betraying no hesitation about where he was going. Guts. Pride. When he knew his way, you'd never guess he was blind.

He found the garage's side door and slammed it, the kitchen door and slammed it, and now he was banging around in the pantry setting ingredients on the counter with a thud. All of it without a speck of assistance from her. As a teacher, she should have been proud of herself.

"Damn proud," she muttered, forcing herself to concentrate on one more pot.

Suddenly she realized Kane was standing, the hair on his back upright, body quivering.

"What is it, boy?"

Her eyes followed his. A chipmunk was standing in the woodpile, frozen in place. The animals were at a standoff.

"Now, Kane," Annie said soothingly, "you don't need a snack that size...." Rising from her bench, she approached cautiously. If she could get his collar before—

Too late. With a series of ferocious barks and madly waving tail, Kane gave chase. The chipmunk dashed through the woodpile, out the other side and was lost in a tiny flurry of dead leaves and downed twigs.

"Kane!"

There was a crash in the kitchen.

"Cliff!"

Annie raced to the kitchen to find a jar of pickles shattered, a can of tuna hanging from the can opener, Cliff holding a bleeding thumb, and the roll of paper towels unrolling across the counter and onto the floor, where at least ten sheets were soaking up the mess.

Cliff launched into a full-length, expletive-packed explanation ending with, *"And what's that blasted dog barking about?"*

"He's chasing a chipmunk!" she shouted back. "I'll bandage your thumb, then we'll go look for him."

"What do you mean we'll look? Is that some kind of sick joke?"

"He'll come when you call."

"If he did, he'd be a better trained dog. Let's go."

"I have to bandage this!"

"I'll live!"

Why were they both shouting at the tops of their lungs? Annie took a calming breath and held his hand under running water. "It doesn't look deep, but it's jagged. He sounds like he's getting closer."

"Maybe somebody will mistake him for a bear and put him out of my misery."

"That's not funny. He's a faithful friend, and if he goes a quarter mile farther, he'll be out to the main road."

"He doesn't have the brains God gave that chipmunk, and if he finds the road as often as he spots my house, we've got nothing to worry about."

They made it as far as the garage where Cliff stopped, asked how close the neighbors were, then let loose a string of curses Annie hadn't heard from him even in art class, each of which began with, "Kane, you worthless..." He then put two fingers in his mouth and whistled three short blasts. The barking stopped.

In a matter of minutes the dog came trotting through the underbrush, panting heavily, covered with burrs, and grinning to beat the band. He circled Cliff once, then sat at his feet. Cliff had only to reach down to pet him. "Your hunting luck must be as rotten as mine, pal."

Surprisingly the next three weeks went more smoothly. They settled into a routine of lunch, laundry and the housecleaning tasks Cliff would need to manage the basics—making beds, vacuuming, dishes. Although his progress was rapid, Annie didn't want to build too fast.

There were still things he refused to bow to. He walked way too fast, and Annie winced every time he banged a shin. When she removed the coffee table to another room, he insisted she put it back. All part of denial, his refusal to live within his limitations. Annie had yet to teach him that the most important lesson of all was accepting himself as he was.

When a rare free weekend came along at the end of August, Annie decided to put it to good use. She'd show Cliff that life, as is, was worth living. There could be fun as well as lessons. With certain reservations, he could do many of the things he used to.

Cliff packed the lunch and Dave drove them to the marina in Leland where Cliff's speedboat had been docked all summer.

"One small question," Annie asked after Dave had helped them both into the boat. "How do you start one of these things?"

Dave crouched on the dock above them. "Well, you see that key—"

The engine roared and bucked to life.

"Then there's the throttle...no there. Yeah, that. You pull back on that—"

The engine sputtered, choked and died. A thin film of gasoline leaked out into the water.

"You gotta pull back on it a little faster. Here—no, wait."

"Dave, stay out of the boat," Cliff ordered. "Let me handle that." Hands on her shoulders, Cliff firmly moved Annie aside and started the boat himself.

"Hey, great." Dave sunk his hands in his pockets and stood grinning. "You're teaching him a lot."

Cliff spoke before Annie could. "I didn't take you and your friends waterskiing for six summers without knowing how to start a damn boat."

"Now if you could work on his manners," Dave added.

"I'm afraid that's a lost cause." Annie laughed. "We ready to go?"

"Just don't let him back it out of the slip. The marina would have a fit."

"Cliff, how about if I steer—"

But Cliff wasn't about to relinquish the wheel. "Just tell me where to point it. Dave, cast off!"

Annie caught the rope and Dave's attention as the boat puttered away from the dock. He merely shrugged and rolled his eyes. A lot of help he was.

"Tell me when we hit open water." Cliff couldn't hide the beginnings of a grin.

"I won't have to tell you if we hit anything else. This has to be illegal."

"Who's to know I can't see? Everybody on this marina's wearing shades."

"True," she murmured between clenched teeth, standing beside him at the wheel. "Stay to the right here."

"Starboard."

"Aye-aye."

The idea had been to get him into the open air, to do some of the things he used to, to show him life didn't have to be reduced to staying in your house or walking down the beach just because you couldn't see.

Instead, she was in a speedboat being piloted by a blind man! She had to be crazy. Maybe that explained her laughter floating across the wind as they reached the marina opening and Cliff, after checking with her about incoming traffic, revved the engine to maximum speed and headed out into Lake Michigan.

"Wide open," he shouted, putting down the throttle and lifting his chin above the slanted windshield. The wind rustled his hair and whipped through Annie's. She grabbed a ribbon from her purse and tied her hair in an impromptu ponytail.

"How far are we going?" she shouted.

"How about Wisconsin?"

Her laughter ran up and down Cliff's libido, but the wind was great, the speed greater. God, he'd missed this, and he had Annie to thank. He pulled her to him for a quick hug.

Annie glanced up at him. With the wind in his hair, those shades and that scruffy beard, he looked like a cross between a *Miami Vice* cop and a pirate racing off with his treasure. For a sudden, piercing moment she wished that could be true.

"Maybe I should go sit in back," she said.

"Who's going to watch for innocent civilians?"

"There's no one for miles."

A full-blown smile broke through. "Just what I wanted to hear." He spun the wheel hard right, and she tumbled against his side, clamped there by a strong arm. "Oops," he lied.

But she stayed, one arm holding on to his waist. He knew she could feel the muscles there, expanding with his breathing, the pinery scent of his soap, which came to him on the same breeze that brought her perfume, the rasp of his shirt against hers as they bounced over the waves. For the moment he enjoyed nothing more than that.

Soon a sheen of cool spray lightly covered them. Cliff could feel the blue skies and deeper blue water in the noise, the roar and the splash. The aroma of gasoline grew fainter, the air fresher, and Annie's perfume— He dipped his head to see if he could smell it again. She stiffened, but she didn't say no. School was out. This whole day was a distraction, and he meant to make the most of it.

The boat cut across a series of waves, jarring them both.

"What was that?"

"The wake from a freighter."

He knew she was joking. The bouncing gave him an excuse to move his hand up and down her back.

She had on a loose cotton shirt, like a man's. His palm itched to find out how low it hung. Did it just cover her derriere? Did the tail end flutter around her thighs? His hand strayed as far south as his thoughts.

"Cliff." Annie tried to push off, splaying her fingers ineffectively against his knit shirt and the muscles beneath.

"What's wrong? There aren't any boats around."

"What if I told you that freighter is about to mow us down?"

He killed the throttle right there and the boat came to a rocking halt, her body once again balanced against his. "Then give me a last kiss."

What Annie had dismissed as vibrations from the boat didn't stop with the engines. She backed out of his arms. "Maybe we should have lunch instead."

He grinned and held his hands wide in a gesture of surrender.

Except for the waves slapping hollowly against the fiberglass hull, the day was still. She opened the cooler while Cliff took a bench seat along one side. Kneeling in the center of the boat, she tried not to notice the gap where his cutoffs ended, where she could follow the hair on his thighs so far up.

Who had she been kidding when she'd promised them a day to relax? She was miles into Lake Michigan with a virile, frustrated man. If she thought they'd be safe because they were out of the pressure cooker her house had become . . .

A glistening can of beer slipped through her hand and rolled across the floor.

Cliff followed the sound of the roll and found it. Coming back to his seat, his leg brushed her thigh.

"You're going to have to sit," Annie said. "There's no room for both of us down here."

She steadfastly ignored his quiet "Oh, yeah?" But her nerves didn't.

"Your sandwich," she said bluntly.

He recognized that tone. It meant he was getting out of line. Good. She'd noticed. He'd been in line entirely too long. He stuck his hand out for the sandwich. "I'll behave. Is this my beer?'' He raised the one he'd picked up.

''Sure.''

He popped the top.

''Yeow!'' Annie jumped at the shower of ice-cold beer. ''That's freezing!''

''Hope you like domestic,'' he said, laughing.

''You did that on purpose!''

''I didn't aim it, did I? Look, Annie, it's been bobbing all this way. It's bound to be shook up.''

Annie knew exactly how it felt.

''Want me to dry you off?'' he asked, leering.

''Only if you want to get snapped with a towel!''

''Getting kinky again, but I'm game. Oh-oh, I can hear that glare from here.'' He hefted the half-empty can to measure its contents. ''You must be soaked. Tell you what. Take your shirt off, rinse it in the lake, then spread it on the windshield to dry.''

His suggestion sounded so practical that she couldn't argue. Still, she made no move.

''If you take off yours, I'll take off mine,'' he offered, stripping with one quick overhead motion and ducking his head to prevent dislodging his glasses. Then he sat back, his arms stretched across the back of the seat, emphasizing his bare chest.

He had to be doing that on purpose, Annie thought.

''Amazing how hot it gets when you stop moving.'' He stretched his legs halfway across the boat.

His chest rose and fell. Some hairs were dark, some bleached against gold; he'd been lying out in the sun. She wondered where the tan ended and the tan line began. Maybe it was that vivid picture that made her feel downright wanton standing before him unbuttoning her shirt.

Fortunately the chilly water she rinsed it in got her mind off bodies for a moment. She stepped over Cliff's feet to get to the windshield to hang the shirt up. There was a pulse pounding slowly in his bicep. She could see it. Could he feel it?

He slouched further for maximum sun and patted the seat beside him. "Come eat your lunch."

The way her pulse skittered he might have said, "Come *meet* your lunch." Annie perched dutifully on the far edge of the seat.

He grinned and scratched his beard, and her heart fluttered like a landed fish. Funny that she should be having trouble breathing, what with all this fresh air. The vinyl seat made a squeaking noise as she squirmed.

"Tell me more about this ex-husband of yours."

She raised her eyebrows, but the look did him no good. Annie realized she'd have to respond to the question. "That's very specific, isn't it?"

He shrugged. " 'Tell me more about yourself' seemed too pat."

"Easier to answer."

"With pat answers." He downed the rest of his beer, frowning. Maybe he was going about this all wrong. It was so hard to gauge her reactions when he was literally in the dark.

The pause gave Annie an excuse to fumble in the cooler for another beer. "Be careful opening this one."

"Was it the wrong question?" he asked cautiously. "I'm sorry if I'm prying—"

"No, it's not that. It's painful."

"Not the great love of your life?"

"I've been in love before," she said, sitting beside him again. "I'm sure I will be again. It just gets a little harder each time."

"Scar tissue," he replied quietly.

She smiled in response to his gentle grin. He was very sensitive sometimes. It didn't gibe with the cavalier image he tried to project. "Have you been married?"

He shook his head. "I lived with a woman until I moved to the Upper Peninsula. It's remote up there, and she didn't want to move."

"That's too bad."

"She helped me pack the U-Haul."

"Nice of her."

The muscle in his jaw tensed and relaxed, covered by a beard that was filling in more densely every day. It looked like mink. Annie wanted to comb it with her fingers, running against the grain. She closed her hand around the beer can.

"I thought that one would work out," Cliff said, still lost in thought.

"That one? How many others?" she asked lightly.

He laughed out loud. "Hundreds! Very tactful, Annie."

"You do give the impression that there were dozens, at least."

"I do?" He would have looked at her then if he could have. At least those occasions when he played the flirt had worked. She knew he was capable. "Let me see if I can count them all...." Mouthing the numbers, he ticked off each finger, then crossed one ankle over his knee to count his toes.

Long, bony, masculine toes, Annie noticed, sprinkled with dark brown hair. He had a high arch, blue veins. She'd never thought of toes as particularly sexy. Which was why she was surprised to picture herself massaging that arch, washing those toes one by one.

Finishing with his other foot, Cliff grumbled, "I'm running out of digits."

Annie snorted. He was making fun of her. "You need a calculator for all your conquests?"

He leaned over to slip his Topsiders back on, and found her ankle. "Aha. The numbers above twenty." Sitting Indian style on the deck, he counted each of her toes, starting with the littlest, small and humpbacked. Then the next, the pad of his finger covering the pink-polished toenail, his thumb on the underside, making her toes involuntarily curl around it.

"That tickles."

"Shh. Don't make me lose count. I'll have to start over. This is Cissy, and this was Virginia, and this was Valencia..."

Annie was laughing so hard that she hiccuped. "That is *not* Valencia!"

"Funny, they kind of blur after a while."

He still hadn't answered her question—*how many others?* "You like women. I get the point."

"Nothing else like them," he replied lightly. His fingers found the bones radiating from her toes to her ankle. He wasn't surprised he could circle that ankle with one hand. "That doesn't mean I'm the playboy you think I am."

If he wasn't, he'd certainly learned somewhere. She'd heard of feeling something down to your toes, but what happened when it started there?

"Sure, I was kind of wild in college," he continued, massaging her Achilles tendon, working his way up her calf. "I'd been housemother to Dave for so many years, I was ready to break out. Girls were fun. They looked after me for a change. But when Linda wouldn't come North with me, maybe it was the scar tissue thing." His hand stopped. "I settled down and stopped looking for a while."

"Completely?"

He shrugged, running his hand through his hair. "I always assumed I'd get around to meeting someone." Then the accident happened. What if the next twenty years were as empty as the past three had been?

Cliff sat up straight. He'd wasted enough time. "What do you think of me, Annie?"

He waited for her reply, listening with every nerve in his body. Annie suddenly wished they could go back to the playfulness of a moment ago. Instead she got up and went to the front of the boat. "You know I don't think it's a good idea, getting involved now."

"No?" He grinned, or tried to. There was a furrow between his brows that showed he was taking her answer very seriously.

"I want to help you."

"You have."

She could see that it wasn't what he wanted to hear. "I think getting involved would interfere with that."

He walked toward her, cautiously for once, feeling for the break in the breeze where her body was. "And if I learn my lessons like a good boy?"

He was angry. He didn't want to win her by behaving. Rewards for performance. An apple for the teacher. He wanted real life, getting close to someone who understood him. That meant Annie. She put up with him, excited him, and although she kept denying it, she responded every time he came near.

He moved in closer, blocking her body against the captain's chair. Let her deny this.

"Cliff, this could ruin everything we've built."

"We could have more." He pulled her to him, legs to legs, waist to waist, her breasts against his chest. He might be six inches taller, but every inch of them matched.

"Don't," she pleaded in that breathy voice.

"Did you know you make me feel like the sexiest man on earth when you do that?"

She trembled. The desire between them was hard and pronounced. The boat swayed as if they were dancing.

"I'm a man, Annie. Treat me like one."

She didn't want to. The student she could handle; the man made her weak and dizzy and ready for anything. She struggled.

"Afraid of me?" he whispered.

"No."

His voice dropped with his hands. "Is it because I'm not a threat?"

"No."

"Do you have another lover?"

"No."

"A sensual woman like you with no one? Maybe you're using up all your caring on people who can't return it. Students you won't let get close—"

"I'm not afraid." But her tongue felt papery and dry until his head dipped, came closer, and their lips met.

She'd seen that coming, even tilted her head for him. Why did it shock her? Like lightning finding a lightning rod. Her hands were limp at her sides, but her mouth was his to plunder. He probed, she took. He sucked, she gave. A moan escaped but got no further than his mouth.

He spread his hand on her naked waist until his little finger touched her bikini bottom, his thumb the top half. He traced the lower edge of her breast and found a bow between them. He tugged. It didn't untie.

That's when his mouth released hers, his voice harsh. "What color?"

"Blue."

"Look good on you?" He put his hand on her bare skin again. It quivered. So did he.

"Yes," she said.

His mouth was inches from hers. "Say that again?"

She cleared her throat, anticipating, hoping. "Yes."

"That's what I thought you said."

His mouth covered hers, slowly. He didn't want to think about how long it had been, how many times he'd imagined what he couldn't have. Her lips were moist but closed. He didn't need them to open right away, not this time. Now while there were a hundred other things he could feel—her breasts in the Lycra suit, full and heavy, just touching his chest. Did they press over the top of it? His hands would have to find out. That too could wait.

There were still her knees to feel, brushing his legs, her thighs, smooth, ruffling the hair on his as he spread them to draw her closer. She hesitated.

"I want the bare skin between here." He touched her bikini bottom. "And here." He touched the top. "Pressed here." He rubbed her hands across the rippled muscles of his abdomen and stretched them around his back. That brought her hips in contact with his. "I want you to feel everything you're doing to me."

Not as obvious but just as potent was what he was doing to her. She felt milky, melting, rolling inside like the waves. Her knees were weak, or was it the motion of the boat? "Cliff this is going too fast."

"Do you know what I want?"

She didn't dare say.

"Put your tongue in my mouth."

Five

Annie couldn't breathe. Her eyes opened and his face was there, dark, brazen. Her eyes closed and she couldn't escape. Tumbling, falling sensations she couldn't deny. She let him fill her with his tongue.

Never had she felt so surrounded, speared. His beard scratched her chin, too long to be stubble, too thick to be soft. It was like a camel hair brush, stiff from one angle, erotic and silky from another. He brushed her cheek with it, her neck, the cleft between her breasts.

His lips tugged the bow on her bikini. She felt that tug to her toes and back again. He was holding her, he was hard, was there anything happening that she hadn't wished for these past three weeks? Was there any reason they couldn't just keep going, ignoring who they were, what she was to him? She wanted to show him life could still be lived. But what price would she pay for that lesson? Although her mind fought it, her body had long since surrendered.

Cliff felt her growing hunger. She stroked his chest with the flat of her palm, one hand tangled in his hair, tearing a ragged groan from him.

Her body, voluptuous and warm, sidled against his in a shimmy he didn't have to see to appreciate. He felt it the length of his manhood. He heard it as he tugged one breast free of her bikini, handling it like precious gold, kissing it, rasping it with his tongue, vainly trying to fill his mouth with it.

There was something in her he needed desperately. She believed in him, as he was, saw him at his weakest and didn't turn away. For her sake he wanted to be as good as he'd ever been, confident, strong, sure. He reached around her back, fumbling with the bikini's catch.

"Let me," she said.

"I can get it," he replied hoarsely. He didn't. The catch eluded him again. He cursed to fill the silence.

"It's okay, Cliff." She reached behind her, but he was already stepping back.

"Never mind."

In the cool air suddenly separating them, Annie watched him walk back to his seat. She covered her breasts with her arms, swallowing the taste of him still on her tongue. "Talk to me," she said, louder than necessary. "Don't hide behind those glasses."

He shook his head roughly. What was he feeling guilty for? If he couldn't see the hurt in her eyes, how did he recognize the hurt in her voice? He cursed. They couldn't build any kind of relationship on this. She'd been telling him that all along. Why hadn't he listened?

"I could say you owe me an explanation," she said, her voice steadier.

"What do you want from me, Annie? Some high school kid fumbling his way through an idiotic parody of lovemaking? I haven't been this clumsy since I was seventeen."

"It's always awkward the first time. People need to learn each other."

"Very wise," he answered with a laugh. "When they can see, maybe. We both deserve better. I'm sorry I got out of line."

The sea gulls overhead mocked and cawed.

Annie rearranged her bikini and plucked her shirt off the windshield. It was almost dry. For some reason she wanted to wrap as many layers around her as she could. They were flimsy armor; the hurt had already been done.

Speckles of sweat on her neck cooled in the breeze. Or was that moisture from his kiss? She shivered and buttoned one button at a time, refusing to let her hands shake.

"This was a kind of first for you," she said. "I'm sorry. I should have been more sensitive to that."

"For Christ's sake, don't apologize!" he exploded. "I'm a man, Annie. I won't be less."

"I don't want less."

He hadn't meant to hurt her. He'd been up and down and angry as hell the past month. "How you put up with me, I'll never know."

The boat bobbed. The gulls circled. Annie watched the triangle of a sail float between them and shore.

"Maybe we shouldn't go any farther with this," she said, not at all sure that was what she wanted. She *didn't* want him humiliated.

"I thought you wanted me to do everything I used to."

"And how often did you used to?" Annie joked.

Luckily he took it as one. "You caught Dave's reference to the Party Barge, eh?"

"Is that what this was used for?"

"If you only knew." Knew he'd been damn near celibate for the past three years, for starters. He thought he'd have all the time in the world for the right woman to come along. And what if she had, at precisely the wrong time?

He found Annie with an outstretched arm and tugged her toward him. He stroked her cheek, his head tilted as he listened. "Tell me what you look like?"

"Again?"

"All I've got is your hair." He ran his hand across it, found a comb and touched it with his fingertips. "I want the shape of your face. Your eyes. Your skin."

Annie braced herself for another onslaught of sensation. Knowing that his senses were so acute made her keenly aware of every part he touched.

He outlined her face with both palms, measuring her cheekbones with his hands, her lips with his fingers, her nose, short and straight. The texture of her skin. Curved brows.

"Smile," he commanded softly, and felt her cheeks lift, the lines beside her eyes, the wide mouth. Her chin was round, her jaw subtle, her throat smooth. As were her shoulders, the warm skin at the base of her neck.

He didn't know the smile was gone, replaced by doubt. "You feel beautiful."

"I'm not."

"Says who?"

"You are," she said, changing the subject. "Beautiful, I mean."

He shook his head.

"Handsome then. You work at it." She couldn't prevent her hands from outlining the muscles on his arms. "It shows."

"Is that a compliment or a judgment?" Hands resting on her shoulders, he felt her shrug.

"A man who's careful of his appearance wants a woman with similar interests. I've never been that concerned with looks."

"It's what's inside that counts, right?"

"Yes. Not everyone thinks that."

"If I'm good-looking, I must be as shallow as your ex. Is that it?"

Annie pursed her lips for a minute, then looked back up at him. All she saw was her reflection. "This is where I'm supposed to say touché, right? It's a kind of pride, Cliff, wanting to be the best you can. But it's not a perfect world."

"And I have to accept me as I am."

"You want to be perfect."

"Not perfect, just me again. I know you've seen the bad side. There is another side of me. I wish I could show you."

Running his hand slowly down her body and back, he showed her a world of sensual intent. "Can't you feel what that does to me?" His hand closed on the outside of her thigh, his thumb tracing the high-cut leg of the bikini from the outside in, finding the narrow triangle of fabric, the curled hair.

Annie gasped. "Please."

Once again he was left guessing. "What does that mean?"

"It means I'm not ready for this. Neither of us are."

A flash of doubt, maybe anger, moved across his face like a fast-moving cloud over the sun. He didn't know, couldn't see what she wanted. She let him get close, then— Words weren't enough. What he needed was a good cold shower. "Do you think there are rocks in this water?"

It took her a moment to realize he was speaking literally. "Out here? Maybe thirty feet down."

"Good."

Cliff reached up and removed his glasses, calmly setting them on the seat. Then he placed one foot on the side of the boat, and in an arcing move, dived over.

"Cliff!" Annie screamed but couldn't stop him. He came up fifteen feet away, shaking the water out of his hair and keeping his eyes clamped shut. "What are you doing? Get back here!"

"I need the exercise!" he shouted. "And to tell you the truth, I need the cold water! Stay there."

She had no intention of moving. "Cliff," she said reprovingly, "nobody warned me you were self-destructive."

"I'm an excellent swimmer. There are no rocks, no sharks, and no boats for miles. I plan to work like hell for the next fifteen minutes. If I get too far, yell. Like you did just now," he murmured, smiling faintly. She might not want him, but she wasn't too keen on losing him, either.

Then he was off, doing a butterfly stroke that was exhausting to watch. Annie counted off the minutes on the dashboard clock, keeping one eye on the orange life jackets stuffed beside the engine compartment and one on Cliff's back, diving in the bright blue water.

She wanted to toss one of those life jackets at his head. "If he doesn't drown, I'm going to kill him," she muttered to herself.

By the time he'd followed her voice back and was grasping the ladder, Annie had reconsidered. He was obviously an accomplished swimmer, and the reasons he'd given her were sound and well thought out. About the only thing she could fault him for was the old wives' tale about not swimming after eating.

"A towel and a beer," she said, handing him one, then the other.

"Glasses, please?"

She handed him those and tried not to watch the water droplets glistening on his body as he perched on the edge of the boat in his clinging cutoffs. That spurt of exercise should have cooled them both off.

Cliff was grinning and breathing hard. "I didn't drown, did I?"

If he thought she was going to stand there and swallow his "I told you so," he could think again. With a cocky strut, she headed toward the front of the boat. "I've been telling you for three weeks you could do anything you used to."

Cliff lowered the beer in midgulp.

"Want to get this bucket started again, Captain? I've got packing to do for tomorrow's fair."

He headed toward the front, neatly sidestepping the cooler. "Keys in it?" he asked.

"Ready when you are."

From the sound of her voice he knew she was facing away. Figuring the width of the boat, and the length of the towel, Cliff wound it up, took aim and snapped his wrist.

Annie shrieked.

Cliff chuckled, imagining the part of her anatomy she was clutching. For once he'd gotten in the last word, not counting the unladylike expletive Annie tossed his way.

"Do you want to sell this?" As they crouched on either side of a packing crate, Annie held out one of the pots

Cliff had made. Another week had passed. He was help-ing her get ready for the first September art fair.

"Are you kidding? Sell *my* stuff? That's misrepresen-tation. It's your booth."

"This has your name on it. You marked it here."

"Defaced it, you mean. It's just a pot."

"I like it. It's sturdy, masculine. The whorling on the sides has your touch."

He reached out and she placed the bowl in his hand. Their fingers met and skimmed briefly, then his hand curled over hers, trapping it against the rim.

"You're flirting again," she said in a breathier voice than she would have liked.

"No, I'm not." They'd agreed, silently perhaps, to keep their distance. They were too naked, too needy, too vulnerable, each in his own way, to get into a deeper re-lationship. It was true on the boat; it was true now.

Annie tried to bring them back to pottery. It was con-crete, three-dimensional, easily set aside. "I'd buy your work. It has style."

He broke into a grin that sent her pulse scurrying for cover. His fingers followed that pulse up her wrist.

"Are you saying I have a distinctive touch?"

There was no point denying the effect he had on her. Through sense and touch, he saw through her defenses. "Cliff, I thought we agreed—"

"We did?" He ignored her words, concentrating on that elusive beat beneath the flesh of her arm. Soft and pale—at least that was how it felt. How would it taste? Would her thighs match it for softness?

Annie jerked her hand away and the bowl crashed to the floor. Cliff only smiled. "A priceless work of art ru-ined. What a shame."

"I'm sorry. That was really stupid. Let me get the broom."

He stopped her by touching her arm. "You ought to pay me for that."

"How?" His grin was easily interpreted. "On second thought, don't answer."

"You won't even guess?"

"Look, can we not crouch next to this crate like this? My thighs are killing me."

"You don't know what they're doing to me." His hand ran down the cotton of her slacks, taut over her flesh, warm toward the inside. She closed her legs but that only trapped him there. They sprang apart; he took it as a license to go farther.

Her voice was a soft threat in the dimness surrounding him, breathy, intense. "Don't."

"Why not?"

"I'll say yes." Her admission shocked them both. They'd reached a turning point neither was prepared for. "But if you reject me one more time, Cliff Sullivan, I swear..."

"I seem to be in the uncomfortable position of put up or shut up."

She sighed. "I didn't mean it that way."

"Close enough."

Cliff sat back on the concrete floor of the studio and ruffled his beard. Blind, sighted, what the hell difference did it make? But when it came right down to doing something about it, he wasn't ready.

That didn't mean he didn't ache for it.

"You're not the only one with doubts, you know," Annie said.

"Don't make up any on my account."

"I wonder sometimes whether you'd want me if you could see, or will when you can again."

"What do you think I'm waiting for? I don't relish making a fool of myself chasing after you when I can't do anything about it."

Annie spoke carefully, subduing her optimism about his operation with the caution her heart required. "You can't predict how you'll feel then. We should wait and—"

"And see. Ha."

They returned to packing the pottery in excelsior, Cliff ruefully congratulating himself on the growing acuteness of his hearing. He was getting good with voices. Like Dave's when his brother humored him. Or Annie's when she sensed he needed encouragement, or a hard-nosed knock at self-pity. And yet he wasn't really sure how she felt about him. If anything did develop between them, he had to be. He couldn't guess about something this important.

"That's the last crate." Annie slipped her hands into the loose pockets of her cotton slacks and played with her car keys. There was one more step Cliff needed to take, perhaps the biggest of all. "Why don't you come along?"

Cliff stopped scratching his beard. "To the art fair? And do what, look at the paintings?"

She wasn't sure she was helping or hindering him in the personal relations department, but at least he could joke about his handicap now.

"I admit it won't be a thrilling afternoon. I let the customers look without hassling them. But it'd be nice to have someone else along."

He took his time answering. Doubt from Cliff was rare. He was more likely to give her a flat no. "You wouldn't want me there."

"I asked, didn't I?"

"And this mountain man look? I haven't shaved in over four weeks. My hair's getting downright shaggy. I look like a throwback to the sixties."

"So do half the people at art fairs." That elicited a chuckle from him. "If you don't like the beard, shave it off."

"And cut my throat?"

"There are electric razors."

"Not to handle this forest. It'd have to be trimmed first."

"We'll stop at a barbershop on the way."

Cliff considered. Maybe the drive to the fair would be the perfect chance to talk to Annie, really talk.

On second thought, he should have cut his throat.

They drove in silence up I-75, an hour passing before they could mention the fiasco at the barbershop.

"Are you going to say anything?" Annie's voice was as tight as her hands on the steering wheel, or the outline of Cliff's jaw.

Even beneath the beard.

"So the barbershop didn't work out," she continued heatedly. "So yell. Blame me, blame him, just don't sit there like a mummy!"

Cliff replied with a unique, very foul expletive, then turned to look stonily out the window. Seeing nothing, he pictured it all. The barbershop, the mirrors, people sitting and waiting. And watching. Him being led in by Annie. He hated being led, so he took her hand as they came through the door. The curious would see no more than a couple holding hands.

They sat. He didn't look at the magazines, didn't check the end of season box scores in yesterday's paper. He listened to the humming razors and the ball game on what sounded like a radio old enough to have tubes. Cliff responded when the barber said "Sir" for the fourth time.

Or rather, Annie did. "Honey?" She leaned over and nuzzled his ear. "Forty-five-degree angle to your left, six paces." The woman was marvelous.

Cliff walked tall, knowing the barber would have the chair facing him. That's when he bumped into the part he forgot. The footrest. Smacking it with his shin, he tripped and grabbed the armrest for support. With all his weight unexpectedly thrown forward, the chair spun.

"Excuse me, sir," the solicitous older man said. "Are you all right?"

"Sorry." Cliff rubbed his shin and tried to get into the chair. He had the armrest firmly in his grip now. Problem was, it was the wrong armrest. His butt almost ended up in the hair clippings.

"Is he all right?" the barber had asked.

"Yes," Annie said, rushing over. Letting Cliff break a leg for the sake of pretending was pointless. "He's blind."

"Oh."

Cliff felt all eyes on him. How many? How many voices had he counted in the room before he'd gone into this slapstick routine? How many mirrors replaying it from how many angles?

"Come on!" He grabbed Annie's arm and headed out. This time he was leading. Somehow they made it to the street. "Where's the goddamn truck?"

Riding in silence now, having earned no replies to her outburst, Annie had had enough. "I'm a teacher," she began quietly, getting a better grip on the wheel, "not a miracle worker. If you would learn to take things a little slower, to ask for help, to walk slower instead of full speed ahead as if nothing's wrong..."

She hit the turn signal and it ticked steadily. The engine whined as she downshifted on the exit ramp. "Cliff, I'm sorry about what happened. But I am not going to handle all this guilt on my own."

"Guilt?" He blew. Annie was ready for it. "Why should you feel guilty?"

"Because I dragged you into something you weren't ready for."

"I've been going to barbers since my first haircut. Don't give me that—" He let loose with another series of curses to describe exactly what he thought of her analysis. "I should have known there'd be a footrest."

"Don't blame it on yourself."

"Look, my life is not your fault!"

"Agreed!"

"All right!"

"We're here!"

"Good!"

"Now can we stop screaming at each other like some kind of married couple?"

Annie parked and jumped out. This was as ridiculous as the disaster at the barbershop. Of course it was her fault. She'd gotten him in too deep too fast. She knew Cliff wouldn't slow down; she had to pace things for him. She'd have to find another way to counteract this setback.

Maybe her best alternative was right before her. "Will you help me set up for the fair, please?"

Cliff clenched and unclenched his fist. He couldn't very well sit here and sulk, like Kane, who had been left behind. His shin throbbed, sunlight streamed through the windshield, and the draft of air coming in her opened door was brisk and smelled of cider and the first sharp days of autumn. Maybe he could show her he wasn't totally helpless. God knows, he needed a dose of confidence right now. "What do I do?"

Annie breathed a sigh of relief. "That's what we're going to find out."

The fair went as smoothly as the barbershop had gone badly. The awning went up without a hitch. Annie held her breath every time Cliff insisted on pounding in the stakes, but he managed. The shelves were readily assembled on tables provided by the local Lions Club. Annie and Cliff covered them with cloth, unpacked her wares and sat back in mismatched director's chairs.

Making conversation, Annie shared the lowdown on the local art world. Chimes tinkled along the edges of their awning.

"Excuse me," a woman interrupted. "I have a niece in Tennessee. Would it be safe to ship her these? They'd make a lovely wedding gift."

"Thank you," Annie replied, rising. "Cliff, would you please get me one of the smaller crates while I write this up?"

"Sure."

He ventured two strides behind the awning, felt among the crates and gingerly stepped back inside. Annie kept the conversation going so he'd know where both women stood. He handed her a crate and sat down.

So the day went. Errand boy. Trained but not very useful. Questions directed at him by customers were deflected, "Sorry, she's the artist." He was feeling good and sorry for himself and he knew it.

Racking her brain for things he could help with, Annie kept an eye on the lines furrowing his forehead. That's when she noticed the woman coming around the back of the awning toward him. Fortyish, well groomed, impeccably blond.

"Excuse me," the woman said.

Cliff barely turned his head. It sounded to him as if Annie would be busy for the rest of the day.

The woman touched his arm. He jumped.

Her tinkling laughter sounded through the awning, leaving Annie hard-pressed to explain what was so immediately irritating about it.

"I'm so sorry," the woman said to Cliff in a honeyed voice. "You were lost in thought."

"I'm sorry myself," he said, nodding politely.

Annie itched to get over there, but she was quoting prices to a local couple and customers were browsing three deep at the other table. Even out of the corner of her eye she couldn't miss the blatant way the woman raked Cliff's body with her eyes. Small consolation to Annie that he didn't catch it.

"I was wondering if you could show me some of your bigger pieces," the woman said.

"I'll bet," Annie muttered under her breath. Blind or not, this woman was sending out signals a two-by-four would pick up.

Cliff showed her to the first display table, turning on that slow smile of his. Annie's blood became a curdled stream.

Exclaiming over every piece Cliff touched, Blondie put her hand on his arm and wrapped herself around it like a vine.

Completing a sale, Annie pulled the charge plate handle across the card so hard that it grated. She snapped it back with a satisfying thwack.

"Oh, I *love* that." The woman ran her hands over a pot. "I've watched potters at work, you know, the way they use their hands. Will you be having a demonstration today?''

"Not today," Cliff replied.

Annie's mouth dropped open.

"I do think it's one of the more sensual arts, don't you?"

Cliff scratched his beard. "Now that you mention it, I've been told I have a good touch."

The woman grinned like a barracuda. "I hope you don't mind my getting personal, but I've always loved men in beards."

Probably always loved men in pants, Annie thought blackly.

That's when Cliff rubbed his knuckles against his beard and ducked his head in a patented James Dean move.

That bastard! He'd used that move on her. What was worse, it had worked then, too. If Annie hadn't been holding up a four-gallon urn to show the price tag, she'd have thrown it at Cliff Sullivan's head.

"What would you suggest?" the woman asked, eyeing the pieces once more. "It's for my bedroom."

"Of course it is," Annie practically shouted, but the cozy couple was too engrossed to notice.

"How about this?" Cliff asked.

Oh, no. Annie held her breath. He'd accidentally picked up the same pot he'd put down moments before.

"Aha!" The woman's laugh was tinkling and false. "Artistic and humorous, too. What other qualities does the man possess?"

"I can think of one that would surprise you," Annie remarked, coming up beside them.

Squeezing between the two to set the pot back down, she wasn't above physically disengaging Blondie's hand from Cliff's arm. Better than breaking it off at the wrist, she reasoned. "I'm Annie Rosetti and this is my work." She might as well have said "my man." "I'd be happy to show you anything *else* you're interested in."

"That's quite all right," the woman responded frostily. "I like to discover them on my own."

Cliff smiled and nodded, seeing nothing. That he'd missed Blondie's meaningful look as she departed was the only thing that gave Annie any satisfaction. As her next four customers came and went, she was fuming like a chimney stack.

"I suppose you thought that was funny," she said.

Cliff put his arm out like a railroad crossing barrier to stop her charging past. She'd been avoiding him while sending out sparks for the past fifteen minutes.

She batted his hand down. "You enjoy misleading women?"

"Are we talking about her or you?"

Annie shot him a look, then ground her teeth at the uselessness of it. "She thought you could see."

"Harmless fun," he said, shrugging.

"Harmless?"

"Why shouldn't I respond to a woman who admires me? All's fair—"

"In love. This was just . . . just lust!"

"Were you worried I'd actually go off with her?"

"She doesn't even know you."

"Doesn't know about my eyes you mean."

"You! Anything about you!"

"The woman I want keeps turning me down."

Annie crossed her arms. "And so she should if you treat her like this."

"Like what? Ever since the boat you've been keeping away from me. You never let me touch you!"

"Shh. There are people around." In fact, two of them turned their heads as they passed the little argument in stall 51.

Explaining as tersely as he could, Cliff said, "I can't sit here and do nothing. I was feeling useless."

Annie heard only the excuses he was making. He was everything she'd taught herself to avoid. Gorgeous, vain; if a woman pawed and babied and praised him enough, he'd respond. Just like Ken. "Let's just stick to business for the rest of the day. Can you do that?"

"Please, I need to drive."

His arm was stretched across the back seat and he was playing with her hair. Again. His fingertips managed to brush her neck just often enough to make the hairs rise.

"I need to know where I stand with you, Annie."

"Out in left field, or haven't you figured that out?"

She was still fuming. He'd given her enough time to simmer down. "I'm tired of playing student. I want more."

"From anyone who will give it to you?"

Her head was pounding from hours of wanting to scream instead of smiling and waiting on people. Never had she wanted more to be alone.

In wrinkled cotton slacks and a silk T-shirt, she didn't feel the least bit sexy right now, no matter how his fingers strummed those traitorous raised hairs. If he had seen her these past few weeks in her Indian cottons and loose men's shirts, smocks and coveralls spattered with clay, he'd know she couldn't possibly compete with that woman at the fair. *Any* of those women, pushing baby strollers, holding hands with their husbands, picking out wedding gifts.

Cliff hadn't been able to compare. Someday he would.

"We've got to talk."

"We've got to talk," Cliff agreed.

Annie sighed. "We really do. About us. This can't go on the way it has."

"Hear, hear." He traced the shell of her ear until she thought she'd scream or run off the road.

"Annie?"

"What?"

"We have to talk about when we're going to make love."

Six

Annie ground the gears as she downshifted. The screech could have been her nerves. "Don't start."

"Give me one good reason."

"There's no future in it."

He sat back stiffly. He hadn't expected her to be quite so blunt. "You don't think the operation will work?"

"I do. That's why I'm being honest. You'll see I'm not your type. Take my word for it." It tore her a little inside, like a seam coming apart, but it was better to say it now. All her daydreams about their going to art fairs together, talking, joking and sharing, would never come true.

"You think I'm looking for a 'type'?"

"You're good-looking," she hedged. "Women flock to you."

"Not lately." He meant the past three years.

Annie thought of the past few weeks. "Thanks a lot."

NO COST! NO OBLIGATION TO BUY NO PURCHASE NECESSARY!

PLAY "LUCKY 7"
AND GET AS MANY AS SIX FREE GIFTS . .

HOW TO PLAY:

1. With a coin, carefully scratch off the silver box at the right. This makes you eligible to receive one or more free books, and possibly other gifts, depending on what is revealed beneath the scratch-off area.

2. You'll receive brand-new Silhouette Desire® novels. When you return this card, we'll send you the books and gifts you qualify for *absolutely free!*

3. Unless you tell us otherwise, every month we'll send you 6 additional novels to read and enjoy. If you decide to keep them, you'll pay only $2.24* per book—that's 26¢ less per book than the cover price! And $2.24 per book is all you pay! There is *no* charge for shipping and handling. There are no hidden extras.

4. When you subscribe to Silhouette Reader Service™, we'll also send you additional free gifts from time to time, as well as our newsletter.

5. You must be completely satisfied. You may cancel at any time simply by writing "cancel" on your statement or returning a shipment of books to us at our cost.

You'll love your elegant bracelet watch—this classic LCD Quartz Watch is a perfect expression of your style and good taste—and it is yours FREE as an added thanks for giving our Reader Service a try.

   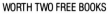
DETACH AND MAIL CARD TODAY

DETACH AND MAIL CARD TODAY

BUSINESS REPLY CARD

FIRST CLASS MAIL   PERMIT NO. 717   BUFFALO, NY

Postage will be paid by addressee

**SILHOUETTE BOOKS
901 FUHRMANN BLVD
PO BOX 1867
BUFFALO NY 14240-9952**

NO POSTAGE
NECESSARY
IF MAILED
IN THE
UNITED STATES

"I didn't mean it that way. You're different." No woman had gotten as close to him as she had. At times it was nearly impossible not to blurt out his frustrations. But he wouldn't burden her with that. He'd already put her through dark moods, bad days, outbursts of temper. She'd stuck by him through all of it. Was she turning him away now?

He listened to her silence and the hum of the tires. They were slowing down. He caught the difference between her short asphalt drive and his gravel one.

"We're here," she said.

His place.

"This is your idea of talking?"

"Cliff, I don't know what you mean when you say I'm different. It's you who's changed, and that's only temporary. When your eyes heal, you'll go back to the mines and the Upper Peninsula. Maybe the women, too."

The sound of crickets and waves rose around them when she cut the engine.

He cursed softly. "I know you have this idea I'm some kind of wolf. It's half my fault. I wanted you to see me as I was, no, *better* than I was. I wanted you to want me."

"I did."

He tried to detect false sincerity, but Annie was never false. Her admission hung in the air. "Then why won't you let me near you?"

She touched his lips with her fingertips. It was late, dark. Without the instrument lights she could barely make out his profile. "I want you too much. That's what I'm afraid of. That I won't want to let go."

"You think you're the only one who's afraid?"

Sitting here talking quietly, Annie knew she'd wanted this with him, the intimacy, the honesty. Aching for him to reach out in some way, not as a student but as a man.

But she'd seen his barriers come and go before. How long would the closeness last?

For now she didn't care. She'd take it as it came. She touched her lips to his and felt his arms going around her waist, pulling her across the seat to him.

She was trembling. That was fine with him. Damn fine, in fact. When he leaned back, she stretched a little farther, her breasts pressed against his chest. She steadied herself by bracing her hand against his thigh. That was fine with him, too.

He tore his mouth from hers. One more thing needed to be said. "I was an insecure jerk today. I don't usually go after women like that. I mean it. Apology accepted?"

"Mmm-hmm." It was all she could answer with him nibbling her lip. She wondered if they'd steam up the windows. The way he was playing with the inside of her elbow made her whole arm shimmy. When he rasped the silk of her T-shirt against the nub of her breast, the arm gave way.

"Ever made love in the front seat of a truck?" he whispered.

Body to body, his mouth against her ear, Annie was having trouble formulating a sentence. Dimly she knew her answer was no. Either way it was only a matter of minutes before that changed to yes. Whatever her doubts had been, they were lost in the swirl of his thumb teasing her collarbone, the silk of her shirt, the satiny underside of his tongue.

A brilliant yellow light pierced her eyes.

"Oh, it's you," Dave called from the porch, briefly blocking the light with his body as he sauntered toward them.

Annie scrambled upright, knocking her knee against the stick shift on the floor.

"So he *is* here," Dave said, grinning. He directed an explanation toward his brother. "Heard the truck and thought maybe you were out here fumbling around in the dark."

"Hardly," Cliff growled. With Annie off him, he pulled himself into a sitting position and got out of the truck. "Point me in the right direction," he muttered. "I'll strangle him."

"Uh, see you later," Dave said, waving as he backed up slowly. "Hey, here's someone who wants to see you!" With that he let the dog out of the house and ducked inside. "Night, Annie!"

In two bounding leaps Kane heaved himself onto Cliff, yipping excitedly enough to send the chipmunks scurrying into their burrows for a hundred yards around.

"Down, damn it!" He might just as well command his body to do the same, Cliff thought grimly, grabbing the dog by the collar and following the woodslat walkway to the pen.

"You keep him out all night?" Annie asked, strolling behind at an amused distance.

Cliff found the chain and hooked Kane up. "Can't keep him in on a night like this."

It *was* a beautiful night, Annie realized. The slosh of tiny stones being washed in the waves, the warm and humid Indian summer breeze rolling in over the water. There was a nip in the air—just enough to spell night.

"I'm here," she said, holding out her hand.

Cliff found it, and they stood side by side as Kane whimpered and panted from his pen.

"There's a moon, almost full. I can see it reflected in your glasses." Annie talked softly. She liked the night, and someone to share it with. "The stars are out. The porch light is on."

"My soon-to-be-ex-brother's addition to the house."

"No-o-o," she chided. "Maybe he thought you were being attacked by a temporarily insane woman in the cab of her truck."

"He's going back to school next week."

"Is he?"

In the quiet and dark, with only their hands touching, their thoughts followed the same path. It was Cliff who spoke. "We won't be interrupted again, Annie."

She suddenly felt hollow, like a vase or a just-fired urn. Some things stood alone; some were only waiting to be filled.

"Cliff," she began, although she had no idea what she wanted or how to say it.

Cliff knew exactly what he wanted, and it sure as hell wasn't temporary. In fact, this first step would take some planning on his part. He released her hand and headed up the path. "Will you come by tomorrow?"

Although her courage had deserted her, Annie found her voice as she stood rooted at the end of the path. It was a night for truth. "I—I wasn't planning on it. I believe our lessons are finished."

There it was. She'd taught him what she could, and in the process had gone way beyond lessons. Her surge of jealousy this afternoon only proved what she'd been feeling for weeks. She loved him. If he didn't return those feelings, better to set him free now.

"School's out," she said lightly, knowing his hearing was keen and her heart heavy. "You've learned everything I can teach you."

Not everything, Cliff thought, not by a long shot. Lessons had never been what he was after. At first he'd wanted a woman to convince him he was still a man. Petty, maybe, but he'd needed that and he'd gone after it. In return, what she'd taught him ran deeper than can openers or clay pots. He heard it every time she spoke; she accepted him as he was—she might even love him. She just wasn't admitting it yet.

Uh-uh, Annie Rosetti, you're wrong about school. The lesson plans he had in mind involved feelings, not pottery. Perhaps he'd start with a session on trust. After his blundering today, they could both use that. And some one-on-one tutorials regarding men, women and their ancient but thoroughly modern modes of interaction. He could think of half a dozen modes right now.

What had she said that first day of class? *Anything you create will be beautiful.* They had thousands of memories to create. And tomorrow wasn't too soon to start.

"I've learned all about your house," Cliff said casually, hands in pockets. "What about my dryer, my dishwasher? All the appliances are different here. How will I run them when Dave's gone?"

Annie stood openmouthed. She felt as if she'd just been slapped by a particularly cold wave. *Was that all he wanted her for? Lessons?* Okay, maybe she'd asked for this by insisting on the teacher and pupil arrangement until the bitter end, but up until a moment ago she could have sworn he felt differently.

Just shows you what a woman can fall for when she thinks with her hormones instead of her brain. "Classes," she said flatly.

Cliff heard the tension in her voice from the back porch. He fought a grin and lost. "Eight in the morning sound okay, teach?"

"What happened to ten o'clock?"

Her voice got sharp when she was peeved. Very sharp.

"I'll make breakfast," he offered, rocking back on his heels and jingling some spare change. "Under your supervision, of course."

"Of course," Annie ground out. So he wanted his free lessons to continue. No more talk of making love, not even a good-night kiss. She'd remember that in the morning.

"Morning, teach." Cliff smiled and slid the beachside door open.

She'd come over feeling decidedly snappish. One look at Cliff and her heart lurched. He was wearing a cutoff T-shirt that emphasized the ripples of his abdomen, cutoff jeans and those ratty Topsiders. She wanted to ask him if that was all he ever wore but decided it'd be safer not to call attention to it. He smelled like soap and looked like he'd gotten out of the shower not long before. His hair was getting so long that Annie suspected it would still be damp. Of course, the only way to test that theory would be to run her hands through it.

She buried her fists in the pockets of her peasant skirt and stepped through the door, using her knees to prevent Kane from squeezing out. "Hi, beast."

The door closed with an airtight whoosh. Annie smelled after-shave. The man didn't shave. That meant he'd dabbed on cologne. For her sake. Under the anger, something began to tingle.

Vigorously she cleared her throat. "Where's Dave?"

"You're not going to ask what that wonderful aroma is?"

She'd already speculated on the wonderful aroma.

"I've got sausage in the skillet and omelet-makings ready to go. We were just waiting for you."

"Smells great." If that was sausage, it was the only kind in existence that smelled like musky male cologne.

She followed him into the kitchen, plastering a smile on her face as they rounded the doorway. The table was empty.

Two place settings.

No Dave.

"I thought you said '*we* were waiting'?"

Kane trotted into the room on cue. "Sure," Cliff said, scratching the dog's ears.

Annie scraped out the nearest chair and plopped down. "How about if I watch my star pupil make breakfast?" The sensation of being out maneuvered finally hit home. No doubt he'd be as competent in his own kitchen as he was in hers. So why the invitation? Her nerve endings went on red alert.

"Anything you say, teach." Cliff patted the counter for the tub of butter, wondering how he knew through sense alone that she was sitting there with her lips pursed, arms folded and legs crossed. Maybe tension communicated itself in waves of some kind.

A pat of melting butter hissed in the pan. Cliff poured in the eggs. "Aren't you curious about the makings of a legendary Sullivan Omelet?"

Annie squared her shoulders and decided she was being silly. She was a grown woman, free to call the shots here, free to say no to anything she felt was getting out of hand. Although, judging from the way her nerves sizzled, if he touched her she might melt like that pat of butter.

She clutched the countertop, a good three feet from him. "Secret ingredients?"

"Old family recipe." He pulled a short knife out of the silverware drawer and proceeded to dice a green pepper.

Watching the deftness with which he handled the knife, Annie held her breath.

"Voilà!" he said, scooping a handful off the cutting board.

Annie's breath came out in a rush.

"Wait'll you see me flip these omelets."

"Wait'll you see me scrape them off the floor!"

At that he laughed. So did she. The tension eased out of her like that rush of breath. She *liked* him. If she could keep her hormones in check, they might even come out of this friends. "You've been practicing."

"Always known how. Meet Cliff Sullivan, Bachelor Chef."

And perfect host, Annie admitted. She ceased hovering and let him finish preparing the meal while she set out plates and poured coffee. By the time they were through eating, Annie was scolding herself for being so untrusting. He'd shown her another side of himself, not glowering but not wolfish, either.

"My compliments to the chef."

"*Merci.*"

She patted her stomach. "I could get used to eating breakfasts like that."

"Most important meal of the day. Better when you have someone to share it with, though."

How right he was, she thought wistfully. That could apply to a lot of things. "Cliff..."

He hopped up. "You wash, I'll dry?"

She swallowed her argument for now, almost relieved. Just his being near made her emotions a muddle. "I thought you had a dishwasher."

"Okay then. You rinse, I'll load."

Five minutes later Cliff excused himself. Soft music wafted in from the living room. Soothing. Romantic. Not rock and roll. If she wanted coffee, she'd have to join him in there. Too late, she remembered the red alert.

"Exactly where is Dave?" She was antsy and ready to get to work. Sitting beside him in this intimate setting, even at nine in the morning, was asking for trouble.

But he remained resolutely sociable. With one foot on the coffee table, he unself-consciously slouched back to scratch Kane's ears.

Annie noticed the washboard effect of his abdomen between the cropped T-shirt and the shorts. She suspected it was there to be noticed.

"Dave got himself a part-time job down at the marina," Cliff said, making conversation. "'Tis the season for taking boats out of the water. Said you were keeping me so busy, he had to find some way to entertain himself."

"Oh?"

"Some*one*, I bet. There's no end of pretty girls down there."

"Is that where your reputation got started?"

He gritted his teeth and let the emotion slide. He had a lot of bridge building to do.

"Dave thinks you're a regular Don Juan."

"Dave's got an outdated opinion of me." And so do you, Cliff thought, his face dark. "It applied in college. I've grown some since then."

"I know you have." Annie sighed apologetically. An accident like the one he'd been through would change anyone. But would he go back to his old ways when the blindness was cured?

Cliff was quiet, the music soothing, the couch fluffy and soft. Annie rearranged her big skirt so that she could curl her legs under her.

Cliff reached out quickly. "Where are you going?"

His nervousness caught her by surprise. She wasn't the only one waiting for something to happen. "Just getting situated," she said. If he wasn't ready for a lesson, perhaps talking would ease things. If sharing and closeness were what she wanted, maybe it was time she asked for it. "Will you tell me about the explosion?"

Cliff thought a moment. "You, a handful of inspectors from the Bureau of Mines, OSHA, the Department of Alcohol, Tobacco and Firearms. Who else wants to know?"

"Tobacco and Firearms?"

"They regulate blasting, along with half a dozen government agencies. Accidents like this aren't supposed to happen. Faulty blasting cap, they think. They ran me and the company through a—a cartload of questions before they came to that conclusion. Was I on drugs? Was the mine operating under unsafe working conditions? Were the blasting caps stored improperly?"

"None of which was true?"

"Not a'tall, lassie, not a'tall."

"Ah." She watched him absentmindedly scratch his beard.

"Luckily no one else was hurt," he said. "All I remember is grabbing my eyes. Hurt like hell. Worst part was not knowing how bad it would be. When they told me about cornea transplants, it was like a reprieve from death row."

Annie squeezed his hand. "I can imagine."

His mouth was grim, caught up in his memories, but his hand on hers was getting warm. When their fingers entwined, she knew she shouldn't have touched him. She wanted to be his lover; she just didn't think she could stand him changing his mind afterward.

"Maybe we should wait until you see me, get your job back, get back to your regular life...."

"Maybe we should," he responded. She was still hesitating. Maybe she was right. He cared too much about her to tie her down to his disability. When he was better—hell, when he was himself again he could imagine how great it would be for them. He was better than this, smarter, quicker, less clumsy. That was what he wanted most of all, for the real Cliff Sullivan to meet the real Annie Rosetti.

"Maybe you could do me a favor," he said, disengaging his hand. "Get me the scissors, please?"

"Scissors?"

He rubbed his beard as if it were hairy sandpaper. "I want you to trim this damn thing so I can cut it."

Annie rolled her eyes. Caught off balance again. "Where are they?"

For the next ten minutes they were busy. Annie filled a bowl with steaming water, found towels, lather and soap, while Cliff fetched the razor off the bathroom sink.

Spreading newspapers beneath a kitchen chair, Annie announced they were ready. Cliff sat. She glanced at his thighs, muscular and large, at the way the cutoff T-shirt ended so far short of his belt loops. She hadn't been so close to him all morning. She snapped open a towel and wrapped it around his shoulders. "Okay, Samson, here we go."

"Not the hair."

"I can't do the hair."

"Just the beard."

"Just the beard."

The music softly surrounded them, along with the snip-snip of scissors. With one hand Annie bent the hair of his beard back so that it would stand out from his skin.

With her other hand she carefully trimmed it down to a prickly stubble. Before long she was engrossed in the feel of it against her fingers—bouncy, stiff, springy.

Her breath fell lightly on the side of his neck just below his ear. Cliff turned.

"Don't. I'll poke you."

"Sorry."

She worked around his ear. Glancing up, she realized she could see behind his glasses. He had smile lines; she'd noticed, but not how deeply etched. She'd never seen the dark lashes resting on his cheeks when his eyes were closed. They opened. She saw the milkiness, immediately overcome with guilt. It was something she knew he wouldn't want her to see.

"How much of these sideburns do you want to lose?" she asked.

"An inch maybe. Here." He indicated a spot with his finger, hoping he could keep it steady.

Maybe this wasn't such a good idea. He'd planned a quiet morning alone, without games, to show her he was trustworthy, that he was more than a Lothario. That was lesson number one. He hadn't planned on her driving him wild with her touch. Sometimes her blouse or her breasts brushed his arm. When she worked her way around the front, he spread his knees and she hesitantly stepped inside.

He crumpled a towel across his lap, trying to think calming thoughts, but her hands kept doing those impossibly erotic things to his beard, and her breath kept winnowing through his hair like wind through a field.

His shaving brush clacked against its ceramic cup as Annie whipped up the lather. "Ready?"

"As I'll ever be," he answered, mouth dry.

Annie knocked the lather off the brush. Shave and a haircut, two bits. Chuckling, she smoothed it on, dabbing his nose with a towel when she put a dollop there by mistake. "Now where's the razor?"

"Here." He put his hand on a flat leather box.

"You can't be serious!" Annie stared at the silver straight razor gleaming against velvet. "You could kill people with this thing."

"Now you know what I mean about cutting my throat. An electric razor would choke on a beard this thick."

"But I don't know how..."

"I trust you." He leaned his head back and bared his throat. Lesson number two.

Annie swallowed. He couldn't be this relaxed. After touching him, smelling him, feeling the warmth and power of his body for the past fifteen minutes, she was almost shaking. Her hands certainly were. "You're either brave, crazy or both."

"You work with your hands," he said confidently.

"Clay doesn't bleed."

She put one finger under his chin and got in position to scrape. That meant standing behind him, his head cushioned against her breasts.

"Mmmm," he said.

"Don't grin. Don't move. Don't even breathe. If I cut your throat, I swear I'll kill you."

He chuckled, and she felt the cords in his throat rumble. This was sheer hell. A sneaky feeling of remorse said she owed him after suggesting they visit the barbershop yesterday. That didn't make it any easier. In fact, the physical risk made her all the more aware of his skin, his smell, the cologne intensified by the damp towel draped over his shoulders.

One scrape and Annie was back to business. Concentrating intensely, she came around the side. One hand held the razor at an angle, her arm circling the back of his head. The other hand tipped his chin. She wiped the razor, and silver gleamed. The smooth patches of skin grew larger. She touched them with her fingertip to stretch the skin for the next pass.

Then she reached the front and stepped between his legs. That should have been the easy part. He pulled down his upper lip, bit his lower lip and contorted his cheek to one side so that she could shave around his mouth.

The funny faces didn't register. All she felt was him reaching out to pull her closer. Her own cropped top left her midriff as bare as his. He found it.

A dollop of lather fell from the razor onto his jeans. Rushing to wipe it off, she touched the fullness behind his zipper. "Uh, sorry."

Suddenly the tension was as thick as the razor was thin and sharp.

"The music," she said, her voice husky, her throat tight, "It's stopped."

"Okay," was all he said, his hands falling to his thighs.

She walked over to the stereo and turned the record over with trembling hands. This just wouldn't do. Half his face was bare now; he was a man she wasn't sure she recognized. That should be a warning. He kept so much to himself. How much did she really know?

Unfortunately one thing was certain—she couldn't leave him half-shaved. Only two more passes along his right cheek and she'd be finished. "Ready?"

Can't you tell? he thought.

Annie stood on his left to reach around and shave the right side, tipping his head against her. Once again she was engrossed, her face inches from his hair. Yes, it was still damp.

Her breasts were warm, the silk of her shirt, well, silky. Cliff knew all he had to do was look up and he'd be inches from her lips— "Ouch."

She jumped. "You shouldn't have turned like that!"

"My fault. I know." He wiped his face clean with the towel.

Annie peered at the small cut. "Guess you'll live."

Cliff touched her cheek with his hand. It wasn't hard to find her lips from here. Full, moist and coffee-warmed. Her lips paused, then parted. His tongue probed, then he waited. When the kiss was over, she said nothing. "Aren't you going to argue?"

Again nothing. Her fingertips stroked his cheek. In a way the beard had softened him. Now the planes of his cheeks were sharper, indelibly defined. The lines around his mouth were clearer. She ran her hand up his cheek to his glasses.

"Leave them on," he said. He could only bare so much; he didn't want her seeing that.

She knew if she wanted him she'd have to accept him as he was—no promises, no excuses, some things kept to himself.

And let the hearts fall where they may. That's what love was. It wasn't conditional; it didn't wait for operations or guarantees. It was suddenly important that she let him know that.

She ran her hands over his face, unable to stop touching his skin, pink from the hot water. "There's something about kissing a man in sunglasses. It's very erotic."

He turned and kissed her palm. "It's sexy in the dark."

"Cliff."

"Shh. Let me kiss you, touch you. I can't gaze into your eyes. This is all I have." He found the opening under her blouse and ran his hands over her love-tight breasts. From there he wrapped his arms around her and coaxed her onto his lap. "Are you going to stop me, Annie?"

"Are you going to make love to me?"

"Yes."

"No."

Their mouths met, explored, luxuriated. It could have lasted for hours; Annie wouldn't have known. The only change was the progress of his hand tracing up her thigh. "I'm too heavy," she said, feeling self-conscious, feeling what this was doing to him.

"Let me say that," he mumbled against her neck. "When I'm on top."

The sound of her moan made him ache, especially when she pressed against his arousal. Her thigh became warm as his hand moved along it.

She shifted. His fingers found lace. "Panties?"

She nodded weakly as his finger outlined the opening. His hands were everywhere, and no matter how she ran hers through his hair or down his clean-shaven face, she couldn't stop thinking about them, feeling them through silk lace until it felt like he was seducing her soul.

The chair was hard and small. If he tipped her back any farther in his arms, they'd fall. There were things he wanted to do that couldn't be done sitting up. Like stretching her out and examining every recumbent inch.

Her lips were wet and hot against his, as moist as the lips his fingers parted under the damp silk between her legs.

She let out a muffled cry.

"Don't stop me now, Annie."

"No...I...maybe we should go upstairs."

Cliff tried to picture a bed, with Annie looking up at him. What if he fumbled, made mistakes? "We could turn off the lights."

"It's morning," she reminded him gently.

"Damn daylight saving time."

She chuckled, burningly aware of his fingers touching her, leaving a trail of honey down her thigh.

"I wanted to make love to you in the dark. We'd be equal then."

She wrapped her arms around his neck. He couldn't withdraw into his doubts now; she wouldn't let him. So much of his self-esteem depended on how he felt about her and them together. "I'll close my eyes," she whispered. "I just want to feel you. Inside."

Seven

He wanted her, but he was going to lead this time. They stood, Cliff reaching behind her knees. "I'm going to carry you to my cave, woman." He waited for her protest.

She nodded, letting her nose skim his cheek so that he sensed it. He needed to show her he could do this. Besides, she doubted her trembling legs would hold her up much longer.

He knew where the stairs were. A short command to Kane stopped the dog at the foot of them. Cliff found the loft, then the bed, and set Annie down. He found the skin at her waist, his thumbs hooking into the waistband of her skirt. "Is this a button?"

She touched his arm in an up-and-down motion and heard the button ping across the room.

Hands trembling, she lifted her blouse over her head. When he found her hands covering her breasts, he tilted his head quizzically.

"I feel so naked around you. You see so much with your hands. I don't know how to hide."

"Do you want to?"

"Not anymore."

He drew his own shirt over his head, flinging it where he'd probably never find it. He brought her hands to his sides, their bodies meeting above the waist, tingling and bare.

Cliff dipped his mouth to her collarbone, tracing the lightest of perfumes, catching the scented powder under her arms, heating to musk. Tangy, sweet. As sweet as her own mouth murmuring his name.

He slowly unfastened the button on his cutoffs, drawing down the zipper but leaving them on. First he had to pull her close, the small circling motion of his hips rubbing denim against silk panties. The sound made them both hot.

"That's hearing. What about taste, Annie? What do you want me to—"

She had only to open her mouth and he was there, sliding her back onto the bed, holding her head in place while he thrust with his tongue and she took.

She was wrong about his sensing everything. He couldn't see what was in her eyes. If he made a fool of himself, he'd never see the pity there. That made him all the more determined there would be none. Only desire, the way he showed her how to stroke him, and excitement in her small gasp when he licked, then bit. His whole body was pumped. The need to make love, now, overrode any anxiety.

He found her with his hand, and entered. "Lord, you feel good," he breathed. "Tight."

She murmured something nonverbal; it didn't matter. He heard her hair whispering against the pillow as her head swayed back and forth, sensations rocketing through her.

"Don't stop," she pleaded.

She must be looking at him, intense, imploring. Damn.

"What is it? Don't stop."

"I feel like I'm on a stage, performing for an audience who can see me, but I can't see them."

She stroked his hair.

He flinched. "Don't."

"Maybe I'm not exciting enough to keep your mind off your doubts."

"Exciting? Lady, you're what got me here in the first place. If I could give you back even half of what you've given me ... You've stood by me. God knows I haven't earned it. I've given you one hard time after another."

"Love isn't a matter of earning. It's either given or it's not. If someone doesn't love you, it doesn't matter how many points you try to rack up. You'll never please them."

Cliff lay back on the bed, one arm thrown over his eyes, his body stretched and taut, his desire heavy.

Love. Is that what she'd been giving him all along? Probably, and he'd been too self-centered to realize it. But did he have the guts to return that kind of feeling? Especially in the condition he was in, this limbo between seeing and not seeing?

"What are you thinking?"

He didn't answer. He was thinking he wanted her to be in love, because that would make two of them.

"Mind if I just look?" she asked after a moment's quiet, resting her hand lightly on his chest.

He laughed, or rather smiled that primitively male smile. "At least I have a couple good points."

"Shall I count the ways? There's this," she said, stroking the ridge of his abdominal muscle. "This." She brushed the lateral muscle that ran from his back around to his hip.

He quivered at the lightly tickling touch.

"This," she continued, running her fingers up his thigh. "And this. Is this a muscle?"

Every muscle in his body was rigid by now, particularly the one she was touching.

He cleared his throat. Twice.

She touched her lips to his chest, one kiss for each nipple and one in between. "Your eyes have nothing to do with your being a man, Cliff. Not to me."

When he finally spoke, his voice was as tight as the self-control reining him in. "This I don't need to be taught, Annie."

"I wouldn't dream of it."

"What do you dream of?"

She touched his cheek. "Making love with you."

Cliff grabbed her arms, part anger, part naked need. "If that's the case, don't touch me with kid gloves anymore."

"All right." She kissed him then, hard, open, one leg across his. She had never done anything as wanton in her life; if Cliff minded, he didn't show it.

In fact, she was under him so fast it took her a moment to get her bearings. That fast he was on her, spreading her legs and uttering her name as if it were some dark magic spell. Then he was in her, a quick, blunt thrust.

Cliff caught his breath, startled by her cry. What the hell was he doing? "Are you all right?"

"I'm fine," she replied, stunned and breathless. "Please."

She rubbed her cheek on his like a cat, her body trembling like a woman. He groaned and slid in and out on honey. Long, slow. Her skin shimmered beneath his like a heat wave. And he heard his voice whispering words to which she responded, with motion and sound, unleashing something in him, something it took two to quench.

Their bodies were solid, matched, physical. His was heavy. The hair on his legs grazed hers until they wrapped around him. Running her foot down the back of his leg, she found a bony ankle. Even that was sensitive.

But nothing like the part of her he found with his thumb. "Do you like that?"

What a question, she thought, laughter rumbling up inside her.

Cliff gritted his teeth; he almost lost it right there. "Don't do that. It makes you quiver. Here." He put the flat of his hand on her abdomen, pressing softly. She moaned and clenched around him.

How masochistic could a man get? He was practically exploding. He tried to distract himself, to hold on.

"Right down here," he murmured, stroking her softly, listening to her pleasure. "Where babies come from."

He lifted himself off her slowly, completely. "I don't know if we can go any farther with this."

"What's wrong? What did you say?"

"We've got to think of what might happen."

"Let it." She couldn't keep the flash of anger out of her voice. Her skin was flushed, her body clamoring for release. But her heart, when he left her like this, was gallingly empty.

"I'm talking about birth control," he said. "We forgot that."

Annie flopped back on the bed. Cliff heard her soft curse. "You don't have any... ?" she asked.

"They're hard enough to put on when I can see."

"Oh."

His jaw was tight, more obvious now with the shave, Annie noticed. She knew he was right. And thoughtful. And she'd almost gotten carried away into what, emotional risks aside, could have been a major mistake. "Do you like children?"

"I hadn't planned on having any quite so soon."

She chuckled and stopped abruptly. Even the memory of him inside her made her blood pound. "That's not what I was getting at."

"Making polite conversation?" He was the frustrated one now. Boy, he was blowing this. Why hadn't he thought ahead? "Maybe Dave has some in the medicine cabinet. He ought to. I've lectured him on it enough."

He got up and strode to the bathroom with that unhesitating walk. Annie lay back and simply admired the walk, the way his muscles moved. "Cute buns," she whispered to herself. She rested her cheek on her bent arm and laughed softly. Good thing someone was thinking here.

Cliff was banging around in the medicine cabinet.

"Find what you're looking for?" she called after a moment.

He cursed as a variety of items came crashing down into the sink. "I can't find them."

Annie came in.

Having heard the noises downstairs, Kane loped into the small bathroom, pushing Annie and Cliff closer together.

"Go lie down!"

"I hope you're talking to the dog," Annie murmured wryly.

Kane wandered into the other room and, sighing, took up his usual position at the foot of the bed.

Cliff shook his head, fighting back a smile. What was supposed to be a sizzling morning in bed, more importantly their first, was turning into a nightmare. "I wonder if this is what they call bedroom farce," he grumbled.

He felt Annie closing in behind him, her arms wrapped around his waist, her body conforming to his. The shock, the intimacy of skin against skin, warmed him all over, reminding him they were far from finished.

She felt his buns tighten and grinned. Running her hands up his chest, she watched his nipples peak in the mirror. "You're sexy naked."

"God, I hope so," he said. That elicited a laugh. He held up a foil packet. "Is this what I think it is? I'd hate to be putting on a premoistened towelette."

Annie laughed so hard that her breasts shook against his back.

Cliff stood up straighter. "Do that again."

Their smiles faded as she rubbed slowly against him. "They're so tender they hurt," she said.

"Anything I can do?"

"Kiss them and make them better?"

He handed her the packet over his shoulder. "Ladies first."

She tore it open. Reaching around, her hands did the work, smoothing, fitting, admiring. By the time she finished, he didn't think just kissing would make anything feel better.

"Does that feel right?" she asked.

"I can think of better things to be inside."

Annie pressed her cheek to his back and glimpsed the rumpled bed. They were ready; no turning back now. Maybe fear and uncertainty would always be a part of it, part of the feelings he awoke in her, too strong to be contained any longer.

He turned in her arms, sensing her hesitation. "I don't expect you to say you love me."

"But—"

"Don't say it because it's expected. We're both adults."

Annie promised herself he'd never know how much that hurt. "You haven't even asked and already you know how I feel."

He caressed her cheek. "Just don't decide now. There are things I can do, but I can't be the man I was. Not yet. Until then I can't make you any promises."

"I don't expect any. But they wouldn't change how I feel."

"I wanted to hold off. However," he said, rubbing his belly against hers, "you make that very difficult."

She wanted to argue. Even with her bones melting and her stomach hollow, she wanted to tell him how much he meant to her. She loved him, the anger, the courage, the doubts. But it was a love he wasn't prepared to accept, a love she knew he'd refuse to believe.

"How I feel about you won't change, Cliff." She touched him, there, tracing the tight curls near his manhood. "Let me show you."

She led him toward the bed, but when the tussling was over, he was on top. Stronger, rougher than she'd expected, more demanding and more exhilarating. There were no concessions to his lack of sight now. The movements he made were elemental, primitive, learned before time. The way he reacted when she moved against him, the way he took her breath away.

"Cliff?" A kitten's mew, a woman's insatiable plea. "Keep your hand there. I like the way that feels."

Smells setting off depth charges of desire all their own made him shake down the length of his bow-tight muscles.

And sounds. Her breath catching in the back of her throat, a tattered moan. Those sounds had him coming unglued. Grasping her head with both hands, he kissed her once, softly, and thrust all the way.

He listened and felt. It was like the first time—everything he should have known years ago, the way a woman's body moved, with, against, around, the irresistible places of ecstasy. For a moment he felt awkward. For the first time in weeks he felt in control. For the first time in a lifetime he wasn't alone.

She wrapped her arms around his back. "Come down here and kiss me."

He answered her throaty command. "Then I couldn't do this," he reminded her with his thumb and a slow circle of his hips.

Another gasp. "No, yes, you can do that anytime."

"And would you react like this?" Again, and again she clutched him, arching.

He coiled her hair through his fingers and gently forced her head back to the pillow. She stiffened, unused to any show of force. "Do you like that?" he asked.

She nodded, and he felt her uncertainty, her excitement.

"It's all part of trust. Trust me. Let it go. This is for you."

She believed him, clinging to that as the rush began to build. She was calling his name, bucking, rippling, crying out. Endlessly, mindlessly. And he was with her all the way, in their dark, giving her something he knew no seeing man ever had.

A few minutes, a lifetime... The ripples subsided and she clung to him. He lifted part of his weight off her, leaning on one arm, locked and rigid.

He was shiny with sweat, his head bowed, his hair tousled and damp on his temples. For a second she loved those spikes of dark hair more than she'd loved anything. She wanted to kiss them, comb them, lick them.

She only had to lift her head to kiss his cheek. So she did.

He was breathing heavily, wrung out. And yet with each subsiding tremor inside her, she felt him stiffen, respond, still hard.

"Thank you," she whispered in the shell of his ear.

It was his turn to shudder.

She'd never given herself that completely—no inhibitions, no self-consciousness, nothing but love. Maybe it had something to do with not being watched. Maybe it was how badly she wanted to show him what he meant to her. Sharing was everything. If only she could tell him how free she felt, how totally and absolutely free to love. But his continued silence, his reluctance to resume until he too finished, worried her. "I didn't embarrass you, did I?"

Cliff knew he hadn't finished; he didn't have to. There had been a minute he'd almost given over to it, but he'd held back. Her ecstasy was more important. Now she thought he should be embarrassed. "You mean, because I didn't reach climax?"

"No," she said quickly. "I was kind of wild."

"You were fantastic. I didn't want to," he said, answering his own question. A moment's silence. He laughed hoarsely. "To tell you the truth, I forgot."

"You what?"

"I've never felt a woman do the things you just did. Never paid as much attention, to be honest." Stretching his body the length of hers, he rested against her legs as she drew them together. "I was so wrapped up in you. Are you always that great?"

Only with you, she wanted to answer, touching his hand where it rested on her breast. Somehow her throat was too full with emotions she couldn't express. Had he really paid more attention to her than to himself? That certainly wasn't the sign of the conceited man she'd once feared he was.

He ran his hand down her body, wanting to "see" it, reclining, supine and satisfied. Her skin felt flushed, rosy. He'd done something just for her, and yet she'd done so much for him, opening a whole world of sensation. He wanted to explore every nuance.

"I won't be blind forever," he said.

"I know." Something about that thought nagged at the edges of her contentment. All this could change. But for now his hands were roaming her body unfettered, a garden of sensation.

"It never felt that intense when I could see."

"No?"

Of course, he suspected that had as much to do with how he felt about her as it did with the blindness. But he couldn't tell her that right now.

"Maybe this is my body's way of compensating for lack of sight. Makes it almost worthwhile."

She laughed, and he paused just to feel it. Then he headed toward the bathroom.

Annie watched him walk. "Maybe you'll believe me now when I say you're pretty good just the way you are."

"Another lesson?"

"There are lessons in everything." She trotted after him, wanting to touch him, be near him. "Even if you stayed blind, as long as you accepted yourself, it wouldn't matter." Not to her.

"You know damn well it matters!"

Annie stood in the bathroom doorway, stunned at his outburst.

"Are you trying to tell me something? Have the doctors told you? Is the operation off?"

"No, I—"

"Is it off? Tell me!" He grabbed her arms, not caring if it hurt. He would not be this way forever!

Kane's growl rumbled in the other room. Horseplay was one thing, but even he knew real anger.

Cliff abruptly let her go, turning away. But where could he hide? He wasn't even sure which way he was facing.

"I didn't mean it that way, Cliff."

"You must think I'm a coward, or worse, coming unhinged like that. I don't want to be this way."

She touched him lightly. "You're the bravest man I know."

"Then why am I so scared?"

In the harsh antiseptic light he looked so isolated, so hopeless. But she was there. She reached for him. It didn't solve everything, didn't prevent fear from coiling in her stomach. Making love hadn't broken down every barrier. The way he shut her out was nearly unbearable now that they'd been so close.

Slowly she wrapped her arms around him. "You don't have to be alone," she said. Body to body, she comforted him, as intimate as a man and woman could be. He'd let her inside his deepest fear and she'd blithely told him everything would work out. She cursed herself briefly, but holding Cliff was more important. "I'm sorry I was so callous."

He shook his head but said nothing.

Fear. Intimacy. Sharing. It was part of risking and part of love. You could be hurt most by the things you valued most, the things you let inside. She'd let him in in every way, until everything he felt mattered to her. As for her own doubts and fears, the future would have to wait.

"Will you come back tonight?"

They were standing at the back door. An hour had passed, taken up with getting dressed, talking softly, doing laundry and the sheets from his bed. Emotionally it had been a rocky morning. Cliff knew Annie had a class at two o'clock, but he was reluctant to let her go.

"You could take a shower here, you know."

"I know," she said. "I should have an hour ago when we . . . I will at home."

He reached out and she stepped into his arms.

"I'll be back at six."

"Dave'll be here. We'll have dinner and try to keep our hands off each other."

She hugged him close and tried to land a peck on his cheek. The kiss he caught her with instead had her legs turning rubbery, her bones melting at an alarming rate. "Don't do that tonight," she said, catching her breath, "or we'll have an audience."

"Maybe I'll send him back to the marina," Cliff growled, listening to her steps retreat in the sand.

She should have thought about it during the day. Somehow she made sure she didn't have time. Between showering and dressing, class came and went so swiftly that she was standing at the back door to Cliff and Dave's cottage before she had a chance to really think about what had happened this morning, how their relationship might change.

As it was, in the seconds between ringing the bell and waiting for the door to open, a dozen thoughts and emotions tumbled through her mind.

She loved him—that she knew. He hadn't told her how he felt, but that would come. Judging from his actions this morning, his tenderness and passion, he had to feel something for her. But unless he said so, it remained a closely guarded wish.

And the future?

What would he do when he got his sight back?

What if he didn't? Would he blame her? She who was so quick to say it didn't matter. She cursed once. She'd meant it wouldn't change her feelings for him if he remained blind. Instead she'd come across as a Pollyanna, unsympathetic to his pain.

Sometimes she had such a strong belief in his good qualities that she forgot to have respect for his limitations. He, however, was all too keenly aware of them. She'd have to remember that.

Eight

The door opened.

"Hiya, teach! Come on in."

Dave waved Annie through with a grin and a curious look.

Annie didn't have to look for Cliff; Dave was motioning her toward the living room.

"He's looking at the mail," Dave said, "or holding on to it. Surprised me when I got it out of the box this afternoon. He usually pounces on it the minute the mailman's truck leaves."

Annie stood in the doorway to the living room. Butterflies had taken possession of her stomach; now they took possession of her voice.

Cliff was standing there, hair combed, neatly dressed. She was surprised all over again to see his clean-shaven face, although she'd memorized it, run her palms over it for what had seemed like hours this morning.

If he noticed her, he didn't let on. He was skimming his thumb back and forth over the corner of an envelope. Annie's skin knew exactly what that felt like. She took a deep breath. From here she could just make out the raised black logo. What did it mean?

For the time being she was more concerned with the simple things in life, like how to say hello to a man six hours after making love with him.

She swallowed. "Hello, Cliff."

He started and turned, the tension in his face obvious. There were deep lines around his mouth, lines that hadn't been so noticeable under the beard. The smooth, bare skin brought out the resemblance to Dave and made him look younger, but no less worried.

"Annie." He said her name as if it had been years. Then he took a deep breath of his own, consciously relaxing. The world was right again. He held out one arm and she went to him.

Put off by Cliff's distracted demeanor, self-conscious with Dave there, Annie tried to feel welcome.

Cliff kissed her forehead and rested his cheek there. When he spoke, it was low and meant only for her. "How you doing, honey?"

"Fine."

"No second thoughts?" He squeezed her to his side but never let go of the envelope. "Where's your mouth," he said, momentarily playful.

Annie lifted her face to his. His kiss was warm, slow and deep.

Dave cleared his throat and made sure his presence in the kitchen was known. Way back in the kitchen, by the cupboards and the rattling pots and pans.

"No," Annie said, smiling. "No second thoughts." That she'd ever had doubts was hard to believe. That she'd spent the afternoon alternately worrying and avoiding the future, was irrelevant now. She felt dizzy and half-pulled off her feet. Cliff's iron grip was making sure of that. But it was more. The way he smelled, the way he felt, the body she'd known this morning was beside her again. "And you? Any second thoughts?"

Just that I love you, he almost said. The smile faded. "None. Until this came along." He dropped his arm from around her shoulders.

Annie felt her stomach constrict. "What is it?" She bit her tongue. Obviously he couldn't have read it. "Has Dave seen it?"

"I wouldn't let him open it. I wanted you to be here." He picked up a letter opener, found an opening in the flap and sliced through the envelope so quickly that Annie winced. Then he handed her the contents.

The sound of rustling paper brought Dave, with Kane trailing briskly behind. "What's it say?"

It was from the university hospital, Annie realized, the one that conducted cornea transplants. Her hands shook as she scanned it. She handed it to Dave and sank down on the couch. "I can't—"

Dave started right in. "'Corneas have become ready for implantation... Please check in by three o'clock, Thursday, September twelfth, at the University Medical Center on Carter Road... The operation should take place sometime on the morning of September thirteenth.' That's Friday the thirteenth," he interjected.

Annie groaned. Cliff stood rock-still, listening with his entire body, his jaw clenched so tightly that Annie could count the pulse beats in the vein there.

Dave continued, "'Your doctor has been contacted for all pertinent records and confirms that you are prepared to undergo the transplant procedure... Please call the number below to confirm your arrival...'"

The air was rent with an earsplitting "Yahoo! You're gonna do it, bro!" Dave grabbed Cliff and the men hugged and slapped each other's backs until Annie thought they'd hurt themselves. Dave was unashamedly crying between shouts and laughter.

Annie was crying, too. Everything was happening so fast. Cliff would see again in a matter of days. It was wonderful; she was overjoyed. But it was all too soon. Their relationship was too new. They hadn't had time to even talk about it. If lovemaking could change a relationship irrevocably, what effect would Cliff's regaining his sight have?

"Where is she?" Cliff asked.

"Come on," Dave said.

Annie wiped the tears from her cheeks and laughed in spite of herself. "I didn't want to get crushed!" She let Cliff pull her to him with his free arm. He kissed her quickly, all over her face. She felt Dave tugging to escape Cliff's other arm.

"I'm getting outta here before I get smooched."

"Wise child," Cliff grumbled, giving Dave a shove toward the kitchen. "Get us something to celebrate with."

"Beer's all we've got. Unless you want me to shake up a couple of wine coolers and dump 'em over your head."

"You do and I'll pulverize you," Cliff joked. He turned to Annie, growling in her ear until she quivered from the sheer sensation of it. "And I'll make love to you until the sun comes up, goes down and comes up again. You may not be able to walk for a couple of days. Is that okay with you?"

She nodded, her cheek to his. Her knees went weak. Everything was hitting her at once. How much she loved him, how much she wanted him, how desperately she wanted him to be happy, to be himself again. And how much she wanted him to still love her after the operation. That, more than anything.

"I'll have you right where I want you." He smiled, more dashing and self-assured than ever. "I'll *see* everything." He licked the edge of her ear.

Annie crumbled inside. "Please, please do that."

"Hey, I've got an idea!"

Annie jumped as Dave came back in, beers in hand.

"How about ordering out?"

"Pizza again? This kid lives on pizza," Cliff groused. "Just fix us something in all those pans you're banging around out there."

Annie was abashed to hear herself actually giggle. Cliff kissed her again.

Dave cleared his throat. "I'm not cooking for company. You're the only person I know who deserves my cooking."

"Hey, bud, I've had it up to here with being self-supporting. For the next couple of days you can wait on me hand and foot, fetch my slippers, read me the paper—"

"You don't wear slippers, and if you think I'm going to wait on you, tell it to Kane."

In half an hour dinner was ready, and Annie's sides were sore from laughing. The kitchen became the Cliff and Dave Show, featuring vaudeville routines, corny jokes and plenty of slapstick. "We slice, we dice, we make julienne fries!"

How the spaghetti and salads got to the table intact, much less edible, was a mystery Annie never resolved.

They drank a toast to the future, then Cliff coerced Dave into handling the dishes alone.

"Don't you want to show off for your teacher?" Dave asked facetiously. "Run a couple of loads in the dishwasher?"

"I'm walking my teacher home in the moonlight."

"How do you know there's a moon?" Annie asked.

"You told me last night." He opened the back door, and Kane scooted out in front of them. Cliff took her arm. "Besides, if you're blind, there can be a moon every night."

They walked down the road, their steps scratching in the gravel. With a short command from Cliff, Kane turned around and trotted back to the house. "Catch this, he actually obeyed me," Cliff said.

"Mmm."

"Why so quiet?"

Annie shrugged, smiling apologetically, though she knew it didn't help. "It seems like our little moment has been surpassed."

"You think I'd forgotten making love to you because of that letter?"

"I wouldn't blame you."

He slowed. "Have *you* forgotten?"

"Of course not. It's just that you can put this all behind you now. Go back to your normal life."

"Is that what you want?"

Her throat was so tight that it was painful to speak. She was warring with too many emotions. How many more nights would they have? "I—I just wanted it to last longer, that's all. Before everything went back to the way it was."

He took her in his arms. "It'll be better, Annie. It has to be." In a matter of days he'd see her. He could stop being this shuttered man and show her the real love he was capable of. But for now— "We'll see. Just a few more days."

Was that all she'd have? Lost in her thoughts, Annie was startled by his next question.

"What time is it?"

She laughed, her body hugged tight to his. She'd changed clothes from this morning, he noticed. She was wearing a one-piece sundress, stretchy material that clung everywhere before flaring to a full skirt that flitted around his legs. He could tell from the smoothness of her back that she wasn't wearing a bra. Somehow feeling that was ten times more exciting than seeing it. "This morning was unbelievable. I'm still not sure I didn't dream it."

"You didn't."

"Are you sore?" he asked.

"No."

His fingertips were on her cheeks. "Are you blushing?"

She laughed again. "That's a very personal question."

"So's this one. What time is it?"

Irritated, she would have stepped back if it weren't for his arms. "Getting bored already?"

"Hardly. There was something about making love to you, with my hands and my senses." He ran his hands possessively down her body.

Her heart went still.

"I'd like to make love to you again."

His body was growing taut and hard, his breath quickening at the sound of his words and their effect on Annie. She knew if she put her hand over his heart that its beat would be like hers, galloping and erratic.

"Is there a moon?"

"Yes."

His hands searched her dress, trying to find the way in. "I want you in the dark, feeling it the way I do." It had buttons; he unbuttoned them, opening it to her waist. He cupped one breast in his hand.

"Are there shadows beside your house?"

"Yes," she gasped as his mouth claimed her. She threw her head back and looked at the moon, the stars, the shadows of the pines on the road.

"I couldn't let you go without showing you one more time how you make me feel."

One more time. It suddenly seemed like enough to last a lifetime, Annie thought, enough to fill a universe to bursting. Her heart was hammering, her legs shaky. Honey started between her legs, hot and sweet. Her doubts shifted like the sand beneath them. No matter how things changed, they'd have this night.

They made it to her house, kissing, clinging, desperate for the one thing each was sure of. She fetched a packing blanket from the studio. There was a sandy spot beside the house, cool and private. The air was brisk on their skin as they removed their clothes.

It was pitch-black. She had to rely on her hearing to know exactly where he was. When he came closer, she sensed his presence before she felt him, masculine, powerful, ominous in the dark. Naked to the sky, buffeted by the night breeze, they were like strangers, bodies meeting in the dark. His hand on her breast was electric, her response instantaneous.

"What if someone sees?" she asked with her last shred of common sense.

"What if they do?" he replied gruffly. Coaxing her to him, he made it clear he didn't give a damn about anyone but them and the love they were going to make.

He found her tension with his fingers, massaging, easing, reading her body the way no man had, lowering her. The blanket was scratchy against her back, the sand pliant as they moved to accommodate each other, caressing each other's special places. A wash of emotion and rhythm rose and receded and rose again, joining their hurried breath and urgent words. The waves whispered and rolled with them.

It was different in the dark. The feel of skin, smooth and taut, pulsing, covered with fine goose bumps. Slick hair, the taste of a mouth, the fine stubble of a beard already growing back. She teased, tasted and vowed to remember. If there were lonely nights to come, they wouldn't be empty of memories.

And when it was over for him, she responded to every aftershock with the only words that mattered— "I love you." She touched his face once more and said, "I love you." She ran her hands through his still-long hair and said, "I love you," all the while knowing none of the memories would ever be enough if he left her.

His entire body shuddered as he rested his chin on her shoulder, exhausted. He felt her quivering around him. Kissing her cheek, he felt the wetness. "Are you crying?"

Her body trembled. There was no hiding from him, not even in the dark. Hot tears ran down her cheeks and into her hair. "I'm sorry. I didn't mean to."

"Why?"

She tried to laugh. "Too much emotion, maybe."

He cursed softly. "Annie, it was wonderful. Tell me."

Maybe it was too wonderful. She shook her head. "Don't make me explain it. I love you, that's all. I'm sorry."

He kissed the salt on her lips, the puffiness under her eyes.

"Don't. I look terrible when I cry." She hastily wiped her tears with the back of her hand and sniffed.

"You look beautiful," he said with complete sincerity. "And you taste even better." He licked her cheek, placing tiny open kisses on her lashes. "Mmm, salty."

She stroked his back, his neck, the plastic of his sunglasses. "First you lose the beard, next these. When the sun comes up, I won't even recognize you."

"I'll recognize you."

And how would he look at her then?

Both were lost in thought for minutes. When Cliff withdrew, they lay side by side. Picking up a corner of the blanket, he covered them, then surprised himself by saying something he'd been thinking all evening. "Come to the hospital with me."

She huddled in closer to him. "I thought you'd want to go it alone."

"So did I." She understood him a lot better than he'd realized. It was scary. After all, if she was there when the bandages came off, she might be there when they told him the operation hadn't worked. How would he say goodbye to her then? How avoid her pity?

He hugged her to him, warming her back with his front. Nothing was going to go wrong. This nightmare would end, and Annie would be waiting for him on the other side. Only then could they make promises, plan a future together. Only then would he be able to say the words that she'd said to him tonight. *I love you.* "I want you there when I wake up," he said.

She touched his hand where it rested on her breast, signaling her assent.

"Of course, if we sleep out here all night, we may never wake up," he joked past the lump in his throat. "It's freezing out here!" He gave her fanny a smack. "Last one in the house is a rotten egg!"

Annie jumped up after him, kicking around in the sand for their pile of clothes. "You'd desert a naked defenseless woman in the middle of the wild outdoors—"

"Not ten feet from her own house—"

"What's worse, you probably can't even find the door!" She shook out the blanket and tossed him a scrunched handful of discarded clothing.

"I can find the deck on the beachside," he retorted.

"With your shin, maybe."

"That does it. I've been insulted enough." He made a lunge for her.

Because she hadn't expected it, he almost caught her. "What are you doing?"

"That's it. Say something so I can find you."

Annie backed up, the blanket clutched to her chest. "I'm not going to say anything."

"Aha! That's all I needed."

He lunged again, and she jumped out of his way, backing cautiously toward the deck. "What are you going to do if you catch me?"

"For beginners, I thought I might toss you into the surf. That'll teach you to tease a blind man. Now, where are you, hussy?"

One lunge to the left, one squeal as he caught her arm, and then she slipped agilely out of his grasp. In a few steps she was up on the deck sliding the doors open. "Last one in is a rotten egg."

Cliff rammed his shin against the planking and let out a curt expletive. "I'd settle for last one in the shower," he muttered blackly, rubbing his leg.

"Oh, Mr. Sullivan-n-n-n," she cooed.

Her throaty voice made chills run up his spine. Not to mention the fact he was sitting there plumb naked on a freezing September night in northern Michigan. "Yes, Ms. Rosetti?"

"How about if we both head for the shower?"

He found the steps and limped across the deck to the sliding doors. "I thought you'd never ask."

Sitting in the hospital corridor, Annie remembered that night. She was keenly aware that she and Cliff had been lovers for no more than one complete day. In the shower his body hair had looked black as it had stuck wet and clinging to his body. The way she had, pressing soft kisses to his throat.

She hugged herself and leaned back in a plastic molded chair that certainly must have been designed for human beings shaped differently than she. Amazing that a hospital would provide something so completely unsuited to the human form, she groused as she watched another nurse parade by.

Dave sat hunched forward, staring disconsolately at the blue, green, yellow and red tape leading up and down the linoleum, heaven knows where. Who'd come up with this system anyway? And who was the poor lug who'd spent all that time on his hands and knees laying it out? Dave would have gotten right down beside him if it would make this wait go any faster.

Cliff, being Cliff, was determined to go it alone. They shouldn't have been surprised. They'd checked him in last night and arrived this morning to find the operation already in progress. He wanted them here, but he'd lied about when it was scheduled. Dave planned to throttle him.

In twenty-four hours the bandages would come off, and they'd know the results. "When he's better, *I'm* going to pulverize him," Dave muttered darkly.

Annie laughed softly. "It'll work out."

"A high success rate for a transplant," Dave said, repeating the doctor's words. "Miracle of modern science."

Annie nodded, then retreated to her own thoughts about miracles. Like love itself. She reminded herself that "I love you" was no magic phrase. On the other hand, if Cliff had only said it the last time they'd made love, she'd be holding on to it with all her heart right now.

Smelling hospital coffee, Annie opened her eyes. "Thanks." She took another Styrofoam cup from Dave. He needed to be up and walking around. This was the fourth cup he'd brought her. She would have preferred herbal tea. "I was just going to ask you to get me another," she lied.

"Bullfeathers. You didn't even know I was gone."

She shook her head sheepishly and smiled. "True."

The elevator door squeaked open. Annie was beginning to hate that squeak. Dave was on the verge of finding an oil can and fixing it himself. Then they recognized the doctor and knew it was Cliff's stretcher. Within moments they were beside it.

"Cliff?"

His face swathed in bandages, he turned his head on the flat pillow. "Annie?" He sounded groggy, and his hand was limp as it rose.

"I'm here," she said, grasping his hand until she felt a returning squeeze.

"You're not supposed to be here," he muttered. "I sent you away for the morning."

"Wild horses wouldn't keep us away, and you know it."

"Yeah, whose bright idea was it to lie about the operation, huh?"

"Dave," Annie shushed.

"Dave," Cliff muttered, lifting his other hand before he faded out and it dropped back to the sheets.

A nurse stepped between them to jockey the gurney into his room. "He'll need some time to recoup, then he'll have a splitting headache. A couple of hours ought to do it. In twenty-four hours we'll remove the bandages."

"You're sure?" Dave insisted.

"Promise," she said, stripping off the green operating uniform.

"Annie?"

"I'm here, Cliff."

He said nothing for a moment, a faint smile on his lips, her hand clutched in his. He lifted it to his lips and kissed it. "I knew it was you in the corridor. I heard your bracelets."

She laughed. "Are they that loud?"

"When your head is pounding, they are."

"I'm sorry."

She made a move to remove them, but that required his letting go of her hand, which he wasn't about to do.

"I love you," he mumbled.

Her heart stopped. "What?"

"Excuse me." The other nurse bustled in. "He's quite groggy. Perhaps you could come back tonight."

Annie realized Cliff was already asleep, his hand limp in hers. Reluctantly she released it. The nurse was right. She couldn't pin her heart on words spoken so soon after surgery. No matter how badly she wanted to.

Nine

————

After two years in college, Ann Arbor was home to Dave, so when an uncomfortable and grumpy Cliff kicked them out of his hospital room the next morning, Dave showed Annie the sights.

She saw the University of Michigan, the library, the student union, the bookstores and the stadium. It was stop-and-go all the way with September's returning students crossing everywhere but at the lights and furniture-stacked Volvos double-parked outside student apartments.

"That's mine, top floor right," Dave said, pointing as they drove by yet another brick house.

"Oh," Annie said, secretly wishing they'd taken a vigorous walk instead. Obviously Dave needed to drive the way Cliff needed to run, Annie realized, missing her miles of Lake Michigan beach.

More by habit than thought, Dave pulled up in front of Bell's Pizza. "Want some?"

"Don't think I've ever had a more gracious invitation," Annie said wryly.

Dave skimmed over the sarcasm, reciting the doctor's optimistic prognosis once more. "He should be able to see immediately after the bandages come off. Hell, he could drive back home."

"Please," Annie said, laughing. "I had to ride in that boat with him."

"Okay, maybe not drive, but within a week or two, with glasses. Miracles of modern science, eh?"

"Yeah. Just keep repeating that."

They ordered. And waited.

"I'm going to get a microwave," Annie said. "I'm beginning to hate waiting for anything."

"Know how you feel."

Annie played with a paper napkin, wishing she had some good firm clay to keep her hands busy. "When he's better, he'll be going back to work, won't he?" There it was, the big question. She looked across at Dave.

He shrugged and leaned back in his seat, his legs halfway out in the aisle. "Doc said it could be soon. What's his name again?"

"Dr. Tanarawanda or something like that. I can't pronounce it."

"Whew. Glad I'm not the only one."

"So," she said, wondering if he'd changed the subject on purpose, "about Cliff's job. He is planning on going back to the Upper Peninsula?"

Her concern finally dawned on Dave. "He hasn't talked it over with you?"

"He's been waiting for the operation," she said, gazing at the Formica.

Dave muttered a curse. "Pardon my French, but sensitivity doesn't exactly run in our family. Maybe that comes from being a family of men. I don't know. We don't always say what we mean."

Annie left off playing with a plastic fork and clenched her hands in her lap. "Cliff's had enough experience with women. You'd think he'd have learned long ago how to say what they wanted to hear."

Dave winced. "Oh, the ladies. Well, you know Cliff."

"Do I?"

"Sure, he used to play the playboy, but he's subtler now." Dave grimaced at how that came out. "He's nowhere near as wild as I remember."

"That could be because of the accident," she pointed out.

"I think it's because of you." He hoped he wasn't letting everything out of the bag. He'd seen the effect Annie had on his brother. Blindness or no, Cliff was climbing the walls, pacing the floor and practically chewing nails over this woman. If anybody ought to tell her Cliff loved her, it should be Cliff. Hell, it should be obvious to both of them.

"That's okay," Annie said. She sighed and tossed him a forgiving look. Lifting a slice of pizza from the box, she cut the stringy cheese with her fingers. "I should be talking this over with Cliff, not you."

Dave pulled his legs in quickly as a coed with a carryout order walked by. He was so rangy, Annie noticed, more so than Cliff, who was more self-contained. In a lot of ways.

"You know," Dave said, downing half a Coke, "I don't know how much this means, but when Mom was sick, Cliff shielded me from just about everything. I was only five then, but I think I would have liked to know more of what was going on. He doesn't see it that way. He takes everything on himself, doesn't share his troubles. That's his way of protecting the people he cares about."

"Thanks for including me in that." Annie touched his arm.

Dave munched a crust, then dropped it into the box with a clunk. "Yeah, but what happens when he shuts out the people he's trying to protect?"

Annie realized she wasn't the only one hurt by Cliff's determination to go it alone. "It'll be okay. You'll have your brother back good as new."

When they returned to the hospital, Cliff was sitting up in bed. Dr. T, as Dave had taken to calling him, was on the far side of the bed. A nurse was wadding up discarded bandages.

The bandages were off.

The sunglasses on.

"Leave those on to prevent any accidental touching or bumping of the eyes," the doctor was saying. His soothing voice with its lilting East Indian accent carried across the room.

Cliff's head turned. Standing frozen in the doorway, Annie wished that sausage pizza had been milder. Her stomach was doing cartwheels. The bandages were off!

She silenced the bracelets that were swaying and clattering on her left wrist. A hundred questions rushed through her mind. Had he heard them come in? Had he *seen* them? Was he looking at her right now? It couldn't be bad news, could it? She wanted to rush to his bedside and hold him. She couldn't move.

He muttered a blunt, "Excuse me," turned his back on them and swung his legs over the edge. Pacing the length of the bed, he turned and came toward her. This time, unlike any way she'd ever seen him walk, he hesitated.

He didn't have to ask if it was her. Something about the way she held her hands in front of her, those bracelets; the color of her sweater alone stung his sensitive eyes.

She was blurry but getting clearer. He had to get closer to see the look in her eyes.

His chest was bare, Annie thought irrelevantly. Having refused to wear "that asinine hospital gown," he was wearing blue boxer shorts, the same ones she'd helped toss in countless loads of laundry these past few weeks. His legs were powerful-looking as always, darkened with gold and brown hairs. Really, he wasn't wearing anything less than he wore on the beach. But coming toward her, in the harsh hospital light, he looked half-naked and vulnerable.

She concentrated on all those things. Anything to take her mind off the petrifying fact that he was looking right at her.

He stopped in front of her, so close she had to look up. That's when her eyes began to fill with tears. She blinked them back; she *had* to know. "Can you—" She choked on the tightness in her throat.

Up close, she was still blurry. He wanted to blink, but he was afraid she'd disappear. She was shorter than he'd pictured, maybe because she was standing beside Dave. Her hair was medium brown, her sweater a riot of purples and pinks and blues. He heard the bracelets tinkle as she wiped something from her cheek. He touched her shoulders, the fuzzy rough weave of the hand-loomed sweater familiar to his fingers. "You've worn this before."

She nodded.

Funny that he had to touch her, hear her, to confirm what his eyes could see.

"Can you see me?" she whispered, knowing it was true. All he had to do was say the words.

He touched her hair instead. That's how it all began, wasn't it, him touching her hair? There were combs holding it off her face on both sides. He saw the glint of copper, felt its coolness. Her hair *was* frizzy, wild and curly, more erotic than he'd imagined. His fingers got caught in it. He wanted to joke about it, but even through the gauziness that remained he could see traces of uncertainty in her eyes.

How often had that been there without his knowing? How often had he hurt her unintentionally while wrapped up in his own problems? "How often have you looked at me like that and I've been too blind to see it?"

"Cliff!"

He found her mouth, or she found his. With their arms wrapped around each other, it wasn't hard. He crushed her to him, wishing he could take back every irritable moment, every moment they'd wasted not laughing and touching and holding each other just like this. "Annie, honey..."

Dave pumped the doctor's hand, subjecting him to the same kind of hugs and backslaps he would have traded with Cliff had his brother not had something better to do with his arms.

Annie was pounding Cliff's back with fists of her own. "Why didn't you tell us the bandages were coming off so soon? The nurse promised us—"

"I strong-armed the doctor into taking them off early. I didn't want to drag you through it."

She took his face firmly in her hands. "Damn it, when are you going to realize you can share the bad things, too? That's what we're here for."

"Shh. It doesn't matter now." He took her face in his hands instead. "You're fuzzy. You know that?"

She laughed and sniffled.

"Some lenses, perhaps," the doctor interrupted, eager to escape Dave's exuberant embrace, "after the sight has stabilized. Although the initial blurriness should fade within the week."

"This is fine, Doc," Cliff murmured, looking down into Annie's face. "In fact, it's about the most beautiful thing I've ever seen."

Annie made herself smile, not sure she could believe him precisely because she wanted to so badly.

"I probably look terrible," Cliff said, reaching for his sunglasses. "But do you mind if I take these off?"

She swallowed and shook her head. She wouldn't have minded being shanghaied to China right now, as long as he was with her.

He reached past her to flick the light switch, the cloudy day outside providing the only light in the room. Keeping his back to the window, Cliff slowly took off his sunglasses.

"His eyes will be red for a few days," the doctor said.

Annie saw that for herself. The part that should have been white was indeed red and painful-looking. She grimaced, and Cliff hurriedly began to put his glasses back on.

"No," she said, softly touching his arm, "they look like they hurt, that's all."

It was his turn to shake his head. "Not much."

She knew he wouldn't admit it if they did, but at the moment it didn't matter. The eyes that stared so seri-

ously into hers were brown with gold and hazel highlights. Black circles darkened the skin around them. She
traced them with shaking fingertips.

"From the operation," Cliff said. "I look like I just
went ten rounds with Sugar Ray."

"You look like you're gonna have one hell of a hang-
over," Dave chortled.

Cliff looked at his younger brother, at Annie, and back
again. "I shouldn't have dragged you two through all
this."

"Yeah, right, sure," Dave replied. "Like we're going
to hand you a bus ticket and say, 'Call when the operation's over.'"

Cliff laughed and surreptitiously wiped what looked
like a tear off his cheek as he put his glasses on. "One of
the symptoms, right, Doc?"

"Yes, Mr. Sullivan. That is right. You may have tearing."

"Bull!" Dave said succinctly.

"Come here." Cliff grabbed him and held on tight.
"Have you been taking care of this lady?"

"Like you said."

"Better than you took care of me, I hope."

"She's not as grumpy."

"She's better looking, too."

"About time you wised up."

"Don't get smart. I can reach you now." Cliff playfully swatted Dave's shoulder. Dave made a fist to hit
back.

"Ah," the doctor warned, "do not hit a recovering
patient."

Dave grabbed a tissue off the nightstand and blew his
nose loudly. "Hey, why don't we go somewhere and
really party?"

"And make a fool of myself in public like I did at that barbershop?" Cliff retorted. "No thanks. No more public performances for me. This has been nightmare enough."

Nightmare, Annie thought dully. As if all her teaching had brought him nothing but humiliation. She shook off the feeling as Cliff threw an arm around her shoulders and gave her a quick squeeze.

"This thing is almost over. I'll be me again."

She understood what Cliff meant, really she did. He meant the blindness and all its frustrations would be over. Not *them*. The pep talk, for what it was, failed to lift her plummeting spirits. She'd spent so much time with him, given him pieces of herself, pieces he seemed suddenly eager to discard.

"Please, you may all come to my office when you're ready. I have some instructions I would like to give."

"Sure, Doc," Cliff said. Then, as he put on his hospital gown, saying, "The last time I wear one of these monstrosities," he spelled out what a miserable couple of months it had been. Annie stood loyally by, the smile on her face feeling more false and brittle as the minutes ticked on.

"Now where's the doc's office?" Cliff finally asked.

"Down here," Dave replied.

"You two go," Annie said. "I'm going to stop off in the ladies' room for a minute." She sidestepped Cliff's embrace and took a quick left turn.

He felt that all too familiar frustration ramming home again. Damn it, why didn't seeing help? Something was wrong with Annie and he didn't know what it was. At least this time he could catch up to her before the door closed. "Anything wrong?"

"I cried so hard I ruined my makeup, that's all." She wouldn't ruin this day for him for all the tea in China. She just had to get away, anywhere, alone.

As the washroom door closed behind her, she rested her forehead against the cool green tile. She was being petty and insecure. Stupid. Infantile. "And to top it off, I'm wallowing in self-accusations." This was probably Cliff's happiest moment. Why did she feel kicked in the stomach? Just because he couldn't wait to forget everything they'd been through together?

Splashes of cold water did wonders for her face but nothing for her stomach. *Get ready to let him go,* the puffy-eyed woman in the mirror said. No crying, no clinging. She'd tried both with Ken; she hadn't even escaped with her dignity. Not this time. She loved Cliff with everything she had; she always would. She wouldn't cheapen it by clinging when he wanted to leave. He was going back to his old life. He made it very clear that was all he'd ever wanted.

Annie fixed her lipstick, wasted minutes trying to apply eyeliner to wet eyelids, then went looking for the doctor's office.

Except for the unpronounceable name on the door, Annie knew she'd never remember anything about Dr. T's office—just Dave perched on the radiator and Cliff sitting in a leather chair, reaching out for her hand as the doctor issued his instructions.

Tiny shivers ran up and down her every time she caught Cliff glancing her way. Knowing he could see her was both terrifying and exciting. He was hers, for these few moments at least. She forced a smile. Nothing, not even her own doubts, were going to spoil this day.

The doctor cleared his throat. "The symptoms you have now should subside. Meanwhile, you must call us immediately if there are any signs of rejection."

"Right," Cliff said.

"We have a saying here, RSVP. That means four things. *R* is for redness. That is a sign of a rejection episode."

"I already have that," Cliff said, his attention riveted on the doctor. The man was talking failure. Cliff had no intention of failing. Not now.

"I know. I mean the redness that returns. This will fade soon."

"And the other three letters?"

"*S* for soreness, *V* for vision change—"

"It's going to change every day. You told me that."

"It should improve. If for any reason it gets quickly worse, call immediately. We sometimes can treat the eyes with steroid drops and the rejection reverses without surgery."

"And *P*?"

"Photophobia."

"What's that?" Dave chirped.

"Means I hate having my picture taken," Cliff retorted. He squeezed Annie's hand, and she glanced over. That was when he remembered she could see him as well as he could see her. He'd have to be careful what he showed here. He didn't want her worrying. He let go of her hand and crossed his arms, trying to look casual. "Rejection is a faint possibility, isn't it? I mean the success rate is very good."

"Oh, it's excellent, and rejection can be treated."

"And there could be another transplant."

"Yes, we could go so far as a tissue-matching program to ensure even greater success. As long as the eyes aren't damaged by the rejection itself...."

Cliff's mouth was tight, so he purposely relaxed it. He wanted Annie. He wanted out of this mess once and for all. He wanted to get on with his life, with their lives. Above all, he wanted to erase the worry that was on her face when she'd come in. She shouldn't have to be put through this. "How long before I can be certain this operation is going to take?"

"A month is advisable."

"A month," Cliff said flatly.

"Yes."

"When can I go back to work?"

"Well," the doctor dawdled, his gold pen hovering over Cliff's chart. "If this is correct about what you do for a living, I think it would be advisable that you wait until we can fit you with prescriptive lenses—"

"You mean glasses?"

"Or contact lenses. In addition, it is not uncommon to continue to be photophobic to a greater or lesser degree, almost indefinitely."

"Meaning?" Cliff barked.

"Meaning," the doctor hurried on, cognizant of the growing tension in the room, "you may find you need sunglasses on any bright day."

"Luckily he looks sexy in sunglasses," Annie mentioned, smoothing the waters.

Cliff stopped frowning long enough to glance her way. This gnawing frustration was supposed to have ended with the operation. As long as there was any possibility things could go wrong, there would be only more waiting ahead. How long could he keep them both walking this tightrope?

Annie smiled, squeezing his hand. "It'll be fine."
Not for the first time, he prayed it would.

The next two weeks flew by, Annie's doubts withering like autumn leaves. She couldn't stop watching Cliff, and the feeling seemed mutual. Every time they walked on the beach, stopping for a sunset or a sea gull in flight, she caught him looking at her.

Every night they made love.

"Let me see," he breathed, turning her insides to soft flowing honey, her heartbeat to pounding waves. By turns intense then mild, his hands roved over her, his dark brown eyes greedy for everything the light of the bedside lamp revealed.

Annie watched, too. This was another Cliff, a Cliff she'd seen in pieces, never whole. Stubborn and precise, often egotistically pleased with himself for having captured such a beautiful woman while blind.

With very little effort, she could forget her fears and simply treasure each day, refusing to count the days until their month was up. Dave was back in school. They had time together. Time was all they needed. Cliff was restless without work, his vision too blurry to read. He strode the beaches, jogging and working out while Annie taught at the hospital. Today she was stealing a few morning hours to build up her pottery inventory. Her days were booked and her nights had become so full....

"Hi!" Cliff called.

Annie's heart jumped. No matter how many times she saw him, she was helpless against that reaction.

Jogging up from the water's edge, he stopped in the shade of the open garage door. He balanced his sunglasses on his head. "Hot day."

"Isn't it wonderful?"

He grinned one of those "eat your heart out" grins that turned her to jelly, then stripped off his T-shirt in one move, leaving nothing but his blue nylon running shorts, his running shoes and a body glistening with sweat. Although she knew every inch of that body, it never ceased to affect her in the most elemental ways. A sear of desire and a flush of modesty overtook her. She felt the urge to tug up the strap of her sundress as it slouched down her shoulder, but her hands were covered with clay.

Kane, less impressed by his master, flopped down on the cool concrete.

"You're wearing that dog out," Annie scolded.

"He needs the exercise."

"You mean you do."

"But my dear, I have you."

Annie poked him in the ribs with her elbow while accepting a chaste kiss on the cheek.

It certainly was a glorious Indian summer morning, one of those rare end-of-September days, precious because you knew they couldn't last. Annie pondered that thought, watching a pot spin. Can't last, can't last, it whispered.

Cliff toyed with her strap and the skin beneath. Lord, she was sexy. "Got a towel I could borrow, pretty lady?"

"Under the sink."

He found one in a cupboard built under the workbench, rinsing his whole head under the arched faucet before briskly toweling off. "You look good," he said, one hip against the counter.

So did he. Annie shrugged and went back to her pottery. "Don't look too long. I have work to catch up on."

"Am I keeping you too busy? Nights, I mean?"

She tugged down the corners of her mouth coquettishly. "My nights are fine. Wonderful, in fact."

He grinned, swaggering without moving a muscle.

"Did I say that was all your doing?" she replied with a huff.

"Come across a good book then?"

She pursed her lips. "I didn't say that."

"Could be," he said, shrugging, "if that book was *The Joy of Sex*."

Was that all it was to him? She looked startled, then hurt, then angry that he'd caught it.

Cliff swore under his breath. That had been a stupid, macho thing to say. Anything for a quip. He puttered with the shelves. A month, the doctor said. Two more lousy weeks. Cliff couldn't make promises until he was sure, no matter how badly he wanted to. "I know what you want me to say, Annie. We should talk about some kind of future, but I can't, not yet."

"Then don't," she said, stung. "It's not as if I'm pressuring you."

"No, but I hear it loud and clear. You want commitment. You want something I can't give."

Was this it then, the beginning of the end? Annie felt her hands wavering on the clay. She lifted them off, not wanting to destroy something she'd created, something special. "Could we not talk about this now?"

Cliff kicked himself for treating her reasonable expectation like an unwelcome obligation. She wasn't the only one who longed for a life together. "I shouldn't have yelled." He dragged a hand over his slick neck. "Mind if I use your shower?"

"Not at all." She was frosty.

He was thirsty. "I'm gonna grab a drink in the kitchen."

"Fine."

The door to the house closed. Kane looked up to watch his master leave.

"It's okay, boy. He'll be back," Annie said quietly. But how many more times?

Yes, she wanted more. If Cliff couldn't give it, better to settle it now than go on pretending. Unfortunately there would never be a good time to let go. Far from pressing him, she had to let him know he was free.

Cliff returned, his shorts clinging to him in damp places that made her heart beat dull and hard, adding to the pain.

"When are you going back to work?" she asked without emotion.

"Up north?"

She nodded.

"When the doctors give me the go-ahead. The mine requires a doctor's slip. So do all the other authorities. There'll be a battery of tests, no doubt." If only she'd wait.

"You'll be leaving then."

"I have to work for a living, Annie. Lord knows I can't do pottery."

She involuntary glanced at the shelves, her eyes going to the half-dozen pieces he'd made. Why was she doing this? Why ruin their few remaining days? "I like that tall one you made."

"Not bad," he said, coming slowly toward her.

"No, it isn't," she replied, trying to sound cool, feeling the heat still coiled in his body. "At least I taught you something." She got up, avoiding him, lifting the new piece off the wheel. She set it carefully on the shelf, as if it held someone's heart.

Cliff was behind her, running his fingertips across her bare back. "You taught me a whole way of life," he murmured. That way of life included her. If things turned out the way he wanted, it always would. Of course, she could say no, especially to living that far north.

He withdrew his hand and thought things out. The hospital in Marquette might not have any need for an art therapist. Traveling to art fairs would be an extra three hours away. Maybe she didn't want to go. Was this her way of putting him off?

"Will you come visit me?" he asked. He wouldn't insist on an answer now. She could check it out, make a decision when she'd seen the place.

Visit? The word tore a small hole in her heart. "It's a long drive," she hedged. "It'll be longer once the snow hits."

Winters. Linda had hated that prospect, too, Cliff remembered, when she'd turned down his proposal of marriage. It wasn't a question a man asked many times in his life. He wasn't about to stand here and watch his dreams crumble.

It wasn't fair—it didn't resolve the argument—but he reached up anyway, his fingers dancing through the chimes. They sounded through his pulse and echoed in the large room, musical, sensual.

Annie turned as if called, not surprised by the intensity in his eyes.

"They still sound like you," he said.

Ten

Annie flushed. The room felt hot and dry, like the inside of a kiln.

Cliff approached, backing her up against the wall.

Her eyes pleaded with him. She needed reassurance, some idea that he planned to stay, at least keep her in his life. "Making love doesn't solve arguments."

"Yes, but do you notice how few start when you are?"

She held up clay-crusted hands. "I can't touch you."

He pressed in against her with his body, hot, hard, the concrete block wall at her back cold and just as hard. "Have you ever done it with no hands?" His smile was cockier than ever, belying whatever troubled his eyes.

She shook her head. "Somebody's got to—"

The thought went unfinished as he lifted her hands, pinning them to the wall with his, the clay and water oozing between their entwined fingers. The subtle circling of his hips became a not-so-subtle pumping motion that made her knees weak, her own rhythm ignite.

One small voice said they had to talk; she couldn't surrender like this every time he—

His mouth covered her ear, and her knees buckled. Her voice cracked when she tried to speak. "Won't it be hard to take our clothes off?"

"If we don't, I'm going to be mighty embarrassed."

She gave a throaty laugh just as he laved her neck with his tongue.

If she had any idea how close he was... "You wear this when you throw clay. That means you can get it dirty," he reasoned bluntly.

"Not fair getting logical when you're making me crazy." It was her turn to nibble his ear. "How about if I run my hands through your hair?"

"No!" He jumped back.

"Vain."

"I just showered."

She came at him slowly, hands reaching. "So shower again."

"Annie," he warned. He made a motion to run his hand through his hair. Catching sight of a palm full of grayish clay made him stop just in time. He rolled his eyes.

He rolled his eyes.

Annie stopped. She'd never seen him do that before, so rarely did she see him without his sunglasses even now. How could he leave when she was still learning him?

"How *are* we supposed to do this?" he said.

She sighed and looked out the open doors toward the beach. "There are still tourists hanging around. Maybe we'd better wait."

Waiting. That was his line.

Annie watched emotions she didn't recognize flicker across his face. Frustration and anger, she recognized, not the others. She was willing to wait out the silence this time, but he said nothing, turning to rinse his hands in the sink.

"When's your next art fair?" he asked out of the blue.

"Next week, a Christmas bazaar at the high school."

"Christmas, it's barely October!"

She shrugged. "It's in town, so I'll go for the day."

"Can I come?"

"As I recall you were bored last time," she remarked dryly.

"I want to *see* one. I should be more help."

Buoyed that he wanted to take part in something so central to her life, eager for the chance to spend as much time with him as possible, Annie nodded.

"Kane."

The dog ambled over. Cliff picked up his harness.

"You never used that when you were blind. You always insisted on the leash."

"When I was blind, I didn't want to look it. Anyway this keeps him from straining so hard."

"We should talk."

Cliff paused in the doorway. "Wouldn't it be easier to take it as it comes?" He looked at her gently, pausing on the edge of the sand.

And when it goes? she thought.

She watched him walk toward his house. She had to give him space, time to get used to everyday life again. There was love there, she knew it. That he hadn't spoken it, that he was letting their days dwindle, made her wonder about their future, and more determined than ever to seize the present.

*   *   *

A week passed. A week of sweetest attention from Cliff. In a restaurant atop a hotel he ignored every beautiful woman present, teasingly admitting, "Of course, I can't exactly see them in this candlelight."

Chuckling, Annie held the menu closer to the candle and surreptitiously read it to him. At least he could do without the sunglasses here.

But for the past few evenings they'd begun drifting, unsure of what to say, tiptoeing around feelings each was afraid to confront. Annie decided tonight was the night. She couldn't be true to her feelings if she didn't directly confront Cliff about his.

Picking up Chinese food in town, she got to his house at six.

Cliff stepped away from the back to let her enter, replacing the lid on a bubbling pot of spaghetti sauce. "We must have crossed wires somewhere." He stacked the take-out boxes on the counter and gave her a peck on the cheek.

"Perfect example of a lack of communication," she replied stiffly.

Cliff let that one drop, like a stone. "Wine with dinner?"

As they sat on the living room sofa afterward, Cliff congratulated himself on at least getting the fire to crackle. Dinner had been a feast of tension and strained silence.

"Are we ready now?" He set a glass of wine in front of her.

"I thought you weren't supposed to drink," she said. This discussion could be the turning point of their entire relationship. Suddenly she wanted to put it off as long as possible. "The doctor said something about it constricting the blood vessels."

Cliff pursed his lips, feeling strangely touched. "For someone who never stopped staring at me while we were in his office, you heard every word he said." He lifted the solitary glass in a salute to her. "Just a sip, then it's yours."

Annie watched him savor it, seeing his mouth move, imagining his tongue and the dark taste of red wine. Heady, intoxicating. "Potent," she said aloud.

He glanced at her, sunglasses off, brown eyes darkening. Then he threw back his head and laughed. "We know where your mind is."

Coloring, she didn't bother to protest.

He leaned back, comfortably placing an arm around her shoulders. "Have I told you how lucky I am to have found you?"

"Only a few hundred times. And only since you've seen what it is you found."

"No!"

"You never mentioned it before the operation."

"I didn't want to count my blessings before they hatched, or something like that. You thought I was waiting to check you out? Sorry, honey, you're confusing me with another vacuous SOB." This time he took a longer swallow from her glass.

Annie squeezed her eyes shut, denouncing herself silently. "I'm sorry, Cliff. We shouldn't judge people according to the past."

"It's normal enough," he said, sighing. "You know, this doesn't have to be a knockdown, drag-out, souls-bared kind of night. Just come at me with it. What's worrying you?"

Annie sipped and studied the flames. "I love you."

He nodded and let that sink in. "I wanted to wait until I knew about my eyes. I have this thing about supporting my family. Good eyesight is necessary for setting charges, any kind of blasting."

"I can imagine," she said, something shivering inside her. "Is it dangerous work? I mean, look what happened before."

"That was an accident. Won't happen again."

She touched his cheek without thinking. It seemed like anything she did lately was thought out, careful. Why not say what she was thinking? "I like you without your sunglasses."

"I can't look directly into the fire, but I can look at you."

"So I noticed." There hadn't been a day, or night, when she hadn't caught him doing just that. "You look neater without the beard. Not so dissolute."

"That should impress the people from the Bureau of Mines. Don't want 'em thinking I was on a month-long bender." He waited for her laughter to subside. "We're being honest here?" he asked, nuzzling her hair. "There's been a reason I haven't said I love you, although I've loved you quite a while."

Her heart stopped, anticipating.

"I wanted to be free of this worry."

"I understand that."

"I was so wrapped up in my own problems I never realized how badly you might want to hear it."

"That's all right. You've already said it."

"I have? When?"

Her eyes twinkled. "In the hospital."

He'd thought it. Lord, how he'd thought it. But he couldn't actually remember. "When?"

She gave his ribs a good poke. "When you were coming out of surgery and still under the anesthetic. I ought to hit you with one of these pillows for putting me through all that. I understand not wanting to make promises when you don't know the future, but who does? If you love someone, you should tell them. No guarantees, and no, I'm not crowding you, but if you do love me, I'd appreciate knowing how you feel!"

"Simmer down."

"Don't patronize me."

He laughed instead. "How often have you wagged that finger at me when I couldn't see it?" He took her in his arms, clearly enjoying the resistance she put up. "You have a lot of the schoolmarm in you, teach."

"I take it that's not a compliment."

He kissed her nose, insinuating his body next to hers. "As a potter, though, I must say you have great hands." He cupped her bottom and drew her even closer. "Not to mention your creativity."

"And?"

"And I'm glad I'm not blind, so I don't hit this damn coffee table every time I chase you around it."

"And?"

"And I'm glad I can tell you I love you, which I should have said two months ago."

Her heart filled. "Has it been that long?"

"At least."

Their kiss was long, deep and ended in a kind of space and contentment Cliff had never guessed would be his. But there was a question nagging him, too.

"Total honesty, right?" He paused, marshaling his courage, watching her solemnly nod. "I can't move the Imperial Mine."

She gave him a look that said, "That couldn't be it, could it?" His big question? "My business is fairly portable," she told him. "Maybe not the therapy part, but if you don't mind my saying so, on a shared income I might get by with pottery alone."

"Sounds well reasoned to me. I enjoyed this last fair." He'd more than enjoyed it. He'd used a break in the action to seek out a jeweler Annie had mentioned. Hammered gold and silver, rings in particular, matching but individual, handcrafted by someone who cared. He hoped Annie liked his selection. It was burning a hole in his pocket even now. Could it matter if they waited until he was cleared to return to work?

Annie was right, though. There were times when the past intruded on the present. "Linda had this thing about living that far north."

"She missed out, didn't she?"

He smiled a dashing smile of thanks that made Annie quiver like a violin string. "That's what I always thought."

He kissed her again, then leaned back. He couldn't get enough of looking at her. Her hair was full of firelight, reddish-brown, highlights like dancing flame. "I love your hair like this, by firelight. On my pillow, in my hands. Heck," he growled, "I love *you* on my pillow and in my hands."

Tumbling back on the sofa, he found her hands resting exactly where he wanted them, where his desire grew under the soft weight of her palm. "You're getting daring."

"Mmm."

"You know what I'd like? You on a blanket of leaves."

"Want to get me outside again, eh?"

"Just think of the fall colors, the reds and golds and you, pale and pink."

"And Kane, chasing deer and barking his head off."

"And retrieving our clothes every time we drop them."

"Speaking of which."

"He's whining to be let out."

"Mmm-hmm." Annie smiled.

Cliff sighed. "Is it my turn?"

"It's your dog."

Alone for a moment, she sat in front of fireplace savoring the wine and the love. She turned the glass around in her hands, thinking about the sparks given off by wine, firelight and dark brown eyes.

He said he loved her.

She believed every word of it. "Back so soon?"

"He's staying out on his chain tonight. He can sleep in his doghouse or bay at the moon."

"Animal lover."

"This particular animal. Care to claw my back, little cat?"

She did a so-so imitation of a cat's purr, but it was the lowered eyelids and come-hither look that undid him. She was right—talking helped. Cliff felt closer to her, relieved of secrets of his own making. He loved her. And while they made exquisite love in front of the fireplace, and later in a body-warmed bed, he told her so again and again.

In the middle of the night, Cliff woke up. Wine headache, he thought. He didn't usually get them, but it had been quite a while since he'd had any wine. Annie was sated and sleeping and curled beside him in the dark. He could feel her there, just as he'd dreamed long before he'd ever actually had her there.

Not wanting to wake her, he carefully got out of bed and tucked the quilt around her. His teeth felt furry. If he was going to wake her with the kind of kiss he planned, brushing wouldn't be a bad idea.

He was naked. The house was cold. Reminding himself it was October and probably time to fire up the furnace, he shuffled through the discarded clothes at the foot of the bed. That was when he remembered the rings in the back pocket of his jeans. Touching them once for good luck, he hid them in the dresser drawer. In a matter of days he'd be back for them. Proposing, a once terrifying prospect, seemed so easy. She'd practically said yes last night.

He retraced his path to the bathroom. Used to do this all the time, he thought, full speed ahead. Used to have bruises up and down his shins, too. He stepped over another pile of clothes—Annie's.

Lowering himself gingerly onto the edge of the bed, he picked up what felt like silk—her blouse. Without sight he'd had sound. He rubbed the silk between his fingers and listened. Touch, that was there in his fingers, too, the fabric smooth and cool, not as warm as when he'd removed it from her. Smell, he raised it to his cheek, feeling the need for a shave as it caught and slid against stubble. He sniffed it. Yes. That delicate smell women have, the particular perfume Annie made, her body so sweet and loving last night.

Could a hundred "I love yous" convey what she meant to him right now? He wanted to wake her and tell her. He got up instead.

She was still lying on her side, facing the bathroom. He closed the door carefully before turning on the light.

With a burst of profanity, he slammed a hand over his eyes. Damn, why hadn't he brought his glasses in here! That white light was blinding.

He squinted, his eyes instantly sore, and fumbled for the toothpaste. At least he knew this routine with his eyes closed. Turning on the water, he opened his eyes just enough to smear on a rapid line of paste. As he brushed, he glanced up once out of sheer habit.

One look was all he needed.

His eyes were red. Blood red where the white should be. He stood and stared, the light cutting through him like a knife. He didn't care. The pain he'd mistaken for a headache was nothing compared to the panic.

"RSVP. Redness, Soreness, Vision, Photophobia." Three out of four symptoms. He was losing it. The transplant was being rejected. He was going blind again.

It couldn't have been that wine. Not half a glass!

It was a transplant, damn it. Anything could go wrong.

But could it be made right?

He dropped the toothpaste tube into the wastebasket with a thunk; he'd squeezed it flat. He sat numbly on the edge of the tub.

How long will I have to wait this time?

What if it fails again?

Half an hour was gone when he opened the bathroom door, letting a shaft of light fall across Annie. His heart lurched. She was beautiful, incredibly loving, and he'd found her when he'd been blind. "How lucky could a man get?" he thought, overcome with fury at the irony of it.

Why, God? Why now, when he was so close?

To think he'd almost asked her to marry him last night. He almost laughed, then didn't, for fear it would come out a sob. What he wanted, more than anything right now, was a convenient brick wall to ram his fist through.

He couldn't keep her. That's all there was to it. Not if he was getting back on that merry-go-round of waiting and hoping and relying on doctors. Not if there was any chance he could be permanently blind. He might have to face that prospect. There was no way in hell he'd ask it of her. Trouble was something you kept from other people. This was his problem alone.

He had to call the hospital in Ann Arbor, he thought, suddenly calm. He'd find out what he had to do, and whether he could drive there himself before it got worse.

But first, Annie would have to leave.

He took a deep breath, then another. Neither calmed his racing heart or the sick dread he felt. Let me look a little longer, he thought, memorizing her before he said goodbye.

Her eyelids fluttered.

His hand fumbled for the light switch and turned it off just in time.

"What time is it," she said drowsily.

Her voice was hoarse in the morning. No wonder he loved making love to her then. He'd like to right now.

"Don't get up," he said, striding to his side of the bed to grab his sunglasses off the side table. Pulling on a pair of jogging shorts and a sweatshirt, he laced his shoes, his back to her. "I'm taking Kane for a run."

"It's barely dawn."

He stopped in the doorway and came back, giving her a soft kiss on the forehead. "Go back to sleep."

Stay in my bed. Don't leave me.

He unwound her arms from around his neck and left.

Annie showered, humming to herself, laughing sometimes. She felt giggly and giddy and more than a little all right. She smoothed soap over her stomach, thinking how Cliff's lips had pressed there the night before. He loved her. He'd said so, many times.

She was still smiling when she shut off the blow dryer and heard him downstairs making breakfast.

Coming up behind him at the stove, she gave him a squeeze. He was still wearing his jogging suit, a line down his back dark with sweat. "You should change. You'll get a chill."

He didn't answer, cracking two more eggs into the pan.

Annie set the table. "Eyes bothering you today? You don't usually wear your sunglasses to breakfast."

"I do sometimes."

"Why not the adjusting lenses? It isn't that bright in here."

His fist clenched on the skillet handle, but he kept his face immobile. "Annie," he said with great patience, "you know how much I liked being hovered over."

That hurt. He didn't have to see her to know it. It was the way she stopped in midmotion, setting the orange juice so carefully down.

"Want your eggs over easy?" he ground out. What sense was there in keeping up the civilized pretense when he was about to do one of the lowest things he'd ever done?

"Over easy's fine." She ran her hands up and down her arms. "Chilly in here."

He clenched his jaw. If that was bait, he wasn't biting. His gut was in knots. He knew right now he wouldn't taste this food.

Sitting down at the table, he forced himself to eat. It was harder keeping his eyes away from her when all he wanted to do was look.

The toast popped. She was up before he was. "Jam?"

"No. I have to leave."

She stopped moving altogether, staring at the red raspberry jam smeared on the bread, knowing that in a few minutes it wouldn't matter whether he liked her friend's homemade jam better than any store-bought. She remembered the fair where they'd bought it, the sunshine, the laughter.

She'd remember this moment, too.

"I have to go to the Upper Peninsula," he said without emotion. "Check in with the mine doctor."

"What time will you be back?"

He didn't answer right away. This he didn't want to see. "I don't know if I'll be coming back."

He looked anyway; he couldn't help it. From behind the sunglasses he wondered why God let him see again if this was all he'd have to remember Annie by—the hurt and anguish, her determination not to let it show, the courage it took her not to crumble, not in front of him.

All right, look, you selfish bastard, look what you're doing to her. All because you couldn't wait.

Annie swallowed a bite of toast, thinking it would never go down. When he'd left so abruptly this morning, she'd been afraid but only for a moment. He'd kissed her before going and the fear had vanished. How easily she could be fooled by a gesture, one of his gestures.

When she decided her hands weren't shaking all that badly, she took a sip of her juice. "That's it then," she said, swallowing mechanically.

"I'm sorry." They were the only words that would come out, the only words that weren't "I love you." He felt like choking on them.

Eleven

Annie couldn't remember how she got home, only that she was here, hugging herself on the couch, feeling like a scarecrow with the stuffing pulled out.

She'd half expected this. But never, never had she imagined it would end so abruptly. How? Why? He'd said he loved her. He'd meant it. Unless she'd been wrong about him all along.

Over the next few days she went through the motions. She couldn't work on her pottery, something about touching, creating; there were too many memories of Cliff out there in the studio.

One morning she woke up. Here she was hiding from the only other thing she loved in life, the thing that might get her through this if she worked hard enough, concentrated hard enough. Marching into her studio like an army retaking a hill, she purposely sought out the pots Cliff had made. Hurled against the wall, the first broke with a satisfying smash. She reached for the chimes. They sang when she touched them, a plaintive ache, and she couldn't destroy them. That was when she sat down and cried.

How could he? Why? Was she that easily fooled?

And what about him? Was the Cliff Sullivan she'd known through so much pain capable of this coldness? Leading a woman on then dropping her the moment he was healed? She reached over to pick up the broken vase. Like an unsolvable puzzle, the pieces just didn't fit.

"No, Mr. Sullivan, you are not going to discard me like this. I will not go gentle into that good night. In that way we are a lot alike. I'm going to do some raging of my own."

She'd gone it alone, carrying her pain inside, not wanting to burden anyone else with her problems. Wasn't that his way of dealing with things? Well, she'd show him. Real strength meant being vulnerable, reaching out. She'd reach out one more time and demand an explanation. Not yelling, not crying, simply asking and deserving an answer. She loved that man, period. He'd said he loved her.

Annie marched down the beach and pounded on the cottage door. No answer. She went around to the window. It was easy to see inside. The setting sun lit up the inside of the cottage like a movie set. There was no one there. Walking slowly around to the road, feeling the revitalizing determination that accompanied her down the beach seeping away, she noticed the bowls in Kane's pen were empty and dry, his chain hung up. Whatever tire tracks Cliff's car had left were blown over with sand. He was gone, had been for days.

He'd returned to the Upper Peninsula, two hundred miles and a world away. It was over.

* * *

Annie didn't know what day it was, how many it had been. Autumn so far was cold and damp, cloudy and miserable, but the weather had nothing on her mood. She worked because she had to, taught because she had to. She signed up to teach Pottery I, Evening Session, at the local college. And never stopped thinking about Cliff.

That was why it didn't really surprise her two weeks after the breakup to glance up one day and see a man who looked like him walking slowly down the beach, head bowed to the wind. At first she thought she was imagining it, the sunglasses on a stormy gray day, the shoulders hunched. He kept walking, hugging close to the water's edge. She kept looking.

The next time. Two days later. After dawn. The garage door was down, but Annie had used every excuse to get up and glance out, finishing pot after pot, filling up shelves. This time there was no doubt. He had Kane with him, in the harness.

It was a public beach, she reasoned. The man could go where he wanted.

Like hell.

Holding her hand-loomed sweater closed against the October wind, Annie stalked across the sand toward him. "Why are you haunting me?" Let him deny it. Let him say he was just walking the dog. She wanted explanations.

After a long expressionless look, all he said was "I wanted to see you." His jaw was tight and clenched, sprinkled with the beginnings of another beard. He turned his head to the pounding water.

The question tore out of her. "Why?"

He tugged Kane into a sitting position. "I had to leave."

"You could have told me if you needed time. I wasn't pressuring you." And she'd be damned if she'd apologize, either.

"It wasn't your fault. It was mine. I had to be certain about my eyes."

"So we waited."

"We went too far. The first time I made love to you I was past the point of going back. I loved you too much."

Past tense.

Annie swallowed the metallic taste of brittle wind and damned-up tears. Confusion reigned over every other emotion warring within her. Nothing he said made sense; she needed so many reasons and none of the ones he gave fit.

"Annie." He touched her arm the way he used to, when he wanted to know exactly where she was. "I'm sorry I came back. I should have stayed away."

Without another word, not a goodbye, he turned and walked down the beach. Annie didn't chase him, didn't call. He didn't look back.

He couldn't.

It took every ounce of Cliff's shredded patience not to slam the phone into its cradle. He hated asking for help in the first place, and his little brother wasn't making it any easier. "Dave, for the last time—"

"I can't. I told you. It's not a matter of wanting to. The transmission is shot. It's in pieces on the garage floor."

"Why did you take it apart when you knew I needed a ride?"

"Because I can't drive with a busted transmission!"

"Then borrow a car."

"It's the Saturday of the Ohio State game. Everybody's out of town."

"So rent a car!"

"You know you wouldn't cosign a credit card for me. Can't rent a car without one. Or leave home," he muttered.

"This is my operation, damn it! I can't snap my fingers and get another transplant whenever—"

"Don't you think I know that?"

The shouting stopped. Tension and silence hung in the air as Dave thought back over the past two weeks. He'd made four trips up north to bring Cliff down for the steroid treatments that were meant to halt the rejection. They'd slowed it, but it hadn't stopped. And yet after each visit, Cliff insisted on going back to the cottage. Why, Dave wondered, if he was so intent on calling things off with Annie?

The whole situation ticked him off. Was his brother totally blind? You didn't find a woman like that and let her get away. Maybe it was time he lectured Cliff for a change.

Then an idea dawned. Maybe a busted transmission wasn't such a bad deal. "Can't you get a ride from someone up there?"

They both knew who he was referring to. Even picturing going to her for help made Cliff wince. It would mean dragging her into his problems. He'd designed this self-made hell specifically to avoid that. He clenched the receiver in his fist. "You're the only one I've got."

Pride was one thing, Dave reasoned, but Cliff wasn't crazy enough to risk his sight for it. He leaned back on the couch and counted to ten. These day rates must be really adding up. "Sorry, bro, there's just nothing I can do about that transmission. You couldn't get a bus ticket or something?''

On Cliff's end the receiver slammed down.

"Ooh-eee!" Dave whistled. That was one angry, bullheaded man.

Cliff tipped his head back for more eye drops. At the very least they might delay the rejection enough to prevent permanent damage to his eyes. The transplant was scheduled for Monday. He'd been watching his vision blur a little more each day. At least the accident had been immediate, a ripping explosion of sand and particles. This time there was an unreal nightmare quality to it, like slipping down a dark hole in slow motion, unable to claw your way to the light or call out to the only one who could save you, for fear she'd be pulled down, too.

Kane panted eagerly by the back door as Cliff headed into the kitchen. Stopping at the fridge to grab a soda, he remembered Annie this morning on the beach. He hadn't mentioned it to Dave. Furiously he slammed his palm against the counter. How could his brother be so cavalier? He *needed* that operation. He had to get back to Annie as soon as possible. It might already be too late.

This morning she'd looked angry, hurt and confused. Was that all he'd ever see in her eyes? Better than pity, he thought disgustedly. Or the hurt and worry he was sparing her by keeping this to himself. He was determined not to drag her through it, had been ever since he'd admitted to himself how much he loved her.

So why was he reaching for Kane's harness one more time? Why was it so imperative he see Annie once more?

Because he had to.

Because he loved her.

Because bitter, furious or indifferent, hers was the only face he wanted to see—even if it was the last thing he ever saw.

Especially if it was the last.

The sunset was a lustrous red slashed with orange. A shape was coming down the beach toward him. Cliff braced himself. He didn't want to argue with her, just look at her.

Annie wasn't about to argue. She had her explanation. Far from leaving her at peace, it left her feeling as roiled as the waves. "Dave called."

"He what?" Cliff replied sharply.

"He says you need a ride to Ann Arbor and he can't give you one. He asked me."

Cliff said nothing, that unreadable look of his firmly in place. She wanted to snatch those damn glasses off his nose. "You didn't want me to know, did you?"

"I had to make you leave. If this operation fails, I'd have nothing to offer you."

"You should have told me."

"So you'd stick around? Pity me?"

"When have I *ever* done that? You made up your mind what I could take and what was too much to ask, but did you ever ask me?" She clutched her sweater to her and whipped the hair out of her face, waiting until she could trust herself to keep the anguish out of her voice. He was in pain, emotional pain, real pain, and God, he was so alone. "Cliff, please."

She tried to touch his cheek. He drew back as if stung. "Look at this, Annie. This is exactly what I wanted to avoid. It's hurting you just knowing. I didn't want you hurt."

"So you were going to keep it to yourself."

"Yes."

"Has it ever occurred to you how selfish that is? You freeze me out every time you insist on being alone."

Alone? Hardly. She'd always been inside him, able to walk right into his heart. Through his sense of smell, his hearing, his skin, she got in, perfume and jangling bracelets and frizzy hair. He'd never been able to bar the door against her—only by leaving—and then he hadn't been able to stay away.

"You only let me share the good times," she said. "When it came to the most important event in your life, I wasn't allowed to even care."

"Maybe I wasn't as much afraid of hurting you as of losing you."

"How?" she cried. "I love you. I loved you when you were blind, when there were no guarantees—"

"But I believed that guarantee, that I'd get well. I had to. This time I'm not so sure."

"Do you think I'd stop loving you?"

He took so long to answer that she thought he hadn't heard. Then he spoke, more to the waves than to her. "I'm afraid I'd drive you away. I can be grumpy as a bear—"

She hastily wiped tears off her cheeks. "I've lived through grumpy."

"And frustrated and insecure and I'm not above being mean. I don't want to put you through that, either, not again. I don't think I could stand to see that happen twice."

"I told you once that love was unconditional. That means you can be imperfect, too."

She could tell by the way he leveled his gaze at her that he could still see something. The frown said it all. "Like

I was the other morning? Treating you the way I did? Is that forgivable, Annie?''

She could almost count the heartbeats. He was giving her a way in. Anything was forgivable. She named her terms. ''The only thing I can't deal with is you shutting me out. If I had to wonder about every mood, every time, wondering if you were hiding something or if something else had gone wrong, I couldn't stand that. Love is sharing. It has to be. Communicating. Maybe you've lived too long alone, keeping your problems to yourself.''

She kicked the sand. It flew back at her, stinging her legs. He hunched inside his jacket and turned to go.

''You almost asked me to marry you,'' she said to the wind. ''In health but not in sickness, was that it?''

He didn't answer.

She didn't expect him to. ''It's ironic. I was afraid you wouldn't love me if I didn't measure up. Instead, you won't love me because you're not good enough.''

She was baiting him, and he knew it. He stopped walking.

''Let me call in,'' she said. ''Tell them I won't be in Monday. Then I'll give you that ride to Ann Arbor.''

''Annie.''

Half of her didn't want to hear it, whatever he was going to say. In a way it was easier to call it quits, wrap herself up in her memories and never get hurt again. ''Hurry up. It's cold out here.''

He tried to decipher exactly how angry she was. He missed that keen hearing he'd had. But as long as there was a shred of fading light, he'd look. ''I had to see you. I couldn't stay away.''

''Then don't push me away! Let me be part of your life. That's all there is to it.'' She wanted to yell, throw another pot. How could she get through to him?

"I don't want to tie you down."

Letting out an angry sigh, she laughed. "Sounds kinky, but I'm game if you are."

His voice was harsh, choked. "That isn't what I meant and you know it."

"*Ask me then*. Don't decide for me!" She trudged up the beach, trusting him to follow. She was so furious that she wanted to shake him. At the top of the last dune before her house, she turned on him. "Listen to me, Cliff Sullivan. I love who I please. It's *my* choice, and for that reason alone I'll never be tied down. Understand?"

He nodded. She was in front of the most glorious sunset he'd ever seen. Reds, slashes of purple, bands of turquoise and the deep blues of night creeping in overhead. None of them were as beautiful as she.

It was a nasty trick of fate, her coming along at exactly the wrong time, insisting on helping him, on being part of his struggle, when all he wanted was to be alone. No matter what the future brought, he had a feeling he'd thank that trick of fate for the rest of his life. And thank that honesty of hers; that might be the biggest lesson she'd ever taught him. "You don't care how grumpy I get?"

"Of course I do. It's a pain in the butt."

He fought a grin, tugging Kane along as he stepped closer. "In sickness and in health?"

"That's how it goes."

He handed over Kane's harness, and Annie took it with a surprised look. Not as surprised as when he produced the ring from his back pocket. "Turn toward the light. If it's the last thing I see, I want to see this."

His fingers were a little stiff, the temperature having dropped as the sun set behind the horizon. But when the ring was on her finger, Annie clenched her fist as if daring it to ever get away. "You haven't been carrying that around all this time?" It was a dumb question, but she knew anything else might result in a sob of sheer joy.

"I grabbed it before I left the house. I figured if I was going to get down on my knees and beg you to take me back, I'd better be prepared."

A picture of Cliff getting down on his knees for anything was downright unimaginable. Annie's doubtful expression said as much.

"If I came here one more time, I would have been. You're marrying a desperate man." He kissed her, quickly catching the tear that spilled onto her cheek. His lips were far from satisfied with a little salty water. They wanted the true taste of her, musky and womanly, lips and tongues and places that opened only for him.

Annie rasped her cheek against his, loving the familiar scratch of the new beard. When it was long, she'd love it even more. And when he shaved it off, and when she asked him to grow it back, and...

He pressed his lips to her ear, inhaling the sweet smell of perfume that lingered in her hair. "Want me to get down on one knee and ask you to be Mrs. Annie Sullivan?"

"Oh, no!" she gasped, tearing her mouth away from his. "I couldn't do that."

"Why not?" For a second doubts flickered across his brow.

"Annie Sullivan was Helen Keller's teacher! I'm no miracle worker."

"To me you are."

"This Rosetti is going to stay a Rosetti. Okay with you?"

She wiped the hair back from his forehead, took off his sunglasses and looked into his eyes. They looked sore, tired, worried, but they looked at her with unmistakable love.

"About the operation," he began.

"All doubts and fears you share with me," she stated unequivocally. "I love you now. I've *already* loved you through good and bad, grumpy and happy, sleepy and dopey and all the other seven dwarfs."

He tried very hard to reverse his smile to a frown. "Do I have to do all the worrying in this family myself?"

"Definitely not," she insisted. She shook her head and pursed her lips, realizing she could skim them over his that way very easily. Pleasantly, too. "But for now, stop worrying and tell me you love me."

"I love you. Now what about the future?"

She quieted him with another kiss and a smile. "Want to rent a hotel room in Ann Arbor? If we go down tonight, we could practice making love in the dark."

"This is your idea of worrying?"

"No, this is my idea of sharing. You can share the good things, too, you know."

"Teach me."

"I will, Cliff," she breathed. "I will."

"And forgive me?"

"Yes."

"And love me?"

"Always."

Epilogue

Walking through the crowded art fair, Cliff knew people were looking at him. The guide-dog harness on Kane made them clear a path, eyes averted more often than not. Sometimes he heard them pointing Kane out to their children. Or the women commenting on Alice, walking like the rambunctious two-year-old she was, one chubby leg in front of the other, clinging to Cliff's other hand.

Funny how he didn't really mind what people thought anymore. Let 'em think what they want, as Annie always said.

He heard the chimes from her booth tinkling up ahead. They'd set up on the first left-hand turn. The sounds made it easy to find. Even Kane noticed, tugging harder, Alice bubbling along in her made-up language.

Annie glanced up, her smile spreading wide, her heart turning over at the sight of them. It always affected her that way. Her bearded, blond husband in those mysterious and sexy shades, striding ahead as confident as ever, their towheaded toddler in tow. Alice was the only thing that could make Cliff shorten his stride. And then there was Kane, the sturdy black tugboat bringing them safely back to her.

As Alice made a detour for the carved wooden toys, Annie took the opportunity to simply watch. Cliff's hair was shorter now, neat, above his ears. Thanks to the beard, she didn't miss that wild Samson she'd met on the beach so long ago. It seemed like a million years, or a handful of days. Either way she had a heartful of memories, the greatest of which was their daughter.

The corner of Annie's mouth turned up in a smile as she attempted to listen to a customer.

He could still turn women's heads, she couldn't help noticing. And she could work up a bout of jealousy at the drop of a hat. Not that it was necessary. He seemed to love her more as time went by, not less.

"We're back," he said.

"No!" Alice said.

Annie bid farewell to the customer and sank back into her director's chair. The child needed attention first. "Want to climb in Mommie's lap?"

"No!"

"Her favorite word," Cliff murmured.

"You don't say."

"Don't you contradict me, too. I even got 'no' to an ice-cream cone."

"No!" Annie laughed. "Even that?"

"How would I have carried it back?" Cliff shrugged. The motion made Annie picture the shoulders and chest covered by his knit shirt. She caught her breath. "You did look like you had your hands full."

He rested one hand on the back of her chair and leaned over to whisper in her ear. "I can think of a couple of things I'd rather fill my hands with."

Alice decided that now was the perfect time to clamber onto Annie's lap, tugging herself into a sitting position from which she could pat Kane's broad black head. "Kay," she said, sweetly offering her two-year-old's version of the Lab's name.

"Maybe later," Annie said softly, touching Cliff's hand. "I missed you while you were gone."

He bent to kiss her across the little girl's head. Alice reached up and pulled his sunglasses off.

Cliff squinted and stifled a curse.

"Don't, honey," Annie said, retrieving the glasses where Alice had tossed them onto the ground. "The light hurts your father's eyes." As she handed them back, she stroked his cheek with her hand. "And he has such beautiful eyes."

Cliff looked at her, long and silent. The love they shared had been spoken, nights in bed, mornings over coffee, evenings making love. In hospitals and a maternity ward, they'd shared their fears and hopes. But there were times, like now, when Annie smiled up at him with their daughter in her lap and love in her eyes, that a look could say it all.

*　　*　　*　　*　　*

COMING NEXT MONTH

AVAILABLE NOW:

You'll flip . . . your pages won't!
Read paperbacks *hands-free* with

Book Mate • I

The perfect "mate" for all your romance paperbacks

**Traveling • Vacationing • At Work • In Bed • Studying
• Cooking • Eating**

Perfect size for all standard paperbacks, this wonderful invention makes reading a pure pleasure! Ingenious design holds paperback books OPEN and FLAT so even wind can't ruffle pages — leaves your hands free to do other things. Reinforced, wipe-clean vinyl-covered holder flexes to let you turn pages without undoing the strap . . . supports paperbacks so well, they have the strength of hardcovers!

Pages turn WITHOUT opening the strap

SEE-THROUGH STRAP

Reinforced back stays flat

Built in bookmark

BOOK MARK

BACK COVER HOLDING STRIP

10 x 7¼ opened
Snaps closed for easy carrying, too

Coming in November from

❧ SILHOUETTE®

Desire®

TAGGED #534
by Lass Small

Fredricka Lambert had always believed in true love, but she couldn't figure out whom to love . . . until lifelong friend Colin Kilgallon pointed her in the right direction—toward himself.

Fredricka is one of five fascinating Lambert sisters. She is as enticing as each one of her four sisters, whose stories you have already enjoyed.

- Hillary in GOLDILOCKS AND THE BEHR (Desire #437)

- Tate in HIDE AND SEEK (Desire #453)

- Georgina in RED ROVER (Desire #491)

- Roberta in ODD MAN OUT (Desire #505)

Don't miss the last book of this enticing miniseries, only from Silhouette Desire.

Indulge a Little, Give a Lot

To receive your free gift send us the required number of proofs-of-purchase from any specially marked "Indulge A Little" Harlequin or Silhouette book with the Offer Certificate properly completed, plus a cheque or money order (do not send cash) to cover postage and handling payable to Harlequin/Silhouette "Indulge A Little, Give A Lot" Offer. We will send you the specified gift.

Mail-in-Offer

OFFER CERTIFICATE

Item:	A. Collector's Doll	B. Soaps in a Basket	C. Potpourri Sachet	D. Scented Hangers
# of Proofs-of-Purchase	18	12	6	4
Postage & Handling	$3.25	$2.75	$2.25	$2.00
Check One				

Name _____

Address _____ Apt. # _____

City _____ State _____ Zip _____

ONE PROOF OF PURCHASE

To collect your free gift by mail you must include the necessary number of proofs-of-purchase plus postage and handling with offer certificate.

SD-1

Harlequin®/Silhouette®

Mail this certificate, designated number of proofs-of-purchase and check or money order for postage and handling to:

INDULGE A LITTLE
P.O. Box 9055 Buffalo, N.Y. 14269-9055

NOTE THIS IMPORTANT OFFER'S TERMS

Offer available in the United States and Canada.

Requests must be postmarked by February 28, 1990. Only proofs-of-purchase from specially marked "Indulge A Little" Harlequin or Silhouette books will be accepted. This certificate must accompany your request and may not be reproduced in any manner. Offer void where prohibited, taxed or restricted by law. LIMIT ONE GIFT PER NAME, FAMILY, GROUP, ORGANIZATION OR ADDRESS. Please allow up to 8 weeks after receipt of order for shipment. Offer good while quantities last. Collector's dolls will be mailed to first 15,000 qualifying submitters. All other submitters will receive 18 free previously unpublished Harlequin or Silhouette books and a postage and handling refund. For every specially marked book purchased during October, November and December, Harlequin/Silhouette will donate 5¢ to **Big Brothers/Big Sisters Programs and Services** in the United States and Canada for a maximum contribution of $100,000.00.